MARGARET STORM JAMESON

was born in Whitby, Yorkshire, on 8 January 1891. Her forebears had lived in Whitby, then a small fishing and shipbuilding port, for uncounted generations: her grandfather was a shipowner, her father a sea-captain. She was educated at a private school, followed by one year at the Municipal School in Scarborough. Awarded one of the only three County Scholarships available in the North Riding of Yorkshire at that time, she took an honours degree in English Language and Literature at Leeds University in 1912 and was given a one-year research scholarship, to be held at University College, London; she found University College dull, and transferred herself to King's College. Her thesis, on Modern Drama in Europe, finally approved by Leeds University, was rewarded by the Degree of Master of Arts; it was published in 1920, by the firm of William Collins. In the meantime she had married and had a son.

In 1919 she returned to London, becoming for a year a copywriter in a large advertising agency. She published her first novel, and began a two-year editorship of an obscure weekly magazine, *New Commonwealth*. From 1923 to 1925 she acted as the English representative of the American publisher Alfred A. Knopf, and later, for two and a half years, was co-manager, with her second husband, Guy Patterson Chapman, of the short-lived publishing house of Alfred A. Knopf in London. She married Guy Chapman in 1925, a deeply happy marriage, broken in 1972 by his death, after a distinguished career beginning with the publication in 1933 of *A Passionate Prodigality*, his classic account of trench warfare in France, and ending in a study of the politics and history of the Third Republic of France.

Between the years of 1919 and 1979 Storm Jameson published a total of forty-five novels. She has also written short stories, literary essays, criticism, and a two-volume autobiography. In 1939 she became the first woman president of the British section of International PEN, where she was an outspoken liberal and anti-Nazi, and a friend and helper of refugee writers. In 1952 she was a delegate to the UNESCO Congress of the Arts, held in Venice. She was awarded a D.Litt. from Leeds University in 1943, and is a member of the American Academy and Institute of Arts and Letters. With her husband, she has been an inveterate traveller, mostly in Europe. She now lives in Cambridge.

Virago also publish *Love In Winter* and *None Turn Back*; three novellas, *Women Against Men*, together with Storm Jameson's two-volume *Autobiography*.

VIRAGO
MODERN
CLASSIC

NUMBER
90

STORM JAMESON

COMPANY
PARADE

With a New Introduction by
ELAINE FEINSTEIN

Published by VIRAGO PRESS Limited 1982
41 William IV Street, London WC2N 4DB

Reprinted 1985

First published in Great Britain
by Cassell & Co. Ltd 1934

British Library Cataloguing in Publication Data
Jameson, Storm
    Company parade—(Virago modern classics)
    I. Title
823′.912[F]   PR6019.A67

ISBN 0-86068-297-8

Printed in Finland by Werner Söderström Oy,
a member of Finnprint.

FOREWORD

THIS book is the first of perhaps five, or six, novels in which an attempt, necessarily incomplete, is made to depict the contemporary scene. The family name of all these books is *The Mirror in Darkness*, and the mirror may be taken to be the mind of the author, or of the reader, or at times only of the young woman called Hervey Russell whose relation to the whole work is unchanging in time, although the space allotted to her in the several volumes necessarily varies. It is clear that a great many characters must be required to play their parts in any illusion of the contemporary scene, and even when the number of these has been reduced to the subsistence minimum (so that one character is forced to do the work of a crowd) it is large enough to make the author's life a busy one, and this first volume, in which the greater number of them must appear, even if only once, in the nature of a *Company Parade*. The author has worked hard to make the reader's share of the work as light as possible, and she begs forgiveness, first for putting herself forward to make what seems a necessary explanation, and secondly, for not being able in one volume to tell all she knows about the men and women in it.

STORM JAMESON.

INTRODUCTION

After more than a decade of writing fiction, a note of Storm Jameson's, dated 25 October 1930, declared her intention 'to write henceforward with the most unromantic plainness'. And some of her finest and sourest portraits of women under stress came from that impulse, notably in *A Day Off*.* But that excellent novella proved to be out of key with the decade that was opening and in 1932 Storm decided to attempt a *roman fleuve* of perhaps five or six novels, to be given the general title of *Mirror in Darkness*. The first of these novels, *Company Parade*, she finished in November 1933, and found a 'good crowded book'.

Storm Jameson was to write only two further volumes in this series, *Love in Winter* (1935) and *None Turn Back* (1936); by the time this last was written she had come to feel impatient with the series. The novel itself had been praised by Edwin Muir for the generosity of the passion and the candour of the prose, even as he criticised it for being more interested in the society it represented than the characters themselves. It was Storm Jameson herself who noted 'The deep reason why I abandoned *Mirror in Darkness* . . . was a stifled instinct that I was working against the grain of my talent.' The series may never have been completed, but as a trilogy the three novels present an extraordinary portrait of England between the wars and of one woman who lived through these years.

Perhaps surprisingly, since Storm Jameson's close friends of the thirties were more often politicians than writers, the subject matter of *Company Parade* is essentially that of her own youthful years through the First World War and its aftermath. The domestic stress of her heroine, as she takes her first timid steps into the literary world, is very much that of Storm Jameson herself. Certainly the name of her central figure, Hervey Russell calls up generations of Herveys and Russells from an earlier trilogy, *The Triumph of Time*

*One of the novellas in *Women Against Men*, a companion volume issued with this (Virago, 1982).

(1932), which chronicles the fortunes of Hervey's ancestors, a shipbuilding family in the North Riding of Yorkshire.

Margaret Storm Jameson was born in Whitby in 1891. By then, Whitby was no longer a shipbuilding or whaling town, but it remained a harbour, looking out across the North Sea. Storm's mother was a restless spirit; the daughter of a one-time shipowner who was no longer rich, but still fastidious and bookish. Storm's father was a seaman, who had not yet been given his first captaincy when he married. He was a brave, obstinate man; but his wife baffled and tormented him. She had a passion for china, rugs and furniture and, even though she bargained for everything she bought, he was made anxious by her expectations. Initially, he must have hoped she would rescue him from his own clumsiness and ignorance, but she had neither the patience nor the gentle disposition for it.

Early in the marriage, when Storm was their only child, the family accompanied him on his short voyages; and Storm's mother travelled as far afield as Vera Cruz and Odessa. After that, there were long separations and all family decisions came to be made by Storm's mother.

It was a fortunate arrangement for the children, since their welfare was her passion; she was determined to ensure they had an education in order to enter the world she felt she had been denied. In spite of the frequent thrashing she meted out to them, all four were filled with an overwhelming desire to do something in the world to fulfil ambitions they sensed had been disappointed in their mother.

It was her mother who entered Storm for a county scholarship, which in due course led to Leeds University, where she took a first-class degree. Her first and strongest ambition was to be a don. When I met her for the first time in Cambridge in 1981, some sixty years later, she continued to insist that she had no comparable respect for the work of a novelist and had 'only written novels for money because writing was the simplest way to earn money when you have a young child keeping you at home'.

In the event, an altogether characteristic fecklessness put paid to her chances of a safe academic job. Awarded a research scholarship in University College to work under W. P. Ker, she chose instead to attach herself to King's College, London, and changed her research subject to a thesis on modern European drama without consulting the university authorities. It was not a shrewd move, but it did open the door into European literature; and in later years, her sensitive understanding of European tensions made her one of the most intelligently European novelists of the period *entre deux guerres*.

In *Company Parade*, Storm Jameson touches on several of those memories she speaks of in her autobiography *Journey from the North* which still have the power to tear at her over the years and which are her idea of hell. All involve breaches of loyalty and failures of love.

After her brother's death in the war Storm watched her mother's life shrivel away. Storm had already disappointed her by making a disastrous marriage to a young man with little sense and a disparaging tongue; and as she saw her mother age, Storm Jameson learnt that for her, at least, what most women mean by love was a paltry emotion compared to the ties of the blood. It is a love that is charted with great poignancy in *Company Parade*.

One of the most sharply observed relationships in the novel is that between Hervey and an irresponsible husband. Anyone who reads *Journey from the North* will recognise how closely the guilt of marital stress and sexual temptation are transferred from her own experience to her central figure. More remarkably, her analysis of the way a marriage can bind people unhappily close 'in an underneath, dragging way' is painfully honest; and she knows exactly how a weak man can come to bully a stronger wife. 'I bring out the worst in Penn . . . I hide things from him—to save trouble—then he finds me out and is able to prove that I'm deceitful. I want to please him, but I try less and less—I don't respect him now . . . He enjoys humiliating me.'

Left to cope with the problem of keeping a child on what her husband leaves from his pay, Hervey Russell takes work in an advertising agency, rather as Storm Jameson had worked for the Carlton Agency. The anguish and guilt of leaving her much-loved son behind with a stranger is a pain documented harshly and without self-pity, biting most deeply in moments of failure; for instance, in Hervey's inability to make an idyll out of a day at the sands. This part of the novel, too, springs directly from her own experience; though, as in all good fiction, it is honed into shape. Hervey Russell's indignation at press reports that suggested German famine in the twenties was exaggerated was very much Storm Jameson's own; but though Storm joined an idealistic newspaper almost as quixotically as her heroine, she took its views much less seriously.

Although it would be wrong to read the novel as a *roman à clef*, one of the liveliest portraits in *Company Parade* (that of the Yorkshire novelist, William Ridley, who bluffs his way to fame) very closely resembles J. B. Priestley as characterised in Storm Jameson's autobiography. It would be hard to miss how the advice Ridley gives Hervey echoes the very phrasing of Priestley's advice to Gerald Bullett: 'Get out, do as I'm doing, get to know people, make yourself felt . . . '

It was not Bullett's style, and it was not Storm Jameson's style either. Beautiful as photographs of the time show her to be, she was as often tongue-tied as her heroine, unless she had prepared what she was going to say. But that social timidity which makes Hervey so ill at ease on the public occasions of the literary world goes along with a 'stiff, self-regarding nonconformist' directness. Among the contradictions Hervey shares with her author are those which arise from a dour lack of self-pity and a readiness to feel compassion (even for her husband whenever his unhappiness resembles that of a child). By and large, Storm Jameson herself entered a sober and decent literary establishment, mainly through the salon surrounding Naomi Royde-Smith. This held none of the writers who were to prove the rebel great of their day. She met Arnold Bennett rather than D. H. Lawrence, Eddie March not T. S. Eliot. She had little time for modernism. No doubt these were losses; but her own authorial voice, with its balanced clarity of syntax, reflects a commitment to the rational and the humane, which arose naturally out of her own Yorkshire shrewdness. This extended in surprising directions.

Few portraits of Jews owning press empires are as sympathetic as that of Marcel Cohen in *Company Parade*. While his business interests make him automatically the enemy of the idealistic young, Storm Jameson recognises in him a restless mind, generous to those whom he admires and able always to recognise honesty in others. The shrewdest assessment of Hervey herself is put into his mouth. 'Unreliable, yes, I knew her grandmother. You can't trust a woman who is as honest as that.' Without in any way sentimentalising his own family attachments (his daughter is shown as silly and grasping, as well as herself prejudiced against Jews), Storm Jameson shows a rare understanding of the sadness of Marcel Cohen's situation as an outsider in a hostile society.

In this there is, no doubt, an element of hindsight. Even while writing the second and third volumes of *Mirror in Darkness*, the dangers of the rise of Hitler were becoming more and more obvious; and Storm Jameson was among the first writers of a generation who found it most natural to oppose war, to urge a stand against the encroachments of that evil. No doubt she was helped in the accuracy of her assessment of the true danger as with so many other decisions, by the close and happy partnership of her second marriage to Guy Chapman, a distinguished historian as well as a fine novelist himself.

Through her travels with Guy, some of her best books came to be written as the nightmare which was developing in Europe deepened through the thirties. Among them, *Cousin Honoré* (1940), draws a portrait of the province of Alsace as a microcosm of the forces undermining European civilisation as a whole. Alsace is not only part French and part German, it was tugged apart by all the rival solutions to contemporary problems; no one had a finer sense of Europe's enemies within, even in France itself: readers of *Gringoire*, Maurras's disciples, all those who thought they could save their fortunes by backing the Nazis when the Germans marched into the Ruhr.

Another late work of some prescience is *Europe to Let* (1940). It is easy to see why Storm Jameson was to be such a gallant and humane president of the British section of International PEN. She loved and understood central Europe as few English writers have; and she threw all her heart and energy into the struggle to help refugees, first from Nazi Germany, and then, after the war, to those who needed to find a place in the West after defecting from the Soviet Empire.

Many of the novels written out of her finest talent were still to be written. Among these was certainly *The Black Laurel* (1948). And she went on writing shrewdly about Europe in the aftermath of the Second World War for two decades after it.

Storm Jameson comes of that generation which had to confront in its own flesh the full mystery of human cruelty and human indifference. 'What I do not know and cannot even hope to understand before I die is why human beings are wilfully, coldly, matter-of-factly cruel to each other . . . What nerve has atrophied in the torturer, or worse is sensually moved?'

Storm Jameson has always been a free-thinker both by temperament and conviction, yet she has nothing but scorn for those who have lost faith in humanist values, whatever scepticism she may have about humankind's right to the planet.

All her life, Storm knew herself tugged between contrary impulses. She joined no party, though she was anti-fascist to the core.

It was no accident that, in the years between the wars, when every sensible intellectual was of the Left, that it should be Storm Jameson who nerved herself to ask Fadeyev, head of the Russian Writers' Union, what was happening to Boris Pasternak in his country of boundless Socialist freedom. Storm Jameson always saw politics in terms of human beings; in that she was true to all the paradoxes of her inheritance.

Elaine Feinstein, Cambridge, 1982

I

COMPANY PARADE

CHAPTER I

DECEMBER 1918

A YOUNG woman comes to London in the month after the
Armistice. She is inexperienced, poor, ambitious, burdened.
This is what happens to her.

The town was crowded, not a room to be had in any of
the cheap hotels; for all she knows, none in any of the dear
ones. President Wilson had arrived that day, drawing people
from all parts of the country to look at him, the bright star
of their hopes. She slept the first night in a Hostel for Young
Women near Victoria. The manageress, a bony creature,
refined, with no bowels, was surprised to see her come with
a large black leather trunk, her mother's: it was of the
kind known as a dress-basket, with a domed top and straps.
'You won't need that taken up to your room,' she said in
a gritty voice. 'You can only keep the room for two nights.
As I informed you in my lettah. Leave it in the passage.'
The girl agreed anxiously. She was tired but at first could
not sleep for thinking of her baby. This child, who was
three years old, and very beautiful, she had left in Yorkshire
with a lady trained in the care of young children. The
more she considered in her mind the perfections of this lady,
the less comforted she was and scarcely able to bear being
parted from him. What would he think and feel when,
falling asleep in a strange room, he awoke to find it stranger
by daylight, and the door opening, and looking round for his
mother, Miss Holland came in?

The next day, Sunday, she tried a score of apartment houses
without finding room. Towards dusk, very tired, she came
on the blue Y.W.C.A. hut in Trafalgar Square and went

9

timidly in, prepared for charity gone cold. There was no such thing—but there was a chair, a good cup of tea, and they told her where to go to find a room. The day after she and her dress-basket shared a bedroom in a Temperance Hotel, in Bloomsbury, the room very narrow, cold, dingy, and the bed a penance. She took possession of it in the evening of Monday, after her first day spent trying to write advertising ' copy.' This day had convinced her that she was a failure, and now the room drove other thoughts home. Too cold and uneasy to sleep, she lay and thought about her baby. When it was wet, the coarse stuff of the pillow-case scraped and burned her cheeks.

She was young, and each morning ran out gladly. She could not stay quietly of an evening in that dreary place, but sauntered about London, pleased with trifles. London to her was a brightly-coloured web, from which now she drew the sound of violins in a café, now a voice crying Victory, now a boy and his sweetheart laughing as they passed, now furtive encounters of which her mind retained a gesture or a glance. In a time and a city of easy meetings no one spoke to her. She was always alone, all her friends dead, or in France or Mesopotamia. In the first months after the War London was gone to pieces and noisy—not gay. She was too young to feel this and wherever there was music and bright warmth and they were cheap there she was, living in her eyes.

Her bedroom in the hotel was so uncomfortable that she never unpacked the dress-basket, and after three weeks of it she moved to a room in St. John's Wood. It was at the top of a house, really a large attic, and when she had stowed her things it looked as though no one was living in it. On the third evening she was going upstairs behind a middle-aged woman. This woman turned and smiled at her and said in a fine jovial voice: ' You doing anything ? Come in and eat a bite of supper.'

The girl followed reluctantly into the first-floor room. It was all white whiskery rugs and low chairs, the very pattern of Edwardian demi-monde ease. She sat stiffly in one of these chairs and watched the woman put beer and sandwiches on a tray in front of the gas fire. She knew she would not be able to drink the beer and said: 'Could I just have sandwiches?'

'As you please,' the woman said. She was a big well-built woman, surprisingly quick. The girl could not help looking at her face, which was coarse and pleasant, with deep merry lines. There was a superb impudence in the way she threw her voice about, slapping it down on things. With the tray between them she began to question the girl. 'What's your name?'

'Hervey Russell.' She could not overcome a dislike of giving her name to strangers.

'What's that? Is it your own?'

'My very own, as it happens,' Hervey said quickly and shyly. 'I'm married, but I don't use my married name very much.'

'What's it, then?'

'Vane.'

'Ha. Well, Miss Russell-Mrs. Vane, did you see *my* name on the door?'

'No,' Hervey said.

'You never heard of Delia Hunt? All the worse for little Delia. I saw when you came in you were married. Where d'you come from? You have a country face.'

Hervey was not offended by the woman's curiosity. When you have answered such questions you have not told anything of importance about yourself. Soon Mrs. Delia Hunt knew that she was twenty-four, had a baby called Richard, and was earning her living (or not earning it—since as yet she had done nothing well) as a writer of advertisements.

'That's fine,' Delia Hunt said. 'I like spirit. I began earning m'keep when I was six, and if I told you all I'd done you wouldn't believe me. Don't talk to me about the horrors of war. I was in Johannesburg in 1890 and if the front line was as raw I feel sorry for the troops. I do so.

I had my husband, but my dear life, he was no sort of protection against drum fire. When I came home I left him there. I been a stewardess, a cab-driver, second cook to a troupe of monkeys, and dear knows what else. You don't learn much more after you've learned the first things.'

Hervey felt ashamed of knowing so little. She had no idea that she was staring until the woman told her so with a rich laugh. Afterwards, in her own much colder room, she felt excited and able to do anything. It was too late to go out and she sat still trying to read. She felt her heart beating as though she were caged. It was the same excitement she had felt as a child when the wind rose to a gale round the house. She wanted to run shouting in the windy darkness. She did not know yet that her thoughts and flesh were the cage. Suddenly she jumped up and began to beat her hands on the window-sill.

CHAPTER II

JANUARY 8, 1919

1. *Hervey*

THERE were two moments on waking in the morning when she was unhappy. The first was her waking thought of Richard, turning his head the moment the door of his room opened, but not asking for her. He would look for her but he would say nothing and no one would know from his face that he was looking. The second was when she opened the door to her breakfast tray and there were no letters on it. After that there was nothing she had to do except run to the window to know which of her two coats to wear. If there was a letter from Penn, her husband, she read it over breakfast, disappointed because it was short and told her nothing and then forgetting it suddenly as she stepped into the street. He was stationed in Kent, a ground officer in the Air Force: his War had been a pleasant tour of stores depots, parks, and aerodromes in England. When she thought of him it was with impatience and kindness, as we think of a person we can neither like nor leave off liking.

At the office she shared his room with an experienced copy-writer, and was his assistant. In practice, she was useless to him. She had no notion how to write the advertisements for a new soap and he could not show her. His name was David Renn, he had been lucky enough nearly to die of wounds in 1917 and then not to die and to be discharged—so that he got out and got work before returned heroes were being sold two for a farthing. He was quick and reliable—to look at, you would say a willing soldier. He was thin and had been good-looking, with very fine bones. Indeed his head was still beautiful, if you looked only at the bones and then at the quick steady eyes.

This morning when she came in he gave her eight type-written pages about an arc welding process and told her to get the facts into two hundred words. As he turned away he said : ' I don't suppose you can do it, but you can try.'

But this was something she could do. When she brought it to him he was holding his leg where the pain started. He read it through, nodded, and said : ' Now try to find just six words about Charel's new soap, to go with the pictures. Take my copy and read through it.' He spoke carefully, with an effort to seem calm. A drop of sweat trickled over his temple to the cheekbone.

' What kind of words ? ' Hervey said.

' My dear God, don't you know anything ? Think. Have you ever walked down Oxford Street of an afternoon and seen that mess of women, as thick as glue on the pave-ment ? They haven't had a fresh thought since they were born, they read the *Daily Post* and believe it, and get their first and last notions of life from the women's magazines and the cinema. Write six words to make every one of those women think that Charel's Almond Cream Soap will save her. Don't shout. Whisper in her ear. How to be more beautiful than other women. How to look young. How, how, who told you, who, listen I'll tell you. Almond Cream Soap.'

' Is your leg very bad ? ' Hervey said.

' What are you trying to do ? Sell me an ointment ? ' Renn jeered.

She went back to her desk and read eight different descrip-tions of the soap. The six words did not show themselves. She tried writing down short phrases and tore them up in despair. Her head felt like leather and the more she dragged at it the heavier and more stupid it felt. I'm wasting my time here and I'm no good, she thought. She was too angry and ashamed to answer Renn when he spoke to her.

In the afternoon the managing director, Mr. Shaw-

Thomas, sent for her and Renn.   He wanted to talk with them about the Charel sales scheme, but first he asked Hervey how she was getting on.   'Not very fast,' Hervey said curtly :   'I can't write slogans.'   She had no natural respect for authority, and Mr. Shaw-Thomas never took any trouble to snub her.

He looked at her as though she amused him.   She was sitting on the edge of her chair, like a nervous boy, her face angry and frowning, as if she were setting her teeth over the notion of being laughed at.   Its stubbornness had a soft look.

'You're not going at it the best way,' he said, with his sharp smile.   When Mr. Shaw-Thomas wanted to thrust a word into your ear he pressed his hand down flat on his desk and smiled, showing small very sharp teeth.   There the word was, pinned through the living body, like a strange moth. 'I know you can write, but writing advertisements is a *subtle* art.   Perhaps we must say *could* be.   To be honest— advertising still lacks its Shakespeare.   There's a peak for you to conquer, Miss Russell.   And the field is—if I may put it so bluntly—pregnant.   How many novelists or poets manage to get themselves read by rich, poor, superior, ignorant, successful, cultured, happy, miserable, unimaginative, snobbish, resigned ?   Remember that people choose to read novels, but you must trick them into reading an advertisement.   You can only do it if you believe in what you're saying. You must know with your *heart* that Charel's Almond Shaving Oil is the purest of all oils before you are fit to write about it.   If by some error you know at the same time that the oil used is somewhat impure cottonseed, you must practise what philosophers call a suspension of belief.   In that way you will achieve the sincerity needed in order to write well.   Great advertising is the expression of deep emotional sincerity.   The risk a clever young woman runs is of being merely clever or cynical.   Do avoid cynicism.'   He considered her for a moment and added :   'It is incompatible with real emotion.'   He nodded at her.   'And now I hope

I have removed some of your doubts about yourself, Miss Russell. I am sure you will do me credit before very long.'

' I'll try,' Hervey answered.

'When is your novel coming out ? ' Mr Shaw-Thomas asked, smiling into her face.

After a moment Hervey said : ' Not until May.'

' I don't think you told me you had written a novel.'

She did not say anything.

' A great novelist is not necessarily a great advertiser,' Mr. Shaw-Thomas said genially. ' Remember, to rise in *our* profession requires more than ordinary talent. You must be willing to give your *whole mind*. Novelists ! I wouldn't pay H. G. Wells two pounds a week until I had trained him. He's probably too old to learn anything. Do you think Miss Russell is learning ? '

' She'll be all right,' Renn said.

Hervey had listened anxiously. She wanted to be praised for writing brilliantly about soaps and packets of breakfast food. In the same moment, she felt herself turning away, with a dreadful flat misery. She was impressed, and at the same time she was sceptical and half-consciously revolted.

When they went back to their room Renn said quietly : ' You've got to accept all that to get on, but all the same don't accept it.'

Hervey looked at him ' How can I do both ? '

' You can't. Either you tell yourself lies or you don't. Perhaps you're the Shakespeare of advertising ? One day you will be so moved by a new purgative that you will write your *Lear* to induce people to buy it. I shall now read you a genuine advertisement from a genuine trade paper. Listen. " *For Christmas, our luminous Crucifix shines in the dark and makes a wonderful Christmas present. Our agents always clean up with this Crucifix at this time.*" If you can play on women's sexual needs to sell them a cold cream why not on another emotion to sell crucifixes ? Behold I stand at the door and knock offering an illuminated crucifix.' His face twitched. ' The answer is that good

business it not always good business unless you suit yourself
to your company. You can't sell decent women illuminated
crucifixes, but you can sell them something else as easily and
get their money.'

Hervey had forgotten to listen in her interest in Renn
himself. It was not at all the interest of a young woman, but
belonged to a part of her mind which drew the same pure
nearly unrealised delight from the flattened planes and creases
of a man's face; the running of a wave; London when a
clear sky gives its buildings that air of delicacy and remoteness;
a big careless woman in full sail; a hill; the curve of a
lighted road at night. If you deprived her of her other
senses and left her her eyes she would be happy. Why not?
She only half listened to what was said to her and did not
enjoy speaking, but her eyes could never look enough and
she lived in them.

When Renn stopped talking she had nothing to say and
pretended to be engrossed in her work. I ought to listen
more and stare less, she thought. The rest of the afternoon
went in the exasperation of trying to write six words and
failing. When she left, she was too fretted and restless to go
home.

She had a shilling to spend on the evening meal and knew
where she would spend it. She walked with an awkward
movement of her young body, as if she did not know or care
what her arms and legs were doing. She half longed for
someone to speak to her, but the moment she saw, or thought
she saw, the beginning of a smile on the face nearest her,
her own turned quiet and sullen. Her awkwardness and her
country face were both a defence.

In her haste, and deep absorption in herself, she missed
the wheels of a cab by seconds. The man shouted at her.
She did not look round. Head down, to hide her embarrassed
face from him, she hurried along the pavement, pushing
between people as though they were trees, submerged with
her in the light flowing between the street lamps. Above
the light, darkness began abruptly.

B

After the cold and the hurrying the Corner House closed round her with a familiar smoothness. Here no one knew her. She could open her book, and keep her eyes in it, only moving when the girl put coffee and scones before her. She was not reading. Her thoughts went back over the day with a nervous fury. I can't do it, she thought, I can't write their six words. I've failed, I'm useless, a failure; this is what I left Richard for, to get this. To sit days in that room thinking how to sell soap, and at night coming here every night getting nothing, knowing nothing, at times happy, unhappy, no doubt a fool but could have been used. Her wish to see and touch her son overcame her. She felt that she would cry, and pretended to drink her coffee, holding the cup at her mouth; her throat was rigid.

Without thinking she knew that she would not go back. She was too dissatisfied, possessed by a devil of energy and ambition. At the least notion of giving up it sprang in her; she could not go back to Yorkshire, to become nothing, unknown. She had to have something to show.

I should have no money, she thought, her mind turning from Richard to Richard's father. It was a fortnight since Penn had written to her. She was not anxious and she did not mind seriously, but she wished he would resolve to leave the Air Force as quickly as possible and find work. His carelessness angered her. If he had work, between them they could contrive to live decently and have Richard with them. That's not a great deal to ask of him, she thought, with growing anger.

Her mind turned back on itself and brought a much younger Penn to sit opposite a young ungrieving Hervey. At once she felt that though he had disappointed her since then, in a multitude of ways failed and outraged her, she was still bound to him. The nerve holding them to each other was alive when she touched it. If she looked up and saw him this moment crossing the crowded room to her she would feel the familiar lift and shock of her blood. I shall never be free of him, she thought: unless he left me himself, because he was tired of me, and then I should be free.

I don't want to live like this, she thought, with surprise and fear. She looked for the first time at the people round her. The sharp light, warmth, and music, washed over them, accepted by them without interest or wonder. They drifted into the room, clung for a time to one of the tables, and drifted away, into streets and rooms she could not imagine, more than a million of them, squatting and pressing on the earth, pressing out grass and trees, killing the roots of many living things, so that these rootless creatures could exist. She thought, I left the place where my own people lived hundreds of years to come here. I was mad.

Almost at once she saw the waitress looking at her and knew she had stayed too long. There was a soldier in leather-cuffed khaki seated at the next table. He was drinking coffee and his eyes over the edge of the cup had a puzzled stare. He seemed not to know any better than she did what he was about. Behind his eyes were roads leading to trenches and the sights and sounds of that life, and he could not relate it to this nor this to anything waiting for him in the future. He stared, his worn uniform investing him with a quality of innocence and awkwardness. He was young, as young as Hervey. He felt her watching him, and his eyes examined her for a moment calmly. Hurriedly getting up, she walked past him and out.

In her room she took up the manuscript of her second novel, but she was too tired and too restless to write. Deliberately she began to think of the American with whom during the War she had had the misfortune to fall in love. She thought of it as a misfortune. She was still in love with him; still, though she did not then know it, imitating his ways of thinking and acting; and still resolute not to give in to him. She would never give in to him, knowing with something firmer and deeper in her than her senses, that he was not *safe*. What she meant by safe was precisely what it had meant to any woman of her family, at any time during the last five centuries. When she was vexed and restless, as now, she would think of him, and then it was as though he came into the room, with that light springing step, and smiling. To imagine him there gave her an exquisite pleasure and happiness. She would never have it in reality, since when he was with her she had to keep her mind sharp and steady against him. This was an instinct for which she never tried to account. It was part of her early discipline and beyond that a dry obstinate pride of blood, something that had been given her and which she could not give back.

She undressed and began to brush her hair. It fell almost to the arm of her chair, fawn-coloured and very fine. I shall cut it off, she thought. As soon as she was in bed she remembered Richard's trick of taking the pins out of it while she pretended not to know what he was doing. She had to pretend to be asleep. He was trying not to laugh out while his hands felt along the plaits, warm and clumsy. When at last the plaits slipped and fell down she opened her eyes and jumped up. His face and wide brilliant eyes were alive with laughter. It broke from them, spilling over his round body.

She turned on her face in bed. I won't think about it. I'll go to sleep now, he's sleeping he can't count the days since I went he won't remember anything oh my little little love.

2. Renn

David Renn left the advertising office at seven o'clock, an hour later than his young assistant. He was thinking of her as he prepared to go, and retrieved from the floor a sheet of paper on which she had been writing phrases about soap. They were all quite useless. He smiled a little, tore the paper across, and forgot her as he walked downstairs.

The street was empty except for a dray waiting outside a fruiterer's, horse and driver frozen into the same attitude of passive endurance. As he crossed the street Renn imagined that the man had been one of his drivers in France but coming closer he saw that it was only the pose had deceived him. He walked on, quickly, wondering whether to go home or to try to find company for the evening. In the end he stepped into a post office and telephoned to his friend Earlham. Earlham's wife answered for him and in half an hour Renn was opening the door of their shabby flat in the Euston Road.

Rachel Earlham was a very small shy Jewess, of nineteen, dark-eyed, with a delightfully gentle manner, like a well-brought-up child. She and her husband were Socialists, very poor, very ardent. Louis Earlham intended to stand as Labour candidate for a North London division. In the meantime he earned a very little money as a journalist. They lived like young birds on what they picked up. There were sandwiches on the table and two bottles of beer, but Renn had brought his own meal. He ate one of the sandwiches, to please Rachel.

There were only two chairs in the room, the table, and their bed, made to look like a couch. It was little wider than a couch and if they had not been so young and thin one of them would certainly have fallen out when the other moved. The second room of the flat was Earlham's 'study.' With a visible effort it contained his desk, a chair, and their bicycles.

Earlham began to talk about his newspaper, which was Radical, independent, and very popular, through its habit of uncovering scandals in public life. It ran these until the excitement waned or the interests which had been attacked bought themselves off. He was violently angry—because he had been sent down to investigate charges of sweating in a bicycle factory, and it was far, far crueller than he had expected : he wrote the article, and at the last minute it was thrown out. The firm booked a series of full-page advertisements.

' I know,' Renn said. ' I have to lay out the pages. They are our clients.'

'Then,' his friend shouted, 'you can write about a skinny child of fifteen who is compelled to jump like a cat between two machines, covered with dust through which her sweat pours.'

Renn smiled his polite gentle impersonal smile. ' On the contrary. I shall describe ideal bicycles made in an ideal factory.'

' You are very wicked,' Rachel said, blushing.

Renn looked at her with a mixture of affection and irony. ' You two babies,' he said, ' imagine that when your Party comes into power there will be no more skinny overworked children. What nonsense ! The system demands them.'

' We shall alter the system.'

' Peacefully ? '

' Of course.'

Renn laughed. He was peeling an apple. He cut the peel off carefully, not to break it, and draped the glossy coils round the neck of Rachel's cat Habbakuk. Offended by their laughter Habbakuk fled through the window on to the roof of the next house. Beyond him a Sahara of roofs gleamed in the moonlight. He sprang feeling his whole body stretch and quiver, and disappeared in the shadows.

Rachel turned from the window to scold Renn, but his smile made her confused. She smiled shyly and happily and went away to make tea. Her husband's voice, raised and vehement, filled the room and sent a shiver of excitement through her small body. She thought of the tiny mole on his arm, of the way he held his cup and drank, looking at her, and of sleeping beside him in the thin creaking bed. Her heart beat quickly in happiness. When she carried the tea into the room Renn was leaning back in his chair with an air of contentment.

' I know what is wrong with you,' Rachel said, ' why you are always so superior and laughing at us. You ought to be married.'

' Who would marry me ? ' Renn answered. ' I am bad-tempered when my leg hurts—and besides—I do not believe in committing oneself. If I could find a woman who did not feel that she had the right to turn my mind upside down to look for a safety pin, I might be able to live with her. Women are unbearably possessive.' His voice was so kind that Rachel did not feel hurt. But she felt glad that Louis had other views on love.

Renn walked home through nearly empty streets. He was very tired and his mind plagued him with visions of his friend and Rachel absorbed in each other, in their shabby room, to the exclusion of everyone and everything else. Habbakuk and I are both in the cold, he thought, amused : I shouldn't get very far over the roofs with this leg.

His landlady had turned the gas off on the stairs and he had no matches. He groped his way up to the second floor, opened his door and felt round for the box he remembered leaving on the cupboard. At last he found it. There was a letter and parcel on the table, both from his mother. He opened the letter first.

'My darling boy, I am sending you a small cake and some apples from the second tree. They are wrinkled but sweet. I am sure you do not eat enough. Sometimes I wish you would give up trying so hard to make your way and come home. Surely there is something you could do here, in Hitchin ? I miss you very much. It is as if you were away at school again but then there was always the holidays to look forward to. However you know best what is best for you, my dear boy. And perhaps you are in love ? Your aff't mother Kathy Renn.'

He undid the parcel and put the cake and the apples away in his cupboard. Then he undressed quickly and glanced for a moment at the sunken scars on his leg. For the hundredth time they made him think of a railway junction, the lines crossing and meeting on the inside of his leg from knee to groin. He lay down, closing his eyes, and saw the yard of his mother's house, with the second apple tree in the corner. Half smiling, he fell a little and then deeply asleep.

Habbakuk poured himself round a chimney stack and moved arrogantly along a narrow coping. His eyes gleamed with the pleasure of heights and loneliness.

3. *Delia*

Delia crossed Piccadilly Circus with the insolence of use. The cold stung her face but her body in its fur coat felt warm and easy.   Once across, she halted to look up at the clock before turning into the Monico for her meal.   Seven.   The room was half empty.   She sat forward, balancing herself on broad white thighs, all that sagging and still vigorous flesh held and moulded into shape by her clothes.   Once she had been so thin that, smoothed neatly over her bones, her flesh needed no other support, but since then so many layers had been added that the early Delia was quite cut off from the world and could only signal now and then in a smile or a gesture which no one recognised.

She ordered oysters and stout and swallowed them with unconscious relish.   Her mind was busy with the problem to which it had to find the answer before midnight.   While the waiter, an old acquaintance, was clearing away the things and placing others, she took the letter from her bag and said to him :

' D'you remember me coming here with Tim ? '

He hesitated in surprise.   ' Your husband ?   That was a long time since.   Let me see—— '

' 1889,' she said curtly.   ' The same year I went with him to South Africa.   Nineteen.   That's what I was— nineteen.'

' I was beginning here then.'   A world sprang alive in his mind, crumbled and vanished behind the curtain dropped by the War.   He felt almost dizzy for an instant, and steadied himself, feeling the used plates under his hand.   ' Funny. The lights weren't nearly so bright then in this room.'

' I left him there in '92 and came home.   I had me reasons. Now he writes, it came this morning even his writing's changed, asking if I'll have him back.   Where's he been ? Would you do it ? '

The waiter moved his shoulders.   ' I haven't seen him in

here,' he said.   'When they come back after a long time
you'd think they was ghosts—or dreaming.'

'I'm forty-nine.   If I don't find a man to live on the
premises as you might say, I'll often be without one.'

'There's that.'

'If you ask me,' Delia Hunt said loudly, 'the lights weren't
so big anywhere.   This town's changed for the worse.
Vulgar I call it.'

The waiter recalled with pleasure stories he had heard about
her.   It seemed that even in the Johannesburg of 1890 you
could go too far, and shock that community.   She'll have her
own ideas of vulgarity, he thought.   He was surprised as he
went off to find himself in strong sympathy with her.

Delia re-read the few lines of the letter.   She sent her bold
smiling glance round the room.   Changed.   I too.   A shudder
started in the depths of her body.   You were young, did as
you pleased, enjoyed yourself, and all at once you felt your
flesh, as they say.   She thought without regret of her life :
which was not over.   A strong excitement moved in her
when she thought of her husband.   He was brutal and had
thrashed her when she misbehaved herself—but lord what's
that, she thought comfortably, I've been worse handled.
I remember I ran away from him that night in camp—and
eight of them—I remember the noise outside and the heat,
I'd me fill certainly.

A smile at once gross and amused crossed her face.   She
finished her chop quickly, pulled at her dress—it always
rode up—and went away.   On the way out she looked with
some interest at a young and very pretty woman entertaining
a Canadian officer.   She had a round laughing face, black
hair cut in a fringe across her eyes, and painted lips.   Delia
experienced a definite conviction that the new growth had
not the stamina of the old.   She saw that the girl was prac-
tising a part, not, as Delia herself at that age, revelling with
a nearly brutal zest in the turns of her life.   Without thinking
it, she felt the strong coarse flavour of the past fading from
the present, leaving it poor and uncertain.   The show is

beginning to run down, she thought grimly, then with a familiar jerk of her blood, It'll last my time.

The thin searching wind caught her as she breasted Regent Street. To pass time until midnight she turned into the cinema. After the cold the over-warmed air made her drowsy. The branches of a tree, moving with the movement of bright water, filled the screen. Involuntarily she remembered that great tree she had admired as a child. In spring its branches came down like wide green steps—she could never look at them without a troubling excitement in her half-starved body. Now the tree was gone and a room, a parlour of the 'nineties, took its place. It was empty, then the door opened and a young woman came in. Delia was seized with a powerful and mysterious emotion. Half trembling, she murmured to herself: ' She's going to light the gas.' As the flame jetted up she pictured the blue spring raying into yellow. A dozen scenes from her past offered themselves rapidly one after another, and it seemed to her that the whole of her youth with its coarse vital ardours was released when she thought of a gas-lit room—it was the same room whether it existed in Brixton or Johannesburg.

The music that went with the film was quick and noisy, and suddenly she felt like dancing. Her body grew tense and warm, with excitement. She felt as strong as brass. No one had ever got the better of her and she had never cared what they said about her notions of pleasure. A sudden contempt for her husband (she could only think of him as a young man) filled her, and at the same time, with a light shiver of pleasure, she thought that she could have him with her that night if she chose. I can do as I like, she thought. At once it seemed to her that her life had been very extraordinary. She felt exultant and reckless, and began to recall days and nights in which she had lived with a gross happiness. Suddenly —she had forgotten where she was—she saw that the picture was over and it was time to go.

Regent Street was nearly as noisy and crowded as by day— only the sky was missing, and the light sprang from below up.

This part of London still quivered with life while the rest lay asleep. Miles of darkened suburbs and the empty streets of the city proper spread away from this one wakeful nerve. One other, the river, remained alive and vibrant, but its activities went on with less noise than those in which Delia felt herself at home. She always said that if she were blinded she could make her way from the Strand to Shaftesbury Avenue by the sounds and smells. But to-night for the first time, she noticed a difference between this London and the London of 1913. It was not only that there were more cars in the streets or that the late posters bawled Make Germany Pay or that dances seemed to be going on everywhere —it was something in the people themselves, there were more of them in the streets for one thing, and more women, and they had more the air of spectators than revellers. A faint uneasiness crossed her mind. It vanished almost at once, as she pushed her way confidently through them with her burden of memories and instincts, towards the Underground telephone booth in Piccadilly Circus. Her good humour made her want to please somebody and she stopped to give sixpence to an old matchseller who had long since resigned himself to selling nothing and was only standing there from feebleness.

She reached the Circus at the moment when Rachel Earlham turned towards her husband in their thin bed with a sigh of infinite solace, and when, almost asleep, Hervey moved her cheek away from the rough patch made on her pillow by her tears. Twenty minutes to twelve. For another moment she stood watching the people hurrying this way and that past the telephone box, weaving another thread into the multi-coloured fabric of London, so strong, and yet frailer than the trees which grow of themselves between its houses and one day will push them over. Her mind darted backwards and forwards along this fabric, as pliant to stretch itself in time as her fingers to close round the receiver. As soon as she touched it the present came about her with a rush.

CHAPTER III

1. *Unsatisfactory conversation*

HERVEY RUSSELL had been in London more than three months without seeing her husband. One evening she was putting on her coat when the porter, a cynical ex-sergeant by name Jaffers, came up to tell her that a Lt. Vane was asking for her downstairs. Jaffers smiled knowingly as he said it.

'That's my husband,' Hervey said to Renn. Her heart beat quickly. She wished she had put on her better coat that morning. When she came into the hall, Penn was leaning against Jaffer's desk, making himself agreeable. He was always affable to subordinates unless these failed to respond in the right way. Hervey was pleased to see him. He looked very well and satisfied. His Air Force uniform attracted some glances in the street, from people who were less used to it than to khaki. He noticed it and began to tell Hervey about an old lady who had spoken to him in Oxford Street and insisted on his driving home with her to dinner.

'But when was this?' Hervey asked. 'You've just come, haven't you?'

Penn looked at her quickly. 'It was last year some time,' he said. 'Where d'you want to go, my dear?'

'Usually I go to the Corner House for some coffee,' Hervey said. 'More for your money there.'

'Still pretending to starve yourself?' Penn laughed.

'I don't starve, but I can't spend much. My room and breakfasts cost thirty-two shillings.'

'Leaving forty-eight shillings a week for coffee,' Penn said.

Hervey struggled with a familiar rage. 'Leaving eight shillings a week for everything,' she said quietly. 'You know I send that woman two pounds a week every week for Richard.'

'Well, well. Quite the little business woman,' Penn said amiably. 'I don't suppose you'll refuse to share dinner with me. I'm going back at nine.'

Too disappointed not to show it, Hervey stood still. ''I thought you had leave.'

'No. No leave yet. I came up to collect some stores, and the transport is going to wait for me until nine. Do come along, my dear. People are looking at you.'

Hervey swallowed her disappointment in silence. Her spirits rose again in the café, because of the people and the crossed yellow lights. She liked the impersonal excitement of sitting in a place like this, where she could watch without talking. Her mind sprang awake, like one of those table-maps on which arrows of light dart from point to point, marking the passage of trains, ships, aeroplanes.

'This is a splendid place,' she said to Penn, in a happy voice.

He rested his hand on her knee. 'I ought to be coming home with you.'

Hervey was surprised to feel herself shaking. 'You'll have leave soon, won't you ? '

'Oh. Probably next month. Can you find room for me ? '

'You don't write to me,' Hervey said.

'I knew you would say that sooner or later,' Penn exclaimed. He made his voice sound patronising and amused. 'You're pricelessly funny when you think you're being subtle, Hervey.'

Hervey was astounded by this answer. When she did not see Penn for a long time she forgot how suspicious he was and being reminded of it she was startled and afterwards angry or depressed.

'I know you so well that you don't surprise me any more,'

Penn said. He was smiling. ' I knew, the moment you began about having no money, that you meant to get at me somehow. Well, well. I don't write to you and I don't send you money and you're starving. Ha, ha. It just happens that I'd come meaning to ask you if you wanted money. I suppose it never occurs to you that it costs a great deal more to feed in the mess than in rooms. And mark, I didn't ask you to leave me and betake yourself to London. You're doing it entirely to please yourself.'

' Don't let's quarrel,' Hervey said in a low voice.

' Certainly not,' Penn said. He had talked himself into very good humour. ' You haven't told me how you like working in an office. I somehow gathered that you weren't finding it such an easy life after all.'

' I don't find all of it easy,' Hervey said. ' I'm not really quick-minded.'

' You're quick enough,' Penn said kindly. He began to talk to her about his life in Canterbury. His face altered, becoming younger and softly attractive. As Hervey listened to him she could not help seeing that he enjoyed his life without her. Well, she thought, with a sigh, I can understand that. Though she was three years younger than her husband she often felt towards him as she did to Richard. But at the same time that she wanted him to enjoy his life she wanted to feel helped and supported by him. In the end she was often neither so kind nor so sensible as her instincts, and then everything went badly for them.

She felt full of unfamiliar food, and sleepy. To her half listening, the life Penn described sounded curious and improbable. She did not believe everything he said. Anxious to seem interested, she smiled and nodded. Penn interrupted his story to chaff the waiter who brought their coffee. She disliked this and sat with a fixed bright look until it was over. Then she said: ' But who is it you take to these dances, Penn ? '

He looked sharply up : her face, smooth and round with well-being, satisfied him. Sinking himself easily in his chair, one booted leg crossed high over the other, he said : ' Surely I told you in a letter ? Ferraby and I made friends with two V.A.D.'s from the hospital. They live in rooms and old Ferraby's quite sunk by his. Priceless. Mine's curly-headed and buxom, and just nineteen. She's been well brought-up, too—she's priceless. She knows I'm a married man. I told her that at the beginning, to make sure. So we toddle off together to the dances, and I see her home and shake hands with her at the door, and it's exactly as it should be.'

While Penn talked he looked at her face to see the effect of his words. It would have done him as much good to watch the back of her head, since she was not listening to him. When she was interested, emotionally or even only for a purpose, she knew what was going on in the other person's mind. While he talked she would be listening to have the sense of his mind, sometimes excited by the difference between two voices. At other times, when she had lost interest, she gave the least possible attention and effort. She seemed to be listening, her face alive and quick, but her ear only listened—she caught the physical sense of the words, and missed their meaning, and what was at work in them. The rest of her brain had gone on some business of its own. She would be sunk in this and perhaps watching for the right moment to speak of it. In all this she was not the simple direct person she seemed. A great many things had contributed to make her what she was becoming, and not least her mistrust of Penn. Not to trust the person to whom you are committed more deeply than to anyone, is a serious misfortune. Hervey never allowed that she had to guard herself from her husband, but she expected it. There were certain things she wanted from him still—of which the head and chief was that he should work for their son.

She was thinking about this now, with a stubborn passion, having already planned what she meant to say. All that Penn was saying was so much noise—until the moment when she heard him say that he might be moved to Netheravon.

' But, Penn,' she said quietly. ' I thought you'd be demobilised before very long. Have you heard anything ? '

' Not a word.'

' You haven't done anything about it ? Would they release you if you applied ? '

' Why should I ? I'm quite comfortable and snug, thank you.'

' But you can't stay in the Air Force always,' Hervey said gently. ' The longer you hang on the less chance there will be of getting work. Just now there are plenty of jobs but in a few months, you'll see there won't be any.'

' I'm not worrying myself,' Penn said.

' You ought to. Listen, Penn. If you're going to be a schoolmaster again why not try now to get work in London ? Then we could have a house and a nurse for Richard, and both earn money.'

She could not help something coming into her voice. Penn laughed. ' How you do like to arrange my life for me, don't you, my dear ? '

' It's my life, too,' Hervey said.

Outside, it was not yet dark. They walked along the street to the Park, and sat down inside, facing the gate. There were people walking under the trees and cabs going between the gates and along inside the Park. All the time Hervey was thinking what she could say to force Penn to some action. The longer he stayed in the Air Force, working easy hours with subordinates to do the real work, irresponsible, because nothing depended on his efforts, going to a great many dances, well-fed, and his boots polished for him by a servant, he was becoming daily unfit for reality. She had had no effect on him this evening, and suddenly depressed she became silent. Penn was in a softened mood. He reminded her of an evening before the War when they sat at this same corner and talked about being married. To her embarrassment Hervey felt tears in her eyes. Penn noticed them and drew her arm in his.

' My poor puppy,' he said gently, ' are you so miserable ? Tell your tiresome dull Penn about it.'

' You're not tiresome,' Hervey said. She gripped his hand. ' I don't want to go on living by myself.'

' You'd rather have me than nothing,' Penn laughed.

' It needn't be just dull and responsible,' Hervey said. ' We could go about together. I don't want you to turn into a grub because you've lost your fine uniform.'

' Don't you ? Only into a schoolmaster.'

' You'll have to turn some time.'

' But not before time.' He drew one glove on carefully and stood up. ' I'll get leave soon and we'll discuss everything. You look after yourself until then. Don't run away from me with an advertising magnate—ha, ha. I shouldn't like it, you know.'

' I wish you weren't going,' Hervey said. She looked, trying to think about them, at the leafless trees. Where a lamp came directly behind a tree the branches of the tree were elongated by a shadow which streamed from them upwards, into the darkness.

' That's very good of you, my dear,' Penn said seriously. ' I wish it too. I know I'm a bad boy in many kinds of ways and a disappointment to you and all that, but you can't tell yourself I don't love you. You can, but it would be a lie.' He looked at his watch. ' Damn it, I shall have to take a taxi. Coming to see me off ? '

' I don't think so,' Hervey said.

Kisses given in the street, in a hurry to get away, are no satisfaction. As Hervey walked off, taking care not to look after the cab, she felt embarrassed and angry. She was angry with herself because she had talked emotionally. There was a falseness in the emotion, which made her ashamed now that it was over. She tried to think herself into calmness, walking quickly and carelessly, as if the Park were a lane. I don't want to live with Penn, I only want not to be alone the whole time. Why have I no courage ? She jerked her head, confused and now tired. A sense of her own inadequacy

c

overcame her. I'm useless and clumsy, she thought. And should work harder. She recalled Penn's face, kind and suddenly serious, as it had been in the moment before he drove off. He's still Penn, who knows me better than anyone else—and he *has* helped me and been kind to me.

There was a deep tenderness for him in her when she came to it after her anger. Really he angered her because he was idle and easy-going; because he refused, not openly but as if he were indifferent, to be responsible for Richard; because he had no sympathy with her in her anxiety about their future—she said she wanted them to have their place in the world, to be rooted, known, secure. He had no feeling for them as a family. He would like a little money, and to have a great many friends who took him at his reckoning—and that was all.

Alas, Hervey's own impulses to vagrancy, and fear and hatred of a settled life, sometimes had the better of her, and she said then vehemently that she wanted nothing, nothing, except one room and peace. Penn never failed to remind her of these wild speeches.

She had reached her room before she became calm. Then, while she brushed her hair and undressed, she tried to think of Penn and herself and Richard in London. Can I do it? she wondered. She knew already how the weight of it would be on her. Before, when I was free, she thought confusedly, work was easy. Now half my energy is mortgaged —to be divided by Penn and my baby. What is left will not be enough for me to write my books. Lacking conceit, she did not give more than a flying thought to the last. The impulse only was there, urging her not to give, to save herself. It accounted for the dry reluctance she felt in committing herself to own a house of her own, with all that owning involved. Only for Richard she would force herself to it.

I can't bother on with my hair another day, she thought suddenly; I shall cut it off. She threw the brush down with joy. At once everything seemed easy and simple, and before she got into bed she wrote part of a letter to Penn.

2. *Conversation in a field*

In the morning she went to a hairdresser in Oxford Street and asked him to cut her hair short. She did not watch the shearing. There was a mirror in front of her and she sat looking down, hating the man's fingers on her skin. When it was finished he gathered up the long dust-soft strands into a plait and gave it to her. She touched the plait delicately: she thought it felt faintly warm still, like a bird that has only just died.

'It's a very unusual colour,' the man said. 'The only colour we can't copy.' She sat rigid, just able to endure him, while he arranged the cropped hair. When she looked at it, it was terrible—harsh, ugly. She did not know how to alter it. All she wanted was to get away, out of the place, which was hateful to her.

She was an hour late at the office. When she walked into her room Renn gave her one glance, under raised eyebrows, and returned to his work.

'It doesn't suit me, does it?' Hervey said, in a deliberately jeering voice.

'No, it doesn't,' he said briefly.

She went red with shame.

The next day she appeared with her hair raked straight back. Thus exposed, her forehead domineered over her face. There was so much of it, and with its four clearly-defined swellings, that it seemed out of proportion with her body. Renn looked at her without smiling. But he was more friendly than he had been.

It happened that evening when she came home that she found two friends waiting for her outside the house. One, Philip Nicholson, was still in khaki; the other had been demobilised and sent back to his research. In a moment, when she turned the corner of the street and saw them, five years vanished like a puff of smoke—a great mercy of time, to make it appear that there had been no War. But in the next moment, as she ran up to them, she saw the

shapeless pockets of Philip's stained, leather-patched jacket.
He was smiling at her. T.S. said in a severe voice:

'You're damned late, young Hervey. We've been here
forty minutes. Your landlady wouldn't let us in to wait.'

'You can come in now,' Hervey said, as happy as never
was. 'There's no food, though.'

'How like you,' Philip said. He put his arm in hers,
and with one accord the three marched along the street.
There revived in them, only by being together, their country
contempt for Londoners. 'Look at that son of a banker,'
T.S. said, pointing to a man walking innocently at the other
side of the road. He stood still. 'Let's put up a practice
barricade in this street.'

They were standing near a shabby two-seater car, so old
that it must have been held together by the rust. 'Look,
our Hervey, that's my car,' Philip said.

'He gave a fiver for it,' T.S. said. 'But he can't drive
yet. All that happens is that the thing acknowledges his
superior intelligence.'

They squeezed into the car, after Philip had started the
engine, and drove off down the road. The car lurched like a
camel. When he put the brake on at the crossing, it dug
its front wheels into the ground and leaped. Off they went
again, with all the effects of a tank in action. Hervey held
on. She was not in the least frightened, but she wished
she had on a thicker coat. She was shivering and T.S. put
his arm round her to warm her. 'Where are we going?'
she shouted.

T.S. shouted back: 'To Philip's country house.' His face
was relaxed and young, the strain lifted from it by the
excitement. He was twenty-four and looked a hard-living
thirty, as did most of the young men of that age who managed
so survive four years' war. 'Have you ever felt such a car?'
he shouted. It reminded him of one night they moved the
companies by bus: he had his arms round Peters, who was
cold. Wish I'd pushed him over the side, he thought,
remembering something that happened to Peters.

Hervey stared round her. They had reached an outskirt of London no more repulsive than the rest. Two rows of new brick houses festered by the side of the road for another quarter of a mile. Then fields began, breathing mist into the evening air. The sky beyond them was like the dusk-coloured glass in old windows. They drove for another hour. A few yards ahead, on the left of the road, a hut made of sheets of corrugated iron advertised itself as The Dug-out. A Good Pull-in. Open All Night.

Philip stopped the car. There was a caravan at the far end of the field beyond the Dug-out. It was a very small caravan. A packing-case of books took up more than a third of the space. Between the case and the door Philip had set a canvas bed, a chair, and two large oil-paintings of horses. Although there was no room to move, the effect was neat and soldierly. Even the horses stood in line, as if on the parade ground. His army valise, hanging from a nail, held his few clothes. He took his meals at the Dug-out, where, he said, the food was very bad and the company excellent, consisting of tramps, lorry-drivers, and an odd soldier or two.

'You never asked me what I was doing,' he reproached Hervey. 'The King dismissed me last week, with a generous tip, and leave to wear his uniform for a fortnight. Thoughtful. I took this place by letter. It's damned nice, isn't it? The Dug-out is the best of it—no worry about your rations coming up—it's kept by a friend of mine. He was my sergeant in 1916.'

Hervey smiled at him. The old Philip, untouched by war. No, that was not true. The touch was there, but for the moment it could be ignored. T.S. had gone over to the Dug-out to fetch coffee. He arranged cups and glasses on the packing-case between two candles, of which the flames blew out level, like yellow leaves, in the draught. A plait of wax hung from the edges. Hervey poured the coffee. Philip stooped behind the case and brought up a bottle of red wine.

'But, Philip, your mother,' Hervey said. 'Doesn't she mind your living here?'

'Not a bit, she died last month,' Philip answered.

He had spoken about her in a light voice, but with that convulsive narrowing of the space between his eyebrows which his friends knew well. Hervey said nothing. Neither did T.S. and after a moment Philip said impatiently :

'Don't sit like owls. I want to know what you have been doing, Hervey. I'm told you've written a book? You would seize the chance, when the rest of us were off killing Germans, to get in first.'

'I write mostly about soap now,' Hervey said gloomily. 'My novel is coming out in a fortnight, in May.'

'You s'd have made friends with my wife,' T.S. said. 'I know I wrote to you from France to go and see her. Why didn't you?' Hervey looked at him blankly. 'Don't tell me you've never heard of Evelyn Lamb,' he said, in a jeering voice.

'Is Evelyn Lamb your wife?'

'Evelyn Lamb has been Evelyn Heywood since June 1918. She married me in a most unusual outbreak of emotion about the War. That's not fair, but why should I be fair? I'm among friends, ain't I? The fact is I didn't know I was marrying half the sparrow-hawk writers, editors, and what not in London. It's awful, awful.'

Hervey had seen quite a number of portraits of Evelyn Lamb. There was always a new one in one of the independent galleries, by a young artist whom everyone would soon know. Young artists began by painting Evelyn Lamb, exaggerating the flattened line of her face and the length and narrowness of her hands. After that they went on to paint the well-advertised young women who move social diarists to their daily or weekly droppings in the newspapers. So that Evelyn Lamb's name carried always a faint flavour of something not merely literary.

Her father was an assiduous surgeon—among his colleagues known as Butcher Lamb—who left her a very respectable fortune. She wrote sparingly essays of a biting, railing kind, and besides this was the literary editor of the

London Review. She had a gravely-earned reputation as a critic and director of taste. Hervey had known about her since a long time—but when T.S. wrote that he was married, and when he spoke of his wife, it did not occur to her that his Evelyn was Evelyn Lamb. Only the notion would have seemed absurd. Why, thought Hervey, she must be ten or twelve years older.

As if he knew what she was thinking, T.S. put on his sharpest and most malicious smile.

' How's Penn. And *where* is he ? '

' He's in Canterbury,' Hervey said, waiting.

' Didn't he get to France, then ? Pity.'

' You know he didn't,' she said fiercely. She was more vexed with herself for her want of dignity than with T.S. Also she was ashamed of Penn before these old-young warriors, and ashamed of her feeling of shame. Why am I so disloyal, she thought.

' Give over teasing our Hervey,' Philip said. He smiled, looking at her with his clear, very clear, blue eyes, as if he were alone with her in the little space. She was afraid T.S. would notice and jeer at him. ' You've neither of you asked me what I'm doing. Nice pair of friends I've got. Well—my mother had over eight thousand pounds put away. I always thought she had only her pension. She scraped and skimped all our lives as if we hadn't a farthing to spare.' Again that contraction of his brows, like a slight pain. ' Now I'm going to spend every penny of it. I'm going to read economics, and then I'm going to start a weekly paper.'

' Oh my God,' T.S. said.

Philip's face was alive with delight. He stood up and put two fresh candles in the place of the old. A globe of light sprang round them, fine and wavering, as though it were a motion of the air. Outside the caravan there was black, still night. ' You're going to write for it, my lad. You'll write the scientist's notes once a month. And our Hervey can write, too, if she behaves herself and does what I tell her.'

' What kind of a paper, Philip ? ' Hervey asked.

He looked from one to the other with a serious air. ' Pacifist, socialist, and classicist,' he answered, in a slow voice.
Listening to it, Hervey remembered that it was always Philip
who, in their life together, had taken charge of it. It was he
who made them empty their pockets for the dock strikers.
He who had the idea of giving away socialist leaflets at the
Principal's garden-party. He ordered and they obeyed. It
never occurred to either of the others not to obey him.

' Socialist—because even to tolerate the idea of there being
rich and poor is vulgar—disgusting and ill-bred. Well-to-do
persons who want to remain better-off than others are very
under-bred. Pacifist—because it is always the young who
die of wars, and this creates for the time an elderly experienced
world, which smells *used*. And classicist—because it is your
romantics who cover up wars, dictatorships, and the other
nastinesses with their bad sentiments. I detest romantics.
Nearly as much as I used to detest our heroic civilians and
the indecent women who gave away white feathers. I know
a number of very high-minded old gentlemen, but they are
not much use.' The draught was now so hard on the candles
that their flames nearly left the wick. Philip put his hands
round one, so that it flew erect again, like a strong stem.
' Because we have survived the War, we have to keep a
channel open between us in 1914—do you remember us ?—
and the future. Before long something new will begin. We
three are going to watch for it, and watch the others—the
practical ones, who support crucifixions on behalf of the nail
and timber interests—watch them that they don't pop the
old greasy clapper of their facts on it at sight.'

T.S. put one hand over his eyes. His eyelids had begun to
twitch, as they did now when he was tired. ' Nothing keeps
fresh for longer than a moment,' he said.

' I'll help you, Philip,' Hervey said.

' It's no use,' T.S. screamed. He jumped up and banged
on the wall of the caravan. 'No use. We're all beasts. Here's
a story for your first number. In December I was in Berlin
for a fortnight. Coming back I fell in with two journalists

on the train. I thought I couldn't do any harm showing
them photographs of the starving children, like abortions.
They swore they'd write about it in their paper. When I
read their article it was headed : Germans Whining For
Help. Stop the Hun Coddlers. How's that for your something new ? '

He shut up suddenly and sat down, collapsed. He was
grey with fatigue, drawn and old. You could not believe
that his youth would ever come again. Yet he was only
twenty-four. Younger than Hervey.

' I'm sorry. I'll help, of course,' he said. He looked at
Hervey. ' Poor Hervey,' he said, with a grin. Hervey
nodded to him, trembling a little. Since the shock when he
screamed, she had not looked up. Now she thought that for
all they had known each other so long and were more intimate
than a many brothers and sisters, never, never would she be
anything better with them than a stranger in all that touched
the War. There, the distance between them was absolute.

During it all, Philip had sat quiet, shielding the candle.
You would think he had been through it before. He now
opened a book and put it behind the flame. ' I've got a
fourth man,' he said quietly. ' He was in my company
until he was shot up. There were five of us in the battalion,
but the others had themselves killed. We used to plan the
paper together. Name of David Renn.'

' He's in my firm,' Hervey said, glad to have something
in the pot with them. ' He is said to be teaching me to sell
soap.'

' Well, what do you think of him ? '

' Only this morning he took the blame for a disastrous
mistake I made, and afterwards gave me such a gruelling
I nearly broke down and cried.'

Philip divided the last of the wine carefully among them.
' We'll drink this to Hervey's book,' he said.

There was peace in the caravan again. T.S. roused
himself, and drank with a flicker of mischief and pleasure
on his face. It really did amuse him to think of Hervey's

book. He felt sure it was queer, stiff, and unreadable. So it almost was. Hervey knew what he thought and did not care. She was by much too happy. These moments when she could feel herself accepted, without having to make any effort, were the happiest in her life. With everyone except these two she felt impelled to take trouble to please or to impress. She was then never free, never herself. Too nervous and mistrustful to give herself away, she was forced to appear the person others wanted. Only with the two who knew her she could be as slow, careless, and violent as she liked.

' Wouldn't it be a fine thing if we had three caravans here, one each,' she said suddenly.

Philip broke into his ridiculous wild laugh. He never learned to laugh with decency. ' You and T.S. are both lost, and I'm the only free man among you.'

T.S. looked at him scornfully. ' You make me very tired, Philip. Do you know what you are ?—you're a doomed young man. Zero hour of you and your new spirit ! '

Towards midnight, Philip led his cohort back to London. In the extraordinary stillness of that night the noise was shattering. Every sound rang again, in the arch of sky and dark earth. It was certainly not the fault of the car if any creature on their route slept through the arrival of the new age.

T.S. chose to get out at the first Tube station. As soon as he had gone Hervey fell asleep. She woke suddenly when the car stopped, and stumbled out. Still only half awake, she forgot to speak, and after waiting a moment Philip called to her softly out of the darkness. 'Good night, Hervey love.'

Words so familiar that they were scarcely spoken before they became a memory.

3. *Philip*

Two miles from the Dug-out the car coughed gently and stood still. Philip smiled to himself. He recognised the

foolishness of trying to argue with the creature, at this time
of night. Resigning himself to walk the rest of the way,
he stepped out, and pushed the car gently into the ditch.
At least no one would abduct such a wretch. In the morning
he and his friend Frank, of the Dug-out, would turn out as a
crash party and bring her in.

He walked comfortably in the darkness, between hedges
where as yet no green showed. The lovely freshness and
thinness of the air between dark and day flowed over him
like cool water. He loved this country, so plain, forgotten
between two roads. It was a comfortable country for a man
who was rarely alone, since there was always a ghost or two
to step up and keep him company. Not that his dead friends
worried him. He liked to feel them about when they came,
but he never encouraged them. Sometimes he thought it a
pity that they gave themselves the trouble to come back at all.
Thin young men in shabby khaki, their eyes embarrassed
the old and were themselves baffled by the flippant stare of
the very young. He himself took care not to speak of the
War except with soldiers. He was not resentful. The War
had given him something, a new poise, without taking away
even one of his early dreams. He still believed that he could
help the world—but now he had a sharpened sense of time's
urgency.

It was not only that he had lost four years. The rude
shock of the War had done invisible damage to his dear
England. He was now like a man escaping from a battle
who looks round him for his friends, to save what he can.
Part, indeed, of the little company of the days before the
War was missing, but the others would not fail to answer.
We must close the ranks, he thought. In the darkness his
face wore that smile, half childlike half mocking, with which
in those early days he had rallied his followers to support
him—it might be in an attack, delivered with stink bombs
and cushions, on a meeting of the Tory Club, or to form
a bodyguard for the fluent and intractable French anar-
chist he had invited to the university, or only to empty

their pockets for the benefit of a strike failing for lack of funds.

He was not, even yet, willing, as were the other survivors from that time, to take up a smiling air of patronage towards these incidents. He would have said that they were necessary —the discipline a platoon needs so that later on it will obey, and which its officer himself needs. But for the habit formed in 1913 T.S. would now be refusing his share of work. Our Philip had too much simplicity to see that his friends loved him without, always, sharing his faith, and that it was for him they slaved.

As he walked he came to a pond, and stooped to dip his hands in it, for the sake of the cool water. He thought of Hervey, whose hands were always cool, with a kind of living cold, like the feel of a leaf. He loved her so much, and without subtleties—only wanting to live with her, and be able to touch her, and hear her voice, which was so thin and clear that he had never heard any other woman with such a voice.

He knew her so well that he could see just how her honesty, that biting tooth, was being turned in on itself by her life—married to that unedifying fellow Vane. He even realised that something in Vane woke a kind of pity under his loathing—Vane was *der Mann ohne Schatten*. But to think of Hervey in his hands—that was too much—Philip groaned aloud. ' My darling, my little child, how could you ? ' Involuntarily he had quickened his steps and now stood still. When he lifted his eyes he saw that the light was coming, more a strange lifting and thinning of the darkness than light itself. Beneath his hand a gorse bush showed some few early flowers and he took one and began to rub it between his fingers. The bitter scent—it was a thick scent like oil— disturbed him profoundly. He stood with bent head, trying to recognise the emotion which had seized him and which belonged, he felt certain, to an incident so far back in his life that it had nothing to do with Hervey.

At once the moment he was seeking gave itself up. He saw

the long school slope and the lines of boys and girls drawn up outside the building, answering Here to their names. He stood at the end of one line, full in the morning sun, and he could see the trees in the valley garden, and one of them, an ash, was just coming—its leaves, widely spaced, and of a very young bright green, gave him an extraordinary feeling of happiness, as if he were listening to music. He stood and looked at it, and at the same time he was crushing between his fingers a piece of gorse pulled from the growing bush at the top of the slope. In time his own name was called and he answered.

Now, standing in the half darkness, he thought that he could say Here with precisely the same feeling of ecstasy and enchantment, since in fact the two moments were identical—there was no flaw of time, no dovetailing of Now and Then, since time had no authority over this experience shared with his younger self. The Philip of both moments was the same person and would live on in him unaltered until he died—and perhaps after.

But that was not all. He smelled the gorse again, and now as if it were one of those quite ordinary objects which an animal or an old woman gives the youngest son and tells him that he has only to hold it in his mouth to have his wish—there again was the school slope, and the marching lines. He marched with them, and just at the door turned his head to look back up the slope. Hervey, late as always, ran down it to take her place. She wore her school cap, and her plaits swung back as she ran, head up in a pretence of confidence. The boy next him smiled widely. ' Look at young Hervey. You'd think she owned the place.' Philip looked.

I looked too long, he thought, smiling. Suddenly he was very tired. The Dug-out was only a few yards away now, but he could not manage them. He lay down on the short grass and felt the cold entering first his hands and cheek and then his whole body.

About six o'clock Frank came out of the Dug-out,

whistling. He saw Philip lying asleep at the side of the road. He looked so like other figures Frank had seen lying in just that attitude that before he could stop himself he thought, Oh my God, they've got the captain. He ran forward.

CHAPTER IV

1. *Evelyn*

EVELYN LAMB's writing room, where she received friends, was a fine, severe room, the walls finished to resemble plaster, and lined for half their height with oaken shelves for books. A sixteenth-century oak table, taken from a church, stood in the window, flanked by a day-bed. There was nothing else in the room, except the chairs, and a rug on the painted floor. Next door to this room her bedroom had been decorated by a Mount Street firm. The floor, of polished steel, reflected as in a dark, smooth lake the dressing-table with its thin ebony pillars, the bed, made of ebony with an ivory inlay, the great candlesticks, deliberately out of keeping to add that touch of the incongruous demanded by the modern scheme, and the open doors of the cupboard in which she kept creams and lotions for the ritual of her face. Those for her body were stored in the bathroom. Two hours in the morning and an hour at night were not enough for these deities, and she attended to them with her own hands. A book was propped against the mirror to distract her mind.

That evening she was brushing her hair before dinner when her husband came into the room, leaving the door ajar, so that the curtains blew out slowly in the tepid air. He watched her for a moment, and said :

' I do want you to ask Hervey Russell to come here. You could do something for her.'

' Are you very devoted to her ?' his wife asked.

' Not at all, I like her, and she shared our rooms, mine

47

and Philip Nicholson's, before she married. Before the War, Your hair is as smooth as water.'

Evelyn laid her brush down, frowning. ' Did you truly live together in all innocence, a young girl and two young men ? I know you say so now.'

T.S. smiled sharply. ' If you had known Hervey in those days. She was very young, shabby, and careless. She didn't know anything. Besides, we were interested in a great many other things.'

There was a long silence. Evelyn's fingers opened and shut in a nervous spasm. She waited for him to speak, to go away, do anything rather than sit staring at her in that absent way. His body had sunk forward, as if the life were leaving it. His eyelids twitched in the way she found maddening to watch.

' Why won't you go to a doctor about your nerves ? '

' There's nothing wrong with them,' T.S. said.

' You have no energy.'

When he had gone she looked closely at herself in the glass. There were no lines on her face, which at thirty-six was as smooth as an egg. Indeed she had become younger during the War and more avid of living. She married a young man, a soldier, for passion and with the nearly conscious wish to identify herself with all that invisible pervasive excitement, springing from the presence everywhere of young men who were going to die in a few weeks, or even a few hours. A sharp sensation, neither grief nor joy, seized her whenever during this time she touched her husband. For the first time in her life her senses got the better of her intellect and she felt herself carried away by an emotion. He was in France several months without leave, until the end of the War. On this, his second return, she scarcely recognised him in the hagridden young man, hardly able to keep his eyes open from fatigue, who fell asleep in the cab. The War is over, she thought. It seemed to her that already some brightness, some mystery, had departed from the world.

The book she was reading fell forward and she turned it

sharply over. '*Au hasard ! A jamais, dans le sommeil sans hommes, Pur des tristes éclairs de leur embrassements. . . .*' Why read ? Why brush your hair ? Why do anything ? She wanted to hurl her books about the floor, to run as she was into the street. Everything bored her, everything was dry, tasteless, finished. She curved herself backward, gripping the sides of her chair. Choking with nervous anger, she repeated 'Let something happen, let something happen,' until her voice stopped of itself. She heard the first of her guests arriving. With fingers over her eyes she grew calm and began to arrange the evening in her mind so that it should seem informal, a quite spontaneous meeting of friends.

2. *Hervey at Ephesus*

About the middle of May Hervey had a letter from Evelyn Lamb, asking her to dinner.

Hervey's first impulse with an invitation was to refuse it. She would go to any lengths to avoid meeting new people. This was partly her nervous fear of being a failure, but more a rooted, unconscious arrogance, vexed by having to make any effort to be agreeable to strangers. I don't want to know them, why should I ? she fretted. Very often she was, as she had known she would be, a failure, sitting wooden and silent, made stupid by the pressure of so many alien minds. Everyone except herself seemed to her to possess a public face, which he wore to perfection. Now and then she came out of herself with a rush and was astonished to find that she had something to say. Afterwards she endured torments, feeling certain that she had made a public clown of herself.

She refused Mrs. Heywood's invitation. In a few days she had another—this time inviting her to coffee at nine o'clock. At the same time she had a note from T.S., ordering her not to behave like a fool. This was like the old days— she accepted, and towards nine o'clock that evening was walking along the Chelsea Embankment to his house. In

D

front of her was a short ungainly figure of a private soldier, sauntering along as if the pavement belonged to him. Hervey was in no hurry to arrive and she kept behind this figure. Nothing warned her that she was present at the birth of yet another new age. Its short thickset legs and broad shoulders held her glance—they were so solemnly self-confident. To her small surprise the soldier turned in at the gate of number 97. Seeing him on the step, she hung back, but the maid held the door open and she had to walk in after him.

The light fell on his cropped head and sergeant's stripes. She had to edge past him, following the maid. She was already taut and on the defensive. She laid aside her coat and looked at herself carelessly in a glass. Then the maid took her downstairs again and opened the door of a large room, filled with people. She heard her name spoken—' Miss Hervey Russell '—and went forward.

It was a nightmare parody of all the times she had pictured herself arriving, already known, in the world of writers. Her arms and legs felt like lead. She glared round the room, with an effort to appear self-possessed. A woman with a tall elegant body, thin almost to emaciation, smiled at her and said : ' I'm so pleased you've come. You don't know me. I'm Evelyn.' So much kindness was almost too much for Hervey. She turned red, grasped the very long beautiful fingers held out to her, and muttered two words.

Evelyn Lamb was a master in the art of placing strangers. She knew at once whether a new acquaintance was likely to be useful or do her credit. Her first notion on seeing Hervey come in, with an air of morose indifference, was that she had made a mistake in listening to T.S. Then as she was salvaging her hand from Hervey's she was struck by a curiously massive quality in the young woman. It was as though she had run up against something she thought soft to find it as heavy and immovable as stone. She felt a spring of interest and curiosity. At the same time she noticed Hervey's old-fashioned dress, and slippers which had evidently been worn a great many times.

' I must have a talk with you later,' she said, in her slow, hushed voice. She always spoke slowly, with a smile, as if she were the gentlest and kindest of creatures. ' Now you must talk to Mr. Ridley. He's come up to take London by storm, too. You must compare notes.' She moved away, leaving Hervey face to face with the young sergeant. He was an extraordinary figure in this company, standing in his thick khaki and thick clumping boots planted widely apart, as if he would refuse to budge. Hervey looked from them to his face, large, sallow, and complacent, and tried to think of something to say.

' Are you a writer ? ' she said at last.

' When I get free o' this uniform I'll be one quick enough,' was the answer, given with terrific gusto, in a rough voice. ' I suppose you're writing something or other.'

' My first novel came out yesterday,' Hervey said.

' And I suppose it's damn bad,' Ridley said, with a broad smile.

' I don't know why you should suppose it,' Hervey said mildly. ' You haven't read it.'

' Because you're like all the rest. Out with a novel, before you know how to write, and then write another, and another, and by the time you've learned something you've written that many rotten books no one takes y' seriously.' He jerked his head. ' Come on, let's sit down over here and I'll tell y' something worth knowing.'

Hervey was glad to be in a corner, away from the centre of the room. Ridley was too blatant a companion. Now that they were apart she did not mind him. He talked to her in a patronising voice, as if she would be incapable of understanding him. She had never known anyone so filled to bursting-point with conceit. At the same time she almost took to him—only because he was pleased with himself. There was something engaging in so much vanity. He was young, her own age, very broad and heavy, with reddish hair.

' I don't mind telling you,' he said, smiling. ' Some would keep a good thing to themselves. I'm not like that. Here's

what you ought to do. Don't write novels. Write criticism
and essays. Get a reputation for saying something a bit
different from other people. Make friends with th'other
writers. Get about among 'em, get known. Then when
you're well in then bang down your novel. Creeping about
the way you're doing is just damn silliness.' He looked at
her out of little twinkling conceited eyes. 'Now I suppose
you're offended.'

'Why should I be?' Hervey said simply. It was true.
If you were only unusual enough she did not mind how
uncivil you were, so far as it concerned her. She never
felt that other people's behaviour touched her at all. Even
when she was trying to please them she did not take many
people seriously. Once out of her sight they ceased to exist
for her.

Evelyn Lamb came towards them, and Ridley planted his
great feet and stood up. 'No, sit down,' Evelyn said gently,
putting her hand on him. 'I'll sit between you.' She smiled
at Hervey, then turned half round, ignoring her, and talked to
Ridley. She seemed to have known him already for some time.
She asked him when he expected to be demobilised. He was
stationed at Dover, where, if you believed him, there were
few men of his metal.

His manner had changed. Without becoming any less
self-confident—as when he thanked her for sending him
books to review his voice suggested that in doing him a good
turn she had done an even better one for herself—he managed
to convey a not too subtle flattery by the way he hung on
her words, nodding his big head when she paused, as if he
were learning from her.

In her delicate fashion Evelyn seemed delighted with him.
She made herself smooth and very friendly, as if his bullying
voice and thick overbearing body attracted her. Hervey sat
stiffly through it all. She supposed she had been dismissed,
but did not know how to leave. So she sat on, inwardly
mortified, with a fixed air of interest. She hoped that other
people would think she was taking part in their conversation.

After a few moments Evelyn rose. A man had come in whom it was important for this Ridley to know, and off they went, leaving Hervey quite by herself. She sat for a long time, ignored, knowing no one, and ashamed to move. An older woman glanced at her curiously, as if she would speak, but Hervey returned the glance with so forbidding a look that the woman went past. The feeling of being isolated shamed her. She could neither endure it nor go. She felt herself turning cold with shame, and yet she burned, she was on fire, conscious in every nerve of the clatter of voices and of figures moving before her eyes. At last she thought she would stand up and walk slowly down the side of the room to the door. Once there she could whisk out, unnoticed. And never, never, would she enter this house again.

She was just about to move, her head thrust blindly forward, when a man halted in front of the couch. He was a big middle-aged Jew, handsome, seeming very pleased with himself. Directed at the air, his smile took in Hervey on its way. Immediately he stepped closer. 'Why, I know you,' he said, in a high resonant voice. His eyes, dark, brilliant, and womanish, examined her with surprise and an impersonal pleasure. He stood in front of her with his powerful head on one side and his fingers pressed together, gazing at her as if she were a painting which he could well value, knowing deeply how fine it was and also what it would fetch.

Hervey was past civility. 'No, I don't know you,' she said coldly. A short time before she would have been glad of him, of anyone who took away from her the disgrace of sitting there ignored. But she had made up her mind to go and he was a hindrance.

'You're related to old Mrs Mary Hervey, the shipbuilder. I'm sure I'm right. Of course I am—I don't make mistakes. Let me tell you you have her very expression.'

'Mrs Hervey is my grandmother. I belong to a part of her family she chooses to have nothing to do with.' She spoke sharply, because she was ashamed of not having any part or lot in her powerful grandmother, and yet scornful. Without knowing it, she lived through the phases of her mother's life each time when, as now, she had to confess her grandmother.

'So much the worse for her,' Marcel Cohen said. 'Now what are you doing here ? You don't know anyone, you have no money, you want work. Our dear Evelyn only helps young men. Try somewhere else. Try me.'

'I am just leaving.' She could not for her life keep her voice altogether steady. She thought in the same moment of the time it would take her to get home, of her slippers, her book, of which no one here had spoken, and of Richard—they stuck in her throat and she could not speak. How shameful if she should cry.

'Na ! What a pity ! Just as we meet. Well, I shall walk to the door with you, then you will be grateful to me— and I shall say to your grandmother——'

'You'll oblige me by saying nothing to her,' Hervey said in a tense voice. The whole of her rage and humiliation went off in the words. She looked at him, at his big genial face, lined and pouched with intelligence and good-living, and detested it. She thought he ought to have known better than to be sorry for her. Head held down, she walked towards the door. Evelyn Lamb spoke to her as she went by and she answered, not realising until afterwards that she had actually accepted another invitation. She took her coat, scarcely waiting to drag it over her arms, and went out.

The cold night air shocked her, and sent a ball of blood to press against the root of her head. She walked without thinking about the past hour. The look of the river, dark, like dark glass with infinite gradations of light under the surface, soothed her : she thought of her home, of the sea, with the cliffs and the town clinging to them and the river going back between the hills, softly, turning this way and that, into the silence between two moors. Truly, to her it was as if it turned in her heart. She followed it with her mind, rapt, until she came to herself again in London. And then she hated so thoroughly the street, smelling of dust, sweat, and oil, and the flattened voices and faces of townsmen, that it revolted her to touch them. She took a bus at last, but when it filled so that the people standing pressed against her knees she stood up and pushed her way out. She would walk.

She thought about Richard. Suddenly there were tears running over her face in the darkness. It was for this she had left Richard, and was living in this man-heap, for such an evening, for such days, spent in racking worthless labour. This was what she had got, and given up her only son for it.

With a great effort she became quiet. She would not think any more, since it was useless. She went home, went to bed, and slept.

In the morning, as soon as she awoke, she felt a change in the air. The room was full of sunshine, like bright running water, everywhere, from the floor to the ceiling. She stepped out into it from her bed and went over to the window. There, in the yard behind the house, a miracle. Only the day before the bush of lilac had been black and dead, with a few hard spikes of buds among the tightly-furled leaves. Now it was quick and alive. The young green of the leaves and the lavender-hued flowers sprang up together in the strong light. Beyond the wall a row of poplars had broken into leaf. Yesterday, nothing—and to-day, flower and leaf together in a swift radiant flight.

3. *Philip and Hervey*

So it was everywhere. That year there was no coming of spring. One day it was winter, no sap moving, the air cold and lifeless, and the next full spring, with the flowers quickening among the young leaves so that both were new, young, and perfect in the same moment, as those mediaeval painters and weavers of tapestries imagined them.

Hervey went to her work like a creature in an enchantment. She was so happy she did not know she had ground under her feet. It was hard to go home at night. Much she wished for company. Her mind teemed with thoughts

as her body, a violin with nerves for strings, vibrated with
pent-up energy. She sauntered in crowded streets, an odd
careless figure, part Yorkshire bumpkin, part spy in enemy
country, heartening herself with words.

T.S. had sunk himself in his work. He was vexed that
Hervey was not at home in his house and vexation worked in
him to keep him away from her. Philip Nicholson had gone
off into Cornwall. One evening Hervey came home to find
him waiting at the end of the street. Cornwall had tired
him, as she could see. He greeted her with his familiar quick
smile, loving and nervous. If he liked me without loving me,
Hervey thought, I could be happy anywhere with him.

'I've dined,' Philip said. 'Have you?'

'Why yes,' Hervey said, to save trouble, and not caring—as
young still—whether she ate or not. But she would eat fast
enough if any offered a meal.

They went into Regent's Park and walked between the
water and the flowers. 'I don't like your novel,' Philip said.

'Isn't it any good at all?'

'You ought to read some French,' Philip said seriously.
'Your book hasn't any *form*.'

'What's worse,' Hervey sighed, 'I haven't the least idea
what you mean. I'm always reading about this here form
and I could write about it myself, but I——'

'Oh Hervey, you're such an idiot, and you've got a broken
lace in your shoe, and I do love you more than anything
else in the world,' Philip said. He laughed, and made her
sit down where she could see a lilac, a chestnut tree, and a
triangle of water in which silly ducks stood on their heads
for sport. He took his hat off and the breeze lifted his hair,
very fair and thick it was, but Hervey noticed that what
she had taken for the shadow thrown by his hat was still there.
It was cast from within outwards, as though something hidden
in his young body were beginning to show through the flesh—
like the almost imperceptible mark of a bruise.

'You're tired, aren't you, Philip?'

'Cornwall was very fine,' Philip said. 'You could lie in

a field and watch it come alive. Like the Creation. I swear
I saw an orchis unwrap itself and all the buds spring open in
the time it took a green caterpillar to clear off. He thought
it was the beginning of a barrage. It's a pity young Hervey
isn't here to see you, I said. So then I came home.'

Hervey smiled at him. She hoped he would talk about her
book. She had a review of it in her pocket, torn from a newspaper, but the moment in which she would bring it out,
carelessly, had not come.

' Do you smile at everyone like that ? ' Philip said.

She took her hand out of her pocket, without the review.
This was not the moment. ' It's my only social aid. I can't
talk—I'm so afraid of not understanding that I listen with
both ears, and my tongue goes to sleep.'

' It took me a quite a time to realise you didn't mean
anything by it—I *know* it doesn't mean anything, but my
heart turns round in me just the same.'

There was silence for some moments. ' Can't we just go
about together ? ' Hervey said at last.

' When I don't see you, I think we can just be happy
not talking or thinking about it. Then I see you, and it's
no good. I know it's no good. I'd always be making you
feel awkward.'

' You do now.'

' It 'ud be different if you were a little more pliant and let
me kiss you,' Philip said. He looked at her with a young
serious air.

' I could be *false* and let you kiss me,' Hervey said swiftly.
A biting impulse to tell the truth seized her. ' Don't you
know what I'm like, Philip ? I always want people to be
pleased with me, I pretend to agree with them when they
talk as I think wickedly or nonsense. I can't *write* lies but
I speak them and if I had to write about a friend's books
I'd tell the strictest truth about them, but if he asked me I'd
answer him they were very good. When I'm with people
I try all the time to be pleasant, I think my own thoughts
but I *say* theirs, and I'd let you touch me, smiling, dear

Philip, and as if I liked it and I should not like it, I don't like being touched, not even by you—it isn't anything to do with Penn, it's something altogether different; if you make me kiss you I'll seem to like it, but it will be meanness and cowardice, and wanting you to approve of me.'

'After this I wouldn't kiss you if you asked me to,' Philip said fiercely.

'All right,' Hervey said. She felt herself shaking.

'How d'you talk to your American?' Philip said. 'Do you tell him all that?'

Hervey did not speak.

'T.S. said you were going to run away with him; I don't believe that, but you've changed, my dear. You're not so simple and fine as you were—maybe it's the War. It's always the War. Did you like him very much?'

'Yes.'

'Did he ask you to leave Penn?'

'Yes. Do we have to go on with this?'

'Did you stay somewhere with him?'

'No.'

'Meanness and cowardice,' Philip said. 'Why didn't you run away with him, our Hervey? You're not religious, are you?'

'I couldn't run far with Richard,' Hervey said quickly. She looked at him, 'Don't quarrel with me. I have to live my own way.' Way of a blind mole. Blindly working its way in the heavy earth. She felt the energy in her veins. One of these days I shall surprise them.

Philip jumped up. 'Come, Hervey,' he said, laughing. 'You're too much for me. You have finer reasons for doing only what you want to do than anyone I know. Richard indeed! I suppose you'll tell me you came to London for Richard's sake.'

'I came to make my fortune,' Hervey said.

'Dear Hervey. I'd send you one by post if I could. You'd take it up, with that look on your face no one recognises but me, which means you're pretending to be indifferent—all the time you're so excited you can scarcely unfasten the knots—you never cut a good piece of string, do you?—well, at last you get it open thinking What's this? why, it's my fortune, hurrah, hurrah. At the bottom of the box there's a card—From Philip. With Love.'

'Why thank you, Philip, I'm much obliged to you,' Hervey said.

They walked past big houses like dowagers, flounced with gardens. Night coming slowly made their trees a sound and a shadow. The sky was very far off, filled with a warm May darkness. There were lighted windows in the houses, and one stood open, framing between curtains a group of three men, two holding violas and the third seated, his cello between his knees. A fourth was partly hidden. Philip and Hervey stood against the railings to listen. Proud, loud, triumphant, the sixth Brandenburg concerto came among the leaves. Tears were in Hervey's eyes. This music was mixed in her with evenings of 1913, with a careless student life of any age, with no bitterness of war's or time's anguish. She touched Philip's hand. He was thinking only of the music: which stopped, and they walked on. They were too happy to care to talk.

4. *The realist*

Ridley's forefathers had been peasants, and farmers in a small way, until his grandfather, another William Ridley, moved into London and became an auctioneer's clerk. The son did a little better and became an auctioneer in his own right, married a good woman, the daughter of a schoolmaster, and sent his son to the university in the hope that the boy (who was prudent, intelligent, and energetic) would become at least a schoolmaster if not a master among auctioneers. He was short, inclined to be fat, with a large head and small bright eyes, like the country-bred Ridleys. At eighteen he no longer looked young. When the War broke out he had just taken his degree and was about to begin work on a newspaper (he had his own plans). Much as he disliked the idea of being killed he was impelled to join up, in order not to feel inferior to other young men and because he had decided that a war, in which he would acquire the reputation of being a hero, might be no bad beginning to his career. The War disappointed him by lasting four years.

He did his duty in it. He could have stayed at home—he had defective eyesight—and shown his father how to profit by it. Moreover, that side of war which could be summed up in thinking of the latrine, with its torn piece of sacking, filled him with loathing—so much so that he never got the better of it. But he went to France and was an efficient soldier. There were many hours when he went nearly mad with rage at having wasted so much time. In February 1918, finding himself in England for a spell of home service, he began to send essays and short sketches to the *London Review*. Some of them were printed, and as soon as he could get leave he called on the editor and by him was handed on rather gingerly to Evelyn Lamb.

His first interview with her, at her house, abruptly altered his life. Up to now he had imagined himself earning a competence as a literary journalist, marrying comfortably and settling down to life in the near country. His one secret ambition was to make a name as a writer. At the first sight of Evelyn's house this changed. A dozen impulses lying loosely about his mind rushed together with a deafening explosion. When the smoke cleared away a whole man, purged of romantic weakness, stood up—the eternal William Ridley had been born.

His small shrewd eyes noted the value of every piece of furniture in the room. The paintings baffled him, as did the tea service. He turned a plate over surreptitiously, made a mental note of the mark, and looked it up afterwards in the British Museum. Later he bought a book on china and old silver and another on the French Impressionists. Here his inborn shrewdness came to his help. If he knew nothing about painting from the artist's side he quickly learned to distinguish a good Manet from an indifferent one. Just as, without having any music in him, he was able to seize at once on the essential form of a piece of music, and by listening intently to musicians to make use of them for his own ends. This was something more than shrewdness. He would have laughed his loud jeering laugh if you had told him that he had a hunger for beauty. This hunger was more vehement in him than in other men. But he was ashamed of it.

He was deliberately brusque with Evelyn Lamb. He saw at once that to seem impressed would only force her to underrate him, and he lolled on her day-bed, his clumsy army boots sticking out across the rug, as if the house was his. He criticised her part of the *Review*, told her that So-and-so was no good, a wind-bag, and offered plump out to write a weekly page for her.

' You don't want all this impersonal stuff. It only bores people. You want something personal. Let them hear the voice. Not " This is a bad novel," but " *I* think this is a damn bad novel." That's what people are going to want now. The War's knocked all your gentlemanly reviewers off their perches. Down to brass tacks—Is this what I like or isn't it ? That's what we want. Now when *I* write an essay, I don't ask m'self, Is this as good as Charles Lamb ? I say, It's not Lamb, Lamb's been done, I know all about Lamb, now you listen to Ridley for a bit.'

Evelyn was impressed by his uncouth ways. Since she did not need to pretend anything, she let him see that he had impressed her. This pleased him, fed the growing vanity which was part of his spirit—and gave him a little contempt for her. In spite of it, he could not shake off the effect her rooms, and her own elegance, had on him. He drove his heel against his chair at the same time that, without anyone seeing him, he had crawled under it on his stomach to guess its value. He was quivering with longing to possess a house in which every object was of more value than anything in hers.

Again, this was not only greed. Somewhere he was as

vulnerable as a new-born crab. If he had great possessions
he could in his soft moments scuttle into them and be safe.
Not that he thought about it in this way. He did not admit
that he was vulnerable. The squirmings of the blind, naked,
terrified part of him went on in such darkness that he could
pretend they were not going on at all.

He was shaking with excitement when he left Evelyn this
first time. His heart thumped, and his neck was squeezed
inside the collar of his jacket so that he thought something
would burst there. He went into the Popular Restaurant
in Piccadilly and ordered a meal and a glass of beer, eating
and drinking slowly, to quiet himself. At the next table
there were two young women, recklesssly made up, very
gay and plump. They stood up to go out, and the girl facing
him smiled : without thinking about it he beckoned the
waiter, paid, and followed them. The streets were already
dark, with a thin wash of light from the blackened lamps.
At another time he would have shown himself polite and
generous but now he made no bones about what he wanted.
The young woman who had smiled must come with him
at once or not at all.

Later, she could not take herself away quickly enough to
satisfy him : he hated her. To get rid of her in the most
humiliating manner, he put her out of the door himself. He
felt exactly as he had felt one evening during his schooldays
when, to please him, his mother let him attend some ceremony
in his best suit and beside the other boys' suits it appeared
cheap and ill-cut. That had made him ashamed of having
been born poor ; now as well he loathed himself for having
been born at all.

In the morning he took a happier and more sensible view
of things. Lacing his boots, he saw them again planted on
Evelyn Lamb's rug. ' Why, I'm getting on,' he said aloud.

He smiled slyly. There was nothing like being proud of
yourself, to impress others. His face in the glass seemed to
him that of a fine self-reliant man, a sound man of business.
The idea for an essay on war-time cafés came to him as he

ran down the stairs. His mind bubbled with happy phrases. One day I'll write a novel about a café, he thought. A deep, almost painful excitement seized him. He drove it out sternly : this was not yet the time.

5. *On being young*

One day David Renn praised Hervey, saying that she wrote special copy better than any other person on the staff. She was so pleased that she sat at work late. It shortened the evening, and she would have less time to saunter about London, dreaming, and less to drink coffee to Puccini beating through the clatter of plates and voices and less time to think. Her body was restless with vitality and if she went home to her room it would drive her out again.

Sometimes as she walked about, she saw something that made her laugh out loud in the street. Sometimes she felt menaced by the people and the buildings, and she had to reason with herself not to run. She was happy without knowing it—anything made her laugh just as anything made her cry. Her mind was never still, balanced like a leaf in the wind. Now there is music, it said ; now the street lamps are lit ; now the sun shines and the flower-women have sprinkled water on their flowers. Once she saw a man reading her book in the street and thought, Now I am becoming famous.

CHAPTER V

1. *The voice of the people*

RENN left the office early, to have time to change his clothes before the meeting. In the office he wore his only good suit and he was afraid to risk it in what might turn out badly—ever since the first notice of the meeting one daily paper had been calling on all true-born Englishmen to signify in the usual way their dislike of unEnglish gestures. In the view of this newspaper the truly English gesture would be to starve all Germans to death, or, if that was a trifling severe, at least to lay them under tribute for an astronomical period. Renn shook the creases out of his second suit. It had been folded up ever since the day his mother packed it for him. Three moth-balls having a poisonous smell fell out and rolled away under the bed : he bent his head to sniff the sleeve of the jacket. ' It smells like mustard gas,' he said to himself. ' That ought to keep patriots away.'

He had promised to call for Rachel Earlham. She was waiting for him with an air of ridiculous courage but her hands felt cold. ' What's the matter ? ' Renn asked.

' Louis rang up from the office to say he heard there was trouble. They're going to break up the meeting, David ! '

' But, Rachel,' Renn said gently, ' you knew it before. Why not stay at home ? '

' No, I shall come. But don't let anyone take hold of me, will you ? I always think they'll do something dreadful to me.' She smiled at him like the good obedient child she was.

As they approached the hall they saw the beginnings of the crowd, women of the neighbourhood, young men, roughs,

and a few soldiers. A dozen bored policemen were holding
them off the steps of the hall. Rachel drew her arm from
Renn's and walked boldly beside him, head held firmly. A
gross comment from the crowd made her blush. Inside the
hall she drew a long gasping breath and smiled with relief.
' I am *very* angry,' she said.

They were early. Half an hour later, when the meeting
should have begun, the crowd outside had swollen to fill the
street, and stones thudded on the shuttered windows—the
shutters were inside and every pane of glass vanished. The
most terrible noise in the world, more terrible and destroying
than any merely mechanical terror, the noise made by human
beings who want to hurt each other, made speech impossible.

Renn put his ear against Rachel's lips to catch part of what
she was saying. She asked anxiously : ' Will they make us
pay for the windows ? ' On the platform the speaker of the
evening opened and shut his mouth without a sound audible
to the woman nearest him. At last he came down into the
room and spoke a sentence to a man here and another there,
who passed his words on. Those left on the platform were
writing the resolution in large letters on a sheet of paper,
which they held up : ' That this meeting contemns the
vindictive clauses of the proposed Peace Treaty and demands
a humaner and more sensible attitude to the defeated.' In
less than a minute they turned the paper over and wrote :
' Resolution carried. It is suggested that we are less likely
to be attacked if we leave the hall in twos or threes.'

' Come along,' Renn said.

Rachel had meant to walk bravely, but her first sight of
the crowd frightened her so that she turned and caught
hold of Renn's arm. It was a much thinner arm than her
husband's. Ah, if only Louis were here, she thought. Her
knees shook so that she could scarcely move them. Suddenly
she saw something which made her press her hand on her
mouth. In front of them an elderly man had lost his hat,
and now someone in the crowd brought a stick down on
his bald head, which cracked across like an egg. He fell,

E

and was dragged into the crowd.   Rachel looked up at Renn's face—he was pale, his mouth lifted in a smile she was not able to recognise.   Something struck him on the shoulder, making him stagger.   Now they were in the crowd between the lines of police.   She stared, fascinated by it, into the curiously distorted face of a woman who was shrieking : ' Cowards—beasts—murderers.'   This woman was well dressed.   As Rachel passed, she leaned forward and struck her on the breast.   A policeman shifted his bulk in front of her.   ' Why you people hold these meetings beats me,' he said in a disgusted voice.   ' I believe you *like* trouble.'

Rachel's little body refused to obey her.   She clung to Renn's arm because it was the only support left, but she felt no confidence in it.   There was nothing left but prayer. Rachel was a Christian—and she began a pitiably incoherent one :   ' Please deliver me from this crowd, please help me. Dear Louis, come and help me.'

Just in front of them a soldier ducked under the arms of the police and spoke quickly to Renn.

' Can I help ?   What's the best thing to do ? '

Renn shrugged his uninjured shoulder.   ' I think if you'd just walk along with us to the bus,' he said.   ' They'll leave you alone.'

' Right.'

Rachel felt her strength returning to her.   Still trembling, she walked along between Renn and their rescuer.   He was a young man, tall, strong, very sunburned, with a country face. His eyes twinkled, and his mouth, short and firmly closed, turned upward at its corners.   When he had seen them on to the bus he smiled and saluted in a friendly eager way, like a boy.   Rachel looked after him until she was almost ashamed, and turning to Renn she caught an expression on his face that made her feel sad.   ' I could not have walked through that crowd without you, David.   I'm a wretched coward.'

' You're a wretchedly poor liar,' Renn said, smiling at her. He had meant to answer roughly, but Rachel looked at him with so young and innocent a desire to please him that he changed his mind. But when they reached the flat he refused to come in to wait for Louis. If I stay, he thought, Rachel will have to wait until I leave to tell him how frightened she was with no one to protect her except poor crippled David. He walked away quickly, ignoring the beginnings of pain in his leg. His spirits were strangely high. I should like, he thought, to drink a little too much, in good company.

The thought barely crossed his mind that good company was hard to come by since so many had gone. Happiness sprang in him from a full source, and in spite of his leg he felt the pavement as light under his feet as grass. What's to do with you ? he said to himself, smiling. Almost at once he knew that he had begun to feel happy in the moment when he came down the steps of the hall into the crowd. The feeling of danger had excited him, stirring other, less simple feelings that he had thought dead. So that the moment when the young soldier joined him followed naturally on other moments, in which he had been sharply and radiantly alive. Those were the days, he thought happily.

Hands plucked at his sleeve as he walked up the stairs. Eyes looked into his with the confidence of a shared knowledge. When he unlocked the door of his room someone who had not waited outside laughed, and said : ' Bless me if it isn't our Davy.'

2. Delia's voice

In another part of London Hervey Russell was enjoying— you can put it in that way—a good dinner in company with Mrs Delia Hunt. Delia had invited her for half-past seven. Punctually at that time Hervey walked into Verrey's and stood staring round her with a pretence of ease. She felt that everyone in the place, and especially the waiters, had remarked her with contempt. For a moment she was seized with panic. The expression her face wore was exactly one it had when she arrived late at school and was forced to walk past the others to reach her place in the ranks—an air of exaggerated calm: here I am, I, Hervey Russell, I'm not at all hurrying myself, why should I?

She said stiffly to a waiter: 'I'll sit here until my friend comes.'

Beneath her panic she was being amused by the extravagant discreetness of the place, the last faint ripple of a wave which broke in the Victorian heyday—or it might have been in Babylon. Delicious days when Verrey's was fast (as fast as hansom cabs). All gone—except this carpet, the discreet cloakrooms, this subdued light. She waited ten minutes, between the extremes of shame and doubt. When at last Delia entered, she was half overjoyed, and half embarrassed by the clothes Delia had seen fit to wear. An immense hat, pinned down at one side, allowed you the finest view of Delia's lively eye and richly recklessly puffed hair. She wore many rings, a dress of lace and satin, and an excessively grand fur coat. As Hervey walked down the room behind this grotesque figure she tried to imagine what the other diners thought of her. Do they think I'm like her, she wondered. It was a disturbing thought.

The room—it had no windows and was lighted from above —accepted Delia without demur. Hervey was the intruder, the speck of grit it could neither digest nor turn into a pearl for a woman's ear.

'Lord, how I do love this room,' Delia said. 'Blue and gold and red—and all those drops and what d'you call 'ems. I love it. I suppose they'll tear it down to-morrow and put up something Broadway could use. Aha, the fools!'

Hervey kept her gaze strictly in the small area of their table, persuading herself that she was invisible. She did not forget to eat as much as she could. This dinner was providential, coming towards the end of a month when, thanks to a bill for Richard, she was poorer than usual. When the waiter cut their *filet de bœuf* she was vexed to see that he gave more than half of it to Delia. Just because she is bigger he thinks she needs more, she said to herself. However, what she received was more than enough for her—it went down with a delicious ease, between mouthfuls of a coarse white bread and two or three sips of the wine. She was relieved that Delia did not insist on her emptying her glass. Without that, the food was making her feel light-headed, and as the meal advanced Delia's voice sank into harmony with the other noises of the place. They flowed over her with a confused pleasing warmth, so that inside and out she felt soothed and well.

' You don't make the best of yourself,' Delia said loudly. ' That coat now—it's what I call tame. You won't get so far with a coat like that. What d'they pay you ? '

' Four pounds.'

' Tch ! Did I ever tell you what I started with ? Fifteen shillings and find your own clothes. Well I found 'em. I knew where to look between m'legs.' She nodded her head with an air of sharp good humour. ' You've got to look out for yourself in this world. In the next, if it's like this. My God, I've heard there are such things as saints and disinterested men, but I never met one. Mind you never do anything for anyone, man or woman, without you get some good of it—if it's only a good laugh.'

' What will you get from giving me this splendid dinner ? ' Hervey said.

' The sight of your face waiting for me,' Delia said swiftly. She gave her great laugh. ' You thought I wasn't coming, and I suppose you hadn't more than a few shillings in your bag. Look here—I could do with an assistant in my business. You can call it that. I'll pay you six—no, look here, you got a boy to keep, haven't you ?—I'll pay you eight pounds a week.'

' But I don't know what you do,' Hervey said calmly. A familiar impulse had taken its sharpest hold of her. Though she had not the least intention to become Delia's assistant in her business—it was probably not reputable—she could not resist playing the cards in her hand. It was an instinct out of her control. Every crafty, hard-dealing ancestor in a long

line of them sprang to her elbow in the moment they saw a
chance to profit. They quite stifled the other Hervey, the
careless one. She rested her chin on her hands, and looked
seriously at her companion. ' Tell me what you do.'

' Eight pounds a week ! I should think you'd take it and
then ask,' Delia grumbled.

Hervey smiled at her. ' I might be no use to you.'

' You're not disinterested, by any chance, are you ? ' Delia
Hunt exclaimed. ' It's all the same to me if you are. I run
a business—Women in Council Ltd. It has three doors, as
you might say, two in and one out. Two pages of questions
and answers—Delia writes th' answers, hundreds of them a
day, Lord, you never read such a book of revelations—in two
mealy women's papers, and gets well paid for it, bless her, and
refers the finest cream dela cream to Women in Council,
which charges them five shillings for consultation by letter.
It's all your mouth to my ear, in strict confidence, and I sell
the names and addresses, a guinea a thousand, to who can use
them. You being a troubled and so wife write an' ask Mrs.
Delia Hunt's advice about your husband, I send you th'
advice—mark me, good advice—wasn't I *born* a hundred
years old ?—in a month or so you get a letter from a skin-
food specialist and husband hears what is to his advantage.
By this everyone's pleased to death, and it all works to the
benefit of th' Empire in which a sucker is born every minute,
an' why not ? Why shouldn't they be born ? They have
as excellent leave to live as I have. So God bless us and make
Delia a good girl. What is it ? Where was I ? Ho me, I
sell a hundred thousand names to Ira Fisher, who guarantees
to cure your constipation thank God I can't complain with
extract of bark and water—a hundred thousand men and
women made glad and happy. You take my meaning ? Ah
yes. The motto of this world is Deliver the goods and mind
to get a receipt. Eight pounds a week. It's a good offer,
isn't it ? The first time I saw you I thought—there's a girl
has got some character. That's what I want—character.
I could teach *you*.'

'Thank you very much,' Hervey said. She gave Delia one of her soft intimate smiles. ' I'd like to think about it.'

She was half enchanted by Delia. The very grossness and boldness of Delia's face, the air she had of being sunk in life like an old boat in mud, so pleased her that if the ' business ' had been less revolting she might have agreed in it. Delia had so much life—and Hervey Russell loved the coarse old-smelling roots of life perhaps more than its delicate flowers. The innocence she kept to the end of her days came in here. So did a cynicism she could not have learned so young—it must have been given her.

She set herself to flatter Delia, and succeeded so well that the woman swallowed all down.

Afterwards, how tired she was. When she had escaped she forgot her at once and her eight pounds. She dreamed. I am twenty-five, my novel is a failure, yes, I must face it. The work I do is useless, I did wrong to come to London, leaving my baby. For what ? For this. I have no money, no one has heard of me yet, I have not even a husband. This last thought jumped into her mind because she had just seen at the far side of the road one who might have been Penn, so alike were they in this light. A deep longing for him seized her. Her body felt light and relaxed.

All the streets were lit up. A river of light from the street-lamps ran down the centre of the road and joined the pools widening outside the big shops. Hervey did not know what she wanted to do. She had walked—bristling with interest, like Habbakuk among his chimney-pots—along Regent Street and down on the other side. At the Circus she hesitated and turned towards Soho, where in a narrow half-lit street the shops were still open, and men and women were at their business—staring, chaffering, touching—in a warm odour of decaying food, sweat, dust, tripes, cheap clothes, and their breath. Between the houses, the air, breathed by so many, was never pure. She turned aside to this street. This or the next, what did it matter, since no one knew her or was waiting for her.

She was in that state between anger and exaltation when fatigue works on the nerves like excitement. Look at that sorrowful woman, her mind said; look at the old Jew; look, is it a dog or a child running in between their legs? She pushed a way through the crowd, impatient, her mind alive with thoughts, with impulses she could not wait to examine before, turning head over heels, they dragged her the other way, like a young animal prowling for what to kill and eat. She thought now of the time when she would be famous. She was eager to write a book, a masterpiece, which at one bound would place her above criticism. Another notion, not displeasing, was to take Shaw-Thomas's place at the head of the firm and be signalled in two continents as a ruthless woman of affairs. She was even prepared—this proves her not quite unreasonable—to become famous through a superb gesture. She rehearsed scenes in which she saved the life of a royal person and was rewarded at once with a sinecure at Court. Or perhaps more suitably, the life of the director of the Ritz Hotel, who would allow her a modest room looking over the Green Park, with the privilege of dining in his restaurant for life.

Suddenly—as she lifted her eyes to see where she was—she saw an elderly man standing in front of her with a tray of dead toys. His face was that of a monk or a scholar, patient, delicate, with sunken bones. He was not trying to sell his toys. He merely stood there as though giving himself every chance to be the object of a miracle. Without looking at him again she laid a penny on his tray. As she walked on, it seemed to her that her mind had taken a plunge downwards into darkness. It flowed silently in the darkness, bearing away with it her dreams and the years of her life.

3. *The voice of Lt. Penn Vane talking to himself*

There was a group of young men in the centre of the room when he came in. One or two greeted him with offhand friendliness, without ceasing to listen to what had been going on for a long time—the story of young Newcomb's adventures on leave. The point of the story was that nothing had happened to him. With peals of laughter, they followed him from anti-climax to anti-climax. . . . ' Go on, Dan, what did you do then ? . . . What did she say to you ? . . . I don't believe it.' Newcomb's cropped fair head almost touched the ceiling—he was a young giant—and the ease with which he laughed at himself infected his hearers. A current of smiles ran from face to face. They became crazy with joy. Penn turned his back on them, as ostentatiously as possible, drew his wife's letter from his pocket, and sat down. He pretended to be engrossed.

He did not dislike the boy because he was young, insolent, and very brave—but because, coming fresh to the aerodrome, he seemed to imagine that the Equipment Officer was a willing kind of dog, useful for fetching things. Penn had set himself to teach the boy his lesson.

' I say, Vane, listen to this.'

Penn glanced up. ' Sorry. Not interested,' he said in a contemptuous voice. If there's one type I can't stand at any price, he thought virtuously, it's the man who runs after women when his wife is safely out of the way. Newcomb hasn't been married more than six months—yah !

He read the last page of the letter four times. Fortunately it was closely written—Hervey had been anxious to economise paper while writing a great deal he had heard before, about their future. He heard the end of the story and the last dying explosions of mirth. Without lifting his head he was aware that Newcomb had strolled across the room, and was eyeing him. ' Going to get me those new struts soon, Vane ? I've been waiting a fortnight.'

Penn glanced at him and returned to the letter. ' All in good time,' he said curtly. ' You're not the only pilot in the Air Force.'

' What a rotten brute you are,' the boy said calmly. ' If you can't fly, you could at least see to getting the rest of us what we need.'

Someone laughed, a young sound without malice. Penn folded Hervey's letter, stood up, adjusted his tie carefully, and without glancing again at Newcomb strode out of the room. He was too sick with anger to eat. *He can wait now —I'm going to teach him to behave himself if they put me on the carpet for it : it's no pleasure to me to dine in mess, I can't stand this new crowd. Ah, the best have all been killed. Poor Perry—Salmson—Griffith—all gone. Only this child left.*

For a moment he left a throb of deep pride in his survival. He might easily have been killed—there was the day young Rose crashed within a yard of his Stores tent. The thought of his wife, and what she would have suffered if he had died then, pricked his eyes. *Poor Hervey.* A sentence in her letter returned to him in good faith. ' I wished for you so much, dear Penn.' *Ah, she misses me all right when I'm not with her, nothing like a spot of absence.* He thought tenderly about her for some time. *I'll write and cheer her up. Why not this evening ? I might send her something, a surprise. With Penn's love.*

He had paused to look carefully in the windows of a shop for the surprise. A loud merry voice calling his name brought him round. There stood Miss Len Hammond, smiling, overjoyed to see him. All the tenderness which had suffused his mind found an outlet in looking at her. They walked along together, very happy, he looking down into her face with a brotherly indulgent smile. She liked him and admired him so much that it would be cruel not to be fond of her. In his room he took her on his knee and began to unfasten the hooks of her white blouse. He could feel her heart quickening under his hand—*perhaps not fair to rouse her, but after all*, he thought easily, *she likes it or why come here ?* He was startled and a little annoyed when Len pushed away his hand.

' What would your wife think of us if she could see you ? ' she said, in a rough unnatural voice. Her round face, not pretty, but fresh and a little foolish, was crimson with emotion.

'But she can't see us,' Penn said reassuringly. He did not want to think about his wife now.

She drew herself suddenly from his arms. 'Really, I'm not a bit happy about us,' she whispered. 'I feel we're behaving wrongly, and if your wife knew she would be terribly unhappy.'

Her distress was clearly so genuine that Penn felt sorry for her. 'My poor child,' he said fondly. 'Why do you worry your head about what can't happen ? We haven't done anything to make you ashamed. So long as we don't—you know. I told you long ago—you can't say I didn't—I'm in love with my wife, and I wouldn't hurt her for anything in the world. I feel certain she loves me too, even though she looks down on me—oh yes, she does—for not being a success and all that, and not flying.'

'But,' cried Len, running to him, ' you're shortsighted, you can't fly. When you wanted to, they wouldn't let you. Doesn't your wife know that ? '

'Of course,' Penn said quietly. 'That doesn't prevent her despising me in a mild way.'

'I don't understand how anyone can despise you,' Len said. She was looking at him again with a lively devotion.

'Don't you ? I do,' Penn laughed. 'She's ambitious— I'm not. Success at any price and all that—it's not in me. She wouldn't like me if it were, but it gives her an excuse to criticise me. Ah well ! '

He found himself thinking of Hervey and young Newcomb in the same moment. A trace of bitterness came into his voice. And he had been about to spend money on her, on a surprise, poor fool that he was.

Len was so eager to comfort him for his wife's hard nature that he felt a fresh access of fondness. He began to caress her again, cupping first one round pretty breast in his hand, then the other. His hand slipped farther, moving gently over her skin. Half pleased, Len gave a convulsive shudder. Her knees were pressed tightly together ; but the upper part of her body had surrendered and lay slackly on his arm. Her eyes were closed. Only when his fingers began to feel at the fastening of her skirt did she make a light movement of resistance. 'What's the matter?' Penn said softly. 'Don't you like me any more?'

'You're taking my things off,' Len murmured. Her head, drooping, turned away from him towards a darkened corner of the room. She was seized with another of those shudders which gave him a delicious feeling of strength and tenderness. 'Don't, Penn—not now, please.'

'I'm not going to touch you,' Penn said. He meant it, with his whole heart. An ecstasy of emotion filled him. It seemed to have nothing to do with his body, which pressed itself against her without his being much aware of it. 'I'd like to see the whole of you. Why shouldn't I? I've seen quite a lot of it, you know.' He looked at her with a mischievous coaxing smile.

Len made it difficult for him at first by clinging to him closely, but at last she began to help him. He had to put her off his knee and she stood in front of him with her hands on her face. Her teeth chattered a little.

'Cold?' Penn asked. His head had begun to throb. He pressed her down into her chair and crouched in front of her, trying to warm her with his arms. He held her firmly, and at last she began, with an air of distraction, to return his kisses. The resolution he had taken seemed ridiculous. He felt more than slightly ridiculous, crouching in a uniform and field boots in front of a naked girl. 'Wait a minute,' he said abruptly. He stood up and walked to the back of the room. He could not struggle with his boots under her eyes. The chair groaned as he dragged at them, and he wondered with some uneasiness what she was thinking about it. The whole affair was a little awkward. He made as few sounds as he could. His belt dropped on the floor: pricking with nervousness he took it up—and dropped it again.

When he approached Len she made no attempt to refuse him. He had a few minutes of happiness such as he had never experienced in these circumstances. Afterwards she began to cry limply in his arms, and he was filled with pity for her. Poor child. He soothed her, feeling her grow quieter until she opened her eyes and even smiled at him. Fervently he hoped she would have the good sense not to speak of his wife—after all, he had not meant this to happen. All this time as he stroked Len's shoulders he was determining to spare Hervey all unhappiness. At all costs, this must be kept from her, and from now on he would give his life to it. Not for his own sake—I'm ready at any time to face the music, he thought firmly—but for hers. What the eye doesn't see the heart doesn't grieve, he said to himself. He stroked Len's breast. A gentle sense of well-being spread through him. He rested from his labours in quietness and felt at peace with the world—in which, almost without effort, he embraced his wife, yes, and young Newcomb. In an obscure part of his mind he felt that he was behaving with delicacy and sensibility. No one had been harmed. He did not love his wife less for loving Len in a somewhat different way. The excellent lucidity of his mind delighted him. There was nothing Hervey could say to him for which he had not one good answer at the least. For a space he saw and heard himself disposing of the whole episode in bold, simple words. My dear Hervey—perhaps, Hervey my dear—all your phrases about sin and—he cleared his throat—purity, are a little revolting. There is no justification for the worship of monogamy, neither in heaven nor on earth. I ask you to observe that it is a convention, not held by a third of the world's inhabitants, and denied—he cast down his eyes —by enlightened men in every civilised country. Men not of the herd. Yes. Many men have loved two women. Yes. After all, my dear girl, a man is an animal. A man has his hungers. The time must come when any man will be prompted by appetite to take someone who will respond to him differently—here he gave her a frank pleading smile— you couldn't understand that, of course.

A poignant and suffocating emotion filled him. He felt that every breath he drew of it made him more sensitive and more mature.   What could be so exquisite as the little shocks of tenderness he felt in himself, each swelling gently the tide of his well-being ?   He felt that he was becoming a new creature.   Even on his eyes the light struck with an early-morning vigour.   Unconsciously he renewed his caresses of the body lying beside his.   Dear little girl.   He drew her closer to him, in a spasm of gratitude.

CHAPTER VI

ON A FINE MAY MORNING

At dawn in summer the country enters London by all roads. Country carts whip up behind lorries and vans carrying in the food the city needs to keep alive during the day. On the main roads the incoming stream meets another which has been flowing all night from the railway depots and the north, and a Hertfordshire farmer halted by the roadside on his way into town is hailed in a foreign dialect by a driver to whom these roads and gently swelling fields seem too smooth to be real. Ships moving with the first tide stand away from wharves emptier than those where the work of loading has gone on noisily through the night: on other wharves the business of feeding London has scarcely ceased and the light only draws another piercing design on the canvas. In the city, in streets which were the first to fall silent the evening before, and in squares which are the last stand of the seventeenth century in a more disorderly age, a sluggish subterranean life of cleaners and caretakers begins, four hours before the first trainload of clerks and typists empties itself into the street, to be followed instantly by another and another like the waves of a sea in which each tiny drop is part of a human body, its eyes, legs, arms, thoughts, and hopes.

These are the late-comers. At the Dug-out Frank has been boiling coffee and cutting slices of bread since three o'clock: now and then he looks across the field, in which the grass shines so fiercely that it is the colour of light without green, at the caravan, anxious not to miss the first flutter of a rag from the doorway, sign that the captain is waiting to drink his coffee. The river, the markets, are crackling with life, before the sleepers in their beds have wakened for the first time, at that zero hour when the life which left their bodies as they slept has scarcely turned to flow back—so that if by some evil chance they fail to drop asleep again at once a strange experience awaits them. All their actions, ambitions and intentions pass through their minds in a light so denuded of all colour that, now, if never before, they see these without the enchantments they secrete during the day.

It happened to Hervey Russell to wake up at this hour—which must coincide with some change in the earth's movement. At once, as though it were the continuation of her dreams, she found herself thinking of Richard, sleeping in his bed in Miss Holland's house in Danesacre. Her mind presented her with the sharpest possible outline of his head on the pillow, cheeks flushed in sleep on which the long dark lashes appeared drawn with a fine brush, tiny beads of damp where his hair clung thickly round his neck.

She realised, with a dreadful clearness, that nothing she had gained for herself by coming to London compensated what she had given up. She saw her work in the office as a mean, mind-destroying ritual, the refinement of trickery, by which she earned what just kept her alive and hired Richard a place in another woman's life. Beside that she was not even a success at her work. Some knot in her own mind kept it from flowing freely in the channels Shaw-Thomas engineered for it. She did some things well, but more baffled her so utterly that more than once she had retired to the lavatory to weep tears of despair and rage. I have deserted my baby, and I am a failure, she said to herself. She opened her eyes. The room, on which after five months she had not left the faintest impression, confirmed the sentence.

But already a subtle change (like the change which takes place in a chemical compound when another element is added) was at work in her thoughts. She recalled praise David Renn had given her. A notion—that it was time to ask Shaw-Thomas for more money—came for the first time close, and the excitement it started brought her upright in bed. She began to rehearse what she would say. Her spirits rocketed, and an air, that her mother would have recognised, altered her face. From being dull it became shrewd and lively, with something unyouthful, a prudent politic smile, in the eyes. She wants me to give her something, the mother would have said.

She fell asleep again, woke, looked at her watch. Six o'clock. The bedclothes, except for the sheet, had spent the night on the floor. She got up, lifted them on to a chair, and walked to the window. A street opened away to the left, going south-west. The near house was awash with light, clear, dazzling; the others were in shadow, they were like cliffs, and the shadows were blue and soft. Directly below her a tree sprang like a fountain, its quivering upper leaves bright. Water in sunlight, they poured this way and that in currents of air. Then, from far above her, a brown feather dropped slowly, straight, turning as it fell, like one of the darts children make. She watched it until it touched the ground, when instantly its turning ceased, it keeled over and lay still.

Now I must go out, Hervey thought. She remembered that her mother, when she and they were young, would run out in the early morning in that bright air, happy, as if she were the only creature in a new world. Her mother, Danes-acre, and Richard were her roots, from which her life thrust away. The thrusting away was pain, and a part of her was never done longing to return, as if a tree should try to send its sap downwards, into the earth. She even knew that the growth was not straight—there were too many things hindering her. Yet here she was—she had got so far, to this room—and not even the agony of her love for Richard could turn her back.

There was the light sound of a letter being pushed under her door. She ran, and stooped quickly. It was from France, from the American, Jess Gage. The bold left-handed writing sent a shock from her eyes to the centre of her body.

She did not open the letter. She put it in her handbag,

F

dressed quickly, and went downstairs. Not willing to face her landlady (silly Hervey, she was never easy with strangers), she had written on an envelope ' No breakfast, please. Hervey Russell,' and left this in the hall.

In the street she felt free, and skipped off gaily. There was nothing in sight but an early hunting cat. You could think you were in a foreign city, except that no housewife had hung her bed over the window sill. Soon she was in a main road, with the early traffic prancing down it. She pranced beside it, pleased with London and with herself for being abroad in it. When she looked at her handbag the leather became transparent and she could see the letter lying inside.

Suddenly she was seized with the pangs of hunger. She walked a long way down the Edgware Road seeking a café. None were yet open. At last when she was dejected and very empty she saw a coffee stall, with a glittering brass urn, and ran across to it. The man in charge was better than obliging. He cut fresh bread to her order, and both bread and coffee tasted so fine that she felt herself in heaven. It seemed now as though her handbag opened of its own accord. She drew out the letter.

Like earlier ones, it was long, written in an idiom as sharp, lively, and common as Elizabethan English. She did not read it so much as hear Gage's voice, soft and peremptory. Its very difference from English voices lent it some of the effect of music on her nerves. She had to listen to it more than with her ears. She was trembling when she turned the last page. ' I'll give you two three months, darling child. You'll see me in England in August. If you can't bring yourself to leave that thing your husband, all right, have it your own way. I'm not going to coax you. But if you decide to have me I'm yours, and I never told you lies—except about other people to amuse you. You know I love you. Don't you want to marry me and go live in a real country ? Jess.'

She swallowed the last drops of coffee, thanked the man

smiling, and went on. The letter glowed in her hand like a hot coal. Its heat made even the sun less bright to her. She walked slowly, trying to harden herself to the notion that she would see her American again. As she thought of him, of the way he walked, of his eyes, narrowed and lively, her body was roused and tense. Her hands shook. She would have to decide : but already the decision was made. It had been made for her, by her terrible will.

She reached the office before time and found David Renn at work. She had built up what was nearly a friendship with him. She was very silent with him, and tried to create in his mind the notion that she was a lower kind of batman. In that way she hoped to use him to seeing her about his room. In time he might even trust her.

She saw at once that it was a bad day for him. Pain made him short-tempered, and she sat nervously at her desk, at the work she had left unfinished the day before. It would never be finished by her, being what she could not, by any means not, do—that was to find a trade name for a jam. In the year 1868, a poor widow, Mrs Susan Martin, of Norwich, began to supply herself by making jams for her neighbours. She prospered, and her sons built themselves a factory, by which it was necessary to change the character of the jam when it was no longer bought and carried fresh from its pantry. The factory was now, in 1919, sold for a good sum to a syndicate.

An evil crow an evil egg, as they say. Having got this sound family business into its hand, the syndicate proposed to swell it out. They changed the jam again (to a hygienic mess Widow Martin's neighbours would have poured to their pigs), voted money to blare it about the country, and called in Mr Shaw-Thomas to help them. A pot of jam costing twopence to make, now cost—with sales-psychology and what-not, pressure advertising, and the labours of poor Hervey—eightpence to get it sold. An artist was preparing the sketches—English cottage interior, 1870; the young widow admiring her jam ; at the window honeysuckle.

'Martin's Cottage Jams,' Hervey wrote. 'The subtle delicacy and flavour of a home-made jam, as pure as science can make it. . . .'

'For pity's sake, young Russell, don't mutter,' Renn said curtly.

She blushed, and looked at him with an ashamed smile. The door opened; Mr Shaw-Thomas came in, followed by an American.

This American's face was so expressive of decision that it might have been made of papier-mâché. Hervey was delighted with him. You could make a door-knocker of this face, she said to herself. What was very strange, when he opened his mouth an odd whirring noise came out before the words.

'This is Mr Harriman,' said Mr Shaw-Thomas.

'Hr-r-r-r-r, very glad to meet you,' Mr Harriman said, smiling and nodding.

It was soon out that Mr Harriman was the agent of a firm of chemists. This firm had been cleaning up America with a disinfectant called Saloxide, containing (but he forgot to mention this) 75 per cent. of a violent corrosive poison. They had done it by the use of what he called War copy. He was very proud of this copy. He had conceived it himself, and he was so fecund a father that you would hardly find any corner in America where the disinfectant was not in use, whether for pigs or babies.

'Now, in England,' said he, whirring, smiling, nodding, 'you boys didn't have exactly the War ours had. We're going to sell Britain, but the copy has got to be adapted. Not written over. Oh no, no, no, no, no.' Mr Harriman laughed with all his teeth. 'Hr-r-r-r. You couldn't write over this copy. Why it's Hamlet Prince of Denmark. It would sell elephant meat. All I want is for you to go over it very carefully, like you were laying out your grandmother for her deathbed, and make it one hundred per cent. British. Yes? At home we had an Army doctor check up on every line and we didn't let a one go out without he passed it.

Maybe somewhere I wrote "top sergeant" and maybe you people didn't call them top sergeants. I didn't partake in the War myself.'

'One moment,' Renn said, 'was the stuff used in your army hospitals?'

'It was not.'

'Oh. Then where does the War come in?'

Before answering this Mr Harriman whirred for so long that Hervey became alarmed. It must be his works, she thought. Fancy if he went on like this for ever. He'd go whirring along Piccadilly, frightening people. They'd have to arrest him for a breach of the peace. A spasm of laughter seized her. She controlled it, but it came at her again and again. Little gusts of laughter went on rising inside her until her body felt bruised and sore. Her face was crimson. At last a choked sound escaped her. Renn looked at her in contemptuous reproof. She was ready to die of shame.

Mr Harriman turned to look at her: his mouth was still open but the whirring had ceased. It was too much. Jumping up, she went quickly out of the room.

She walked upstairs to the half-landing and leaned against the wall, feeling weak and disgraced. She no longer wanted to laugh. After a time she heard the door open and Mr Harriman going away. She slunk into the room. Renn did not speak to her. He was looking through the heap of papers Mr Harriman had left with him. At last he looked across at her and said:

'Why did you behave like that?'

'I'm very sorry,' Hervey said anxiously. She was relieved that he no longer looked angry. He looked tired to his death, and his mouth was drawn into a nervous smile. She walked over to his desk.

'My God, what brutes,' Renn said quietly. 'This is an account of a battalion going over the top, wounded coming back, clearing station, stretchers, field hospital, "Am I for it, nurse?" operating room . . . what saved thousands of lives in the Great War? peroxide and saline. . . . What will save

millïons in the Peace ?   Saloxide. . . . These pictures will
have to be redrawn.'   He held up a full-page drawing of
an American soldier, smiling and insolently handsome. ' This
one reminds me of——'

Without warning, he was sick over his hands and the
drawing.

He refused to let Hervey touch him or his desk.   When
he had finished washing the desk he sat down and laughed
at her face.

' My poor Russell,' he said unamiably.   ' I'm as sorry as
death, but I had no time to help myself.   Would you like
to go home ? '

Hervey looked at him and scowled.   ' You wouldn't say
that if I were a man,' she said.

' Neither I would,' he answered calmly.

Twelve o'clock.   Mr Shaw-Thomas called a conference
of copywriters in his room.   Hervey sat at the back of the
men, conscious of her hands.   Lunch time returned her to
herself, with an almost physical sensation of ease and lightness.
Going on the way to the office she saw a fair tall girl, clad
from head to ankle in pale blue, striding along like a man ;
a poor woman's little merry baby, in a frock of red velvet,
and gold rings in its pierced ears ; a soldier without legs or
hands ; and a woman and a child begging.   They were
figures in the front of a vast frieze, a faceless anonymous
multitude, which flowed past her without stopping.   The
afternoon exasperated her, pressing on the nerves at the back
of her head.   At three the ferret-faced manager from the
Charel Soap Company came in to complain about her copy.
He said it lacked passion and the poetic note.   His smile
was stretched out on his face like a filthy rag.   Four o'clock.
A page which had gone safely to press was ordered to be
changed and Hervey ran with it to the printers.

She then should have gone back to the office but went
home instead.   Her landlady came out to her, with a sly
jeering smile on her face.

' Miss Russell.   A man who said he was your husband

came. He asked if there was a room he could have.' She watched Hervey closely.

Hervey jumped round. 'Where is he now ? ' she said in a sharp voice. A shock of hatred for the woman went over her.

'He said he'd come back.' The woman stepped closer. 'I suppose you *are* married, Miss Russell ? ' She knew that Hervey was Mrs Vane, but she wanted to see her embarrassed and vexed. It was less malice than curiosity—she had been a countrywoman and she could scarcely use herself to closed doors, to not knowing what your neighbour does and is.

'I explained it to you when I came,' Hervey said. She felt that she was losing self-control. 'I use my own name at work. My husband's name is Vane.' Her eyes started at the woman.

The landlady turned away, now a little afraid of her. She was lame, and as she went she made the most of her age and lameness.

Though she was trembling with anger, Hervey felt conscience-stricken. 'The photograph in my room,' she called, 'is my son.'

The woman did not answer. But when Penn came she gave him the small room next Hervey's at a low charge. Hervey felt more remorseful than ever. But she hated the woman, and would not have been sorry to hear her fall down the stairs with her lame leg.

She turned to Penn with a cry of relief and pleasure. He seemed so cool and definite, untroubled, she forgot her vexed mind and clung to him. It was enough happiness not to be alone for this evening.

He was looking, she thought, young and engaging, and her heart warmed to him. She ran from her room to his, helped him to put away his things, fetched the manuscript of her unfinished novel to show him, talked and talked away, altogether unlike herself.

'Are you going to read this to me ? ' Penn asked.

'No, I must finish it.'

'This evening ? ' Penn grinned.

'This evening we'll go out. We'll enjoy ourselves.' She gave him a sudden bright look, as though she had felt shy. Deeply moved, he came over to her and kissed her, holding her body against his. It felt light and thin.

'Your dress is too large for you,' he said smiling. He drew a fold of it between his fingers. 'Look.'

'I bought it,' Hervey said, as if that explained enough the question of its size. 'Where shall we go?'

'Where do you want to go?' he said, humouring her.

Hervey knew that he felt pleased with her. He liked her when she let herself behave as a schoolgirl and not when she talked to him about their future and reminded him that he had responsibilities. It hurt his pride and he retorted by refusing to take any interest in them. Actually he could not endure her when she was managing and ambitious. He wanted to knock all that flat in her; to listen patiently to it was one thing he could not do. The more she strove and was anxious, the less he cared. It was as though he felt that her vitality diminished him in some way.

This evening she tried willingly to please him. If he would look after her for a short time she would be anything he wanted. Very gladly she let herself be young, as if she were still a student. She recalled what she enjoyed doing then, and off they went, in good spirits, to Richmond.

They had a late tea in the café which provides succulent cakes called maids-of-honour. In the year before the War, when she came here, Hervey had not been able to afford to eat more than one. Determined now to have a fat feast and a jolly banquet, she ordered twelve. 'When I am old,' said she, 'and the *doyenne* or aunt of English letters, young cake-eating men with an eye to favours will ask each other what does the old girl like, then bring me here, and stuff me to the ears with maids-of-honour. Then I shall—or shall not—praise their books.'

Alas, the fifth finished her. It was a proper finish. Penn laughed at her look of dismayed greed.

Afterwards they walked along the towing-path to Kew,

The river was still and cloudy, with a barge moving slowly towards London. Hervey lingered to watch it. ' If we lived like that we should be free,' she exclaimed.

' You'd tire of it in a week, and of me, at close quarters,' Penn said.

' The house we lived in until 1917 was almost as small.'

' Yes,' Penn said, ' and were you happy ? You grumbled day and night. No, no, my dear, you never forget you're Mary Hervey's granddaughter. You'd like to be as wealthy as the old girl. And if you were, you'd be as intolerable a bully. You bully me hard enough as it is.'

Hervey did not say anything. When you accused her she could not defend herself until she had looked to see whether you were right. These words hurt her.

Penn glanced at her face. ' All right, puppy,' he said gently. ' I didn't mean to upset you. Look here—what did you want from our marriage ? Tell me. Tell me now.'

An extraordinary sensation passed through her, a shiver which began so far below the surface of her life that she felt it in the pit of her stomach before she felt its cold touch on her skin. It was disconcerting and familiar—her nerves had sent out a warning message—something wrong somewhere, hidden from you, it said—wait—listen. The sensation lasted less than a second, while she was looking at Penn. When it went she forgot it.

' Don't you know ? ' she cried. ' I wanted us to live together and be kind to each other. I don't know what else a marriage is for. There is so much unkindness.' She struggled with herself, to find words for what was better without words. ' I'm safe, so long as you approve of me,' she said, with a smile.

' Ah,' Penn said lightly, ' but do you approve of me ? No, no, no, you don't any more. You think I'm lazy, irresponsible, slack. One of these days you'll leave me for a cleverer chap. Run away from me, and what will poor Penn do then ? '

' I shall never run from you,' Hervey said quickly.

The river was empty, and the towing-path empty. Warm stillness lay everywhere. Penn put his arm round her, with a smile. 'Why won't you ? Tell me.'

A deep certainty seized her. 'I couldn't leave you after we've lived together so long,' she exclaimed. 'It would do too much damage. It would destroy one of us.' She looked at him—thinking, odd as the thought was, that it is the dull, tiresome things you do for one another in marriage that seize and hold. 'Are you beginning to be tired of me ?'

'My dear child !' Penn said.

They walked on in complete accord. The thought crossed her mind that again Penn had said nothing about leaving the Air Force. She was too anxious for the success of their outing to risk the question. Perhaps in the morning he would speak of it. She felt closer to him again, as if their conversation had been important—a revelation.

CHAPTER VII

RICHARD

RICHARD VANE, son to Hervey and Penn, was between three and four years old when his mother, on whom he depended, left him to make her fortune. His if she succeeded. He knew nothing about this. One morning his mother bathed and dressed him as usual and in the evening a strange woman called and took him away to her house. When she left him alone for a few minutes he looked in one or two places for his mother. The woman returned, gave him supper, bathed him and put him to bed. He did not ask for his mother.

In the morning he sat up in bed and looked about the room, waiting for his mother. The woman came in smiling. He had begun to accept her as part of his new life. When he had lived in the house a short time other children came. Excited by their voices and faces he rushed to the door to meet them, surprising them. He had an idea that his mother had sent them. The woman, to whom he had now given a name, sometimes spoke to him about his mother. He listened but said nothing. No one knew what he was thinking. He disliked the question sometimes put to him, 'Do you remember your mother?' and did not reply. He was often alarmed by shapes and sounds, and his defence against them was always silence.

One day he was looking at a white flower. He pulled it closer and looked down into the deep cup. He saw dark violet lines, and spikes covered thickly with a bright yellow powder. I am living down in there, he said to himself; I am hidden, no one sees me. The extraordinary feeling this gave him was scarcely pleasant, and it was in spite of himself that he went on looking into flower after flower. The feeling lasted, and when at tea he tried to eat he was very sick. When this happened he had been with the woman a long time. His other life, with his mother, in some other house, had not vanished from his mind, but it was at times something which had been endlessly long ago, and at times as close as yesterday. One morning he was playing by himself in the garden. He heard steps coming up the path at the other side of the house and put his things down to listen. The bell rang, then an interval without sound, then his mother's voice. His heart turned round in his side. He got up and began to run. 'Is that my mother?' he called.

Before she saw him Hervey heard him speaking in this high voice. She was struck through by it. When she went away from him he was—both by being obstinate and an only child—backward in speaking. He would say a single word and point. The thought in her mind was : Without me he has been learning to speak. She was never able to reason away the ridiculous pain of this thought.

To come, she had travelled by the night train and was going back the next night. When she came in the early morning, her mother was watching for her from the window of her house. She had turned her head aside and Hervey had a momentary glimpse of her staring, it seemed, at nothing, her blue eyes fixed and empty, with the look in them of one used to distances, mouth drawn down and bitter. Hervey stood still on the path, looking at her mother's face, the skin still clear and pale, but the look of bitterness fixed on it, and the lines deeper.

With a kind of anger in her, she ran into the house, deliberately noisy and gay. Anything to rouse her mother from that set staring immobility. She could not bear it.

After breakfast, before going out to get Richard, she looked round the house to see if anything was new there. She saw a chair in her mother's room and the newly-framed photograph of her brother. It was one taken only a short time before he was killed.

' I like your new chair,' she said eagerly.

Mrs Russell touched it gently, caressing the old wood. ' I'm going to have this room painted in the autumn. I told your father and he looked as black as thunder. Ha! he'd let us live in a barn if he had his wish. I take no notice of him.'

She spoke with a quiet steely anger. ' When Jake's things were sent home,' the mother said, ' he wanted to take them. " I'll take those," he said. " Oh no you'll not," I told him : " they're mine, *my* son's—and you don't lay a finger on them." And I put them away. He never thought anything of the boy ; when Jake got his first medal he wrote to him that other men had done as much and not been given medals for it. And then saying, " I'll take those." ' Her mouth worked.

Hervey watched her with the old feeling of rage and pity. She could not bear it when her mother showed so plainly her disappointment with her life. She was in truth disappointed. With all her young rage Hervey could not make it right for her.

After a pause Mrs Russell said : ' Your grandmother is building herself a new house.'

Your grandmother ; *your* father—but *my* son. She puts as far away from herself as possible, won't have, the things she dislikes, and grasps the others. ' Where ? '

' Almost on the moors. The place is about five miles from here. They've cut a road from the main road and great cartloads of stone were being taken along it. I saw it. Carlin and I were up there one day and we saw the road. Like a cut made in the moor. You'd think she had houses enough without building another.'

Hervey did not look at her. At last she said : ' Five miles. Suppose she came here to see us ! She might be thinking of it ! '

' Not she ! ' Sylvia Russell flashed. She laughed, in the loud contemptuous way that had hurt Hervey as a child. ' She'll not come here ! ' Pulling at her mouth, she said quickly : ' I'll tell you a thing I've never told anyone. One day, it was before you were born, your grandmother came to see me—not in this house, in the house I lived when I was first married. I hadn't seen her since—since just after I married. I asked her to take your father into the firm and let him make a career for himself. Mind you, I was very young. And she refused Your father was out of a ship after that for over five months. When she came that day I thought she'd come to offer him a post. I opened the door to her and I said, " Have you come to offer William a place in the firm ? " When she said No, she hadn't, I shut the door again. I wouldn't have her in the house. From that day to this she hasn't been near hand. She didn't come when you were born. She never offered to do anything for any of you. All that Jake did he did for himself. The time when she could have helped him is gone.'

' I suppose you never wrote to her,' Hervey mumbled. She was afraid of saying the wrong thing. There was something dreadful, the ugliness of a wound, in her mother's bitterness. After all these years she was no less bitter than if it had happened yesterday. Why, she thought, even I have forgiven my grandmother. Wincing inwardly, she saw herself, a stiff, badly-dressed schoolgirl, asking Mary Hervey to give her work. To herself she laughed guiltily, wondering what her mother would say if she knew. She had not the faintest wish to tell her.

' Why should I write ? ' Mrs Russell said loudly. ' I was poor, not she. It was her place to write, not mine. Nay— I was done with her after that.'

' Of course,' Hervey said quickly. ' You couldn't do anything, she was mean and cruel to you.'

She wanted to assure her mother that she was on her side. Mrs Russell's face had a sunken defeated air. At this moment Hervey hated her grandmother. In the same moment she could not help thinking how different, easier, and happier, their life would have been if her mother had relented.

As if she felt this Mrs Russell began a violent justification of herself. It was not she, it was Mary Hervey who had been relentless, grudging, hard. Hervey listened and nodded. With one of its strong leaps her mind saw how everything in Sylvia Russell's life had been coloured by her quarrel with her mother. Everything she did had to justify her. Everything she did was right. If she broke a cup, it was not her fault, nothing was her fault. Am I like her ? Hervey wondered. With her usual savagery towards herself, she answered : Yes, I am like her, I can't bear being in the wrong.

There was one person in the house who could best Mrs Russell. That was the nine-year-old Carlin. In the afternoon, while Richard was sleeping upstairs, the little girl played quietly in a room with Hervey. All at once she dropped her doll. Its face cracked into bits. Carlin did not cry. After one glance at the wreck she flew across the room and began to beat Hervey. 'You broke my doll,' she cried, her fine delicate face scarlet. Hervey was taken by surprise and laughed out. At that the child lifted up her voice and wept loudly. Mrs Russell hurried in and Carlin rushed to her.

' She threw my doll down.'

A flash of anger passed over the mother's face. She glanced at Hervey.

' That I did not,' Hervey said. ' I was sitting here where I am now. I was nowhere near her.'

Mrs Russell said nothing, and took Carlin away. Hervey heard her comforting the child in a soft voice. It seemed that Carlin, too, was above the law.

In the evening, she took Richard back to Miss Holland's house and put him to bed there. He did not ask her how long she was staying. She waited a short time downstairs and then went up to see if he were sleeping. He must have fallen asleep without moving, his small body curled up, one arm flung out. How heavily the dark lashes lay over his cheeks. She bit her lips in her hard grief.

Mrs Russell looked closely at her when she was saying

good-bye. ' Do you ever feel sorry you went away ? ' she asked.

' Something had to be done,' Hervey said.

When the train started she stared across the harbour to the old town. In the light without sun every stone, tile, chimney, was as sharp as glass. The green edge of the cliff struck the sky. A few gulls turned and rose above the houses and the boats with reefed sails. To keep herself from thinking of Richard, she thought of her mother. There was the strange pattern of Sylvia Russell's life, with threads woven into foreign ports—the young spoiled girl becoming the stubborn woman, refusing defeat. Who could say that her mother's life had been wasted ? Touch it anywhere and it fell apart, revealing fresh skies, a street in Vera Cruz, wharves, storms at sea, a toque made of tiny silk flowers, gifts, anger, and joy coming in the morning.

That so much should end in so little, Hervey cried. The loveliness of Danesacre hurt her, because she thought of all the women who had walked in its streets, of whom through their eyes it had become part, until they died and saw it no more. She felt angry, and shivered.

CHAPTER VIII

TWENTY-EIGHTH OF JUNE, 1919

1. *Philip makes plans*

PHILIP drove away from the Dug-out about five o'clock. It was a white morning, with the promise of heat, but at this hour the grass was still silky and shining, and the distances clear. Four aeroplanes crossed the blue of the upper sky, one beside the arrow-head of the other.

He chuntered through two villages without noticing the flags thrust from the windows, and was surprised when he reached the main road to find himself in an ever-thickening stream of traffic. Nursing the car, he kept round the northern skirt of London, to reach Renn's lodging without much driving in streets. When he drew up there he saw the large dirty flag drooping from the window above Renn's. There were others. The shabby street had broken out into a red white and blue rash. Philip ran up the stairs and opened Renn's door. 'Well,' he said, 'what are you celebrating with this show ?'

Renn had been setting the table for their breakfast. He glanced up with a smile. 'Signing the Peace,' he said. 'Don't you read a newspaper ?'

'Only if Frank wins one from a customer. For over a week we've had no luck. I might have known it—wait—*patches will I get unto these cudgell'd scars And swear I got them in the Gallia wars.* Well, that's something done with.'

'I'm not so sure,' Renn said. 'A bad Treaty doesn't settle anything—except the causes of the next war.'

He could not make this gloomy prophecy in any but the happiest voice, because of his delight in seeing Philip.

'All the more reason,' his friend said, with a smile, 'why you and I should assert ourselves quickly. He seated himself at the table opposite Renn. 'How long is it since we shared a meal?'

'The night of the fifteenth September 1917, in Kemmel Shelters,' Renn said at once.

'Well—it's too long,' Philip said.

'You were hit the next day and I the day after.'

Philip was examining the room, as shabby as the house and street of houses. 'You should live out in a field, as I do. It's better than this.'

'I'm warm and well as I am, thank you,' Renn answered. He did not think Philip would be interested to hear that, of his salary of eight pounds a week, he sent two pounds to his mother, and put three away against the fear of losing his job and having nothing to send her. 'Besides, I live alone. I'm out almost every evening, trying to find an honest man who will tell me what's wrong with the world and invite me to join with him. Note that I still believe an honest man could save us.'

'You won't have time to look any farther,' Philip said. 'From now your evenings belong to the Anti-Clerical Times —unless you can think of a better name. You're my business manager—unpaid. You know all about costs and printing, I want you to draw up an estimate of the best way to spend eight thousand pounds establishing a weekly paper. This paper is to keep an eye on the scoundrels, politicians, financiers, bishops, writers and the like, who want to betray us. Why respect a society which lets little children be nipped by vermin as they sleep and settles difference by ripping open the bowels or shooting the eyes out of hundreds of thousands of young men? You'll see now that the one cry of our scoundrels is Back to 1913. So that they can have the War over again later, with a fresh crop of young bodies! Also they'll cheat everyone to keep their profits. You'll see what will happen to heroes when they become workless workmen again—but like the bugs and the killing it will be excused as facing the facts. We're going to prove that their facts are lies, only fit for honest men to ——. We'll print the real facts. We're for humanity against the devil, and against respectable writers and priests, and for the common man against the people who want to fight to the last drop of his blood—perhaps we shall discover why women are so insensitive about war. Is it because they have no imagination ? or only because they lack self-respect ? ' He stopped, and added in the same voice : ' How do you get on with my friend, Hervey ? '

' She sometimes does what I tell her,' Renn answered. He saw on Philip's face that his friend was in love with her, and that he was no happier for it. ' How long have you known the young woman ? '

' Why, we were at school together,' Philip said. He looked at Renn. ' There's nothing to say about it. Let's settle about the paper.'

' Your paper's finished before it sets out,' Renn said, smiling. ' People don't want to be frightened and disturbed.'

' Are you going to help me ? '

' Of course.'

He stood up to get fresh coffee. The extraordinary thing was that nothing Philip said mattered. Renn did not believe in this ridiculous paper which was to blow up society, but he was going to work for it until all hours and to give up his evenings, and that with joy. The thing was to have found something to do at last. An exquisite happiness and relief filled him. Just as the room from being shabby and uncomfortable had been transformed at the moment Philip entered it into a good friendly place so his life had once more become an adventure. He held the coffee pot in his hands, admiring its colour. Until now he could not have told you whether it had a colour. As he carried it to the table he noticed for the first time that Philip had eaten nothing, nothing at all.

' What's wrong with the toast and honey ? ' he demanded.

' Nothing,' Philip said. A slight look of fatigue or annoyance came over his face. ' The fact is, I can't eat. Something's gone wrong with me in the last five or six weeks. I daresay it's indigestion, due to Frank's cooking.'

'You ought to see about it,' Renn said. His feeling of dismay struck him as ridiculous. After a moment he said: 'You were hit in the stomach, weren't you? Perhaps they left a splinter or two of shell in you.'

'It feels a little like that,' Philip laughed. He drank his coffee, then went over to the window. 'Look at this.'

A shabby dozen of children were lined up in the sunshine on the opposite pavement. Two of them had wound khaki puttees round their match-stalk legs and one supported a German helmet. It rested on the bridge of his nose. All carried weapons of some description, and the tallest struggled with a flag many sizes too large for him. As the two young men watched they formed smartly into ranks and moved off, singing. Their marching ditty was the most scandalous version of a popular song about the Kaiser. They marched swinging their arms and looking slyly into the faces of the passers-by to be admired. The smallest held out a collecting-box.

'There's your future for you,' Renn said.

A little later Philip went off, leaving his car outside Renn's house. He doubted whether its constitution would stand a day of celebrations.

He had to meet T. S. Heywood for lunch and had chosen a restaurant which T.S. could reach easily by tube from his laboratory. The room was discreetly shaded from the sunlight, which nevertheless crept in. Pieces of glass and silver flashed suddenly, and a woman's face, caught in the light, appeared dead, and as if detached from its skull. There was a negro orchestra in blue and silver.

As soon as they were seated Philip began to talk about his paper. He was so absorbed in it that he did not observe his friend's indifference until T.S. said abruptly:

'You know I'm going to write for your paper only out of weakness—because you'll make my life unbearable if I refuse. I don't believe in it.'

Philip smiled at him without malice. He allowed T.S. more licence than his other friends, who were forced, on pain of being cast out, to share his convictions. But T.S. could say what he liked—provided he obeyed. For all his simplicity Philip had a Yorkshire side to his character, which forbid him to throw away what he could use. Others, if they did not believe, would be quite useless to him, but from T.S. he wanted only a supply of facts. ' I'm not interested in your private beliefs,' he said firmly. ' You're my scientific correspondent.' He had asked the waiter to give him the wine list, and while he was looking through it said :

' There aren't many people here. Aren't they celebrating ? '

The man looked at him with a civil smile. ' For to-night we could have booked each table three times over. There is a gala Peace dinner and a dance here.'

At this moment a woman's voice from the next table exclaimed : ' He has a hundred thousand pairs of trousers and ninety thousand tunics on his hands. They will be paid for, of course. But no one could have expected the War to end in that shabby way. People have been ruined ! '

' What a pity ! ' Philip whispered. ' I always felt there'd been a mistake. After only four years' killing any peace would be premature.'

' All I can tell you about peace is that we're experimenting in the production of a new gas. It's economical in use, inflicts really disgusting agony, and has no known reagent. My private hope is to see it used on a meeting of the Imperial League.' T.S. went on to draw a picture of the death antics of a well-nourished elderly gentleman, so unpleasant that Philip was revolted. Quite unabashed by this, T.S. raised his voice and had the satisfaction of seeing the three middle-aged women at the next table turn scarlet and begin to talk in loud quick voices. His eyes sparkled with pleasure.

' That's enough,' Philip said. ' Have you seen Hervey lately ? '

' No. She came to see my wife, to one of her evenings.

I don't know what happened, I wasn't there, but I suppose she felt out of it. You know how uncouth Hervey can be. And Evelyn has no kindness to spare for intelligent young women. She did say afterwards that she felt certain there was something in Hervey. But you saw that she had no intention of helping it out.' He broke off suddenly, looking at Philip's plate. 'Why did you order eggs if you don't like them ? '

' I ordered it because it was the cheapest thing on the menu. I can't eat without feeling or being ill, and I don't intend to feel ill now—I must fetch our Hervey out this evening.'

' What's the matter with you ? '

' I'll tell you afterwards,' Philip said. He had a blind faith in his friend's cleverness, the faith of a layman who mixes up all branches of science and imagines that if a man understands chemistry he must know why you have a pain in your belly.

Afterwards, in T.S.'s room, he spoke rather shyly about his feeling of unease and the slight pain he had. He frowned, and was ashamed to be discussing his health. Yet it seemed as though the uneasiness he spoke of were in his mind. He made light of it and yet he seemed relieved to have spoken, as though he had passed on a warning he did not understand.

T.S. asked him several questions and at last said shortly : ' I know nothing. I'm going to send you to a doctor.' He went away to telephone and when he came back he had arranged for Philip to see the doctor next day. He was unsympathetic and called Philip a fool to live as he did.

' Why, where shall I live ? ' Philip said. ' *I'm* not married to a famous woman.'

When he was alone, T.S. sat a long time unmoving. He was staring across the Embankment at the river, which ran smoothly and was filled with light. Where it met a barge it shattered in pieces and the light sprang up from it. He felt certain that Philip was seriously ill. The little he knew, joined to a memory of his own father's illness, assured him of

it. Perhaps Philip was actually dying. As he thought of it
he remembered that he had already called Philip ' a doomed
young man '—and at once the phrase seemed less apt, because
it was a generation which had been doomed and it was not
worse for Philip than for the others.

Carelessly, his mind offered him a scene plucked from the
files—Philip and himself in St Amand, the room half dark
half lighted, a dish of eggs and two bottles of red wine, thin
and tart, Philip, his thick fair hair all ways, laughing and
laughing, so that the good French housewife thought he was
drunk. T.S. smiled. How bright the water is, he thought.
I can admire it, I'm not suffering. Don't I mind about
Philip ? He searched rudely among his thoughts, but found
that he was searching for a place to lay Philip dead—pushing
first this and then that young man out of the way to make
room. Above all let's be peaceful and tidy, he said to himself.

Evelyn came in, and not speaking she walked past him to
the window. She is beautiful, he thought. A feeling he
much disliked possessed him. He felt ashamed, because
always, at these moments, he was liable to the same weakness,
a schoolboy's snivelling physical longing for some emotional
act. He pictured scenes in which Evelyn became the pro-
tective wife-mother. A vulgar slobbering miracle took place
and he was saved. Speak, his mind jeered ; say ' Evelyn, my
darling,' and fasten your body upon hers.

Evelyn put her hand up to the blind and jerked it half
down. The shadow came to her waist. ' Don't forget
dinner is half an hour early,' she said absently. ' We're going
on, you know, to Mrs Harben's, to hear a concert of Purcell.
Franz-Joachim—how unfortunate his name has been to him.
No one believed he was a Swiss. And then dancing.' Her
fingers twisted the blind cord. ' I haven't danced since last
year.'

' Do you think this a suitable occasion ? ' T.S. grinned.

Evelyn considered. him for a moment. ' Are you going
to be tiresome ? ' she asked, not ungently.

' I hope not,' her husband answered. ' But I don't want

to hear Purcell, and I shan't dance. You had better take someone else with you.'

'Very well,' Evelyn said. She left the window and stood beside him, resting a hand on his neck. His hair was very short but she found a piece at the nape which she could make a show of twisting. 'You take very little interest in me. Am I looking old?'

Nothing responded in him, except that a horrid jangling sprang up in the nerves of his chest. He felt humiliated. He looked up and pulled a clown's face at her. 'You look splendid,' he said, grinning. As she moved away he put his hand out and smacked her across the behind, with a vacant laugh.

He felt a sense of relief as soon as she had gone. Trying to think of Philip he could only see the room in St Amand and Philip's face crimsoned with laughter. His arms in stained khaki sprawled across the table and his shoulders quivered.

2. *The celebrations begin*

To enjoy eating, not for the sake of the food, you must have starved at an impressionable age. Marcel Cohen had been hungry for the first fifteen years of his life. Now, though he was fifty, he found an acute pleasure in thinking of the good his food did him. He felt that he deserved it—the sherry in the strong consommé, the delicate flesh of grilled trout, the firmer flesh of young chicken (in preparing it, port, white wine, and cream had been used), he had almost a sense of triumph as he absorbed them. They fed his intellect as much as his body. From the red gravy of the tournedos, a cut of which he was especially fond, a thin savour ascended to his nostrils and thence to his mind.

That morning, it being his fiftieth birthday, he had looked at himself curiously after his bath. He saw that he had gone thick in every part without losing the outline of his body. It had coarsened like a tree. The skin was yellow and smooth, full of oil. He thought of it now with an impersonal and sardonic friendliness, as though he were merely a spectator of its satisfactions. Just as at times he had a cruel notion of his mind running from cellar to cellar like a rat. This rat had teeth strong enough to gnaw through iron. It could not help gnawing—the very joists on which this room had been built were not safe from it.

This was more curious since Marcel Cohen took pride in his house. The room in which he sat had bulbous pillars, mouldings crusted with figures, and hangings of Italian stamped velvet of the seventeenth century. His taste and vanity were both fully satisfied by it. He had chosen each piece of its furniture—chests of oak veneered with walnut and inlaid with ivory, a drawing table with six elaborately carved legs and fine ivory inlay, Farthingale chairs. He admired them and they were worth a great deal in money. The claret he was drinking pleased him—he thought of the price paid, a fair one, considering the nature of the wine, and of its incomparable flavour.

He set his glass down, and took a look at his wife. Sophie was his own age, and she was fat, fashionable, and unhappy. He knew that she was unhappy, and while he felt no respect for her and no love, he was occasionally a little sorry.

Sophie Cohen's dress was cleverly designed to make her seem thinner, but, as always, a wrinkle had formed in it under each arm, and she wore too many jewels, which winked and glittered above every fold of her neck and arms. Poor mamma, he said to himself, she has no taste. It was to please her that they invited eighteen people to dinner. He liked to dine with one other man, and to spend an hour afterwards dissecting the world—nerves could be severed by this knife— before hearing music. He listened to music as some read poetry, with his bowels and mind, and it did not occur to him to value a concerto by the amount of applause it received.

Sophie was inviting her guests to drink to the Peace. He smiled at her and at them and raised his glass. 'We could have made peace in 1916,' he observed. 'It would have

been a sounder and less spectacular affair and we should not
have spent a great deal of money we have spent.' I forget
how many young men, so many that the number doesn't
matter, he thought, who were living are now dead: it's
funny, I don't like to think of so many hands and mouths
rotting away in the ground.

He reflected that if peace had come in 1916 he would have
been poorer by half a million pounds. The rat underneath
the joists saw a balloon of swollen profits go up from the
battlefields. Garton's Shipbuilding and Engineering Works,
chairman Thomas Harben, were about to issue bonus shares
to the value of two million pounds, out of undisclosed reserves.
That's splendid, splendid—better sell now, sell, now sell,
never touch the price again. He stood up. Sophie's body,
like a badly-shaped vase, steel-ribbed, teetered behind her
guests into the upper room. He followed, and walked over
to the window. At once the thought of his dead son—he was
wounded and died in hospital in 1916—squeezed him so
that he gripped the curtain between his hands. Yes, he was
sorry for Sophie, but there was one thing he would not forgive
her. When the boy was near death he asked for her—' When
will mamma come ? '—and the father had to say : ' She's on
her way, son,' but the truth was that she was afraid to come.
She was afraid to look at disfigurement and death. So David
died without her. Yes, yes, he understood it, poor mamma,
poor Sophie, but he did not forgive her. At this time, too,
he had realised fully how useless she was to him. Why, she
could not give him another son.

The thought of David was leaving him. He had learned
to endure it in a very simple way—by recalling his gifts to
David, the pony, the bathing pool, Eton. David's youth had
been soft. Mine, he thought, and his mind paused—before
the sight of an eight-year-old boy in the room he shared with
his mother and five sisters. The boy was frowningly busy
with the bugs in his bed, squashing them on his hand. After
a time he got up and went out. The water-closet was shared
by five families, and while he waited his turn the door began

to open slowly, and a man came out, but before the boy could slip in a woman pushed past him and past the man and slammed the door. The man grinned. Well, he could not wait any longer so he withdrew a few paces. The man watched until he squatted down, then said quietly, ' You little jew bastard,' and lifted his foot.

But it was so humiliating that the adult Cohen suffered nearly as much as the boy. He had been back to look, and the court was still there, housing five families, unchanged, a place into which no man would put a dog he liked, but there were children in it. Strong, he thought—I was as strong as a rat. David had two nurseries.

A servant had crossed the room and whispered to him that Mrs Groelles was in the library. He smiled with pleasure and went off quickly to speak to his daughter.

She was dressed for some party and greeted him with a smile of impatience. ' My dear Fanny,' he exclaimed, ' you look very well—and you're wearing my emeralds.' Because of her tall shapely body, fine skin, and head of dark red curls, at twenty Fanny Groelles was a ripe beauty. She had married out of her race, the second son of a poor landowning family, which had once had an illustrious member—so long since that the pride they might have felt in him had been transferred to the length of time since his death, during which no one of the family had said or done anything memorable. Her husband was as foolishly extravagant as herself. They were perpetually in debt, Fanny's large allowance from her father scarcely paid for her clothes and her husband's racing stable. Whenever she came to see her father she asked him for money, and this even seemed natural to him. His love for her ate up his conceit and even his common sense—he gave her anything she asked. Now he said fondly : ' Have you come to stay the evening ? '

' Good gracious no,' Fanny said. She was so completely taken by surpise that her father could suppose she had an evening to spend with him that she told the simple truth. ' I don't like Jews, daddy, and you never have anyone else here.'

'You are a Jew,' her father said.

'But I needn't live with them any longer,' Fanny said simply.

Marcel Cohen looked at her with a reserved smile. He found it difficult actually to believe that his daughter was ashamed of him. His mind had formed the habit of avoiding this thought. So now all he said, and with a sigh, was: 'Before you came, my darling, I was thinking of David.'

Fanny heard and instinctively misunderstood him. Her social sense—she had had to defend herself during the first months of her marriage against the biting speeches of her mother-in-law—was so finely organised that she had been able to earn a reputation for 'delicacy' and 'true kindness' simply by detecting in advance and avoiding the occasions on which she would have to display these qualities. She saw that if she were forced to discuss her brother's death now, it would be awkward to ask for money. It was almost without thinking that she said in a gay voice: 'Why, David spoke of you this evening. I went in his room to say good night: he was in his cot, and he looked at me with his funny smile and said: "Are you going to see my grandfather? Give him my love." Don't you think that was remarkable from a child of three?' Her father smiled again. Laying her arm round his neck she said earnestly: 'Daddy, I'm in such a hole. I can only stay two minutes, we're going to Sarah's and I ought not to be late.' Her father stroked her arm and listened. He liked her to talk to him in this familiar way about people to whom she would never show either her father or mother, and now that she was kneeling beside his chair he felt that she loved him.

'Tell me what you want, my darling,' he said gently.

3. *Two comfort each other*

Philip called for Hervey at six o'clock and took her to dine at Gatti's. The rooms were decorated but not indecently so. About eight o'clock they walked to Piccadilly Circus, where the crowd was thickest. Soldiers, women in short frocks, whistles, rattles, flags, men and women in each other's arms, a girl with one breast bare, drunken soldiers and civilians dancing waving their arms, a frenzy of unreal excitement. There was no spontaneity in any of their antics. Feeling had gone cold since the Armistice, and the resurrection was attended with a great inconvenience of worms. Philip felt Hervey pulling his sleeve. He had to put his ear to her mouth to know what she was saying. ' They're not enjoying themselves,' she cried : ' it's terrifying, it's hideous, let's go away, Philip.'

' Very well,' Philip said. They were several minutes struggling out of the crowd, Hervey was afraid of being knocked down and gripped his arm : at last they were able to walk with some ease.

They took a cab to Renn's street. The car looked sulky— perhaps vexed that it had not been shown the celebrations. With a great struggle they started, and then Hervey noticed that Philip had grown white. She touched his hand lightly and found it cold and damp. ' You're ill,' she said. She spoke carelessly because he disliked fuss.

' No,' Philip said, ' it was the effort. If you leave me alone I shall be all right.' His lips were colourless. But it was true—before long he had recovered, it seemed easily, and Hervey was very glad of it. Never ill herself, illness in another person bored her. Unless the other person were her son. Then she changed at once, her whole being drawn to a point, that point her son's life. She still felt that the tide of his life depended on hers and that only she, if he were ill, could save him.

They drove directly to the Dug-out. It was dark when they reached it and a little light came through the curtains. It made Hervey think of night at Danesacre, and of coming home. She said nothing, and followed Philip shyly into the room behind the counter. This room, which was very small, was the living-room of the family ; Frank's father-in-law slept in it, and Frank and his young wife slept in the other

room, which was smaller still.   Both rooms were stuffed
with furniture, and clean, smelling of soap, grass, and of some
kind of string with which the old man was making a hammock
for a child.   The child was not born yet, but he liked to think
that everything he had to do was well forehand.

Hervey smiled, shyly and warmly, at the young woman,
and wished to be gone.   Her mother's anger when a stranger
was brought into her house had persuaded her that no one
ever welcomed chance-brought company.   She was sure that
she was unwanted.   But Frank's wife was pleased to show
off her rooms to another young woman.   'We came here
because of Frank's chest,' she said, with a smile, touching
her own.   'He was gassed, and doctor said towns were bad
for 'en.   I reckon we're well off here.'

'This is a nice room,' Hervey said.

Since this only confirmed the general belief no one answered
her, and in a few moments she and Philip were walking across
the field to his caravan with bread and a jug of strong dark
coffee.   The night sky was immensely blown out and thin,
like a bubble at bursting-point, and except for the sound they
made themselves, whipping the long grass, there was nothing.

Philip left the door open and lit his candles ; the flames
lay over on a current flowing from the darkness into the tiny
cell of light.   At first nothing was said and he watched the
line of Hervey's cheek resting on her hand.   He felt happy
and curiously at peace, as if he had done a great deal of work
that day.   It was a comfort to be with Hervey and without
other people.   He began to talk about his paper to her.   She
listened and nodded her head.   She was thinking how well
she got on with him and how if he were only not in love
with her they could set up house together and be unusually
happy.   The absurdity of this thought made her smile.

Philip stopped talking.   'Please go on,' she said anxiously.

'No.   I've talked about myself too long,' Philip said.
'Come and sit outside on the step and wait for the bump.
It's a minute to one o'clock and at one exactly the earth goes
over the top.'

Sitting with the door of the caravan at their backs they talked and were silent and talked, each speaking into the darkness and receiving an answer from it. A deep happiness possessed Hervey, sprung from the likeness of this long night of talking to others just before the War, when with Philip and T.S. she had often stayed awake all night to talk and discuss life and their future—about which, as it turned out, they were much at fault.

Suddenly Philip said: 'What do you want most in the whole world, Hervey love?'

Shall I tell the truth? Hervey thought quickly. It was not easy for her to give herself away, but for this once she would. 'To be famous and Richard to have a fortunate life,' she said. She looked at him to see whether he were going to laugh at her.

'Is that all you want? I should like to be the conscience of unthinking people.' He reflected that Hervey's ambitions were more human than his. But there must be no more poor, he said to himself.

'You can be that in your paper,' Hervey exclaimed. She did not believe that he would achieve anything with it, but she wanted to help him. She looked at his wrists, lying crossed on one knee, and was struck by their thinness—it gave all his plans an air of uncertainty in her eyes.

'Don't you want to be in love?' Philip said.

'Indeed yes,' Hervey said—she paused—'but then it's so much trouble,' she went on, saying what was in her mind. Speaking the truth, once you have started it, is too exhilarating to draw back.

'Do you really mean that, Hervey? There must be a difference between men and women in these things, because I don't know what you're talking about.'

'I don't know anything about women—I know more about myself,' Hervey said. 'I know what I should like —to share a violent passion with some man. But it must be a physical passion, I don't want to feel sorry for him or to have to change myself to please him. I want to be able

to say what I choose.   And I want it to burn up and be over.
I don't want to have to live with him afterwards and order
his breakfasts and try to remember what he likes.   I don't
want to know what he likes.   Respect—companionship—all
that—that's nothing.   I can respect many things, and be my
own companion—I shouldn't want them to come into my
love affair.   You have to make allowances for a person you
respect, modify your thoughts, be tolerant.   That isn't
anything to do with love.   But it's what all the men I have
known—except one—think of as love, and that's what I say
is too much trouble.'

She is talking about her American, he said to himself.   A
feeling of bitterness crossed his mind.   ' Then you don't
want a husband ? ' he said, trying to smile.

' I have one,' Hervey said calmly.   ' And perhaps I shouldn't
like to live alone.   No doubt that's why marriage goes on.
But why confuse it with passion ?   Or think that you are
having both when you marry.'

She spoke sleepily.   Her mind was full of unsorted specula-
tions—she had not spoken a tenth of them.   It was no use.
What I think and feel has scarcely any relation with what
I do, she thought—if I lived as I feel, I should be a monster.

They were both silent—a little depressed, as the young
are when they are forced to realise how little of themselves
is of use to life, but comforted by each other's nearness.
Philip could see the tuft of soft hair on Hervey's nape.   He
felt a desire to touch it but refrained.   Instead he thought
over what she had been saying—she had described a kind of
love as narrow and brutal as a knife, yet she had been speaking
her thoughts.   All at once he saw that her thoughts did not
determine her life.   Her mind, a strong clumsy instrument,
was blunted and turned aside by her profound carelessness of
herself : it dictated only the least significant of her actions,
a resentful prisoner shut in the same cell with her sense of
humour—which was that of a savage.   For a moment he
was as sorry for Hervey as if he had known that she was going
to be defeated.

The sky, as they talked and waited, was turning from night to day. The earth still slept, but it was visible in a strange light of no colour. To the east the grey husk of sky split apart and showed a naked whiteness. Seen in that way, the whiteness was startling. It was as if they had watched a new continent break from the sea.

Philip looked at his watch—half-past four. Hervey was leaning a little against him and he thought she had fallen asleep. He watched for another half hour, during which short time the edges of the new continent caught fire, and delicate tongues of flame ran here and there across the vast spaces; the waters dividing them became a clear green, with overhead a sky, new, smooth, and flawless. A busy chattering began in the trees behind the caravan.

Hervey was not asleep, she stretched herself, smiled, and said : ' If it was *my* country we should hear a peewit cry.' She stood up. ' Now if you drive me home I can get into the house before it's too late.'

Philip was seized with anguish. He put his arms round her, looking closely in her face. ' Oh Hervey, stay, stay,' he repeated.

Hervey stood perfectly still. ' Must I ? ' she said, after a moment. ' You know I don't want it.' Her liking for him made her speak carefully, not to hurt him, but he felt the ease and finality with which she was leaving him. And he felt not as though she were going but he dying. He released her. His arms strained back to feel the wood of the caravan. ' Yes, yes, stay with me. I only want not to be alone yet.'

' Why, Philip,' Hervey said, troubled and ashamed.

She sat down again on the step of the caravan. ' I can stay,' she said. He saw that she was reluctant and had no warmth for him, and it was no use keeping her.

4. *The celebrations end*

Evelyn pressed her hand down on her eyelids. The nerves behind her eyes throbbed and sent flashes of crimson across

the darkened lids. To look is better, she thought, and
opening her eyes gazed round Mrs Harben's music room.
The concert was long finished. They were dancing in the
next room, and couples passed and repassed the doorway.
Many of them were middle-aged or elderly. She saw one
motion issuing from all their bodies like a snake unfolding and
folding itself along the wall. Some of the revellers were drunk,
and since the floor was crowded these kept bearing off into
side rooms ; one fat elderly woman had let down the shoulder
straps of her dress, to the satisfaction of her partner. Why do
I stay ? Evelyn thought: why go ? why did I come ? She
turned her head and saw William Ridley coming towards
her, walking carefully on the waxed boards. Here he comes
with his boasting face, she said. His face was one large smile.

'How are you getting on ? ' he asked, as if he had brought
her : 'I'm having a grand time. I've made an impression, too.
It's a good thing you asked me to come with you, I've met
some good chaps.' He sat down close to her. 'You look as
if you weren't enjoying yourself. You should let yourself
go, eat something, get among people, drink—there's plenty '—
he tapped her knee—' I don't like to see you looking glum.
I don't like anyone to be glum when they could be happy.'

Evelyn looked at him. He was above himself with happiness at being here. That's almost pathetic, she thought.
Nothing else in him could rouse a feeling of pity, unless it
were the cheapness of his clothes, which squeezed his ungainly
body here and hung on it there. But if he had ever known
they were wretched, he had forgotten it in his satisfaction at
having made his impression. But on whom ?

'What time is it ? I shall go home. Can I take you
anywhere in the car ? '

Ridley hesitated, weighing in his mind her importance
against the richness of a whole new world—which he could
use. She was wrong if she thought this house, these people,
impressed him. 'You drop me off at your house,' he
answered. 'I'll walk on after that. These people here
aren't important—I want to see what th'others, the tarts,

the shop girls, young clerks, policemen, old wives, are doing to celebrate.'

When they were at her house she asked him to come in and talk to her. 'My nerves are bad,' she explained. 'I shan't sleep yet. If we talk for a time that will make the hours less until daylight.'

In her room, Ridley seated himself with his legs widely apart. He was very warm and excited. Her restlessness had infected him and he felt a desire to walk about the room, fingering things, to assert his position here. 'You should be like me,' he said. 'I get moods—when that happens I don't sit brooding, I go out, have a drink, talk to people.'

'What are you writing?' Evelyn asked. She kept her eyes on his face, waiting for him to begin talking. Her Spanish shawl, blue and crimson, had fallen from her over the day-bed. Talk, talk to me, her mind repeated. She leaned forward, twisting a corner of the shawl between her fingers.

He was ready enough. As he talked his inner excitement swelled, but he was determined not to show it. He felt that things were turning out well for him. The mirror between the widows reflected his face and well-filled shirt front, enough and no more. 'I am probably the most important writer you know,' he exclaimed: 'that's because I'm not ashamed to write as I feel. Like the rest of your sex you suffer from too much cleverness.' Here she roused herself to protest, and he said seriously: 'Well—I'm not making conversation, I'm telling you something of importance about writing.'

'One day you will know a little better how to write,' Evelyn answered, in a dry voice. But she felt that already he knew as much as he needed. Nothing she knew was of use to him, though she had more sensibility in her finger than was in his whole hulking body.

'Then we won't talk about it,' Ridley said, with good humour. He rose and came towards her clumsily, his arms knocking against the objects in his path. For the first time she became aware of his excitement. He stood looking down

at her, his body leaned forward, arms hanging.   His lower
lip was thrust out with a drop of moisture on it.   He stooped,
and fell forward with her across the couch.

For a moment she struggled weakly with him.   She yielded
longing trying to feel to feel to lose oneself ecstasy to feel
everything yes to feel.   But there was nothing, only discomfort and the disorder of her mind.   When he rose, she averted
her face from him.   She wished to regain a semblance of
dignity.   She lay silent.   When he spoke to her, a little
blustering, she answered only by a mortified smile.   She was
conscious of nothing but the effort of waiting for him to go.

As the door closed she felt the room settle into silence.   A
burden passed from her mind.   Think, I lay still—it was thus
and thus—I said nothing.   People walking outside in the
road disturbed her, she listened to their footsteps passing and
then to a burst of laughter that began abruptly and went on,
it sounded like an old man, weak and malicious.   Now think.
But trivial things distracted her and she could fix her mind
only on a scratch on the table and the swinging blind cord.

CHAPTER IX

HERVEY BEGINS TO MEND

WAR ennobles few it does not kill. It happened to a great many non-combatants in the last war to suffer a loss less palpable than the loss of a son, a husband, a lover. They lost heart or decency, or only their heads. There is some natural law in this. If some quarter of a modern town or city were set apart for the legalised slaughter of human beings there would spread from it a strange infection through the rest. The very streets, and the children playing in them, would wear an air of listening : what in one quarter ran off in blood would excite in degree the senses of all knowing of it. Now, not a city only but whole nations are involved in modern war, and the law becomes general. This impalpable excitement is the reason why delicate women, who could not bear to see a dog run over, can read without turning a hair : 'Our losses were less than three hundred officers and fifteen hundred other ranks.' And why others give away white feathers. Or take to drink or a lover.

The event is natural, one of the by-products of a prolonged war which, since it is not convertible into five per cent bonds, has escaped the notice of experts. A pity.

Hervey Russell had taken the infection without knowing it.

She was hard at work one Friday in August, and alone in the room, when the telephone rang. It was on Renn's desk. She went over to it, spoke, and heard the American's voice. Her strength left her. Her heart beat in her head, her hands, and in the void between her ribs. She leaned on the desk. 'Dinner ? Yes, certainly. Yes, I should like it if you came for me.'

She went back to her desk. She was not able to do any work. At last she had a coherent thought—it was that she could not go out to dinner with him in a frock that was eight years old if it was a day.

She had agreed to lunch with Philip, and the idea came to her to ask him for a loan. At another time she would rather have starved than ask for a penny. She had a nervous shame about such things. Now the idea took complete possession of her. She went out, met Philip, sat down with him in a restaurant, smiled, listened. All the time her mind was occupied with the thought of the money. Philip's face was not the face of her friend, it was an algebraical sign for a face, and if it was pale and the eyes sunken she did not notice these things.

He asked her about Penn. 'When is he coming out of the Air Force?'

She shook her head.

' Does he come to see you? Write? How often do you hear from him?'

' I haven't heard for five weeks,' Hervey said. Her mind jumped. 'He doesn't answer letters, either. I wanted a little money—bills—I can't pay everything. But he didn't send it.'

' My dear Hervey,' Philip cried, ' I can let you have money—as much as you want. You knew that. I've just come from the bank. You can have ten, twenty pounds.'

Neither relief nor her overbearing excitement showed in Hervey's face. She thanked him and folded the money into her bag, and at five o'clock spent the whole of it on a dress. With the same blandness and want of scruple she knocked at Mrs Delia Hunt's door to ask a favour. It would be kind, very kind, if Mrs Hunt would lend her her room for a few minutes. A little before time she went there in her new dress and waited, polite and stolid. There was a knock, and Delia opened.

Captain Gage looked past her to Hervey. He came directly in, and without speaking walked up to Hervey and kissed her with passion. She had not expected it, and almost fainted. She came to herself in a moment. She succeeded in behaving in a rational way, though her knees trembled so that she could scarcely stand. The familiar tone of his voice, sudden and pleasant, startled her. But she had not forgotten it, any more than she had forgotten that he walked with a dancing movement of his body, very fine and neat. He had grown thinner. There is no one like him, she thought, almost with pain.

She saw him take Delia in at first glance. They're two of a kind, she thought quickly. Both had a quality she admired, a hard impudence in the face of life, but the American was at the height of his physical beauty. He made himself agreeable to Delia, and as soon as he was outside, he asked :
' Known her a long time, darling ? '

' No,' Hervey said.

' She's not the right company for you,' Gage said seriously.

' Kind to me—she offered me work,' Hervey said.

' You won't need any work,' Gage observed. ' I certainly hope to support my wife better than Englishmen seem in the habit of doing.'

' You could perhaps do it by mere moral superiority,' Hervey said. She felt a pleasure in running him through not less keen than the pleasure of watching him and listening to his voice. A delicious sensation—like the surprise of new life after an illness—possessed her. She could have run and jumped for joy.

' You'll be lovely to come home to,' Jess said. He looked at her with a smile.

The cab turned across the Haymarket, and stopped. Hervey stepped out carefully, holding her dress, and walked into the hotel as though she were used to these places. She was afraid of stepping on her dress, which brushed her slippers.

Jess smiled at her across the table. He began to talk to her about France. ' The French are a great nation. If an army of locusts arrived they'd eat them and charge duty. During the influenza I was buying eggs at three francs apiece—each

time one of the boys died they put the price up to offset the
loss of custom . . . I lost my servant. The eggs I was
buying were for him. Hervey, I tried every way to keep
that boy. He lost his nerve. There was one thing he
wanted—that was a cabin trunk like the one I'd got me to
take home. At last I said, " Boy, if you're well by Saturday
I'll buy you a cabin trunk in Paris." That boy certainly
tried hard to live.'

Hervey was watching his face so closely that she had no
comment ready. After a moment he began to tell her other
stories, less truthful. She listened vaguely. The room, the
discreet orchestra, lights, waiters, diners, unfamiliar tastes
and odours, formed in her mind a picture which bore scarcely
any resemblance to the reality. It changed and fell to pieces
momently—now the tables were radial lines with a vast bare
arm filling the foreground, now a bar of music took shape as
a street with lit windows, or an eye, and dominated the
pattern. Suddenly Gage said: ' Last year you couldn't
get yourself divorced because you couldn't leave Richard.
Now you've left him—I want to know how much longer
I'm to wait for my wife.'

Her head cleared quickly. ' I haven't left Richard—
except to earn money. Nothing's changed.'

' I haven't asked you about Penn. You're not living with
him any longer '—Hervey did not speak—' and I don't want
to hear about him. I don't dislike him and I don't want to
talk about him. This is my last leave in England, darling
child. We've got to settle something. You're not tired of
me, are you ? '

' No,' Hervey said.

' I couldn't stop myself thinking about you in France. I
can't say I wanted to marry anyone, maybe I don't love you
—I don't know what you'd call not being able to do without
a woman as irritating as you are. You've got to live with me.
If you don't we'll both die of it—I won't always know that,
but I know it now. I'm not saying what I mean. Do you
want to be half alive and half dead for the rest of your life ? '

Hervey smiled at him. ' Isn't your life worth something ? '
Gage said.

She did not answer. She made some answer, but it was an
evasion. It satisfied him. He talked to her about Texas
and the sort of houses she would live in, and his father (who
wrote him letters beginning, My darling June), and as if she
were remembering she listened. Small things engrossed her,
the unfamiliar sound of familiar words in his speech, the
movements of his hands. She tasted the coffee with surprise
that it did not taste different from other coffee.

' Am I boring you ? ' Jess said.

' No.' But smile, smile, my love, she said silently. Her
heart failed with joy.

She was going softly past Mrs Hunt's room to her own
when the door opened and Delia beckoned her. She let
herself be led inside.

' You be careful, my girl,' Delia Hunt said. ' That
American is a bad type—I know his sort. Greedy and no
conscience. You'll get yourself murdered.'

Hervey smiled kindly and went away. In her room she
gave herself up to the thought of living with Gage. Their
life would be difficult, violent, and uncertain. It was what
she wanted. The violence of change and uncertainty, not
to live in a house with books, servants, the orange juice
before breakfast, at nine the *Manchester Guardian* arrives,
books and more books, writing, a few friends, not added to
hastily, the peace of death which passes all resurrection.

She sat for hours in her window. She had taken her new
dress off at once and hung it carefully protected from the dust
by a nightgown. When she thought of Gage it was to feel
that he was in the room. She experienced thus the finest
pleasure of the senses.

All this time she was careful not to think of Richard. She
was able to overlook him because of a certainty, not yet
admitted but present in her mind, that she could never leave
him. This settled at the roots of her mind, she was able to
dream of a future in which he did not exist. In an hour she

lived with Gage a year and visited China, South America, and the mountains of the moon.

She spent Saturday afternoon and evening with him. He had been in London a week. In France, after the Armistice, he had had the idea of addressing himself to Thomas Harben (that is, to a forest of ships, steel, cotton, oil, coal) with whom his father did business in oil, to suggest ways of selling small arms in China. He refused to stay quietly in Texas, working for his father. ' But won't he be cruelly disappointed ? ' Hervey asked.

Gage looked at her. ' He'll try to get round you. He'll say, Hervey, can't you do anything with June ? '

' Well,' Hervey began. She paused. ' What did Harben say to you ? '

' I didn't see him at once. A fine young draft-dodger interviewed me. I got right up from my seat, polite and ceremonious, downright English—" You can tell Mr Harben I didn't come here to talk to his telephone. I'll be at the Carlton for one week if he wants to make an appointment with me. Good day "—and off I went. Well, thought I, that's finished, and I had a mind to go home without seeing you. Thursday morning—" Mr Harben would like to see Captain Gage at eleven." " Tell Mr Harben I'm obliged to him," I said. Maybe he was pleased to see me. He looked round his nose, spiteful vulture, and held out one finger. " I hear your father is building tank steamers," he said : " very rash of him. Too much competition." " Very rash," said I : " lo, the poor savage. But if you'll forgive me— he's certainly a step nearer his oil supply than you are. It wouldn't surprise me at all if the cause of humanity drove us to clean up Mexico this year. Maybe President Clemenceau wasn't writing poetry when he wrote : Oil is as necessary as blood to the battles of to-morrow." Round came his nose— " Very interesting. But we have oil nearer than Mexico, young man. And the future is a matter for friendly competition." " Until the next war," I said. I was growing fonder of his nose every minute. " The next war may be

fought for oil," said he : " but you haven't come here to-day
to arrange terms, have you ? " Why, Hervey, I laughed out
—thinking of all the highminded buzzards and their League
of Nations, not knowing John D. Rockefeller and Thomas
Harben had it squeezed into a ball between them. Your old
nose, I said to myself. But then we did our business. Next
year I'll be in China and elsewhere, travelling in ammunition.'

'Who will buy arms from you ? ' Hervey asked.

'Why, both sides,' Gage said, chuckling.

Hervey said nothing. A world torn between Gages and
Harbens is in a bad way, she thought. A fine world for
Richard. Words like ' the next war ' filled her with rage.
With rage and a growing horror, she thought that there are
men who make a business of death. They must have wars
in order to live. A swollen louse, world size, sucked the blood
of all the men and women on earth. They worked, married,
had children, and all the time this horror had fastened on their
bodies. If I say what I think we shall quarrel too seriously,
she thought, with contempt for herself. She sat quietly,
seeing Gage, not for the first time, as he was—sentimental
and brutal, the world his forced market : his religion—a
successful deal justifies everything from theft to murder.

My love for him is strictly a matter for my senses, she
thought. They began it in the first place. My foolish mind
is nearly, but not quite, helpless. She looked at Gage. He
has only to lay his arm over me and I have no more strength.
She remembered her thoughts when she was alone. I have
no strength when I think of him, she said. I shall never feel
like this again. Take me, take me, take me, my love. But
this won't last, she thought, it will burn out, I know that—I
am not so foolish. The only honest thing, since I am not
going to give in to him and make a clean fire of all I feel,
is to run away. The only dishonest thing is to lie with him
in my mind.

Gage asked her what she was thinking about. ' You and
your Thomas Harben,' she said lightly. ' You're making a
frightful mess of the world.'

' You can't run a world without doing business,' Gage said seriously.

The next day, Sunday, Gage hired a car and called for her. He would not tell her where they were going, but by the time she reached Basingstoke she knew. They drove through Andover and by lanes to the familiar valley. The road followed the valley, with a clear stream on their right. As they crossed the bridge into Broughton Gage nodded and said : ' Last time I crossed this bridge going back to the aerodrome from your billet, I hated you and your countrymen. You had just jilted me.'

' You weren't mine to jilt,' Hervey said.

' I was and I am. You're probably the cleverest woman I have ever owned—the slowest, too. I'll have to trick you into marrying me.'

' I shouldn't try it if I were you,' Hervey said dryly. 'I don't mind injustice, but I should resent being tricked.'

' Just like you,' he exclaimed. ' But you'd trick me.'

' Only in self-defence,' Hervey said with a smile.

' Don't I have to defend myself against you ? The hell I don't.'

Hervey smiled again. She felt better able to deal with him. The certainty of disaster—this must end in a disaster—perhaps one she would laugh at later—had a familiar effect on her, bringing out the other Hervey, the Hervey she distrusted. This Hervey was a passionate creature, careless, greedy of experience, ribald, unreliable, hating authority, cynical, cruelly clear-sighted. Possibly she was the essential Hervey—but there was another, a young woman shrewd and conservative, who watched her and kept her in order and did what she could to make money and get together a solid steady life. At the moment this other was only a spectator and listened ironically, now and again putting in her word.

Hervey looked out at the village. It was exactly what it had been in 1917 when a colony of Flying Corps officers and their wives were billeted on it. For eighteen months

this colony lived a life as separate from the life round them
as if a Roman legion had returned to the valley. With the
end of the War it vanished, and its traces, in the sensitive
earth, were only the latest and weakest scrawl on a memory
in which the Romans figured as newcomers. Indeed, in this
memory Romans and Flying Corps officers were now coeval.

The car balked at the road to the downs. It was a track
pressed into the chalk, its whiteness blazing in the sunlight.
They climbed up on foot. The grass at the edge of the
downs was thin like hair, exactly as she remembered it.
They could see a long way, to the other side of the valley.
The chalk glittered everywhere, under the grass, between the
roots of trees—it was the hard bones of this country showing
through the delicate skin, the skin fine and unwrinkled, as
smooth as water.

Jess was talking to her about Thomas Harben, and about
a woman he had met in the hotel, who knew Harben, and
was very free with her stories about him. In the end she
offered to sound him on Gage's own business—'He begins
with agents and drops them when it suits him,' she had said ;
' I could find out his real opinion of you.'

' She wasn't going to do that for nothing,' Hervey said.
' What were you to pay her ? '

Jess laughed sharply : ' We didn't get so far. I put her off.
What's your advice, darling child ? '

' I should have nothing to do with her. A dog that will
fetch will carry,' Hervey said. She pulled at the dry grass.

Gage's mouth twitched between amusement and pleasure.
' You're right,' he said. He stretched his arm out and laid
a hand on her ankle. ' I'd decided it for myself.'

' You were trying me ? ' Hervey said with a grin. She
was offended, and unwilling to show it. She disliked giving
herself away and would pretend to be pleased rather than
admit she had been hurt.

' No,' Gage said. He was quick enough to know what
he had done. But he did not know how to put it right,
unless he treated her as he would treat any other woman

in the circumstances.   That he did not do so is to be accounted
for by the vanity which dictated a great many of his actions.
He was physically brave and morally incapable of self-control
at the point where his vanity came into play.   Thus his
bravery had unjustly the air of bravado.   His generosity, on
the other hand, was almost all vanity, without seeming to be.
At the moment he was vexed with himself—a point had been
missed—and ready to be vexed with Hervey because she was
stiff and unmanageable by the most natural methods.   During
the drive home he told her stories about himself, some of
them true.

Hervey had ceased to look forward—she lived impatiently
in the moment, aware that sooner or later a moment would
turn up when she would be forced to act as if there were a
future.   Gage's manner, when they met in the evening,
steadied her at once.   He had drunk enough to exorcise his
vanity.   Without realising what it was, she felt that some
impulse on which she relied in order to govern him had
disappeared.   She felt scornful and anxious.   His vitality,
which drew her so sharply, began to seem only violence.

During dinner, for which they went down to the grill
room, he talked about his country.   'Europe's done, England's
done.   Finished.   But for the War you might have held out
against America for another quarter of a century.   You're
done.   You've nothing left but your diplomatic experience.
Your goddam diplomats will always overtalk ours, and it
won't save you.   Only a young country can afford mistakes.'

'That may be so,' Hervey said.   'Let us hope you will
make as many as will hang you.   Even if another barbarian
invasion is due I don't expect to enjoy it.   When you have
wasted our inheritance what will you put in its place ?   The
largest building ?   The loudest noise ?   Or only the most
motor cars ? '

'You may use your tongue on me if it amuses you,' Gage
said.   'But I am going back to France to-morrow, then
home, to be demobilised.   I should like everything settled
before I go.'   He was speaking quietly but with a passion

that alarmed Hervey. She was afraid he would disgrace her by making a scene.

'What is to be settled?' she asked smoothly. She felt uncertain but not yet angry. If he becomes unmanageable I can leave him, she thought. The idea of walking across the room alone was more alarming than anything else.

Gage looked at her with narrowed eyes. He was full of suspicion. Then he noticed her hand trembling and made an effort to control his mind. But he was too nearly at the point at which his muscles twitched of their own accord, and twitched his mind.

'Do you want to marry me, Hervey?'

'No, I don't think so,' Hervey said quietly, her eyes on him.

'Then go away,' Gage said. 'Go. Go at once.'

Hervey stood up slowly. 'Very well,' she said. 'And— thank you for my dinner.'

She walked out of the room, passed the waiters and the cloakroom attendant, feeling her cheeks burn. Her ignorance was such that she half feared to be stopped in the doorway with questions about the bill. Certainly they looked at her. She walked looking fixedly before her, up the stairs, and into the street. She had no coat and no hat. She walked for a time, then decided to take a cab but uncertain of the cost walked on for another ten minutes, conscious of glances at her bare shoulders.

In her room, locking the door, feeling nothing, nothing, she tried to think. She was too tired. She had enough of force left in her to keep quiet, smoothing out her dress, pouring water for the bath she took in her bowl each night, but no impulse to think. She fell suddenly asleep, with her arm stretched to pull the blanket up.

In the morning her first thought was that she had thrown away her single chance of escaping from this dry life. She lay still, feeling too dejected to get up.

Slowly, another feeling came in over the first, a curious lightness, nearly relief. She held her breath, afraid to move.

In a moment she said gently : ' I'm free, I'm alone but I'm free.' At once, fiercely, she knew that, even if there were no Richard depending on her, and no Penn, her mother's daughter could not have married the American. She could not trust herself to this man who was violent, neither civilised nor primitive, neither cultured nor simple, and with no very fastidious notions of conduct. It is because he has so much more life than other people that I love him, she said to herself : I don't respect him, in a few months I might even detest him.

She was too young not to feel downcast, as well as profoundly surprised, by the discovery that her body had its own conception of the good life. If her upbringing had not made it possible decently to snatch that life !—she closed her mind over the thought. The effort was a familiar one. In time it would be easy.

CHAPTER X

THE SCHOOL FOR FICTION

In bad weather there was no getting into the east-going buses. She must travel by tube, first walking up a long windy road to the station. She had an everlasting dislike of tubes. Her country-sharp senses frightened her with thoughts of the weight of earth above her, and she hated the destroying noise and the pressure of other bodies on her own in the packed swaying cages. One stormy morning in October the trains were crowded. Hervey stood wedged fast between a girl and a stout man, trying to withdraw into herself so that only her body received the insulting pressure of theirs. The earth was riddled with these moving cages, each full to suffocation of uneasy bodies, meek, staring, breath mingling with breath. At the end of the journey she ran thankfully into the street, though her shoes let in water and the rain soaked through the stuff of her coat.

She was still raging inwardly when Mr Shaw-Thomas sent for her. On her way to his room she decided to ask for another two pounds a week, that is, half as much again of her wages. She was in the state of mind which prefers disaster to enduring poverty another moment. She sat down facing Mr Shaw-Thomas with the air of an injured schoolboy. When he had finished giving her instructions for a certain piece of work she said abruptly : ' I should like more money.'

Mr Shaw-Thomas lifted his eyebrows. ' Why, Miss Russell ? '

' I can't live on four pounds a week,' Hervey said. ' I need a great deal more to live properly.' She spoke with great assurance and politeness. Now I am really growing up, she thought, greatly pleased with herself.

Mr Shaw-Thomas was more amused than annoyed by being spoken to in this way. He felt the liveliest interest in the awkward young girl and looked upon her as his pupil. Actually, if she had said that she needed the money to support an invalid mother, or her child, he would have felt less inclined to give it to her. Commonplace worthy persons bored him no less than commonplace advertising (unfortunately for his happiness his finest notions were too heroic for the dull dogs which captain industry). Moreover he was kind. This, too, was the moment in which advertising firms felt the swell of the wave under them—they were going up, up— glorious emotion. Still, there was no reason why Mr Shaw-Thomas should have given her the two extra pounds a week. He did. Six pounds. She remembered to thank him.

' Now,' he said, smiling sharply, ' now a warning. The Charel people have complained that their last batch of copy, yours, is too subtle. *Your* danger, Miss Russell. If the great middle-class—your public—enjoyed subtle writing they would buy it. But they buy Mr ——. Don't mistake me. I should have to get rid of a copy-writer who wrote as badly as a popular novelist. All I am saying is that your copy must make as few demands on the intelligence of its readers as if it were popular fiction. The difference—these novelists are paid to be, forgive me, a little diarrhœtic. We on the contrary pay heavily for our right to speak. Just now and then—quality copy, in a high-class paper—advertising something too costly for the middle public, subtlety may be possible. I deprecate the risk.'

Hervey was sunk, hiding her triumph. She had missed the whole of this speech. Renn saved her by coming in fo orders. She stood up to go, but Shaw-Thomas kept her and talked another five minutes, plunging his fine sharp smile into defenceless words. ' Think of a street of little houses,' he said to her, ' a plant in the window, ivory lace curtains, in each house a woman dusting, making beds, mending, looking in the oven, looking at the scrubbed toes of children's boots. She pushes her hair back with one hand, thinking in the same moment of the price of shoes, the torn place in the rug, and a coat worn by the young woman her neighbour. With all that in her mind, and with the endless work, how can you get her to listen to you ? And having listened, open the rubbed purse in her bag and take a shilling from the handful of silver and coppers for something she had no notion she needed until you spoke to her ? '

' Yes. I see,' Hervey exclaimed.

' The greatest artist ever born couldn't do more with words,' Mr Shaw-Thomas said.

She went back to her room, in one hand grasping the promise of wealth, in the other a half-fledged excitement. Her head throbbed. After all there is something in this copy-writing, she thought. To write with the extreme of precision and economy—that takes some doing. She looked up as Renn came in. He saw that she was excited, and smiled, looking at her from the side.

' Don't you know that part of Shaw-Thomas's job, for which they pay him three thousand a year, is to blow enthusiasm into his copy-writers ? '

Hervey looked at him. She felt foolish and very young. Her ardour died at once, which is not surprising. She blushed and bent her head over her desk; unfortunately there was nothing beneath her eyes except a rag of blotting-paper.

' You're beginning to use your mind on your work—which will be the death of your mind if you stay here long enough. It seems a small pity to waste you.'

' Am I wasted ? ' Hervey asked, pleased.

Renn came over to her and said in a sarcastic voice : ' I read your novel. It's a preposterous novel, but you could learn. If you want to stay here you'll have to learn all the dishonest uses of words. You despise popular fiction, don't you ? Well then—why do you stay here writing advertisements for soap ? What is there to choose between playing on a woman's silliest emotion to sell her a new soap, and gratifying

them with a ridiculous story of life as she would like it to be ?
Both times you're selling women the lie they want—the lie
they want. That's fine isn't it ? They buy the soap, they'll
buy your stories—they'll give you more than money for
them—praise, gratitude. How she understands us, they'll
say ; how lovely our lives are when she describes them to us—
More, give us more, Miss Russell, another of your rich
exciting human books ; persuade us we're happy, fortunate,
noble, pathetic, brave.'

Out of breath with his sudden vehemence Renn paused.
Hervey said sullenly : ' I tell lies about soap to get my
living—*caveat emptor*. I don't want to tell lies about life.'

'Why not ? ' Renn mocked. ' *Caveat emptor* . . . it's
true that lies about life are more insidious. There's a patent
stomach medicine on the market that rots the membranes of
the stomach. Someone should examine for creeping rot the
inside of a brain addicted to popular fiction.'

His face changed and he said kindly : ' You'd better get
out before it's too late, Hervey. These brutes—they're
spoiling all the best words by using them to sell soap. Very
soon honest writers will have to use only the simplest, crudest
words—those which the advertisers rejected.' He laughed.
' Shall I tell you my nightmare ? In the name of efficiency
the world has been taken over by big business : our new
overlords address us in the most natural way, by advertisement.
Thus : Eat More Fruit. Use More Steel. Since no one
has thought to advertise loving-kindness, they fall out among
themselves. Then as you walk along a road, from one side a
mechanical voice blares: Use More Wood, and from the
other : Use More Steel. You rush home and shut the
windows : the voices come down the chimney, by telephone,
by wireless, by post. The More Steel party decides on war.
Every newspaper runs terrific headlines : Fight and Grow
Strong. You and I sweat at our desks writing five hundred
strong words on The Romance of War. We remember the
rule : clinch your advertisement by giving the reader something to *do*—ask his grocer or fill in a coupon. So we write :

Demand War NOW. At this moment a bomb comes through the roof and a fragment of my belly flying in one direction encounters your head going in another. At last the last word.'

'You're wasted on this firm,' Hervey said. 'You should be a revivalist.'

Renn blinked at her. 'You're right,' he said.

Hervey glanced furtively at him when he stooped over his desk. An incongruous thought—the plane of shadowed flesh falling away below his cheekbone reminded her of an edge of Salisbury Plain, smooth violet-shadowed hollows scooped in the chalk. Both gave pleasure.

Towards six o'clock Philip walked into their room and asked them to waste two hours with him. He was leaving London for Germany—to see a doctor who was healing ulcers in your body without the knife. He was excited, his eyes in their darkened hollows wide and pale, as if their colour were leaving them. He had grown irritable in the last few weeks, taxing the love of his friends.

Outside snow had fallen and was melting into slush. Hervey felt it oozing between the thin places in her shoes. Philip did not want to eat, or rest, he wanted to walk. The three of them walked along the Embankment, stopped to argue, walked on again. Hervey shivered. Near Blackfriars Bridge they turned into a small dingy café and ordered coffee. A young man was seated at the next table. After a moment Renn said to him: 'I remember you. You saved me from having my head cracked after a socialist meeting.'

The young man looked at him with a charming smile. 'Lucky I happened to be there. I didn't know what it was about, though.'

'What are you doing now?'

'Starving,' the other said in a firm voice. He had a jester's face: when he laughed the ends of his mouth shot up to form a quarter circle, and his eyes were bright hazel colour. 'Don't look at me like that, it's not catching,' he exclaimed. 'I was demobilised, I've spent all my money, my mother

died at the end of the War, and I haven't a job. I wasn't
trained for anything.'

'What were you before you enlisted ? ' Philip asked.

' A schoolboy. I was eighteen in January 1918. In my
time you didn't enlist—you were conscripted.' He began to
laugh, throwing his head back. 'That last year at school
was very curious. We knew, I and the other fellows, that
we should be called up unless the War ended before then.
We didn't think it would end. We wrote Latin verses and
played games, we read our ancient history, and none of it
was of the least importance. Some of the fellows loafed and
tried to break loose. They said it was wasting their last
months. But what could we have done ? Trained our
minds ? That would have been a pretty good waste of time,
too ! "

' Where are you living ? '

' Last night I slept out—for the first time. My goodness,
it was cold.'

' You'd better come home with me,' Renn said. ' You
can sleep on the couch and we'll discuss your state in comfort.
Comfort compared with sleeping out.'

The boy laughed again, gently. ' Why should you do
such a thing for me ? '

' Upon my word, I don't know,' said Renn. ' Except
that you did save my life.'

In the meantime Hervey was shaking so violently with
cold that she had to keep her knees from knocking against
the table. She spilled the coffee from her cup as she drank.
Her teeth chattered on its edge. Only the newcomer
noticed. ' You're freezing,' he exclaimed.

' Nothing of the kind,' Hervey said quickly.

Philip picked up a morning newspaper from a chair and
became engrossed in it. His face crimsoned with anger.
' Do you see ? ' he said. He held up the page and pointed a
trembling finger at the headlines. *Stolen Hun Cows. Well-
fed German Babies. Justice to French Babies. Hun Food
Snivel.* ' That's how these brutes report a conference of

experts set up to deal with famine in Germany and Central
Europe. My God, it's unbearable. I should like to shoot
the hooligan who owns this paper.'

'Well,' Renn said, smiling. 'You might remember that
lice will go on breeding on a dirty body even if you kill the
largest you find.'

'It's a cruel article to have printed,' Hervey stammered.

Renn turned on her his wide smile. A muscle twitched in
the tightly-drawn skin over his temple. 'You won't face
things,' he said lightly. 'Human beings are cruel by instinct.
Homo homini lupus. The more civilised a country is, the less
scope there is in it for open cruelty. The War was a godsend
to our instincts. In the name of justice you can starve Hun
women and children freely. Think of the relief!'

'I'll become a naturalised German,' Philip shouted.

'They'll soon begin torturing each other,' Renn smiled :
'they have no other outlet.'

Philip jumped up and hurried from the café. Renn paid
quickly and they followed him. They caught him up at the
other end of the street. He was still angry, but he apologised,
squeezing Hervey's arm. His train went in lesss than half
an hour. They climbed into a Liverpool Street bus, the
young ex-soldier keeping shyly apart. At the station he stood
aside while the other two went with Philip to his train. They
stood below the window looking up at him in silence. It
reminded Hervey of the leave trains with their load of doomed
young men. She raised herself on her toes to put her arm
round his neck and kiss him.

'That's the first time you've done it without being asked,'
Philip laughed. 'I must be very ill.'

'No, no,' Hervey said. The train moved. 'Come home
again,' she cried.

They watched him disappear into the darkness.

Hervey went home. She who usually slept like a child
slept badly, and woke with a pain in her side. She stayed at
work, trying to ignore it.

The next day the pain was worse. It caught her under her

waist when she laughed or moved quickly, the twist of a knife. On the third day she could not keep herself upright. She walked with difficulty, stooping forward keeping her hand on the pain. Renn said something that made her laugh ' Oh ! ' and bite her lip. Sweat ran over her.

' What's hurting you ? ' Renn asked.

' My right side,' Hervey said. She felt ashamed as she said it.

Renn got up and went out, in silence. He came back in a few minutes tearing the wrapping from a clinical ther- mometer. ' Would you prefer to put it into your mouth yourself ? ' he said politely. It registered four degrees of fever.

' Now will you go home,' he said in an exasperated voice.

Hervey crept away. It was two o'clock. She went home and went to bed. Her head ached and when she moved her eyes they seemed to be the only movable parts of a solid block of pain. She slept for an hour and woke to find herself in a grey world. It was a moment before she remembered that she had been sent home. Lying still, she had no pain and she supposed that she was cured. She sat up, and it seemed that she was drowning. Grey water swirled to her throat, she fought it feebly, then slipped down and lay still.

From unconsciousness she passed into a state neither waking nor sleeping. The room was there, strangely dis- torted, and filled with a faintly menacing darkness. This darkness was actively at work stifling the little light that came under the door. She lay and watched it. It kept changing its shape. After the light, my turn, she thought. Now Mr Shaw-Thomas was in the room. Smiling, he handed her sheet after sheet of paper until the pile reached from the floor to the level of her eyes. He went away and she began feverishly to work, writing on each sheet and thrusting it into a mouth that opened, with a sucking jelly- like motion, between the bed and the wall. She wrote : Ex when your child is dying, Ex when you fear birth and death in a grain of sand, Ex when you have been mutilated by the spades of the archæologists, Ex for Lucifer, Ex when pity causes foul smells in yards, graves, war memorials, streets, and sick rooms, Ex when Celia all her glory shows, such gaudy tulips raised from dung, Ex against Communism, nose-bleed, Zeno's arrow, and the streptococcus of life, Ex against famine and the wolf. Lines of poetry, single words, the names of villages near her home, fragments of recollected speech, ran through her mind like sand on to the paper. At last she wrote nothing but: I am now going home. She wrote the whole night and fell asleep towards morning. When she woke again she felt heavily tired but cool. Her body when she moved gave her less pain. She lay quietly, looking at the ceiling. Nothing seemed worth the effort of thinking about it.

Towards nine o'clock in the morning, when she should have been out, her landlady came into the room. She seemed annoyed to find Hervey in bed and asked her if she wanted a doctor.

'Not at any time,' Hervey said in a placid voice. The woman went downstairs. A short time later Delia Hunt toiled up the stairs from her room and took charge. She nursed Hervey for six days, with great good humour. On the fourth day, when the pain in her side and fever were quite gone, she made her eat a nearly raw beefsteak. It made Hervey drunk.

She stayed at home nine days. Once during this time she heard Delia's husband speaking to her outside the room. He spoke in a low voice and she did not hear what he said, but his voice made a definitely unpleasant impression on her. Delia never mentioned him to her.

She thought a great deal about Penn during these days. Because she was not in love with him it did not occur to her to feel surprised by the prolonged silence between his letters. Her own feelings and ambitions absorbed her so that when she thought of Penn it was of someone to whom she felt bound by a past life. Therefore it never entered her mind to wonder what his feeling was towards her. Since for

her he belonged to the past she supposed him to be unchanged
—still in love with her and dependent on her even when he
was behaving with the utmost unkindness or brutality. This
blindness of hers was part of her sole vanity—she believed that
she changed but that others did not.

   She made countless plans for their living together. At one
moment she thought that she could live happily with Penn
and her son in a cottage. I shall write books, with which
I shall earn a little money; Penn can teach Latin in the
nearest school and he will earn what may just keep us. As
soon as she had thought this, her ambition sprang up and she
knew that she could not endure a quiet and obscure life.
At another moment she said to herself, with a grave air:
One does what one can, something will come of it. The
one fixed point in all her plans was Richard: the promise
she made him when he was born—to get him everything he
wanted—was always in her mind.

CHAPTER XI

PENN was released from the Air Force in February 1920. He came up to London, and was waiting for Hervey in her room when she came home. She was overjoyed to see him out of uniform, and for a few days, watching him in clothes he had worn in 1917, before he went into the Flying Corps, she felt deeply moved and gentle.

He had made no plans for the future. To the last moment he had refused to consider any life outside the easy pleasantly exciting life of a ground officer in the Air Force. Now he had nothing but his gratuity. Hervey thought that this money should be spent to establish them with Richard in a small house. She grudged every pound he drew from it. When he had been at home for a week without making an effort to start work she became anxious.

Only a few years earlier she would have spoken directly of her hopes. But she had lost the courage for this. A harsh upbringing had destroyed much of her self-confidence and Penn's attitude to her completed the damage. Though no thrashing would now follow she hated to be found out in a mistake. Her unnatural pride suffered, too. And she hated as much to be seen wishing or hoping for something. She expected to be laughed at. Young as she still was, her subtle and slow-moving mind had created a maze of defences for her, through which her impulses had to find their way out—now often so changed by the journey that their own mother would not know them. Astonishing how many twists and turns her thoughts made—even with a simple and honest end in view.

139

She brought home a copy of the *Educational Supplement* and showed Penn that three London schools needed classics masters. Penn smiled. ' What's the hurry ? ' he said amiably.

' Your gratuity won't last for ever,' Hervey said. ' If you were at work you would have it to spend on other things.'

' I'm spending it on other things now. Don't you think I deserve a rest ? '

Hervey looked at him. She felt herself growing red in the face. ' No.' She tried to smile.

' Why are you so anxious to drive me to work ? Have you made plans for spending my money ? '

' No,' Hervey said. She added with an effort : ' Perhaps you'd like to go up to Danesacre to see Richard ? You haven't seen him for a year and a half.'

Penn's face changed instantly. ' So that's it ! You want my gratuity money for the boy. Why didn't you say so ? I have never known anyone with so dishonest and tortuous a way of going about things. It doesn't do you any good with me ! '

' It's not true,' Hervey said. Her pride was roused. She began like her mother to justify herself, in a sharp passionate voice. ' Your money is nothing to me. I have my own. Enough for Richard.'

When she spoke to him in her mother's voice Penn hated her. In her soft youth there were so many hard rocks scarcely beneath the surface. Each time he caught a glimpse of one of these he lost all kindness for her : he wanted to wound and punish. Even if he could make her cry he was not satisfied.

' Don't be too sure you'll always have Richard,' he exclaimed. ' He's my son.'

' Then you should be glad to spend money on him,' Hervey said. She could not endure him and running from his room fastened herself in her own. The past year now seemed to her a period of delicious tranquillity. Forgetting how often she had been lonely she cried tears of rage at the thought of living with Penn for years to come.

Penn had gone out. He was determined not to apply for any of the schools Hervey had suggested. That would look too much like obeying her. He went instead to call on T. S. Heywood, whom he found alone. T.S. made no show of being pleased, but Penn talked affably, and talked himself into good humour and at last said outright that he was here, at Hervey's suggestion, to ask her friend whether Evelyn had room for an intelligent man on the *London Review*.

'Yourself?'

'Naturally,' Penn laughed.

'But I don't know anything about my wife's editorial work,' T.S. said coldly. He did not believe that Hervey had sent her husband. If she wanted anything she would try to get round me herself, he thought. 'Why don't you see Evelyn about it?'

Penn's face assumed an air of idiot cunning. 'Well. I suppose I can say you sent me?'

'No that you can't,' T.S. said at once. 'Leave me out of it.' He stood up, his face twitching with a nervous anger.

There was nothing for Penn but to leave. He went home, turning in his mind reasons for T.S.'s manner. He found them in jealousy and envy of himself. If Len Hammond had been in London he would have run straight to her to be comforted.

He went into Hervey's room and in a grave voice said:

'Oh Hervey, I've had a miserable evening. I met your friend Heywood and asked him civilly whether there would be any hope of his wife giving me a chance on her *Review*. From the way he spoke you'd think I was nothing. I felt miserable, I can tell you. I thought he was a friend of mine.'

Hervey was touched by his look of childish unhappiness. She knew exactly why T.S. had refused and that he did not trust Penn. At the same time she was nearly angry with him. It was always so—Penn had only to tell her in a simple voice that he was unhappy and her heart melted. This voice of his recalled the time when she admired him above anyone. In those days he had discovered how to rouse in her an agony of pity for him, and this weakness of hers—it had become a habit—was the hold he had over her.

Trying to say what would console him, she stroked his cheeks. ' But, my darling, you don't want to review books, do you ? What else could Evelyn Lamb give you to do ? '

' She could make me her assistant editor,' Penn said, with a happy smile.

' You have had no experience,' Hervey exclaimed. She did not know whether to laugh or cry at the singular notion he had formed of his chances.

' What of it ? I have a better head than the run of literary journalists. You'll see, I shall get my foot in somewhere, and then I'll go out after your friend T.S. and make a public fool of him.'

' No, no,' Hervey said, alarmed. ' You must hold your tongue—I don't care yet to offend Evelyn Lamb. We're not rich, we have to make our way yet, and we shall only do it by being more intelligent than other people. We have no friends in London to help us. Why waste energy *going out after* anyone ? It does no good and it is uncivilised.'

' Oh you ! you would do anything to avoid trouble,' Penn sneered.

This was so close to the truth that it silenced her. Penn walked to the door. He waited a moment and said coldly : ' Let me tell you, your cleverness doesn't impress me. When I feel like making trouble I make it, and damn public opinion. That's the kind of man I am.'

He shut the door. Hervey rested her head in her hands. She felt tired and contemptuous. One half-formed thought crossed her mind : I could perhaps make friends with Evelyn myself. At the moment she felt more inclined to give up everything and run back to Danesacre. Surely Penn would not let her stay there, on her mother's charity, but would look for work.

She stood up, looked at herself closely in the glass, and laughed. But of course I shan't go back, she thought.

It was already eleven o'clock. Creeping downstairs to fill her water-jug in the bathroom she heard curious sounds issuing from the Hunts' room—a fall and a woman's groan. Is he cruel to her ? she wondered. Her heart moved quickly and painfully.

CHAPTER XII

HERVEY now did what any sensible young woman, who wished to *do the best for* herself, would have tried a year earlier. The inconsistency in her nature went too deep : she would use all her wit, shrewdness, and tact on behalf of another person or to get something she did not want but only needed for the security which disgusted her—but for herself, to advance her as a writer, she never lifted a finger. This was not the result of delicacy. Only the effort bored her to such a degree that she would never make it for herself alone. Other people might have reproached her if she refused to exert herself on their behalf, but she would not reproach herself for having neglected her own interests.

With the idea of helping Penn to get what he wanted she took endless trouble to please Evelyn Lamb. It was not impossible. Hervey had great natural charm when she could use it, and her childhood had been one long severe training in diplomacy. She had learned young to read faces, tones of voice, and hearts.

Before long the older woman found it natural as well as pleasant to talk to Hervey more freely than she had talked to any woman since the death of her sister. The young girl listened with the whole of her mind. This happens so rarely to anyone—half of your friend's mind is a generous gift—that it is the finest flattery. Moreover, it is a true gift—you cannot make a feint of listening with your whole mind. Hervey felt a deep interest in the older woman. Without knowing why, she was sorry for her. She was also greatly frightened by her. Even when she saw Evelyn two or three times a week

she went through the same tortures of shyness and sighed with
relief when she escaped. Though Evelyn was really pleased
with her, she could not resist making the young girl pay for
their friendship by nipping her sharply several times the
week. Since Hervey could never think of any retort that was
not fatally harsh she blushed and was silent.

She was ashamed of being shy, and she failed to realise that
nothing, in a society of writers, is so dull as civility and a soft
heart. She met a great many well-known or about to be
well-known people in Evelyn's house. Only a few of them
spoke twice to a polite young woman with nothing to say for
herself. On these persons she made a deep impression, but
not in all cases a good one. William Ridley had the wit to
notice that she was obstinate, opinionated, and malicious.

Evelyn allowed her to write short unsigned notices for the
London Review and employed her to check references and
quotations. She did not pay her for these services, which
engaged all Hervey's leisure. Hervey toiled cheerfully, since
she meant at the right moment to suggest making use of
Penn. It was ironical—since she wanted nothing for herself
—that Evelyn kept promising to take signed paid work
from her when she had learned her trade. As to that—
Hervey considered that she wrote a great deal better than
William Ridley, whose weekly essay followed Evelyn's in the
paper.

One Thursday in April she was drinking tea alone with
Evelyn. Evelyn had asked her opinion of Ridley. Hervey
had none. She did not know that he was Evelyn's lover, and
spoke honestly.

' I should say he was a very commonplace writer. He has
so much energy, and he notices everything—I think perhaps
he is a commonplace genius. He's very conceited.'

' He was laughing yesterday over your novel,' Evelyn said
dryly. ' Are you writing another, by the way ? '

' Yes,' Hervey said. She blushed.

' Try to write about what you feel,' Evelyn went on.
' That might be new. Do leave clever talk about problems

to the undergraduates, and write only what you have felt—
about falling in love, or mathematics, or talking to other
women. That will be first-hand revelation. You should
use your mind to search your heart. Anyone can search
the newspapers, for stories of unhappy marriages, suicides,
and all that.'

Hervey looked down. She longed to deserve praise, but
the truth is that she learned nothing by hearing it, and years
would pass over her before she understood what Evelyn meant.
At this moment the door opened and William Ridley came in.
He sprawled on a chair and talked to Evelyn without paying
any attention to Hervey. She walked over to a window
and tried to think of a way of leaving without seeming
awkward. It was clear that she was unwanted, but Evelyn
had borrowed five shillings from her to pay for a cab and if
she went without it she would be penniless until to-morrow
afternoon. At last she jumped up and calling out—' Good-
bye, I shall see you again this week '—she ran from the
room.

As soon as she had gone Ridley said, jerking his thumb:
' I can't stand the airs she gives herself.'

' Airs ? ' Evelyn said. ' My poor young Hervey ? Nonsense.'

' I didn't come to talk about her. What's this someone's
been saying in the *Review* about my friend Mrs Harben ?
She's in a rare temper. I said I'd ask you about it.'

Evelyn smiled slightly. So he is going without me to
Lucy Harben's, she said to herself.

An extraordinary emotion seized her. She shuddered at
the complacence with which he uttered the words ' my friend
Mrs Harben '—never had he looked less pleasing—and in
the same moment she was waiting, rigid, for the clumsily
violent caress she expected. Her fingers gripped the edge of
her chair. It would give her no pleasure, it confused and
wearied her, yet she craved it. It was as though she craved
the confusion, but without knowing what she hoped from it.

Her inner life had fallen into disorder. She felt that for

years she had been keeping up a pretence of order in her mind by an effort of nerves or will. Now that the pretence was finished she looked inward at a life which had collapsed on itself.

Her first thought was that no one else must see it. There must be a rigid outer order—in everything, in her actions and writing, in other people's, everywhere. She wrote the first of a series of unsigned essays condemning romantic licence. In the second, she allowed herself to make fun of Mrs Thomas Harben's taste in art—it was the week the other woman lent her house for an exhibition in aid of blinded soldiers. This was not pure criticism—she had always been subject to impulses wildly at variance with her known character. Already she bitterly regretted the attack. It threatened her social front with disorder, at the moment when order, and more order, was what she wanted.

Ridley was disconcerted by her smile. Even now, though he believed firmly that women are at the mercy of their feelings, he was a little intimidated by her reputation as a clever woman. Moreover she was an editor, one of the creatures upon whom he depended for his life. He threw himself back in his chair. 'I suppose you didn't write the article yourself.'

'Certainly not,' Evelyn said, without giving herself time to think. 'In fact, it was set up in mistake for another with much the same title. You know I was ill last week and left that idiot Kerr in charge.'

'He didn't write it! Come now, you'd better tell me who did. I can soothe Lucy Harben for you.'

'Thank you,' Evelyn said, smiling. She felt a spasm of fury. 'The little Russell wrote it. She writes very well, and though I can't use much she writes it is good practice for her.'

'I never see anything by her in the *London Review*.'

'She hasn't signed anything.'

'She'd better not,' Ridley chuckled. 'Our Mrs Harben won't forgive you for encouraging her after this.'

Evelyn said nothing. She felt as though she were being crushed from all sides. And there was nothing, no force in her, to keep her safe. She would die. But it was her own fault, and her own act had started the destruction. I shall repair it, she thought, with growing energy; my mind is not weakened, I shall repair everything. Shall I at least get rid of this fellow ? She had closed her eyes. Opening them she saw first Ridley's thick short hand on the arm of her chair. It would not be a bad idea to pick it up between finger and thumb and drop it.

She began to laugh.

When Hervey came to see her on Saturday she brought with her the criticism of a play. The dramatic critic of the *Review* was going to resign and Evelyn had half promised to try Hervey in his place. This half promise had excited Hervey so that she was afraid to think about it. She laid the copy of her criticism on Evelyn's desk and waited. Her stomach felt horribly empty.

Evelyn read it through quickly and said : ' You can do another one or two if you like. I'll pay for them but I'd rather you didn't sign them. I've taken on a young man as dramatic critic. He'll begin in a fortnight.'

Hervey fell down an endless flight of stairs. When she could speak she said quietly : ' I don't mind working for you for nothing. But—will you give Penn a chance to do something ? He reads Greek and Latin and knows a great deal of history, he could review solid books for you.'

Suddenly, while she was still speaking, it came to Evelyn that Hervey was responsible for the mistakes she had made in the last few months. There was something disturbing, unreliable, about the young girl. She gave way to a cruel impulse.

' Don't talk to me about that ridiculous husband of yours,' she cried. ' I don't mind your bringing him here in the evening now and then, if it helps you, but I warn you not to let him make a nuisance of himself.'

Hervey walked out of the room.

In the hall she found T.S., half in his overcoat. He asked her where she was going and offered to walk part of the way with her. She nodded. She was trembling. but he did not notice it. In the street he stumped along beside her in silence, head down, until they reached Ebury Street. Then he said : ' Philip's in hospital.'

' What ? ' Hervey felt a shock of dismay. The blood rushed through her body, checked, dropped. She looked at T.S. He did not seem to be sharing her dismay, but only looked more sardonic than usual. Come, it can't be so bad, she thought. Nevertheless she stood still, touching the wall with her hand. ' Why is he in hospital ? Is he worse ? '

' He has cancer, of course. I knew that a year ago, but the damned fools have been treating him for dyspepsia and then for an ulcer. I don't suppose it would have made any difference.'

Hervey bit her lip. She did not want details. ' Is it his wounds ? '

' Oh yes, I think so,' T.S. said.

' Will they cure him now ? '

' Almost certainly not.' He added : ' I went with him to-day to see him in. Visiting hours are between four and six, so you can come with me next Saturday.'

Hervey did not say anything. She had a singular horror of sickness in any form and wished Saturday would never come.

' Do you remember ?—you told him he was a doomed young man.'

' One of my lighter efforts,' T.S. grinned. ' Come on, young Hervey. We'll drink a cup of coffee together. To our good intentions.'

The café they went into was underground, one of those cellars disguised with hangings, carved screens, and cushions, which a single added layer of dust would obliterate. Hervey pulled a face at it. ' Fancy if an earthquake buried us down here. I should turn in my bones at the things the archæolo-

gists will say when they dig us up. "*The places they lived in !*"
They'll label us the Sordid Age.'

'So we are,' T.S. said swiftly. 'Do you remember that
place in Surrey we walked to, you and I and Philip, in 1913 ?
Philip and I went there yesterday—his idea.' He looked at
her and said : 'We didn't take you because we were afraid
you would have trouble with Penn. It was a mistake, too.
The place was torn to pieces. The field of the chestnut tree
is a street of new houses, ending nowhere, so ugly you never
saw, the grey manor house is a tea-shop, the hedges have
been cut down, houses everywhere, like a disease, and the
air reeks of petrol. We couldn't find our way and were as
lost as ghosts. Philip said : "I'm glad I didn't go over to
look at the battlefields. I shouldn't be surprised if some
brute has gone and built houses on them." Rose at the pub
is fat and minus a tooth or so.'

Hervey laughed out. 'I should hate not knowing what
the country was like before the War. We've known better
times. Not much to boast of ; but something to make do,
in another age.

'The War went on too long. Everything's spoiled.'

'You can't see round the next corner,' Hervey said. She
made an incautious movement, and seized the table for support.
'This couch isn't safe !'

'Once Philip and I were summoned to Corps Head-
quarters. It was a castle of sorts. We were waiting, alone in
a room. Philip sat down on a sofa, which collapsed and he
rolled across the floor bringing down with him a *cloisonné* vase
as big as a man. You never saw such ruin, like a hurricane.
I was paralysed with terror. I thought we should be shot
for counter-military action. Philip rang the bell and when a
servant came in he said in a cold furious voice : "Clear away
this mess. It's disgraceful, unheard of." The man ran about
like a hare under Philip's steely eye—the eye of a second
lieutenant !—I think it hypnotised him—and the last fragment disappeared through one door as the G.S.O.2 came in
at the other.'

'Don't you remember?—no, you missed the evening Philip read a paper to the Literary Society at King's on the life and work of a Polish philosopher called Csychewinski. It was just after we'd been forbidden to debate Socialism and this Csychewinski was a socialist, an atheist, and held astonishing views on sex. Hardly a soul in the hall realised that our Philip had invented him until that theological lecturer, the camel-faced one, got up and asked where the eighty-six volumes of the Life and Works could be seen. Philip looked at him and said sweetly: "In the really admirable library of the Gas Light and Coke Company, sir." There was a riot.'

'This idea he had of starting a new paper. He'd have been disappointed, certainly. English people won't pay out good money to read uncomfortable truths.'

'Philip is never disappointed,' Hervey said, surprised. 'He has a religion. If the paper failed he would find some other way to speak. Even if only six people listened.'

'People always listened to our Philip,' T.S. said. 'Visiting generals listened.'

'He was as uncompromising as an early Christian. Do you remember our old librarian, who loved him and lent him MSS. and first editions? You knew Philip had been calling on him once a week? Last March the old man wrote an article in the *Review* on the beauty of war. Philip sent him fifteen folio sheets, in his small writing, of devastating criticism, and added that he would not be coming again. The old man was heartbroken.'

T.S. laughed. 'All the same he'll outlive our Philip.'

CHAPTER XIII

THE EIGHTEEN OLD GENTLEMEN

HERVEY was alone in the room when the old gentleman came in, carrying a portfolio. He had a letter addressed to David Renn in his hand.

'Mr Renn is away ill,' Hervey said. 'I am Miss Russell, his assistant. Can I do anything?'

The old gentleman seated himself shakily with his arms round the portfolio. He was tall, with bright serious eyes, and a fair skin. He looked at Hervey with a little confidence.

'I beg your pardon, Miss Russell. A friend of mine—no, of my wife's, I must be accurate—gave me a letter to Mr Renn. I was to show him my sketches. You buy sketches, don't you? I can draw in any style required.'

'Usually, we employ our own artists,' Hervey said. 'We have a studio upstairs.' She looked, not knowing what to add, at a number of water-colour drawings, careful, lifeless, such as children once copied.

'I can leave these for Mr Renn to see.' He replaced them slowly. 'I had better tell you that I am a journalist—or was. I was the art critic of the *Morning Gazette*. When it changed hands last year the new proprietor engaged an efficiency expert, a profession new to me. He sacked eighteen of us at once, without enquiry. Yes, yes, he enquired our ages. All over sixty were dismissed and without pension. I am seventy-two.'

'You look much younger than that,' Hervey said. She smiled at him.

He looked innocently pleased. 'Do you think that? I ought not to take your time, but you are kindness itself,

I shall tell you why I need money at once. My wife—we have lived for thirty years in Hove—well, now she's going. The doctor wrote to tell me this morning. Well I wrote to her and I said, " Annie, I've got the best job I ever had and we'll go to France as soon as you're better." Was that the right thing to tell her ? When I was at home, last week, he said, " I suggest giving a little stimulant. You know what she'd like, don't you." I knew at once. "Annie, you'd like some champagne," I said to her. She only looked at me. Well, I took eight of my sketches to my wine merchant and I said, " Let me have one bottle of Möet '06. I'll leave these with you until I can pay for it." Just fancy, he sent in half a dozen bottles that evening.'

Hervey had been listening with the intensity, only partly deliberate, which drew people to talk to her. At these times the extraordinary sensitiveness of her finger-tips seemed to spread through her body. She felt it drawn taut to receive a sound, like a touch. ' *How* long were you on the *Morning Gazette* ? '

' Forty-two years, my dear Miss Russell. Please don't think I saved nothing. Why, we saved so much every year. I had invested it in the Northern Counties Shipping Company. In 1918 my Company bought up the Field Ross Line. They issued a great many new shares, over two million pounds worth. Just think of it, and they were all subscribed ! What days ! Alas, this year my Company had to sell back many of the new ships to their original owners—at a fifth of the price paid. A little later it collapsed, and in April it was put into the official receiver's hands. My shares were ordinary shares and I lost all, yes, yes, every farthing. Many of the shareholders were incensed, but I formed the opinion that there could be nothing wrong. Why, the managing director of my Company was a brother-in-law of Field and Ross's chairman ! Still—I had lost all. You can scarcely imagine how startled we were.'

Hervey sat frowning. ' If I can think of a way to help I'll write to you,' she said at last.

' You're too kind.   Just think, there were eighteen of us sacked that morning.   One of us committed suicide.'   He spoke almost with pride, like the survivor of an earthquake. ' Eighteen !   I shouldn't like to blame our one suicide, but I shan't come to it.   Fortunately, it's forbidden.   My religion is perfectly clear on that as on all other matters.'

You're a Catholic, are you, Hervey thought.   She had begun to wish he would leave, but did not know how to get rid of him.   With Renn's work and her own she was certain of at least three hours' work in the evening.   The slackening of her interest was felt.   He stood up, helping himself by touching the wall.   Hervey received the portfolio from him and laid it down with an air of respect.   She walked with him to the door.   The thought came to her : ' I'll pray for you and your wife.'

' Are you a Catholic ? ' the old gentleman asked.

' No.   But I think even a Protestant's prayers may be needed in this.'

He stood in some distress.   ' Oh, you don't think I'm so bigoted as that,' he cried, ' but I never heard a Protestant say that.'

He was neither the first nor the last person to be misled —and comforted—by Hervey's polite heart.

CHAPTER XIV

1. *Hervey meets a minor Power*

His ownership of the *Daily Post* gratified the two Marcel
Cohens who lived, scarcely in amity, in one body.   One
could tear at this and that decayed beam, while the other
did business on a sound basis.   He had never stepped outside
the law in his life, or evaded the least clause of a contract;
but his own lawyer drew the contract.   Thus he could enjoy
his intelligence, without the need to sacrifice to it.   He
flourished on the disorders which have infected our civilisation,
because he accepted the conditions of disorder—that there are
no spiritual standards of reference, no human values—the only
universally acknowledged value is success, and the only
alternative to success is failure.

In his newspaper, which he called a Radical Independent
paper (to allow himself the widest margin of opposition to all
parties), he published articles exposing the filth of the slums.
His city editor advised investment in companies relying in
part on the existence of slums.   The financial page, read by a
few thousands, was better worth a penny than any other
daily newspaper in the country.   A vast public gulped down
the rest of the paper, enjoying its fat feast of exposures and
the assassination of private and public men.   It was a fillip
for the day.   The political leader writer had a turn for neat
festering phrase.   On the middle page well-known novelists
exposed their views and parts.   The cartoonist had been born
unable to respect anything and was paid well for his misfortune.   At times Marcel Cohen was made to feel the dis-

trust his restless mind inspired in the Christians with whom he did business, and a dismayed sub-editor or a reporter, meeting him accidentally after one of these rebuffs, found himself sacked for no reason. Cohen paid his people well, squeezed the last drops of energy from them, and had a clause inserted in the contracts allowing him to discharge without warning.

He was amused and surprised to receive a note from Hervey Russell, asking him in a very formal way for an interview. Now what does she want, he wondered ? He had seen her four or five times since their first meeting in Evelyn Lamb's house, and she had avoided him—he thought, through shyness. He answered her letter himself.

She came in with a look of confidence. It made him smile to himself. I know all about it, *I* have pretended confidence, he remembered. An impulse to take the wind out of her sails made him say : ' You're astonishingly like your grandmother. By the way, are you still on bad terms with her ? '

Hervey only smiled. She had prepared for the question. ' On no terms at all.'

' *Schade !* You're making a mistake. Mrs Hervey is not only the richest, she's the most surprising figure in England. An eminent Victorian. You'd better think about forgiving her.'

' So that she would help me ? ' Hervey said. ' I prefer to help myself. Do you know my grandmother ? '

His mouth, shapely and too expressive, twitched. ' I sat opposite her jaw at fifty board meetings before she resigned from her own firm. Yours is the same jaw. The upper half of your face is different—less, forgive me, less sure of itself. I daresay you're more intelligent, but you won't get so far.'

' I didn't inherit a shipping firm,' Hervey said dryly.

Cohen looked at her with a sharp smile. ' Oh, there's one thing you don't forgive her. Well—why have you come to see me ? '

' Do you want an art critic ? ' Hervey said.

'What do you know about art?'

'Nothing. I don't want it for myself?' She hesitated, forgetting the speech she had prepared. 'Do you remember when the *Morning Gazette* changed hands they dismissed half the old staff? One, the art critic, is my friend. He must know it all. Can't you give him work?'

Marcel Cohen laughed out. 'He will be eighty. The art criticism of the old *Morning Gazette* was early Victorian. The music worse. Policy and methods also—before the reorganisation it was all but bankrupt. It is still as reactionary and unintelligent as before, but it has smartened itself up and it will last until a Liberal government suppresses it. Liberal governments don't suppress—one reason why there won't be another in our time. Ours is a time to suppress or be suppressed. In any case, I don't employ a regular art critic. Who wants it? I get a painter or a critic, not the most modern but the most modern heard of, to write an article on the Academy. Last week we ran a young writer, William Ridley, on public statues, very destructive and funny. That's what people like. Do you ever read ordinary art criticism?'

'I'm not interested.'

'Neither is Mrs Smith. Can your friend write a slashing attack on anything?'

'Bless me, no,' Hervey sighed. She stood up to leave. 'I see it's no use.'

'Sit down a minute,' Cohen said. 'Don't you want to write something?'

An unexpected question usually started cracks in Hervey's mind, through which everything fell. She blinked and said: 'I'll think about it.'

'What do you do? Are you in business? No, you're a writer.'

'A copy writer.' She put her head down, so that he saw her face foreshortened; boulder of forehead; eyes, one perceptibly lower in her head than the other; short upturned nose. 'I could write you an article—"Advertisers are doing the Devil's work"—would you print it?'

' Certainly not,' Cohen said. ' Like any other newspaper the *Daily Post* lives by advertisements. Besides I don't agree with you.'

' I didn't suppose you would,' Hervey said. She looked at him with a warm smile. ' Well then. How would you like one on shipping firms which blow out their capital until they can't afford to pay dividends, and finally blow up, ruining their ordinary shareholders. I mean the Northern Counties Company.' She felt a thrill, the familiar sensation of jumping from a great height. Though she had looked up the figures and details of the affair she had not discovered whether Cohen was on the board of either company.

' You don't want to write for me at all,' Cohen said. He kept his eyes on her face, frowning. ' What do you know about shipping ? ' He gave a sudden laugh. ' Your grandmother ought to have put you in the firm. She had a grandson in it—'

' Nicholas Roxby, my first cousin,' Hervey said.

' First fool,' Cohen shouted. ' He walked out during the War. Left her with her ships in her arms. It was then she sold out—at the top of the wave. Just like her. Heaven only knows what she's worth now.'

' My cousin must be a fool,' Hervey said bitterly.

Cohen looked at her. ' You wouldn't have done it, eh ? '

' No,' Hervey said.

' Not you. Now, that Northern Counties story would have made your grandmother stare, and sneer. To buy at £22 a ton and sell back at £4 ! The government refused an enquiry. Quite rightly. Why all this about the loss of a few millions ! How many millions did the War cost ? A day ! Someone has to lose money in the slump. First in and first out is the rule—known to your grandmother. You're not a socialist, are you ? Comrade Smith proposed that slumps be made illegal. Carried unanimously. Bah ! '

Weakly Hervey nodded. She could not force herself to say that she was a socialist. The figure of Mary Hervey, mouth clenched, eyes cold and starting with anger, possessed

her mind. She admired that ruthless possessive spirit. One
of the masters of an age. Which age ? The great houses
of merchant princes set within sight of the slave quarters.
Her grandmother's house. Succeeded against her will by
Marcel Cohen. The rats are underneath the floors. Am
I a socialist ? *Th-en, comrades, now rally And the last fight
let us* . . . The delicate steel-engraved outline of her grandmother, blood staining her dress, retreated slowly. There
was a darkness over all the earth until the ninth hour. With
pain she tore away the cords fastening her to her grandmother.
Brother, I believe ; help thou mine unbelief. Cold—how
cold it is, said the little lamb. My mother reading from the
book. She could not help smiling.

'Now, you and I are going to get on together,' Cohen said.
His eyes twinkled a little. 'You're a clever girl and if you're
sensible I see a future for you.'

'Thank you,' Hervey said, smiling at him.

'We'll drink a cup of tea, eh ? ' He pressed his bell. With
a feeling of friendliness he talked to her about his children,
about the boy who had died without his mother finding the
courage to see him, and about his daughter. The liking
Hervey had felt for him when he was talking about the boy
died as soon as he began to recite a list of his daughter's
friends ; her house in Bruton Street ; the room she slept in,
like a drawing-room, décor by Charles ; the bed, Florentine
and painted, in the alcove ; two nurseries painted out in pale
green ; the bathrooms—' but only quite a simple house.' She
wondered why he did not notice that she had ceased to be
sympathetic. There were extraordinary gaps in his understanding of other people—extraordinary because of the
assurance in his glance. He ought to know better, she
thought. Such childishness, side by side with such experience,
repelled her.

Cohen wished to interest her. He thought that perhaps
he could use her. The thought crossed his mind, If she's at
all like her grandmother she'll try to use me. That displeased
him. He looked again at her face and saw in it more of the

withdrawn contemptuous old woman. He decided that she
had stayed long enough.

Outside in the street Hervey went over the interview
with a growing feeling of shame. She tried to recall all she
had said and to construe the impression it must have made.
The conviction of her utter inadequacy returned to beat
inside her brain. Her face burned crimson. To forget
what had happened she walked quickly in the May sunlight.
The evening was as clear as glass, mirroring rose and delicate
amber clouds in the sky above Trafalgar Square. Her self-
possession began to return.

2. *Frank reads the* Daily Post

The evening traffic past the Dug-out had scarcely begun.
One lorry had drawn up under the hedge and the driver,
a thin man with blue patient eyes, was gulping down hot
coffee. He looked at the road. ' Going north ? ' Frank
said.

' Middlesbrough.'

' Ah, I was in Garton's Yard the year before the War.'

' You made a good exchange,' the driver said. He wiped
his hand across his mouth and felt for the buttons of his
under-jacket, an old khaki tunic. After he had started the
engine he came back. ' Want to keep the paper, mate ? '
He handed it across the counter.

' Thanks,' Frank said. He laid it down and went into the
back room. His wife looked at him from the bed with a
smile. ' How d'you feel, Sally ? ' he asked. The presence
of the other woman tied his tongue—he felt in the way.
He went back to the shed facing the road and leaned against
the counter reading the *Daily Post*. An article on the
workers and ' direct action ' caught his eye. He read it
through twice. The writer showed that strikes and any such
violent action injured the workers more than the other classes.
They must put their trust in . . . English sense of justice
. . . the ballot box . . . constitutional methods . . . the

slow march of democracy . . . prosperity for all. But what
if our votes don't get us anywhere ? he thought. He read
the article again. No, nothing in it about that. Woman
Found Dead in Tub. Shooting in Ireland.

He read the news, and the sporting pages. A lorry drew
up beyond the Dug-out. The driver came running back.
' Three sandwiches quick, mate. I got to be in Carlisle by
four ac emma.' Frank cut and folded rapidly. He served
eight persons in quick succession. After this a lull. No one,
no lorry or cart in sight. He went back into the house.
Standing, irresolute, he listened for sounds from the other
room. A footstep, the creak of a board, then his wife groaned.
It was an animal sound—he could not believe she had made it.
Scarcely knowing what he was about he opened the door
and went straight to the side of the bed. ' Oh, Sally is it
bad ? ' he said.

' I didn't mean to call out,' his wife said. ' Shan't do it
again. I don't want to frighten away customers.' She
smiled. Her face changed quickly—as though a hand passed
over it, wiping away her youth. He felt his heart stop.

' I'll call you if I want help,' the other woman said kindly.

He was elbowed out of their room and the door shut on
him. For a moment he was resentful without knowing why.
He could not be angry with his young wife, so he hated the
older woman. Spreading herself in the place, he thought.
Too many women—we could have managed.

He went outside. As if to even things his mind took him
to where there had been no women, only men. He rarely
thought about the War. When he did no whole vision of it
stayed in his mind. His life before the War, and after it,
was a plain story. He could say. That year I was in
Garton's ; that summer the strike started. The four years
of war were different : he remembered incidents, single
moments, with a vividness which struck him dumb about
them. But there was no order in his memories, and if, as
he was falling asleep, the corner of a trench in blazing sunlight
leaped from nowhere into his mind he could not be sure

into which month, or year, of the War it fitted.   Yet he could see the texture of the earth and sandbags, feel the heat of that sun in his body, and hear words spoken as carelessly as if no mind were laying them up for the future.   Once, when he was walking across the field to the caravan with the captain's breakfast, he remembered an hour lying out on night patrol, his body taut flattened against the ground.   His hand felt the crack in the ground into which he had driven the ends of his fingers.   The smell, like nothing else, of ground that has been fought over rose in his nostrils, and his heart pounded in his throat.   Another time he stood again at the back of a dug-out watching the officer write on a pad held on his knee—the candle bent over and he watched it carefully, and the hand moving across the paper.

The road outside the dug-out was straight for about five hundred yards.   He marched, swaying with fatigue.   His body was no longer separate, but dragged and was dragged at by the rest of the marchers.   That would be the Tunnels, he thought.

A lorry drove clean through the lines of swaying men and stopped.   Frank shook himself, heated coffee, and listened for sounds from the room.   Nothing.

' Got a paper ? ' the driver asked.   Frank handed over his *Daily Post*.   ' I can't read that rag,' the other said.

' What's the matter with it ? '

' Can't you read ?   Or don't you care what happens ? '

' I thought it was a sort of socialist paper,' Frank said.

' Socialist be blowed,' the driver said.   He swallowed his coffee.   ' You got a nice place here,' he said, looking about. ' Bad luck for you when they begin the bye-pass.'

Frank looked at him for a moment.   ' Bye-pass ?   What's that ?   Where is it ? ' he said.

' 'Tisn't anywhere yet.   It's going to cut out all this '—he swept his arm round—' and save twenty miles on the road north.'

' Far from here ? ' Frank asked.   It was an effort to ask. He kept his voice low.

'About three miles.'

'Have to move,' Frank said.

He stood still, when the other man had gone, trying to think it out. They couldn't go on living here—if it was true. He felt convinced it was true. For a moment his dismay was so acute that he had to hold on to the shelf for support; nothing seemed safe. A door opened in the house behind him; he heard it but did not move.

He felt hungry of a sudden. Breaking off a piece of bread he stood eating it, and thinking. That they could do this, ruining him, and he helpless. A feeling of bewilderment seized him: all round him there were millions like himself, working, eating, looking at the faces of those nearest them, touching things, working, working: who thought about them? who knew them? I'm no one, he thought. He touched his skin and ran his hands over his body, trying to reassure himself. Here I am, he thought; they can't just wash me out, I'm living, I'm here. He felt small and uncertain. His throat was dry, a mouthful of bread stuck there and he had a time swallowing it out of the way.

He had his elbow on the copy of the *Daily Post*. Moving aside, he noticed it, and thought, Newspapers are a lot of words, I can't vote myself a living, can I? He seized the paper and began to tear and fold it into pieces the right size to cover shelves. Make some use of it, he said to himself.

Bustling about, he felt more cheerful and with that and with the idea of making some enquiries—ask people, go across there and have a look round—he began to be confident. He ate another slice of bread, feeling slightly hollow inside.

His name spoken behind him. He swung round, and saw the woman smiling and beckoning. He followed awkwardly, scowling at her because she was all smiles. Sally looked different, his girl again.

'I didn't call out again,' she said.

'It isn't over, is it?' he said, dumbfounded. He knew it was, but his tongue was much slower than his mind.

'Look at him then,' Sally said kindly.

Instead, he looked at her. My lovely girl. He tried to say something.

' Don't you like him ? ' Sally asked.

' If only they'll let us live,' he burst out.

Sally looked at him, drowsy and serene, her pains not remembered now. ' Why shouldn't we live ? We're decent people. Aren't we ? Who's going to stop us living ? '

3. *Thomas Harben makes plans*

Many people knew Thomas Harben—his wife, his fellow-directors, managers of departments, secretaries, scientists employed by him, journalists, foreign industrialists and their envoys, bankers, his mistress. None of these people, not even the last, knew that he could not sit at a square table without running his fingers over the corners. In a strange room he was uneasy until he had touched and passed a finger over every square corner about the furniture. He would stand, carelessly, beside the mantel-shelf, walk past a side-board, feel with his hand for the edges of his chair. Walking in the streets he counted, and touched, the right-angled corners of walls ; he paused at the end of the pavement and his foot felt idly round the edge. He had been doing this for so many years that it had ceased to be a habit and become a pressing need. When he was younger he tried sometimes to break himself of it, but his discomfort was so great, and increased the longer he abstained, that he yielded. Nowadays he performed these small acts methodically as part of his life, and had ceased to reason about them. Occasionally it came into his mind that there was something comical in the spectacle of a man of his importance edging across a room to touch the angles of a cupboard, and then he laughed. He could laugh at himself.

Dressing for his wife's dinner party, he came to a standstill before the dressing-table. By using both hands he could touch all four corners in a flash. That over he gave his mind to adjusting his tie. His long sardonic nose seemed to be taking an interest in the business; it looked down at his fingers fiddling with the ends. He watched both in the glass, feeling almost friendly toward them.

For a man of fifty-six his face was very little lined. You could not say it was a young-looking face, but neither was it old—its long heavy cheeks, long nose, mouth closely gripped, deep eye-pits, seemed made of a substance more enduring than flesh. Such lines as he had were deep. He was a big man, heavy but without much flesh on him. In repose his face was still sardonic and alert. Speech altered it very little. Only his mistress could say whether it changed under a sensual emotion, whether the eyes veiled themselves— perhaps the mouth loosened for a short time. His wife had certainly forgotten.

He was thinking of his wife as he dressed. Of her extra-ordinary habit of mixing people at her dinner parties, regard-less of effect. The truth, he knew it, was that she could not endure his acquaintances, but a vestigial sense of duty made her ask them, not too often, to the house, and then she found herself driven to invite two or three friends of her own, by way of bodyguard. It was simple—not vexing, almost funny.

He admired in his wife her unshakeable self-assurance. She knew her place in the social pyramid, its privileges, its duties. She looked after the tenants on her father's land, now hers. In London she gave the right number of dinner-parties, some large, none noisy, always followed by most excellent music. She understood that, patronised musicians, travelled to Bayreuth, to Salzburg. She knew something, enough, about modern art, and bought judiciously. She read many books—but when ? he had no idea : perhaps in bed. In all these—culture activities (it was thus that his mistress spoke of them to him, but with respect, and with her slow smile)—he took no part. He was entirely uninterested. His life touched hers only in the certainties both felt. Lucy had hers through her family; his were a matter of power and character, he had started with the competence left him by his father and made himself one of the eight richest men in Europe.

Curiously, he could think of himself as a man, a male animal, and compare himself strength for strength with a docker or a furnace-man, but he never thought of Lucy as a woman with the bodily shape and habits of other women. He had once expected children from her.

The thought that he had no son scarcely troubled him. It visited him at odd moments—as now, when he was looking at his face in the glass he saw queerly a young face beneath the bones of his own, and it occurred to him that it might have been his son's. That was a strange thing. Now for a moment he wondered whether Lucy—does she ever think of it? Lucy when young. He frowned in the effort of memory.

The door leading to his wife's rooms was at the other side of the landing. It was slightly open when he came to it, and obeying an impulse he went in to speak to her. 'Who's coming here to-night, Lucy?'

He stared at her long straight back, as if it might split and reveal a much younger woman hidden away there. Nothing short of this miracle would be any use. He could not of himself recall the least smile or word of the lost young woman.

'George Ling again? But I can't stand the fellow,' he said, with abrupt vigour.

'You said he must come once a year,' his wife answered. 'The last time was eighteen months ago.'

'Well who else? Marcel Cohen?' He exploded with laughter. He never failed to find amusing the encounters of Lucy with her Jews. Needing music, she could not do without them, and her very bones protested against their presence in her house. As well as a go-between for Lucy when she needed some celebrated musician to play in her music room, Cohen was his associate on half a dozen Boards. He detested George Ling, who was afraid of everything and yet stank of piety, but not so forcibly as he distrusted Cohen. And they were his allies (but thank God not his only ones) in the struggle he foresaw. He had felt, then thought it, placing his thoughts like sentries. The outlines of the struggle were acid-sharp in his mind—one or other of the nations would make beak and bones out of the post-war remnants; one, with or without satellites, would secure itself, for a generation at least, against the competition of the rest. As he saw it, it was only a matter of prevision and brute energy. America? In all simplicity Thomas Harben believed that the Americans would fumble the catch, because they were American—that is, foolhardy and inexperienced—not English. Japan? sharply more dangerous, he thought, seeing a runner stripped to the skin.

A *cold* enthusiasm kept his thoughts grinding at the mill. He thought in abstractions as concrete as steel rails and the keels of ships. When he used the words ' man power ' he saw a half-naked steel puddler, but far from starting in him the ideas of a common humanity this image only angered him. A sullen will in the half-naked man opposed itself to his. This sweating brute at his furnace had feelings, desires, energies, not used up in work. Strikes, quarrels about hours— crowning impudence, the talk of nationalising this industry and that. To nationalise *my* industry, thought Harben. It was stupefying. It was enough to drive a man mad.

' There's another strike starting in the Garton yards,' he broke out.

His wife looked at him calmly. ' You don't seem able to manage as the old lady did. She had no strikes during the War.'

' And the fault's hers,' Harben exclaimed. ' Her War bonuses to the men ! I warned them, at the time I warned them. The Board used to agree to anything she said. Now she's sold out and left me to carry the burden.' In spite of his anger he could not help laughing. ' The old devil. A nice pudding she mixed us. They've finished with bonuses, of course, and they're going to take wage cuts as well. Do you know—if one could run an industry without men—that would be something.'

' What would you use ? '

' Machines without men,' he said promptly. ' And I don't doubt it'll come to that—but not in my time.'

' Trade is much worse, isn't it ? ' Lucy said politely.

' Worse all the time. This is the moment they strike, and chitter-chatter in their unions about nationalising! Time and energy wasted to argue with them. I'd give something to argue them with machine-guns. Poor brutes of private soldiers who were shot for desertion deserved it far less.'

' You might not have thought so if you had been a general,' his wife said.

' Eh, would I ? ' he laughed.

He felt an impulse to clap her on the shoulder. That was enough—the mere notion was unseemly. He went away, fingering the edge of the door as he went.

The minutes before dinner—well now, he reflected, looking about the room, Lucy has surpassed herself. He spoke to Evelyn Lamb; who answered by asking him, in a languid voice, something to do with the music. ' Upon my word, I don't know anything about it,' he said. He saw Marcel Cohen standing at the other side of the room, and thought, There's a man knows infinitely more about music than this clever silly woman and he has more sense than to talk to me about it. Making his way across he spoke in Cohen's ear.

' You remember my idea of a bureau of information and propaganda. Discourage all this subversive nonsense. I've thought about it a great deal now. I shall want to discuss it with you, my dear fellow.'

When he needs something I'm his dear dear fellow, Cohen said to himself. He made a gesture with elbows and outward-turning hands. ' When you like,' he said smiling. ' Any time, any time. I am at your service.'

4. *Ridley pays a call and makes notes*

Ridley's self-possession deserted him as he climbed the steps to the house. He was not sure—was it wise to call

without an invitation ?   It was true she had said : ' I shall
really be interested, if you can hear who wrote that absurd
article.'   But if it had been better to write ?   A brief amusing
letter ?

He rang the bell.   The door opening, he felt as if he had
stepped over the edge of a cliff.   He fell and then waited for a
year.   When the man returned he looked into Ridley's
face and said civilly : ' Mrs Harben is not disengaged, sir.'

' Oh,' Ridley said.   ' Thanks.'

In the street he experienced the greatest difficulty in walking at a proper speed.   He wanted to run, to fling his arms
about.   Not disengaged.   What a way to put it !   Was it
or was it not an insult ?   Have I been snubbed ?   He stood
still and felt his forehead.   It was dry and burning, and yet
the inside of his hand was wet.   A man passing looked at him
inquisitively.   He hurried on.

In the state he was he thought of Evelyn with dislike and
impatience—as if it were her fault he had overshot his mark.
Not for the first time, he regretted involving himself with
her.   Thank God, he cried, I have better friends.   Grand
chaps.   Working writers and reviewers, no nonsense about
them.   He forgot that Evelyn had first given him these
friends.   Thinking, In future I'll stick closer to my own sort,
he began to be comforted.   The miserable wrigglings of his
lower self dropped out of sight.   He walked on slowly.   The
air was mild and pleasant.   On a May evening London
enchanted, more surely and subtly than any other city.   He
began to notice things.   A pale child passed him crying
silently and bitterly, and he turned himself about.   ' What's
the matter ? ' he asked.   No answer.   Wanting to comfort
her, he felt in his pocket.   ' Here you are, poor little thing,'
he said with a smile.

The bad taste of a city with pavements as wide as Regent
Street and no café tables.   I'll write in the *Review* about it,
he promised.   But with the thought of drinking he began
to die of thirst.   He hurried on as far as Charing Cross Road
and went into a bar there.   A leaning man made room for

him and as he did so looked up. This man had a face as grotesque as a dream. It was long, thin, bent, one grey eye and one green, mouth as wide as a street, rick of black hair. Ridley knew him at once—how could you forget such a face ? —a farm boy who in 1915 had been with him in France. They shook hands with the proper joy. 'Well? How's life?'

' I'm writing—articles in the papers and so forth,' Ridley answered.

' Are you now ? You'll be getting famous,' the other said. His bright eyes searched Ridley's face with the little sharp malice of a peasant. ' Trust you to make the best of yourself ! Now look at me—I've travelled in Germany in style, I married a French wife, I've a grand farm near Dunkirk with a house and furniture all present and correct, and here I am, with a few shillings in my pocket. In December my officer took me to Cologne and Berlin with him and when he stayed at the best hotels I did, too—not in the same part, but it was all right. Investigating. Yes there was children starved so that they had stomachs blown out to a point and the insides of their cheeks meeting ! ' He went off into a fit of laughter. ' And yes when I was snug in Berlin I gets a letter from France, from a friend of mine, tells me she has a fine baby —and wouldn't I come back tsweet and marry her, and look after the farm. Why and mind you, she was no girl, but I said to myself, The best stock comes out of the oldest pot. Here's where I went wrong. Back I went, yes, marries —with considerable trouble—and starts farming. Lord, lord, I soon found I'm married to her mother, father, fifteen great-aunts, a whole tribe of blossoming frogs. Mouldering mumping maggots. Up before dawn working, no money, all scraped up by the old woman and hidden away somewhere. One day what do they do but trust me with five hundred francs. Did I run ? I ran, I ran, I ran.'

' You're a nice scoundrel,' Ridley said, grinning. He took an envelope out of his pocket and scribbled on it : Best stock comes out of oldest pot. The beer and the fellow's crazy chatter exhilarated him. He left the place smiling, and as he walked he took pains to etch the man's face on his mind.   It was a fine item snatched into the Rogues' Gallery he kept there.   All these with the sounds and sights he added daily and with some were not rogues, like that pale child to whom he had given sixpence for her crying, he meant to use, when the time came.   Yes, yes, he could and would use them— but he loved them dearly too.

5. Conversation with Philip

Renn could visit his friend only between six and seven o'clock.   This was after hours, but with T.S.'s help he got himself in, and because Philip was alone now in a private ward, and because he was considered to be dying.   (This had not been in Philip's plans.)   He went every day.

For a long time he thought that Philip had not changed. There are some changes the body conceals within itself until the last possible minute and they are even less alarming to the onlooker for coming in this way, without warning, as when the light dies rapidly from a scene, turning to the grey colour of water all that has been fields and woods.   To-day, looking towards the bed as he crossed the room, Renn had the impression that Philip was half asleep.   Philip smiled at him, began to talk, but remained drowsy, his head drooping over his chest.   He spoke, too, as if Renn had been with him all along.

' What became of your ex-soldier in the end ? '

' Oh, he's learning to think,' Renn said.   ' I give him books and take him to meetings.   Now and then he earns a guinea. He learns as fast as he thinks.   He is as strong as a bear, lazy, and likes being alive.   All his family is dead.   Father a sea captain, the mother had some ambition in her thoughts and tried to train the boy.   He has a head for languages, and speaks French, and he's learning German fast.   Out of all this I'll find work for him in time.'

' I'll talk to him when I get out of here,' Philip said. ' Perhaps I can help him.'

He had been following one train of thought in his mind for many days. It was not new, but it had forced itself on him with threats, and he could have no peace until he dealt with it. How can one bear the evil in man, knowing that there is no justice or pity in life, and knowing that when Jesus said : ' Are not five sparrows sold for two farthings, and not one of them is forgotten before God ? ' He was saying only what He willed to believe ? Children are born into poverty and young men eat their hearts out in it; infinite care, infinite ingenuity, is daily given to the filthy and bloody traffic in armaments. For all these things there is no compensation. The hungry are not fed, the defrauded young are not comforted in another life. They were born to be defrauded. In the last War the flower of England died *uselessly*.

This spectre followed him day and night. At last he came to it that the only good in life lies in one kernel with the evil. Just as death always triumphs over life, so cruelty is stronger than gentleness and hate than pity, and greed than kindness. A man can live until he dies ; so also can he raise his voice against cruelty until his tongue is torn from its roots. I too feel hate, Philip thought. I hate age, cruelty, greed, ignorance, dying. I should be ashamed to submit to what is forced on me.

He was not surprised to look up and find Renn standing beside him. In the last week he had felt pain less. A curious dualism—of body, not of mind—possessed him. He had two bodies, one which sweated and rebelled, and another which remained apart and could think clearly concerning everything except concerning time. Time eluded this self, and he was often surprised to find night falling on a day no longer than the single thought that had occupied him since waking. At one moment his friends were with him, the next gone. After another moment, or a year, there they stood again. His thoughts played with him—one came alone, then a flight passed, a cloud of birds winging strongly across a clear sky. He was not unhappy.

'I made a will before coming in here,' he next told Renn. 'You know I have almost eight thousand pounds. I've left the whole of it to you, to spend on the paper.'

'You're going to spend it yourself,' Renn said.

'I know that,' Philip said, smiling. 'But just suppose I don't—suppose I were to die. The odds are poor—I've had eight doctors at me in a fortnight—eight to one against! In that case, I want you—will you take it on?'

'Certainly,' Renn said.

Philip laughed. 'Do you remember our first week in the line—Hannescamps—and the sudden descent, terrifying us two poor children, of a full-blown Corps Commander? He asked me—rather like Jove, I thought—how I should act if I were in command of the company and a battalion of the enemy attacked at once without warning. I couldn't get out a word. I daren't tell him—if he didn't know—that a battalion couldn't attack in full daylight without warning. I nearly burst into tears. When he tried you, you said in a kind voice: "I should engage them at once." He can't have been such an ass after all—he laughed.'

'I've forgotten,' Renn said.

'Well, I thought I had,' Philip said. 'I remembered it when you said Certainly.'

'I've been trying to write an account of the retreat,' Renn said, after a moment. 'I can't find any words hard enough. They ought to be as sharp and hard as flints. I've given it up.'

'Did you write any more poetry?'

'No,' Renn said.

'Don't give that up.'

Renn did not answer. He was watching the shadow on his friend's face—no trick of the light, but the deepening, otherwise imperceptible, of an inward tide. Where had been clear stream, leaf, sand, and pebble, shining in sunlight, was now a gathering swirl of darkness, nothing to be seen, all, all lost. He roused himself to question Philip about the policy of the paper.

Afterwards he forgot the answers but remembered that Philip said he hated the new standardising of life, which has touched a pitch that whereas even chairs and candlesticks used to be signed by their makers you now, wading chin-deep in the flood of books, can find scarcely one that bears the signature of its maker in any line. The spring that runs living out of our English past is being choked with these piles of rubbish. Rubbish Shot Here.

Philip proposed a patient sifting of the writings and speeches of all kinds of men, from leaders of industry, politicians, divines, bankers, trades union officials, to novelists. We shall wash a great deal of muck for a thimbleful of metal, he said. He thought that a wide public would welcome his efforts on behalf of their inheritance. Really, one cannot be sorry he died without having to admit he had been deceived.

When Renn left the hospital he rang up T. S. Heywood and asked him this question. 'What are they doing to Philip in ———'s ? '

' Trying a new lead treatment on him.'

' Will it cure him ? '

There was a short silence, during which he had the sensation of supporting an immense weight, the burden of the space between himself and T.S.

' No. I don't think so. It will kill him off,' T.S. said.

' Quickly ? '

' Oh yes. Fairly quickly.'

CHAPTER XV

LATE June, there was no shade in the room in which Hervey and David Renn worked. Opening the windows wider availed nothing—bringing in another layer of dust and stench from the narrow street running to Covent Garden. The sun laid its hot dry hands on everything in the room. Renn had grown pale and Hervey scarlet. Strands of hair like wet seaweed clung to her forehead.

The work on Harriman's Saloxide had been delayed and was going forward now by forced marches. They had worked late together for three days. On the morning of the fourth they were both short-tempered, Renn's body ached, and under the surface his mind watched Philip. Mr Harriman was giving trouble. None of the drawings prepared in the studio pleased him. At first it seemed that he disliked the uniform worn by English soldiers; when he had resigned himself to what could not be helped, he disliked the pose. Six times the artist had redrawn his figure of a young subaltern, without achieving the desired air of martial and joyous confidence. This although Mr Harriman gave himself the trouble to visit the studio. He explained patiently to the artist that the air of confidence was essential: ' he's sure confident; he knows that if he's wounded Saloxide will save him.' The artist had a wife and child to consider.

At last—' imagination is not enough,' Mr Harriman said: he begged them to use a live model. Renn seized the chance for his friend the young ex-soldier, and Henry Smith, wearing a uniform borrowed from the artist, posed for some hours. He was in the studio this morning. From curiosity Renn

175

and Hervey climbed up there to see how nearly ready the new drawings were. They saw Mr Harriman going away by the main staircase and Henry Smith dissolving in silent laughter. He had just persuaded Mr Harriman that it would not do for him to stand with a foot on the neck of a machine-gun and an arm waving a rifle aloft. The light fell on him; he had thrown his head back, smiling in pure pleasure. Standing so, he was incomparably beautiful—the sun had warmed him and laughter made him radiant.

Mr Harriman had crept back and was looking at him with a complacent smile. This was at last the right air. He flew whirring across the room, immobilised the young man, and only then caught sight of Renn and Hervey leaning against a door.

He hurried to them with a friendly air. ' I was just calling on you two. I want you to get that lovely confidence into your copy. Maybe I could read us out a few sentiments I took down. I don't want you to quote any of them—but, listen, it's a trifle of spirit.'

He held a notebook out in front of him and raising his voice for all to hear, read :

> ' *Yet say whose ardour bids them stand*
> *At bay by yonder bank,*
> *Where a boy's voice and a boy's hand* '

—waving his hand towards Henry Smith, ' as it might be this lovely boy—

> *Close up the quivering rank*
> *Who under those all-shattering skies*
> *Plays out his captain's part*
> *With the last darkness in his eyes*
> *And* Domum *in his heart.*

How's that, eh ? Listen :

> *So the boys, undismayed,*
> *Walked the dark valley singing as they went.*

That's fine, fine '—squeezing Hervey's arm—' but now
listen : *They went with songs to the battle, they were young.*
See where it says ?—they were *young.* You two've got to
get that idea of youth into your copy—and a kind of wistful
note—*At the going down of the sun and in the morning We
will remember them.* Don't you like it ? Why don't you
like it ? Maybe you didn't lose anyone. Listen, I'm going
to let you keep these sentiments by you. I'm working on
the idea that everyone in this country lost someone, if it was
only a friend. When they look at the picture of this boy
they'll remember—like it says—and here's where you'll
touch in something young and wistful, until they're catching
their breath, then—Saloxide ! '

He tore the page from his notebook and put it into Hervey's
hand. Renn had gone.

Towards four o'clock T.S. spoke to Hervey on the telephone. He asked her to come to the hospital at five. She
repeated the message to Renn.

On the way to the hospital they were more friends than
they had been. T.S. was sauntering in the square formed
by the two wings and because he looked no different silly
Hervey supposed that Philip was better. It was a fortnight
since she had seen him. In that fortnight he had altered
quickly. He was colourless and had violet rings under his
eyes. His head hung forward as though he were falling
asleep.

Hervey did not realise that he was drugged. Out of
politeness she talked as if she did not notice that he left words
half spoken and seemed not to hear what they said. His
half-closed eyelids gave him a sulky air. Except for the
light contraction of his forehead his face was smooth like a
boy's. You would say that dying was doing him good. At
every stage in this journey he was making against his will
another burden of responsibility fell from him. The only
grievous thing was that he was alone and could not communi-
cate to his friends his new lightness and confidence. Renn
and T.S. had been seeing him every day. They did not realise-

that he was already away from them, their words less clear to him than words spoken so many years earlier that they had outlived time. Hervey was alone aware of it. She felt constrained and shy with the new Philip.

She sat close to the bed, and after a moment Philip reached out and took her hand. He held it clasped lightly in his own all the time she was there. She strove to keep herself calm, so that no tremor of her nerves could touch him. She was ashamed of disliking the pressure, dry and lax, of Philip's hand.

He took no notice when Renn spoke to him. T.S. had been looking out of the window, but he came back when he saw that Renn was at a loss and began to talk to him across Philip. ' I tried to speak to you this morning, but you weren't in your room when I telephoned and I couldn't wait.'

' I was in the studio,' Renn said. He bit his lip and smiled.

' Tell me where we can meet to-morrow night.'

' At my rooms,' Renn said after a moment's thought.

' Why didn't you come sooner, our Hervey ? ' Philip said in a distinct voice. ' You might have come. I would have come to you. To seek the unforgotten face. Who wrote that ? They won't give me any of my books, damn them.'

' I'll bring you some as soon as you're better,' Hervey said. ' Which do you want ? '

As if he had forgotten about it already Philip did not answer.

' I had a letter from your old sergeant, from Frank, asking about you,' Hervey said. ' They're going to make a new road and he thinks he'll have to move. He wants you to tell him what to do about your caravan.'

' Frank,' Philip repeated. His eyes opened wide. ' Oh God young Martinson at Loos,' he said. His body trembled.

' You don't have to think about it now,' Renn said.

Philip shut his eyes. In a few moments his head sank lower and he breathed as though he were going to sleep. T.S. and Renn talked to each other in their ordinary voices. They ignored Hervey, who as usual could not think of anything to say; she moved gently to draw away her hand but Philip closed his own over it quickly and firmly. After a time he lifted his head and said drowsily : ' I'll wait, Hervey love.'

Hervey looked anxiously at T.S. She felt her calmness going and he was doing nothing to help her. T.S. looked at her and looked at Philip, his eyelids twitching as they did when he was tired. He stood up and leaned over Philip.

' They won't let us stay with you,' he said in a low voice. ' You know that, don't you ? '

And after a pause Philip said : ' Very well.' He released Hervey's hand when she pulled it gently. She stood up, sighing with relief.

' Do you remember that tree ? ' Philip asked her.

' Yes.' It was not true. She did not remember anything, any tree. She wanted to get away. ' Good-bye, Philip. I'll come to see you on Saturday.'

' No you won't come,' Philip said.

Renn came close to the bed and stood looking down at him.

' Good-bye, my dear,' T.S. said.

Renn stooped lower. ' Good-bye, Philip.'

Philip did not say anything more. He kept his eyes on Hervey for a moment, then closed them and kept them closed until he was alone.

Outside the hospital Renn stood a moment, looking down at his hands, then turned away without a word and walked off. They watched him cross the street and disappear. ' What's the matter with him ? ' Hervey said.

' Nothing—he's hating the sight of you,' T.S. grinned.

Hervey felt surprise and pain. ' What did I do wrong ? '

' You wouldn't understand it,' T.S. said. He looked at her with a touch of contempt. ' He and Philip and I went out together in March '15. I was transferred later. They stayed together until Renn was wounded, in September of '17.'

' Yes ? '

' Yes what ? That's all.'

' Is Philip going to die ? '

'Renn won't see him no more,' T.S. chanted. 'Ne-ver see him no mo-er. They shall hunger no more, neither thirst any more; neither shall the sun light on them, nor any heat. They shall hunger no more. And God shall wipe away all tears, all te-ars from their eyes, and G-od shall wipe aw-ay all tears, all te-ars from their eyes, all tears from their eyes, all tears from their eyes.'

'Don't sing in the street,' Hervey said. She had turned crimson.

'Do you call that singing? I knew a man, he'd sung at Queen's Hall, who used to sing German lieder in the trenches to amuse himself. One morning a board was hoisted in the Boche trench with the words, You sing that too slowly, chalked on it. He said it felt much worse than getting a rotten notice in *The Times*.'

Hervey could not help laughing. She bit her lip to control the spasm but it forced its way out, and she laughed until she felt bruised and aching. The thought of the War, of its insane twisting of natural emotions to unnatural ends, and of Philip, was like the blow given by a clown's bladder. It was too farcical. It jarred your brain and you laughed. T.S. waited patiently until she recovered, then took her arm and walked on slowly, half leaning on her. She could feel the exhaustion of his body. They spent the evening together, drank coffee and sherry in the Café Royal, and went to a music hall. It was a little like the months just before the War. But for what they carried about with them, in their hearts.

Philip died during that evening. T.S. telephoned to her at the office next morning. Her mind swayed for a moment in utter fear. The edge of the table steadied her limbs, then to think of Renn was too much; she turned in her chair and said: 'That was T.S. He says Philip is dead. He says it was time it came.'

After a scarcely felt pause Renn said: 'I'm sure it was time.' He smiled slightly.

Hervey discovered that the dead are not real. She could

not think of Philip, only of herself with Philip. And when she cried it was for herself. The sun warmed her hands, which had been cold for a few moments. She felt thirsty and thought of a glass of iced coffee. Towards one o'clock she went out and went to a Corner House. She asked for iced coffee and sat drinking it and watching the people. A woman with a fat merry face and an ample body pleased her greatly and she kept looking at her until the woman went out.

The vague melancholy that filled her was scarcely unhappy. This scene, familiar and changing, the sun, the ease of her body, soothed her little by little; she began to think earnestly of her son. His birthday was in two days and she had to decide at once what she could send him. Philip retreated to the back of her mind, becoming more shadowy each moment, until at last he came to the place prepared for him.

CHAPTER XVI

THE ROMANTICS

On Saturday she went with T.S. to walk in Richmond. The grass was dry and brittle like straw. A sun as proud as a peacock drew his tail over the sky. They walked to that edge of the Park which overlooks the vale of Twickenham, now veiled in a clear rippling haze, its colours sucked from it by the bright light of the sun. Here they seated themselves and T.S. talked. His short stocky body lay relaxed, fitting into a hollow of the ground. His head, too big for its body, lolled back. The flesh below his cheekbones had fallen in, leaving his beaked nose more prominent than ever. It made Hervey think of a bony mountain ridge between two plains.

'What do you think, our Hervey? Last week I had the offer of two jobs. The first was to write what Marcel Cohen, and my dear wife, call a science column—for the *Daily Post*. You know what. How to split the atom in your own home without practice or drudgery. Will the artists of 2000 A.D. paint by wireless? A column a week at ten guineas.'

'That's a great sum,' Hervey said. 'I wish I had it.'

'I wrote: Dear Cohen, When I want a job tearing up science into pieces small enough for your readers to wipe their ——s, I'll ask you for it, yours faithfully, T. S. Heywood. The other offer was charge of the research department of Stokes Chemical Works. It wasn't offered; I had word that if I asked I should be given. Evelyn's friend Harben is a director of the company—it's a subsidiary of a vast combine with associate firms in a dozen countries. It makes something useful—paying an interest guaranteed by the government—and researches into poison gas to be beforehand with the next war. The wages are eight hundred a year. I accepted. Such a chance. Once and once only.'

' I can't see that it's a better offer than Cohen's,' Hervey said, startled. ' I call it vile work. I thought you had a conscience. Don't you care what happens ? '

' Conscience ! ' T.S. sat up sharply, the skin round his eyes twitching. ' What should I care ? he said softly. ' If there's another war, if after the last another is permitted, I hope it finishes us. I hope every country that goes to war is broken by it, the soil poisoned, the towns festering. I shall do my best to live—if only for the pleasure of seeing how Lucy Harben and my clever wife like living in savagery. They're both disabled from childbearing. A pity. They'll be spared something.' He smiled at Hervey. ' Don't glower at me, young Hervey. I'll look after you. We've been friends for a long time. When you hear the first gas-raid warning don't run into a shelter—they're not really proof, you know, and they'll be very unpleasant when the gas seeps in—come to me and I'll kill you quickly and gently. I'll label you, too. *Stand close around ye Stygian set, With* Hervey *in one boat conveyed. Or Charon, seeing, may forget That he is old and she a shade.* . . . So you think I've chosen wickedness ? '

Hervey felt confused and did not know what to reply. She was afraid of his sharp tongue. To be laughed at was more than she could endure; it filled her with a ridiculous obsessive shame. At last she said : ' Isn't there anything you believe in ? '

' Certainly. Science is a satisfactory life. Clean enough. Decent. No room in it for your little chittering entrail-pickers of writers.'

' You're only a romantic, after all,' Hervey said, with sudden spirit. ' You have to take cover somewhere and you've chosen science. I hope it keeps you warm ! '

T.S. only smiled at her. He said nothing, and Hervey's

anger died away.   It was not in the least necessary to say so.
The warm earth, the sun, held both of them in one hand.
They lay side by side very contentedly in silence.

Hervey sat up with a strong feeling of reluctance.   ' I ought
to go home,' she sighed, looking round her.   ' Penn will be
waiting.   He went over to spend the day with his father
and mother but he won't stay.'

' Why doesn't he get work ? '

' He has tried,' Hervey said.

T.S. looked at her severely—he likes, she thought, to look
savage and disillusioned.   ' How old is your precious Penn,
Hervey ? '

' Twenty-nine—three years older than you and me.'

' He's too old to be looking for work.'   He hesitated, and
said with a quick warm smile : ' You don't like living with
Penn, do you ?   Don't tell me any lies—I've known you
longer than he has.'

It was a relief to speak the truth.   ' I bring out the worst
in Penn.   He distrusts me—and no wonder.   I hide things
from him—to save trouble—then he finds me out and is
able to prove that I'm deceitful.   I want to please him, but
I try less and less—I don't respect him now and I feel it's a
waste of my strength—as if I were so important !—to take
trouble for him.   And so nothing goes right.   I make
resolutions and don't keep them.   I'm not generous enough
to give freely.   And Penn makes no concessions.   He enjoys
humiliating me.   I would give anything to have him out of
my life, but it's impossible, too much is involved in it ; it
would be like unravelling a whole carpet to get at the first
knot.   Yes, impossible.   If I had the courage—I have no
courage, I could never bring myself to leave him.   And you
know yourself, I'm not *easy* to live with.   I like to be in the
right and I'm impossibly moody and careless.   Penn ought
to have married someone much less ambitious, someone who
depended on him.   Every time we quarrel, and such quarrels,
T.S., I blame myself.   And yet I can't help thinking I could
behave better—with another person.'   She forgot what she

had been going to say. ' Don't laugh at me,' she said, turning very red.

' *I* could live with you, Hervey,' T.S. said quickly. ' You're the only woman I'm at ease with. I like you better than anyone. We two could saunter about Europe very happily, and nothing to pay.' He jumped up and gave her a hand. ' Come along, then.'

Hervey laughed. A wind had sprung up, scattering coolness everywhere. They walked at a good pace. It was something, if only for an hour, to be with a friend and to feel free.

Penn was not in their rooms when she arrived there. They must have persuaded him to stay the night, she thought : and in this hope unlocked a cupboard and took from it the manuscript of her novel. More than half of it was written, but lately, with Penn always at her elbow in the evenings, she had had to leave it alone. Her first novel had been such a failure. No one, except the critics, had read it, and she was ashamed to be seen writing the second. Not that Penn had been unkind ; indeed he had encouraged her, but it was no use—the book was a failure and only her stubbornness and a simple dislike of admitting failure forced her to go on. She told no one what she was thinking.

Turning the pages, she thought that only an idiot would go on writing with so little taste for it. I know nothing, nothing, she cried. (One reviewer had said of the first book : ' Miss Russell has every talent but knowing how to write.') It must be true—but what am I to do, how can I learn ? Better to give up at once, before she was utterly disgraced : but not yet—not until she was certain, as certain as repeated awful failures could make her, that she would never learn, never make any money, never reach safety—Heaven knows I don't want safety for myself, she cried : but Richard, Richard—it was for Richard.

She began to write slowly, holding her pen round the nib so that it covered her fingers with ink. The story—it was conceived on a sublime scale and none of the characters was low or ordinary—had to do with a young woman whose husband was unfaithful to her.   But now, now that she had reached the climax—the young woman has the fatal letter in her hand and is about to cry out, or swoon, or clasp her head—she discovered that she had no more notion (she said) than a cat what feelings went with such a scene. What should I feel, she thought, if Penn———?   At once it came to her that she would be enormously relieved—she would conceal it, of course, behave with ease, dignity, kindness ; but all the time she would feel like dancing for joy. (Nothing warned her that in imagining a painful scene which has not yet taken place, we assign to ourselves in it only manageable emotions— emotions chosen not in tranquillity but in ignorance. When the time comes, another self takes possession of us, and the emotions suffered by this self are not manageable and not newly-coined. They spring from the deepest sources and drag in feelings and memories from all sides until the mind sinks under its weight of experience ; a younger, less assured self takes possession of us : the grown woman gives birth to a girl, weeping the uncontrolled tears and suffering the sincere exaggerated anguish of youth.)

She frowned. She laid her pen down. Relief. Joy. This would never do ; it was the last thing she wanted : the young woman in the story was destined to suffer every kind of tumultuous emotion until she died or became reconciled to her husband—but it would take a long time, another hundred and twenty pages at least, before either end came in sight. And to keep the young woman alternately crying out and swooning for that prodigious number of pages was more than she could face. I must think, she sighed, again.

The door opened and Penn put his head in, withdrew it, and went along the landing to his own room.

She put her manuscript away at once. Either he was irritated—vexed by having had to endure all day his father's disapproval (as if it was the poor boy's fault that no one would employ him). Or he was very tired. She felt a prick of

remorse. Had she not given him away to T.S. ? To that
friend—true, he was her oldest, and her dearest, since Philip
was dead—she had presented a picture of her marriage that
falsified everything in it. Penn was lazy, selfish, a bully;
he told lies; he was not to be depended on in any of the ways
a young woman may hope for in her husband : but for all
this he held her; like a child he depended on her; he was
quick as a woman in little things; he could be wonderfully
gentle and simple. More than all this—and something she
could not speak of—he was her first youth, fastened to her
by all the emotions of that time, when to be in love is to
discover a new continent every few hours.

She hesitated over going to his room to fetch him out. He
might snub her, and that, she knew, would start in her the
hideous discontent she wished to forget (having spoken too
freely about it to T.S.). She brushed her hair, looked in
her purse to see what money there was, and sat down with her
hands folded, to wait.

Penn had flung himself on the bed in his room. The sight
of Hervey, writing—as he supposed—had put the finishing
touch to his despondence. It was enough that he had
quarrelled with his father, run out of the house, walked—to
save the fare—from Holland Park to St John's Wood, but
he must come home to a wife indifferent to him, absorbed,
and covered with ink. There was a thick streak of it across
her forehead where she had pushed the hair out of her eyes.

He pitied himself with more fierceness than ever when,
raising his arm, he noticed that the cuffs of his jacket were
frayed and shiny. The sight was too much. He felt tears
in his eyes. Shabby and a failure. That's what I am, he
groaned—a failure. A shabby failure. The memory of
weeks, months, spent applying for posts in London schools
—five months since he left the Air Force—rushed over him.
He wiped his eyes with the back of his wrists. At every
interview, and he had been interviewed dozens of times, it
was the same thing. Too old. They meant too costly.
Under the new scale, the salary they would have to pay him

rose with the number of years he had been teaching, and counting his years in the Air Force. We should like to have you on the staff, Mr Vane—your degrees, your testimonials—your appearance—admirable, in every way—but——. In vain he began offering, after several such interviews, to take less salary than he was allotted—it was no use; that was forbidden. One headmaster said : ' Just after the War you would have had no difficulty——' He refused to believe this. It was what Hervey had always said.

Between emotion and hunger he felt tired and very weak. He rose from the bed, washed, straightened his jacket, with a glance mournfully averted from the sleeve, and went in to Hervey. She looked up and smiled at him.

He felt that he was going to cry. The interviews. The coat. His father's face quivering with his anger, his contempt. Blindly feeling for her, he knelt down and laid his head against her knees.

' Oh Hervey, I'm miserable.'

Hervey's heart ached for him. She stroked his cheek, and said : ' Why are you so late ? I thought perhaps—I have the money for it now—we could dine once a week in Soho. You enjoy it. I thought perhaps to-night—unless you're too tired.'

' I can't dine out. I'm too shabby.' He held out his arm, displaying a slender wrist in its band of threadbare cloth.

' You must have a new suit,' Hervey said. ' Come, we're not so badly off as that. You haven't come to the end yet of your gratuity money '—(he had, but he said nothing)—' a pre-war suit—it's good cloth, of course, better than the new. But you can afford a new one. And if you can't '—she glanced towards the cupboard—' my book, when it's finished —there's always that : if it makes any money. Surely it will make a little which will be a fine help. We can spend it on luxuries—a new suit, for instance.' She saw a brown bear on wheels in the window of a shop in Regent Street.

Penn's arm closed round her. He was comforted, she could feel that, and her body grew strong and light. It was so easy to restore him. She had only to listen, to smile, to distract him with some brightly-coloured toy, like a child. At once, though she did not listen to it, a voice said in her ear that it was too easy, not worth doing. Not worth her doing. She trembled a little, losing all patience with herself, and ashamed.

'My father offered to-day to send me up to Oxford, to read modern languages,' Penn said.

'Another degree!' Hervey exclaimed. She grew rigid. Coming from the Vanes, this offer insulted her. 'What use would that be?'

'He seems to think it would be useful,' Penn smiled.

Hervey was silent. She was trying to think calmly about it, but she could feel only surprise and pain. To send him away, leaving her alone. It terrified her. It would mean another three, four, irresponsible years for him, now, now when more than anything he needed responsibility. Her mind swung between astonishment and anger. Her voice quivered. 'Your father forgets that you have a wife, and a son,' she cried, with bitterness.

Penn sat up. He looked at her with a malicious smile. 'On the contrary, my dear. He and my mother think you're bad for me. The offer depends on my leaving you entirely out of it. Even if you were willing you mayn't come to Oxford with me. And I was to live with them during the vacations, to make sure I worked. If necessary, he said, he would pay you ten shillings a week.'

Hervey felt her anger increasing. She sprang away from him. 'And you? What did you say?' she asked.

'Oh, I refused,' Penn said lightly. 'I told him what I thought of him and came away.' He stood up and put his arms round her again. 'What did you think?'

CHAPTER XVII

THE SIN OF ANANIAS AND SAPPHIRA

THAT year a few people saw that they were living in a new age: it was as impossible to return to the old as to Elizabethan England—both were now historic and the child Richard, born during the four years' destruction, would feel the one no less strange and distant than the other. The many turned back in mind to the past and lived *as though* the change had not taken place, thus sowing the seeds of future disorders, even of madness. Over vast acres of Europe the destruction itself had not come to an end. In what were still called the enemy countries vast numbers of the enemy were still dying. It is true that most of them were under five years of age.

Luckily it cost less to kill these than to kill soldiers. And it happened with decent modesty. No telegrams were delivered: Regret to inform you . . . twenty children . . . death due to starvation . . . Vienna yesterday. What was an even more serious omission, no disengaged poet seized the chance to picture Heaven joyfully preparing nurseries for this invasion of babies.

A Save the Children movement had begun earlier, and saved certain who would otherwise have died. Nine out of ten persons considered the labour unnecessary or perverse. When a well-meaning woman invited George Ling to contribute his mite, he drew up the strings of his mouth and said : ' I see no reason for sending money to the ends of the earth ; we have our own poor.' ' Then give it to me for the East End,' she cried—but he remained true to himself, and his money stayed with him. David Renn told Hervey about an Austrian woman who had five children. She saw that one of them was stronger than the others. The thought came to her to save him at least. Daily she took a little from the tiny portions of the others to add to his. The plan succeeded, but one day she confessed to a doctor at the American Mission and killed herself that night.

This story shocked Hervey so that she could not sleep for it. For a time she lived on one meal a day and gave the few shillings saved to the Fund. But she wanted to do more, and plucked up courage to call on Marcel Cohen again. He received her kindly and said: 'Well, what do you want now?'

'I should like to write an article for the *Daily Post*,' Hervey said.

'Well, why not? A particular article? Do you want to see your name in print?'

'That's not necessary,' Hervey said directly. She felt that she must at all costs keep an air of coolness. 'I want to write about the children dying in Austria. If necessary I can write it for nothing, but if you pay me I could give the money to the Save the Children Fund.' She went on with a pounding heart: 'If I'm to write to order, I mean if you choose the subject, I should charge you ten guineas.'

'Your grandmother couldn't have put it more clearly.' He smiled at her indulgently, while his eyes searched her face for the flaw he expected to find in everything.

'Why must you drag in my grandmother every time?' Hervey said.

'Because you remind me of her. You don't mind, surely?'

'I would rather remind you of myself,' Hervey said, smiling. She felt less anxious, now that she had said all that she had arranged with herself to say.

'You do that, too. Let me think. Could you write a fairly straightforward article on the future of advertising?'

'Yes,' Hervey said.

'I'll pay you eight guineas.'

His liking for her had increased, but it was impersonal, the emotion he felt before a piece of china of which no copy is known to exist. He admired her and wanted to ask questions, and at the same time he was anxious to feel sure that the object was actually valuable and unique. If there was a personal element in this feeling it was the watch he kept on her for any signs of an attempt to exploit him. He felt certain that so much shrewdness could not exist without at least the impulse to take advantage of a powerful friend.

'Very well,' Hervey said. She looked round for her despatch case, a shabby monster that she tried to hide on coming into a room, and usually forgot where she had stowed it. It was behind her chair and she could not see it unless she turned right round.

Cohen had noticed that she no longer went to Evelyn Heywood's house. He had tried to find out from Evelyn what had become of her protégée, and had to content himself with a long involved tale in which there was no central fact but a great many accusations of treachery and ingratitude, all of which he dismissed, cynically, as applying to Evelyn herself. He was curious to know the truth. Human nature, more especially what we call the under side (thus revealing at once our fears and our aspirations), interested him as passionately as music. He liked to pick minds to pieces, and when he could watch a strangely involved motive at work he was as exhilarated by it as by music. He had twenty minutes to spare and he imagined that, even allowing for the eager anxiety of the young to explain themselves, he would hear the whole in that time.

He did not expect to have the truth from Hervey. His practice was by comparing two or more untruths to deduce the truth.

'You don't go to our dear Evelyn's Fridays any more.'

Hervey was instantly alert. I must say nothing, she thought. 'No, I don't go out much,' she said in a placid voice.

'But you used to go there a good deal.'

'Yes,' Hervey said.

He scarcely believed that he was being baffled. 'Don't you like meeting people ? '

'Not very much,' Hervey said. 'Either I talk too much, or I can think of nothing at all to say. I make a fool of myself either way.'

She had discovered her despatch case. Reaching for it in a careless way, as if she had had her eye on it for a long time, she rose to go. It was after she had gone that Marcel Cohen reflected on the extent of his failure. He had not even asked her how she intended to write the article. It could easily be useless. If it is I have been taken in by her specious air of competence, he thought, astonished. He was far from thinking eight guineas a small sum to risk.

The article came in a week later. He read it himself and had no fault to find with it. Mr Shaw-Thomas could have been content with his pupil.

When Hervey got her cheque she meant at first to pass it straight on to the Save the Children Fund. The cheque came by the morning post. During the lunch hour she saw a brown linen frock in the window of a shop in Regent Street. It was marked 'Sale Price £2.' The wish that seized her, as she looked at it, was no mere fancy. It took instant and complete possession of her. Scarcely giving herself time to think—as she well might—that the dress she was wearing to the office was shabby and too thick for summer, she went into the shop, had the dress taken out of the window, bought it and went back to the office wearing it, carrying the old one. Her feelings as she walked in the sun in her new frock were a mingling of joyfulness and discontent.

When she entered the room David Renn, who was in a good mood, said : 'That's a fine new frock, young Russell.'

To his surprise, and her own, tears stood in Hervey's eyes. 'I stole it,' she said, in a rough voice.

She told him what she had done. He listened patiently, her air of young dejection was amusing and touching, and at last said : 'I consider you were entitled to it. I haven't noticed your buying many clothes, I think you needed this.'

N

His voice gave Hervey a happy feeling of relief. It was the being approved by him. For the first time in the months she had worked for him she felt nearly at ease. In the same moment she noticed that his mouth was beautiful. This gave her an impersonal pleasure. It is true that from one cause and another his lips were colourless, but they had been drawn with extreme delicacy. She wished she were an artist, since there is more satisfaction in it than in writing. She said nothing in answer but began to feel that she could in time save the missing two pounds.

CHAPTER XVIII

RENN MEETS A SOCIAL DEMOCRAT

STILL thinking of Hervey—she had surprised him into taking her seriously—David Renn walked out of the office and sauntered towards the Earlhams' flat. He wanted to laugh about the new dress and could not. It seemed to him that there was something strained and unnatural in her remorse. The remorse was genuine—but it was wrong. A young woman ought not to feel that she had committed a crime in buying a new dress, even if the money is part of a sum dedicated to good works. She takes life too hard, he thought. But the smallest thing made her laugh like a boy —and he had himself seen how easily she forgot to think of Philip.

There were violent contradictions in her, under her stolid bearing. She conceals too many things, he thought. That explained her better. He frowned and smiled, wondering what sort of life she had beyond the office. Philip—he remembered now—had distrusted the husband, and thinking of Philip he let Hervey pass out of his mind.

He walked slowly, afraid of catching his friends at their meal. They would invite him to join them and since there was never enough for two——! Moreover he enjoyed the walk. London, he said to himself, is perfect in June. Delicious in May, perfect in June. The trees—if the trees growing in London's streets and yards could be brought together they would make a thick wood—are still green and glossy. No one hurries. The young men loiter along the pavements. He liked to look at them, at their dreaming faces, the child not yet ousted by the young man, almost innocent, only the first, the lightest tracing in their looks of the insolence of experience.

A lorry clattered down the street, driving with its back to the sun. It was carrying a big piece of machinery, the steel and the enamel flung out rays and flashes of light. The cover at the back of the lorry was looped up, so that a wedge of sunlight fell on the face of a boy seated between two men. The men were talking to him. He looked from one to the other, laughing not speaking. Renn noticed everything, the boy's strong white teeth, the light, a branch of green tied to the pole. He felt excited, as though what he had seen was beautiful and significant, a sight he could never forget. I must never forget it, he thought. In some way that he did not understand it released for him his feelings about London, more than that, about life itself. Something had been revealed to him, and if for the moment he did not understand it he could feel the excitement and the elation.

Earlham's flat looked out over the roofs of other houses. He climbed up the stairs, pausing on the third landing to rest his leg. The fourth was so dark that if he had not known where to look for them he might have missed name-plate and door. Henry Smith, coming an hour later, did miss them. He felt round the walls and, the door opening suddenly, fell into the flat.

He stood up, laughing and embarrassed. There were three people, and the Earlhams, in the room already. Rachel Earlham looked helplessly at the newcomer: he seemed to fill it to suffocation, so that she thought the walls might give way. There were no more chairs in the flat. He settled the question for himself by sitting down on the floor with his back to the window. Even here his long legs were in her way. He laughed. His eyes were candid and very bright.

On the wall near him hung a portrait of an old man with a serious kind face. 'Who's that?' he asked.

Rachel looked at him with astonished eyes. 'Keir Hardie. Don't you know that?'

'Oh.' He threw his head back and nodded at Renn. 'I

only know what he has had time to tell me. Do forgive me.
I'm beginning to learn.'

' Are you a socialist ? '

' I'm against society,' he laughed.

' Why ? If you know nothing.'

' A decent society wouldn't tolerate the slums : the existing
society does tolerate them, therefore it is not decent. That's
logic, isn't it ? ' He pleased her with his sunny face.

Louis Earlham said fiercely : ' Mr Marcel Cohen, who
owns the newspaper I work for, owns some of the worst
slums in London. The ground they're built on belongs also
to the Church. That's nice, isn't it ?—the slum-owning hog
supported on the parson's back.'

' Why do you go on working for him ? ' Henry Smith
asked.

' We all have to live. Why does David Renn write
advertisements ? '

One of the two men, strangers to Renn, broke in, with a
sarcastic smile. ' Louis admits that he is selling himself.
He'll go on doing it, too. You all do it, three-quarters of
the Labour Party is only holding out for a better price.
As for Trade Union officials——' He jerked his head
contemptuously towards a big rosy man, middleaged and
stout. ' Like Bradford Joe here.'

' We should starve to death if Louis didn't work,' Rachel
cried. Her clear pale face coloured with her indignation.
She folded her arms and sat upright.

The man who had been called Bradford Joe chuckled in a
placid way. He had a shrewd snouty face and small eyes, a
remarkable but not an agreeable face. ' Don't worry yourself, Mrs Earlham,' he laughed. ' Grassart's mad. Downright mad. No better than a Communist.' He said ' mad '
as only northerners of all races can say it, Yorksiremen best
of all. It sounded like a large square strong hand coming
down flat on a table.

' We were talking before you came about the dockers'
strike on Tyneside,' Louis said. ' Grassart thinks the Unions

ought to have made a transport strike of it and demanded the nationalisation of docks and railways.'

'It's no time for that,' Joe said soberly.

'Ay, and never will be, as long as you think more of your safety and your comfortable places than of the revolution,' Grassart sneered. 'Revolution! You won't move—now or in a hundred years. Your paws are too well buttered.'

Still smiling and good-tempered, the other rose to go. He held Rachel's arm and patted it and told her she ought to eat more. A few minutes later Grassart went, too. He had sat silent, hanging his head, after his enemy had gone and now he went without saying good night to Rachel. She made a funny childish face at his back. Henry Smith shook with silent laughter. He was already enchanted with her. When she brought in the tray of cheese and bread he looked quickly at Renn, and noticing that he took only the smallest piece, helped himself sparingly and made it last out a long time. He was sensitive, for all that he was young and noisy.

Renn said quietly : ' Grassart's not altogether in the wrong. If the Unions were to strike now. They're well-off and powerful. As it is, the controls are coming off everything with a rush. All we used to hear about the rebirth of the nation has been shelved for an indefinite time. It costs too much.'

'You forget the difficulties,' Louis said. 'There's distress —ex-soldiers looking for work. The country's dead against making experiments.'

'Are you going to wait until the other classes beg you to change society for them ? ' Renn said, with growing irony.

He smiled at Rachel. She came over to him and stood stroking his hair. 'Naughty David,' she said, shaking her head. 'You're teaching your friend to be reckless and impatient. Don't I tell you—you ought to get married and have a wife to keep and to look after you. Then you would give up all your wildness.'

'Am I so wild ? ' Renn said, smiling. He looked up at

her, with his fine eyebrows lifted as high as they would go.
She blushed and went back to her chair, pausing on the way
to run her finger across her husband's sleeve. Her childish
air of delicacy and enthusiasm was overlaid now by drowsiness.
Renn saw it—he saw too much, everything—and very soon
went away.

At one point on the dark narrow stairs he caught at Henry
Smith's shoulder. His leg had begun suddenly to pain him.
It was like a knife working between the flesh and the bone.
He controlled himself and walked on. He felt dejected—less
by the pain than by the feeling he had had in his friend's flat.
Those two—he had believed in them. They meant well!
But Louis was too quickly swayed. He had been impressed,
actually, by that Union official—and if ever, thought Renn,
there was a self-seeking complacent hog of a man——

' How many brands of Socialists are there ? ' Henry Smith
asked suddenly.

' As many as of the other religions,' Renn said.

He could not add another word. He felt ashamed of his
evil dispostion. In their rooms he helped the younger man
to arrange his bed on the couch, then went quickly to his
own room. He sat for a long time on the side of the bed,
rubbing his leg, and thinking.

CHAPTER XIX

A FORTNIGHT later Renn gave notice that he was leaving his firm. He had completed the arrangements for Philip's paper, which he proposed to call simply *The Week*. Part of its duty—and these were Philip's plans—was to reprint significant statements made (in speech or writing) by well-known politicians, priests, leaders of industry and finance, writers. Philip's idea of himself as a watchdog was responsible for this. He wanted to keep an eye on these people, who can change our lives, to pursue them with a relentless energy. ' Look, this is what they are saying this week. *This one* is lying again, to soothe you. *That* is an enemy of peace and the common man. T'other grudges you your liberties.'

For the rest, Philip had supposed that, without writing the whole all himself, or making many enemies, he could deal as faithfully with literature as with politics, finance, the Church. He expected the support of tens of thousands of young men and women, as eager, patient, and uncompromising as himself.

When Renn spoke to Hervey she said directly : ' Philip wanted my help.'

' So do I,' Renn said, with a calm smile. ' But I can't offer you as much as you're getting here. I shall take five pounds a week. I can pay you four.' He did not give himself the trouble of explaining that of his five pounds almost half would be needed by his mother.

' I could manage on that,' Hervey said, after a pause.

Renn looked at her. He was still smiling, in a way which accentuated the extraordinary delicacy of his face. ' You

won't leave Shaw-Thomas.   You're much too anxious for his
approval.'

Hervey did not answer.   It was true that she shrank from
facing Mr Shaw-Thomas to tell him that she was leaving.
And this was less because he had been kind to her than
because she disliked the idea of sinking in his eyes.

But there were other impulses at work in her, of which
David Renn knew nothing.   Most of these had to do with
her husband.   Her mind had been busy for a long time on
Penn's failure to find work, and it had produced a plan.   The
more she dwelt on this plan the finer it seemed.   Her mind
was at its nimblest and surest when it was a question of
handling people to produce an effect.

She had thought that if she were to resign her job and by
the next post Mr Shaw-Thomas received a letter signed
Thomas Penn Vane (and no one here except David Renn
knew that she was married or would connect her with it)
asking for an interview, he would seize the chance to fill
her place without the trouble of advertising or examining
a number of applicants.   All this had been in her mind before
David Renn spoke to her.   It sprang from her passionate
wish to help Penn, to restore to him his waning self-confidence.
She could not bear to see him daily losing faith in himself.
His attempts—by an air of arrogance towards her, and
scorning her for trifles—to disguise it, roused in her more
pity than any other emotion.   It is true there was some
contempt hidden in the pity—in so far as she did not believe
that Penn would achieve anything by himself, and she felt
certain that she could very quickly find herself in work.

There was more in it than this.   She had enjoyed making
Shaw-Thomas take her abilities on trust.   That was a
triumph.   It was something she knew how to do, and could
do again, but without being able to understand it.   When
she listened to people in a certain way, she knew what they
were thinking, and could give the wanted answers.   And
this, to her, was the only, absolutely the only moment when
she enjoyed an enterprise.   She wanted to be given something,

a position, a confidence, she delighted in this exercise of her wits; and as soon as the position was in her hands she no longer wanted it. If, as advertising did, it involved the effort of meeting and talking to other people, she soon loathed it. And she cast about for means of wriggling out of it, without discredit if possible—but even with it, if no sound excuse came along.

To help Penn was as sound a reason as she was likely to find, for any occasion.

For a time she told no one what she was thinking.

Now with David Renn's offer in her hand she felt that she could manage Penn. It needed care. He may—he will—she thought, feel offended. He may refuse because I have found it for him. How can I begin? (It is easy to manage, to feel one's way, with others but not with an intimate. The closeness hinders—just as to be passionately in love makes it difficult to behave adroitly.) She would begin by telling him that she was tired of copy-writing. That pleased him. He laughed—and told her that she was incapable in anything of persevering. Yes, Hervey said, yes—she sighed; she feared she was actually very unstable. It seemed a pity that Penn had not taken the job in the first place. He would have done well with it. Yes, of course, Penn said, he would no doubt have been given the job if he had applied. Indeed he had had thoughts of applying, just after the War, but Hervey had nipped in before him. He teased her about stealing his birthright.

Now was the moment. Hervey felt stiff and cold with the excitment. At the same time she felt sure. She had only to speak, to smile, to put a hand on his knee. ' Why shouldn't you do it now? ' she said, smiling. ' If I were to resign, and at the same moment you applied—and with your qualifications and looks—why then—but perhaps you think the work would bore you? '

' Not at all,' Penn said. He rose and began to walk about the room. She saw from his face that he was closeted with a director; he was being fluent and convincing; a movement of his shoulders emphasised a point he had just made : these men knew his worth, they listened to him. In time—nay, at this very moment—it was he who listened with an indulgent air, to the enthusiasms of a subordinate. He came closer to her in his stridings up and down, and stopped. Hervey had meant to say that until he felt sure of himself she would help him ; he could bring work home in the evenings and she would go over it with him. She decided not to suggest this yet. After all, she thought—his mind is quicker than mine ; he may not need help from me.

When Penn stopped, and stroking the back of her neck, said that it was a splendid idea of hers and she must resign— since, he laughed, she had, as usual, made her mind up without saying a word to him, but he was used to that—and he would apply and take her work over from her, she felt herself ready to fall, she was so tired. This kind of thing was exhausting. She felt as though all the strength had gone out of her and she had scarcely enough left to crawl into bed.

A week later—it was now July—she went trembling to Mr Shaw-Thomas, to give him a fortnight's notice. He was surprised and offended, but concealed both these emotions. For the first time he noticed that the lower half of her face was stubborn and heavy. He had never looked at her hands before. The long fingers were untended. There was dust on her shoes and she was wearing cheap stockings. He expressed a merely polite regret at losing her and had the just satisfaction of watching her slink from his room. By a fortunate chance he had just read a letter, written—which had pleased him—on Air Force notepaper, from an excellently promising young man. He beckoned his secretary over and gave her a letter to the young man, with the day and hour for his interview.

Hervey wanted to advise Penn how to behave at the inter- view. She did it badly. She was still smarting from her own ordeal. For the time she had nothing to give Penn. She resented having to be on guard with him. He ought— she knew he did not—to trust her. He ought to know that

anything she said was to help him, not—why did he force her
to say it ?—not to offend or humiliate him.

' Mr Shaw-Thomas enjoys the sound of his own voice,'
she had said. ' You must let him talk. If you listen carefully,
you'll hear what he wants you to say.'

' You're afraid I shall give myself away,' Penn said. He
frowned.

' Not at all,' she answered wearily.

' You'd like to take this interview for me exactly as you
try to arrange the whole of my life. You're as abominably
managing and domineering as your mother. Perhaps you
think I don't see it. I do, but I'm usually too bored by it
to point it out. What a pity you have such a low opinion of
me. It makes you make mistakes.'

Hervey held her tongue. His interview was that afternoon.
The thought that she had been too clever gripped her.

In the very moment when she saw Penn's face of triumph,
the relief in her mind swung over into sharp fear. She
could have wept. What could I have been thinking of, she
cried, to give up a place where I was safe ? If Penn makes a
failure of it I have sacrificed Richard to my folly, and all for
nothing. She could scarcely believe what she had done.
I was mad, she thought. It was like buying the dress.
Something had arisen in her, outside her will, and thrust her,
blind, absorbed in her own cleverness, along a path of which
the end revealed itself only at the end, in a flash of terror.

She kept these thoughts quietly hidden. During the last
days before she left the office and Penn stepped in she was
stolid and more silent than usual. Penn was in high spirits.
This was some comfort to her, but not so great as it would
have been to a nobler character.

Towards the end of the month she went up to Danesacre,
to see Richard. She had now told Penn about *The Week*.
He was inclined to laugh at it, and she herself did not believe
that it would last more than a short time.

She had not seen Richard for over six months. That was
at Christmas, and since then he had had meaasles and recovered

from them with no after effects. Miss Holland had written
every day during the illness, and yet she had been in agony.
It was the first time he had been ill without her to nurse
him. She remembered his last illness when he was a baby
and the care she had taken of him. She hated Miss Holland.
That she, that any woman, should be nursing her child. It
was as much as she could bear.

She thought him paler, and grown. He was now five, tall,
and with his high forehead and eyes of a pure deep blue, very
beautiful. He was so beautiful that she was afraid. She asked
Miss Holland whether he drank his milk, and how long he
slept in the afternoon. Miss Holland, who never failed a
jot in her duty, resented these useless questions. She answered
them but she added, smiling, in that way of hers—it made her
kind brown face look as though she were propitiating and
despising you : ' Richard is sometimes bad tempered.'

' A bad temper ! ' Hervey repeated. She looked at the
woman in astonishment.

' He has fits of senseless anger,' Miss Holland said firmly.
' I never know what causes them. He lies on the floor
screaming, and bites the legs of chairs. Sometimes it's the
carpet he bites and then his mouth fills with fluff and I have
to coax him to let me bathe it.'

' Do you punish him ? ' Hervey asked, trembling.

' Dear me, no,' Miss Holland said. ' I wait until it's over
and then I ask him about it, quietly. They don't come often.
He's really a good little boy. Kind, and intelligent.'

Hervey said nothing. She felt that she was to blame. It
was because she had left him. He was never in a rage when
he lived with me, she thought. But she had forgotten much
of what had happened to them in those days.

In the afternoon she took Richard to the sands. It was
only half a success. She knew how to care for a child, so
that he would grow up strong and handsome, because these
things can be learned, but not how to play with a child. She
forgot, building the castle, that Richard's hands were less
quick than hers. In the end, she built while Richard looked on.

The feel of the warm sand on her legs, and the light shiver as the wind breathed on them, woke in her the memory of long summer days spent here with Jake her brother. Solitary children, they played together alone, between the cliffs and the sea. The days were endless. At one moment the tide was far out, leaving pools and ripples in the dark sand; they turned their backs on it, and in a moment it was licking at their heels and the heel of the cliff. Between the two moments they had built a city with bridges. The city was destroyed daily, and Jake had been killed, shot down in the air and fallen dying into No Man's Land (she felt the shock of it in her body, the terror and the falling). Only I am left, she thought, looking at her hands, stronger and yet tireder than the hands of the builder of cities. As she thought it, she knew that it was not true. The moment itself, that long moment between two tides, was left—it hung like a bubble in the clear air of time itself, within it two young Russells were safe for as long as either of the two lived, and here they had their eternity. The sea rose in her and retreated, tide after tide flowed through her veins. She was the moment through which the whole of this passed and in which it was reflected, as in the sides of the bubble. She moved. She felt the warm sand under her hands. Now she saw that Richard had turned away from their castle and was making a clumsy tower for himself. He piled one bucketful of sand on the top of another until the whole collapsed. Then, knitting his brows, he began it over again. 'Why don't you finish our castle?' Hervey said.

'I'm busy here,' he said briefly. He added at once: 'God helped me to build the first and it fell down. You can't blame him for that, his fingers are not very strong.'

What can he be thinking? Hervey wondered. She watched him until he wearied of the task. They shook the sand from themselves and went away to the pools between the rocks. Richard walked a little apart from her, not looking at the sea, which he disliked.

In the evening, when she had put the child to bed in her

room, her mother talked to her about him. She said that when he came here to tea he always played the same game he had invented. Mr Vane has called to see Mrs Russell. Dear me, what a pleasant surprise; how do you do, Mr Vane? Very well, and how are you, Mrs Russell? 'I take him back to Miss Holland before bed-time,' Mrs Russell said: 'if it is raining I keep him here for the night. When it is almost time he keeps saying, Is it raining? Do you think it will rain? He likes to think this is his home. She's very kind to him. She said to me that he is an exceptional child, exceptionally intelligent.'

All the time her mother was speaking Hervey kept half turned from her. She kept her face indifferent and stolid, as though all this chatter about Richard bored her. She did not know why she was behaving like this. She knew only that she was deeply inexplicably offended by being asked to listen to her mother's praise of him. It was quite another thing that she was afraid of being laughed at if she showed her own pride in Richard. Her mother had laughed at her as a child too often and unkindly—the fear of it was always with her: there was no one with whom she felt safe.

Now Mrs Russell was talking about his illness. For a long time, days, he was listless—as though, the doctor said, he had no interest in getting better, which was absurd in so young a child. Then one night (it was about three in the morning) Miss Holland had gone in to him, and he was awake, and she said, Is there anything you would like? and he said in a thread of a voice, I should like a good cup of tea. Then you shall have it, the kind good woman said, and there and then she went downstairs and made it for him and he drank it and after that night, Mrs Russell said, looking up and smiling, he began all at once to get better.

Hervey did not say anything. She was thinking: he wanted to be indulged, it was me he wanted. She would not show that the story had moved her at all. She listened with a polite smile, as though she must decently be grateful for the effort to interest her. But so that no one could suppose she was interested, she asked no questions. And she would ask none. Mrs Russell was disappointed. She searched Hervey's face for the look of softening she expected. Hervey turned to her with a bright air. Behind it, her mind ran up and down passages, groaned, scrabbled at the boards, beat itself on walls and doors, and all for nothing. There was nothing to be done.

CHAPTER XX

No one could say that as a reformer Hervey lacked zeal. She was short, lamentably, of experience. During their first month David Renn was laid off with his wounds, which were giving trouble in a new way. He said they had suddenly developed an imagination of their own. Whatever it was, it meant that he lay in bed, looked after with loving incompetence by Henry Smith, and after the doctor had been—he came every morning and forbade Renn to sit up or read—he cut extracts from the score of newspapers, English and foreign, lying in the next room, and wrote an editorial and other columns, and sent Smith off with a sheaf of instructions to Hervey. She had to make up the paper and see it through the press.

She also reviewed books and plays. She had engaged the late art critic of the *Morning Gazette* to make the translations from French, German and Italian. He worked at them at home, writing in penny exercise books, and was never late with what he called his *devoir*, but the translations were word for word and utterly unreadable. Hervey spent an hour or more every night turning them into tolerable English.

Their office was the top floor of a thin house in a square behind Fleet Street. The square was old and shabby, and not a house in it but had fallen on evil days and lost its character. A narrow road, always busy with lorries, led from one corner of the square to the printers' and beyond to the river. On fine days and when she had time to leave the office for it, Hervey took her dinner down to the Embankment and sat eating it and watching the boats and the gulls. There is a moment when the gull, turning, to sweep sideways and downward to the surface of the water, makes a movement of such perfection that it can scarcely be watched without tears.

The floors in their two rooms had sunk in the centre, so that chairs slid inwards and desks had to be wedged. In the outer room a typist and a cynical office boy shared unhelpfully in Hervey's days. She pored over David Renn's instructions and did what she could, with a copy of *The Spectator* open beside her, to make *The Week* look a little like a paper. The compositors in their kindness taught her best. One of them showed her how to use space to advantage. She was always behind time. On press nights she waited at the printers' until one o'clock reading the pages as they came off the machines. The room was fiercely lighted and the light took the colour from the men's faces. The noise of the machines destroyed her. Its strong mechanical beat, without any of the intervals which belong to a living rhythm, tore at the fibres of her brain. She wished she could stop her ears. The men drank cups of deathly strong tea, and fetched her a cup. It was the thickest china she ever felt and the tea the strongest.

When Renn was able to sit up, he worked in the office and sent her out on errands. She called on Evelyn, whom she had not seen since their quarrel. She was to ask her for an article (at the lowest level of pay) and for an advertisement. She dawdled in the street, outside the office of the *London Review*, for half an hour before finding the courage to go in. She hoped that Evelyn would be in a kind mood. This hope was vain.

' Dear me,' Evelyn said, ' how long have you been touting for advertisements ? '

' Not long,' Hervey said, with a smile. ' I used to be a novelist, and I've gone down in the world. I now shark for myself and live as opportunity serves.'

Evelyn asked a great many questions about *The Week* and about David Renn. At last she was called into another room and went away, asking Hervey to wait. Hervey waited almost an hour. She could hear the two girls in the room whispering about her with smiles.

The door opened and Evelyn came in. She looked at Hervey in astonishment. ' Are you still here ? '

' You asked me to wait,' Hervey said. She stood up, trembling. Evelyn kept her waiting for another age, to listen to an account of the mistakes made by amateur editors. ' Aren't you going to write for us, then ? ' Hervey said, in a jaunty voice.

Evelyn looked down at her desk. ' I may later,' she said— or had she only said Good-day ?

In the street Hervey walked blindly, with tears of humiliation and rage. She could not check them. They welled up, and ran over her cheeks. With shame, she fled into the station lavatory at Charing Cross.

This mortifying hour was the worst she endured. She called, to ask him for an advertisement, on the publisher of her novel, Charles Frome. He asked no fewer questions than Evelyn. His eyes, quick and brightly blue, watched her with curiosity. Rousing herself, she made him laugh at her mistakes. In the end, and still laughing, he said : ' Well, my dear, I must say I'd rather you wrote us another novel. But if you're resolved to be the death of printers I suppose we must do something about it.' He gave her a half-page advertisement for six weeks.

She was confused and grateful. For a long time her mind kept returning to this interview. She went thoroughly over her words and Frome's answers, trying to feel sure whether he had been more kind than friendly, and whether she pained him by her want of elegance. She was only aware of her clothes when she saw Frome, with whom were involved her earliest ambitions. At all other times she went shabby with a good heart.

William Ridley did not wait to be asked to write for *The Week*. He called at the office when she was on her way to lunch, and came with her. They ate chicken cutlets ('bags o' mystery,' Ridley said) and drank coffee in a restaurant in which even the plates witnessed to the death of society. They had been stamped by sweated Czech workers with patterns which satisfied the American importer's idea of French peasant art. Hervey spoke of this to Ridley. He offered at once to write an article on it for *The Week*. ' That would be very fine,' Hervey said thoughtfully.

She looked at Ridley's large face, in which the little bright eyes were like windows with a watcher stooping behind the candles. The edges of his jacket were shabby. She asked him, Are you willing (she meant, able) to write for us for less than the *London Review* pays you ? We're poor but worthy, she said. He nodded, blinking—and as though the words, and the thought behind them, had released something in him he began to tell her about his youth. His father was an auctioneer, and there were five other children; he was the eldest, he had taken scholarships, worked, at thirteen he was already thinking of his career. So was I, Hervey thought. At this moment she liked him warmly.

' I had a suit I kept for best,' Ridley said : ' when I went to the university I grew out of it—but I had to wear it for occasions. So you would see me, on ordinary days, shabby but covered—and at a luncheon party, my best suit, it was grand cloth, in for a penny in for a pound, said my father, with the jacket bursting across the front and my wrists sticking out. Not that I attended many parties. I couldn't ask back, y'see.'

Hervey listened and nodded. This was nearly her own life. And if the War took four of his years, she thought, so it did of mine, seeing, as though they were poured down in front of her, the interiors of rented rooms, streets, Richard's bath, the edges (as white as bones) of Salisbury Plain, a dress hanging on a nail. And now Ridley was talking of his success, and she stopped listening to him, only a word or two reached her—talk sense . . . make your impression . . . get in somewhere. ' I'm going to write a novel about London,' he exclaimed. ' Crammed with scenes, colour, richness, plenty of fun. It'll take me years—I'm preparing for it, and it'll be worth it. There hasn't been a novel like it.' But he's unbearable, Hervey thought. ' I know I can do it,' he said.

He talked on and on, and about his life, and how he went
here, and here, and spoke to this man, and made friends with
that well-known writer, and again she liked him and was
sorry for him. She saw that his monstrous conceit was a
defence.

They left the restaurant and walked along Fleet Street
together. He jerked his head at the *Daily Post* office and
told her how he had impressed Cohen with his ability. It
meant something, he said, looking at her. Hervey agreed.
She did not mind his bragging, now that she could translate
it. They shook hands, and she smiled warmly at him.
' You're not so bad,' Ridley said. He called the words after
her as she ran up the dark narrow stairs to *The Week*.

Had he really said that ? she wondered. Extraordinary.
He was an extraordinary creature, and infinitely more
complex than she had supposed. She thought humbly that
to understand any single person, deeply enough to pass
judgement on them, would be work for a lifetime. And then,
no doubt, you would be ashamed to judge.

And yet I must judge his deeds, she thought. I don't like
his writing : it makes me think of a grocer setting out his
window—so many sides of bacon, so much sugar, so many
heaps of raisins, boxes of soap, pyramids of tins, cunningly
set out to rouse your appetite and make you buy. You *must*
buy, so that he can live. He has no time to wonder whether
you are happy, whether his food nourishes you, and what
becomes of you when you leave his shop. Perhaps you are
torn by doubts of the value of your life, spent between an
office and a house which is the image of a million other
houses. Or you are a farmer, whose land no longer keeps
you. Or a machine hand, lashed across the machine. You
had dreams, but you have forgotten them, except for a faint
uneasiness when you find yourself alone for a moment. Soon
you are afraid to be alone. You turn the gramophone on,
or crowd into the cinema at the corner, or get out the car.
Something that you thought you had has been stolen from you,
or lost. You are a man brought up as the heir to an estate

who finds on entering upon it that it has vanished—the fields
rotted, the great roof fallen in, and where you expected lights,
servants, music, there is nothing, a heap of stones, the lintel
stone of the door, but the door and the familiar rooms it led
to, gone. And here is tradesman Ridley's chance. He runs
forward with his lusty essays, his great novel ('crammed
with'—sides of bacon and bottles of cooking wine)—a kind
of vast beano, all together now boys, hip, hip, hurrah, we
won't go home till morning. What's this you say about lost
lands? The roots decayed? The wells dried up? Ah,
that's only what you think—take another look at our Spring
offers. Sign here, join now. Stupendous attraction. Real
camels, real sand. For a few shillings you can dream that
you are still the heir, you are fortunate, you are safe, your
dish is prepared for you, in your Father's house there are
many mansions.

Hervey walked past the typist, opened the inner door, and
closed it quickly. She saw at once that Renn's wounds were
hurting him. His desk was set at an angle with hers and as
she came in he turned his back, but not before she had caught
a frightening glimpse of his face, damp with the sweat. There
was nothing she could do. She worked on until six o'clock.
The typist went home. Still Renn went on writing. Sitting
with him, in the now empty and silent office, Hervey imagined
that she was alone with him in the cabin of a ship. Miles
of sea cut them off from their kind. There were dangers,
the sky—I don't much like the look of it, she thought—but
still he said nothing. Stooped over the table, he wrote and
wrote.

'Why don't you go home?' Renn said.

Hervey walked across the room and stood in front of him.
'Is there nothing I can do?'

'No, of course not.'

'What does Henry Smith do for you when you're like
this?' Hervey persisted. She gripped the edge of his desk.

Renn looked at her with a slight smile, full of irony. 'He
rubs my back.'

' Does that relieve you ? '

' Yes, it does. I know no reason why it should. My mother discovered it by accident. One day when the pain ran from my leg to my shoulders she began rubbing them— you can't rub the scars themselves—and after a time it went altogether. Magic.' He laughed.

' Why don't you go home at once and let Smith rub you ? ' Hervey said.

' Why, because he went off yesterday, with five pounds, to walk across Germany.'

' I'll rub you,' Hervey said. She stared at him, her chin poked forward into a stubborn disagreeable line. Her hands were shaking. If he refuses, I shall never forget it, she thought.

Renn only smiled. ' That's very good of you,' he said. He took off tie and collar—his jacket was already lying across his desk—and drew his arms out of his shirt. They were very thin, whiter than Hervey's. She averted her eyes from them, with the feeling that he must be ashamed of his thinness. He turned his chair sideways and leaned forward, laying his arms across his desk, and told Hervey where to place her hands and how to rub deeply. When she had rubbed his shoulders for a time, she kneeled on the floor to rub beneath them. From the quietness in the room and from the quiescent body of Renn she received a strange image. She thought that she was very old, she had been on her knees here for centuries, she was tired, her arms withered and came again, and she went on with her self-chosen task. Once Renn sighed. He sighed with his whole body. She felt the muscles in his sides lift and relax, and it was as though she held him up between her hands.

' What is your mother like ? ' she asked, after a time.

' A small woman,' Renn said slowly. His head was hanging forward, so that his voice sounded deeper than usual. ' Thin and small. Bluish eyes, a very delicate nose, like a girl's. My father died when I was at school.'

Hervey's shoulders burned as though her arms were being

pulled in their sockets. Yet she felt that she could go on. Her strength came from Renn himself, from the fine bones under her hands. At last he moved, straightened himself a little, and said: 'That's easily bearable now. You can give up.'

Half exhausted, she let her arms drop and knelt forward with her hands on the floor. Her head was swimming. Looking up, she saw that Renn had his back to her; he was dressing, and she stood up, swaying, and leaned on her desk. She had recovered when he turned round.

'Did I manage as well as Smith?' she asked.

'Much better,' Renn said, smiling. 'I ought to thank you,' he said, 'and I don't know what to say.'

As they walked down the stairs together he laid his hand on her arm. She felt a pure pleasure, as though she had been rewarded for something, or admitted into something—she was not sure which. Whatever it was, she was happy—and from some deep cause grateful. She had nothing to say.

CHAPTER XXI

1. *Hervey Russell*

WITH Penn at work, Hervey began to save money—a pound one week, the next only a few shillings. At the end of September she had almost six pounds hidden under her handkerchiefs at the back of a drawer. They bore up her spirit in time of trouble.

One evening she was tempted to spend them. She was tired. Her work—not made easier by David Renn's conscience: he checked every figure and date quoted in the paper and felt disgraced by an e printed upside down in one issue—was hard. She felt pulled down by the burden of small duties. Her unfinished novel plagued her. She knew of a farmhouse where she could live for two pounds a week and she was tempted to buy herself three weeks' freedom. Something less than loyalty to David Renn—perhaps kept fear of his contempt—held her back.

She sat waiting for Penn in her room, restless in mind. When he came in he began instantly to say that one man in the advertising office was treating him shabbily. He was always given the dreariest and most unprofitable tasks, and if a client showed signs of becoming dissatisfied he and no other had to attend to him, and take the blame. Hervey roused herself to pull at the centre of this knot. It turned out that he had offended one client, who straightway complained to Shaw-Thomas, to the end that Penn was in trouble.

After listening, with a little patience, Hervey said: ' You will always offend people if you try to put them in the wrong.

217

Why not begin by agreeing with everything ? Then you can insinuate your knowledge so that it seems theirs. You should never argue. If you begin an argument, your man will be on his guard—the very state of mind you wish to avoid. Choose his least sensible idea and agree to it with the wildest enthusiasm. Say, Yes, it will do this, and this, piling one effect on another. In a short time he will feel uneasy, then will begin to suggest doubts and flaws, and before long you'll see him turn right about and agree to any compromise.'

' Dear me,' Penn said. ' It appals me to think that this is how I must have been handled, at least before I married you.'

Hervey did not answer. Yes, she thought, when you married me I had learned none of these tricks : it is through you, and through your distrust, that I came to use my mind against people. She bent her head lower. Yet it was in me, she said—the impulse was there : you did not create that. She saw herself as the badly-dressed student, standing on tiptoe—where was it ?—in a crowded room to get sight of the back of Penn's head. She was in love with him then. She recalled the simplicity of her love in those days. There was no one whom she admired as she admired him. Why, she would have gone readily to the stake for any of the opinions he announced with so much assurance.

She felt on her table for a book and held it up to hide her face. There was nothing to be said. But a slow anger—the overt edge of her memory—woke in her against her life. She hated the room, which contained nothing that was not worthless—as if the whole of man's present ingenuity had been used up in creating more and more elaborate machines ; these did nothing except deliver daily piles of excrement in the shape of just such chairs and tables. And I, she thought, I, who hate them, live among them. I hate my life. She saw a cliff-side in sunlight, the wind stroking the reedy grass ; pavement cafés in a foreign city—what city ? a wide river, bronze-green running into flakes of light. This and this is what I want, I shall grow old without having lived. She

jumped up, went over to the window, and stood peering out.
The street lamps cast yellow circles on the pavement. She
watched a woman run swiftly across one circle, vanish, and
appear again in the next, her dress blown by the wind. A
familiar excitement seized her. Standing quietly, she felt
that she was straining with all her force against a wall. She
beat her head against it. I can't get out, can't get out.
Her hand gripped the edge of the sill. No escape, nothing
for you here, she thought. But what do I get from this
life ?

She turned round. ' I can't endure this room,' she said,
in a low voice. ' Can't we do anything ? Won't your
father help us ? If we had the smallest place of our own
—with decent things—a bed, a table, chairs—I could bear
it. Ask him, if he won't give, ask him to lend us a little
money.'

' You're only being silly and hysterical,' Penn said. ' I'm
sorry I'm not a rich man.' He looked at her with contempt.
' You seem to forget I should now be in Oxford, at least in
comfort, if I hadn't been willing to help you.'

I vex you into showing your unpleasantest side, Hervey
thought. She felt cut off from him, and from herself too,
able only to watch the two of them behaving like madmen.
With her dreadful honesty she owned to herself that though
anxious at the thought of his going away, going to Oxford—
afraid of being left, of failing, of having no money—yes, all
these things—but she had had mean thoughts too, had
resented the contrast between her life and his : why should
I live here while Penn amuses himself in Oxford ?—yes, I
thought that, she admitted—it is true, I am an egoist, I am
selfish. She looked at Penn with a sharp smile. She felt an
impulse to anger him. It was as though she wanted to drive
him out of his senses with her—like a child which is not
satisfied until it has angered its mother to punishing it. ' You
and your Oxford,' she cried. ' You are thirty this month,
and you talk of going back to school. With a son for whom
you do nothing. Nothing, nothing.'

'When you bawl at me in your mother's voice I only feel that I was a fool not to go,' Penn said.

Hervey ran out of the room. She ran downstairs, and into the street, without coat or hat, and walked up and down, until the cold sent her back. Penn had gone away into his own room. She undressed and got into bed.

The door opening sent a shock through her. She looked up and saw Penn coming towards her. He did not seem unkind, but he seemed young and vulnerable. He came into the bed and put his arms round her in silence. Tears sprang to her eyes. Without meaning anything she cried: 'Life is so disappointing.' Penn laid his face against hers— 'Poor Hervey,' he said. The words flew back across her mind, flashing the signal first to this hill and then to that until the farthest bore its fire, and the message was read—but by whom ? Now she grew warmer and began to fall towards sleep. It was very pleasant, to glide, to fail, to sink into sleep. Her mind seemed to hover, like a breath of wind playing alone, above her body. Penn was speaking, but she was too sleepy to listen to him. It is something weak and foolish that Penn comforts, she said to herself. (' My dear, I wish you could have your house,' Penn said.) Is it that weak thing which goes on clinging to him ? Yes—her head sank forward—yes, I am weak, I am a coward—it is marriage (' I'll never call you that again, Hervey, it's silly ') : marriage ties people to each other in an underneath dragging way, she thought, in growing confusion. Her mind stooped to enter a long dark corridor, like the passage in her mother's first house. Her senses were now astray. She felt warmth and the smoothness of the clothes. And now, as if it had come to the end of the passage, her mind was confident and happy. She felt that nothing was too hard for her. I can do anything, anything, she thought. She sank deeper. Light welled round her; where the darkness had been it was now full light. She ran after her mother and they stepped out together into the clear early-morning air ; there was sunlight, the yellow flowers of the broom sent a spray of bright drops into the air when she reached for it. She laughed, looking at her mother; who was smiling. She is pleased with me, the child thought, and her heart felt light.

2. *Delia Hunt*

In the room below Hervey's Delia was in bed, ill. Her nose had sharpened as if she were dying. But she was not, not this time. There was a nurse in the room, and to avoid watching directly she watched this woman's shadow move by the wall. She saw the white end wall of a house and the shadow of herself as soft there as soot. No sun made that shadow. It began then, she thought—no, that was not true, it began months and years earlier, in Brixton. The door opened and an aproned child ran along the street. She dragged her hand by the wall, her fingers touching the stone—yes, night, the walls cold, rough, sending the cold through her hands, and the street, it was behind the market, empty. At last she came to the turning, the dark archway, and the market. The lights of open stalls, roaring tongues, drew her here and there. She ran about between the stalls like a lean cat, brushing against women's clothes. Underfoot the stones of the road were wet, slippery with mud, leavings, spittle. The staring faces of men and women were larger than life, pressed against the stalls; there were so many of them that they moved all together, surging to this side, forward, then back, laughed, grumbled, lifted their hands with spread fingers— she held her own red tiny hand before a gas jet, to see its bones. A sharp excitement pricked her. She felt the prick in her stomach first, it spread, and she swelled with it until she was light as a feather. She rolled on the ground. Two legs overstepped her and a hand gripped her jerking her up. She began to dance. She showed her skinny legs in the dance. A woman's voice saying, ' If she were mine, I'm bound I'd give her a hiding,' filled her fuller than before of wickedness, and the excitement, and dancing, kicking her legs, she made an idiot's face at the woman. It was rich.

' Do you want anything, Mrs Hunt ? '

' No,' Delia said.

' I'll take a nap for a few minutes.'

' Nap your head off.'   Only leave me alone.   She wanted to get back again.   For one moment she had had the strong biting taste of those days in her mouth—but the fool must speak and spoil all.   She could scarcely breathe.   Her body felt swollen.   It felt monstrous.   She made an effort to part her legs but they had grown together and she could do nothing except lie and endure these changes.   No change taking place in her body could be so extraordinary as the one which had overtaken the child Delia.   For some reason this thought gave her intense pleasure.   She considered it for another moment, then closed her eyes.   At once, she felt that she was falling headlong through a black torrent.   She had a fancy that her husband had come in : half opening her eyes she looked everywhere in the room.   Nothing.   The nurse dozing made as much noise as her own laboured breaths.   I was a fool to take him back, she thought, without heat.   She felt only contempt for herself, no pity.   She did not feel injured when he thrashed her more than when he looked at her.   It was all in the day's work, she would say.   Her mind, more resilient than her body, took all such mishaps as they came.   She treated her body as if it were not important, and rolled it in the dirt ; but every pleasure she had had came to her through it.   What alarmed her now was that it refused to obey her.   It's the end of everything, she thought.

The nurse had set two candles on the floor.   Delia turned her face from them and thought of other rooms which the candles had changed and diminished.   Ah, but I was young, she repeated.   In those days London was smaller and grander. You knew where you were.   Women like her, with no weak modesty and no fears, were apart.   There were places she went where no what you called respectable woman could nave gone.   A sense of warm satisfaction filled her, as if her body had its own thoughts.

I never stinted myself, she said.   Loud familiar music

sounded in her brain. The feeling of satisfaction deepened, it became an exquisite joy; shock after shock of this joy passed through her; she felt it spreading upwards and filling her breasts with warmth: even her breathing felt easier. Now I am winning, she thought. When she felt happy she had always a sense that she was getting the better of life. She had had this sense when she rolled on the ground, when she was drunk, when she was merry, when her lusts were filled. She thought of life as a woman of her own present age, and miraculously stronger. No friend of hers, but someone of her own family—a familiar and an old enemy. Times when she was poor, or unlucky, were one up to life. Her illness was another score for that side. I'll pay you out, she thought—you, I'll fetch you a slap in the eye—yes, that's it, she thought, that's the way to live, up and at 'em. The pressure in her side started again, it was like a hand opening and shutting. Damn you, damn you, she said to the other woman. She felt angry that she could do nothing but lie here with life crowing over her. You wait, she muttered. Yes, wait, I'll show you. I'm a fool, but that's neither here nor there, she thought, confused by the pain.

' Nurse.'

She called twice before the inert body in the chair stirred and sat up. With a hurried gesture the nurse straightened her cap. She disapproved deeply of her patient.

' I feel much worse.'

Stooping, the woman felt her forehead and wrist. ' We're going on very well,' she said in a moment.

' *We*, you fool. Are you ill in bed too ? ' Groaning with with rage, Delia struck at the woman's hand. The nurse withdrew in an offended silence. Now Delia felt past all. Her body seemed to be dissolving away from her. She tried to save it by fixing her glance on one and then on another of the objects in the room. She liked her furniture. It was ornate and comfortable. The floor was thickly carpeted so that she could step out of bed without feeling the cold, and with the chairs, the gilt bed and the dressing-table, it was another slap in the eye for life. Who could have expected her to reach this? Not that woman in Brixton who wanted to give her a hiding. Whatever happened to her, these would remain, the marks of a victory.

She let herself drift again into a half sleep. Her body flowed over the room, touching the walls, the ceiling. In a sudden panic she contracted it until it lay huddled and panting in the bed. Doors opened in her everywhere. As fast as she shut one, another sprang apart to let out a rat or a dwarf. The dwarfs were as small as children, dark, with bent legs. They ran everywhere and everything they touched shrivelled. She tried to keep out of their way. A sudden spasm gripped her. Seizing one of the dwarfs she tried to cram him into her body, but in the same moment she woke and saw the room. She was so hot that she thought she was burning. And life was standing by her bed, grinning down at her. 'You've come, have you,' she said to life. Now I am burning, she thought. A slow anger possessed her. As life stooped down and began to choke her she made a sudden effort and sprang forward. She fell on to the floor and still fighting rolled under the bed. She tore her nightgown and tore at her throat in her struggle to breathe. In the struggle she rolled back and forward, sending the chamber-pot flying against the wall; it broke into a dozen pieces and she cut herself on one of them.

The nurse could do nothing to help her. Out of her wits, she opened the door and called for help. It was four in the morning. Hervey heard her and came downstairs pulling a coat over her nightgown. 'She's fighting under the bed with something,' the woman said.

They went in, Hervey reluctant, afraid of seeing an unpleasant sight. Delia was exhausted. She lay with her hand bleeding—a little blood where she had put it to her lip. Dragging and lifting, they got her into the bed. 'She's killed herself,' the nurse said. 'Congestion of the lungs, and that strength. Who would have expected her to do it?'

Hervey was looking closely at Delia. Her big gross face, the mouth gone slack, was as if empty. As Hervey watched, a little colour suffused it. The eyes were open. They were alive, staring, bold, used.

Some impulse deep in Hervey recognised its like in Delia. She stooped closer, trying with an unconscious passion to see the brain moving behind the eyes. A strong excitement filled her, the sense of sharing in a mystery. Behind her the nurse fumbled with the candles. Only one remained alight; the rest of the room was so dark that it might have been underground. Delia's face changed. She moved her eyes and looked straight at Hervey, with her bold cynical gaze, the flame of the candle wavering in her eyes. She's alive, Hervey thought. ' Do you want something ? ' she asked, smiling. Delia winked at her. ' Whoops, dearie,' she said in a breathless whisper. She closed her eyes again and kept them closed. She had no further need of help.

' What's that ? Has she spoken ? '

' She's no more dead than you are,' Hervey laughed. Far less dead, she corrected herself. She stumbled back to her room and slept at once.

In the morning, going out to her work, she looked in Delia's bedroom. A big man, in a travelling coat down to his ankles, stood at the end of the bed.

It was the first time Hervey had seen Delia's husband. She knew that he lived mostly in Ireland—he was an officer in the Black and Tans—and her faint feeling of distaste for his profession strengthened to active enmity. She looked at him without speaking. He had a smooth face, the planes curiously flattened, nose fleshly and strong, narrow guarded eyes—a hard face, hard-mouthed and arrogant. He returned her gaze with an encouraging smile, which increased her dislike. Turning her back on him she spoke to the nurse, took one look at Delia, who was sleeping, her face grey in the daylight, and went out. Her heart quickened uncomfortably. As she stepped into the street she was trying to account for her dislike. It was unaccountable, a breath across a

mirror : it came, she thought, from the past—he had
reminded her a little of Captain Gage.   No—from the future,
she said.   But that was nonsense.   She hurried on, half
running to get away from the image of herself standing like a
stock before that inexplicably alarming figure.

CHAPTER XXII

TIME PASSES

In December of that year it came to Hervey that she had been in London two years and was not famous yet. She was sitting in the editorial room, correcting proofs of *The Week*. Renn at the other desk had raised his head and was staring at the window. She followed his glance. There was nothing to see except the sky, like a river of grey water, between the buildings. She jumped up, seized her coat, and went out. For an hour or more she walked eastwards, through the streets and squares in which half the world's wealth comes to report for service abroad. She passed the tall new offices of what had been, until she sold it, her grandmother's firm. An old shame dyed her cheeks. I asked her to give me work: I went there wearing my thick coat because its length made me, I thought, look older; when she snubbed me roughly I cried. Am I never to forget it? She felt pleased that the firm had been sold because there was no one, no Garton, Roxby, or Hervey, to carry it on. It was a just punishment. *I* could have carried it on, she said.

The sight of a top-hatted man stepping into a car outside the building infuriated her. Had there been a stone near her fingers she would have seized it. He was a usurper, and the lawful heir trudged past him with a crack in her shoes. She turned back, and half running, brushing against people in her impatience, she entered the room where David Renn was still staring at the window, as if he had not moved for an hour, and asked him if she could go to Danesacre for a few days.

'As long as you like,' David Renn said, without looking at her. 'Go there to-day and stay over Christmas.'

Her anger, discontent, fell off like a shadow passing; she was ashamed of them, of herself. I ought to stay with him, she thought. But she turned and went out of the room again —it was four o'clock, she would run across to Penn at his office, tell him that she was going, run home, pack, send a telegram, and take the night train to Danesacre. It meant four cold hours in the early morning waiting at York, but it was worth it. It saved a whole day.

When she came into Penn's room, her old room, it was empty, except for a young woman typing out letters at a desk near the window. My desk, Hervey thought. She spoke to the young woman, making use, as she did when she was nervous, of her dazzling smile. On this occasion it woke no answering warmth. The young woman only looked at her, with a cold inquisitive stare, and went on with her work. Hearing Penn on the stairs, Hervey went out of the room to meet him. She told him her news.

As she was going out she asked, struck through by an unpleasant feeling : ' Who is that girl in there ? '

' Girl ? ' Penn said. He smiled. ' She's the typist I share with another man. She admires me, because I brought her in here.' He could not refrain from telling her this. It gave him a strange quick pleasure, almost as though he were making a confession.

' Did you know her ? ' Hervey asked. She felt something unreal in his manner, under the jaunty voice. But what is it ? her mind asked. What is wrong with him ?

He said, No he had never set eyes on her until she came to be interviewed, then he had felt sorry for her. Why ? Oh—nothing. He laughed loudly again, and Hervey decided that it was all a lie ; for some reason, probably for no reason at all, he had made up this foolish story. She sighed impatiently and let it pass from her mind.

Penn went with her to King's Cross. A moment before the train moved he drew a flat parcel from his coat and gave it into her hand. It was a bag, a small leather handbag. Hervey did not care for it—it was not, she could see, good

leather—but she cried out with pleasure. She was touched
by his kindness.

'I thought I'd like to give you something, you haven't
got many things,' Penn said, gently and smiling.

Danesacre in winter is pinched between a grey jagged
sea and iron moors. The shops are decorated for Christmas
with a little coloured paper and evergreens and holly, and at
night they are brightly lit, some with fancy lights under the
coloured paper, so that there are pools of red, green, and
yellow light on the pavements, and the children press their
foreheads against the glass. The evening before Christmas
Hervey and her mother went out to see the shops. This was
what they had always done, from the beginning, and as she
walked down the steep streets and crossed the bridge over the
harbour, the water black and silent, with the lights from the
houses broken into it, she felt the strong excitement we feel
when some trivial thing we used as a child is put into our
hands. But it is not only excitement, it is pity, a deep wish
to be safe now as then, and recognition, more surprising than
any, that something was offered to us at that time which
cannot be taken away or destroyed. And it may happen
that the thrill of a lighted window in winter lasts longer
with us than any of the great emotions, of love or ambition,
and is perhaps the only one we shall keep at the end.

Mrs Russell was excited and very happy. She talked, a
thing she hardly ever did, of her youth in her mother's house
near Middlesbrough. Hervey had not seen this house, but she
knew that it was a great place and as splendid as her grandmother could make it. She thought of it as old and charming.
Actually it was neither, but for Sylvia Russell too, as for her
daughter, it had become more than a great house. It marked
the defeat she had prepared for herself and did not accept;
and each time she bought a chair or a curtain for her own
it was because it reminded her of one in her mother's house
and when she had it it was another advance, an inch, towards
an ever-receding glory.

'We girls liked Christmas because it was the only time

in the year we could be sure of keeping my mother with us,' Mrs Russell said. 'There were the presents—Clara spent weeks, months, making hers—almost always it was something quite unspeakable, a work-bag or a stool, such things as my mother never used—and then as like as not she pushed it out of sight instantly. I remember one Christmas when Clara made a dreadful woollen scarf, oh dreadful, and my mother's face when she took it, and then weeks afterwards we saw it being used to tie round some books that were going to the office. Poor Clarry. I was sorry for her then, but the truth is she has no idea how to manage anything.' She said this as if she had not managed her own life so that it had been a ceaseless fight to get less than a morsel of the fineness she craved.

'We had very little pocket-money,' she went on. 'My mother never thought that we needed any, and so we had to plan and scrape. Of course any shop would have served us, but we would as soon have set fire to our clothes as order anything we couldn't pay for at once. We were happy, though. We laughed a great deal, and rode about the moors. One summer I had a grey silk habit. It was the thickest silk you ever saw. I wore long black gloves with it.'

Her eyes were very bright, a bright pale blue. She glanced at her hands. The fingers were swollen with much work, the wrists thickened.

Hervey saw her looking at them. She felt a familiar rage and grief. Why have you grown old ? Why are you tired ? When her mother was like this, gay and yet so tired and finished, she felt as though a nerve were being drawn out of her own body. She pretended not to notice anything. 'You must have looked very fine,' she laughed.

'Grey always suited me,' Mrs Russell said.

'Why don't you have a grey dress for the spring ? '

'Yes I might do that,' her mother said. She considered. Was she, Hervey wondered, seeing only the other dress ?

'I'll give it you for your birthday,' she said, eagerly.

Mrs Russell would not agree at once. 'We'll see,' was

all she said. But the idea pleased her. The girl saw that,
and longed to give her something better than she had ever
had. 'When my ship comes in I'll buy you a fur coat,' she
cried.

Mrs Russell laughed. Hervey's presents were a joke in the
family. She would give away her own skin if she knew you
wanted it, her mother said. But her generosity was more
nerves than heart.

The next morning she woke early. Richard was still
asleep in his cot. She saw his face, the skin clear and delicate,
his eyelids weighted down with the black heavy lashes, and
she felt an old fear. I am utterly responsible for him, she
thought. She promised him again that he should have
everything, she would get him everything.

Lying in her bed, she could see as far as an older part of
the town, where they lived when she was a child. She saw
the roofs and the tops of trees, with fields between. Now
she began trying to trace the streets and to recall their names
and the look of the old houses. There was one street she
remembered where grass grew between the stones.

An exquisite happiness filled her as she looked at them
from this distance and tried to recall how they had seemed
to her. What was surprising was the silence. There were
no sounds in her memory, but all was still ; and in stillness
and in bright airs the child lived its tranced life. Surely one
day, she thought, a child will stand by the steps of Number 5
and look at the laburnum with my eyes. And she thought
that when that happened she would come to life again, and
the story would begin afresh. The narrow unfashionable
houses would see her again ; she would run down the hill
to the harbour, and the grass thrusting between the stones
would fill her with the old delight and surprise. Ah, then
I shall be happy, she thought.

CHAPTER XXIII

DAVID RENN GOES TO SEE HIS MOTHER

RENN spoke to Hervey in a sharp voice. ' Is this fellow Ridley a friend of yours ? '

' No, why ? ' Hervey said. She spoke anxiously, expecting that she had done wrong.

' We can't print another of his essays in *The Week*. The first was enough.'

' I haven't asked him for another,' Hervey said. She glanced over the pages. ' What is wrong with this one ? '

' Everything,' Renn said angrily. ' It's just another Now then, boys, all together, hip hip, what jolly dogs are we. I won't use it.'

' He's becoming important,' Hervey said, sighing. ' Can we afford to make an enemy of him ? '

' We can't afford his friendship,' Renn said. He looked at her with a light smile. ' Poor Hervey. You don't like failures, do you ? If I let you, you'd turn *The Week* into a glorious success. But it would have ceased to be an honest paper. Perhaps after all it isn't worth the trouble. But you haven't much public conscience, have you ? '

' I don't like being poor,' Hervey said.

Renn opened his mouth to deal with her, thought better of it, and got up. ' Finish off these proofs for me,' he said pleasantly. ' I'm going home.'

He went out and walked towards the Earlhams' flat. The lights were all lit in the streets. He passed a line of people waiting in the yellowish glare for one of the theatres. Did I once stand there ? he thought. I was just nineteen. He remembered buying a paper to read as he waited, because of

the words on the poster. Austrian Ultimatum. Is that all
I remember ? Six years is a long time.

He heard his name called. Turning, he saw a man who
had been his platoon sergeant in France. He came striding
towards Renn past the waiting lines. A leather strap over his
shoulders supported a tray filled with cheap sweets. 'What
are you doing with that thing ? ' Renn asked.

'It's my new trade,' the other man said, smiling. 'Help
yourself to a stick of chocolate.'

'Thanks,' Renn said. 'I never eat chocolate.' He put
his hand on the man's arm and turned him towards the
nearest café. It was a dark small room, with a Greek
proprietor, who did not object to shabby pedlars. When they
were seated, he noticed that his late sergeant was the colour
of grey wax. His clothes were thin and shabby, and he
wore a muffler in place of a shirt. 'What's happened to
you ? ' Renn asked.

'Nothing unusual. I hadn't a job. My old firm was very
polite to me, shook hands and all that, awfully glad you've
come safe out of it, my dear chap, sorry, unfortunately filled
your place when you left—your successor is a married man
with a family. But I'm married, I said. During the War.
I married in 1917. Splendid, splendid. You won't have any
difficulty in finding a job. Refer to us whenever you like.
Good-bye.'

'And did you ? ' Renn asked. He tried not to notice his
friend's hands. They were shaking so that he could not
hold his fork and it clattered to the floor. The little Greek
picked it up, wiped it absently on his sleeve, and handed it
back with a polite smile.

'Did I what ? I was out of work for sixteen months.
My wife went home in the end. Last week a fund, charity
for ex-soldiers, fitted me out with this thing. You buy the
chocolate from them and make a small profit if you sell the
lot.'

'Is it heavy ? '

'Try it.'

Renn placed the strap round his neck.   He went out,
leaving his sergeant to finish another mess of lentils and
meat, and walked alongside the queue.   One woman asked
him the price of the bars of chocolate.   He had forgotten
to ask, and answered Fourpence at random.   There were
sixteen bars and three boxes of chocolates marked one shilling.
That made about eight shillings' worth in all.   What was
the profit on it ?

'You're a nice one,' she cried angrily.   'Look, they're
marked threepence.   As plain as your nose.   I've a great
mind to give you in charge.'

'Don't do that,' Renn begged.   'I really made a mistake.
Have one for nothing instead.'

The woman looked at him with hatred but snatched the
packet he held out to her.   He waited to see whether she
would thank him.   She examined it in a cold silence.   He
went up and down between the queue and the street.   A boy
bought three pennyworth from him.   The strap dragged at
his shoulders and he felt horribly exposed.   The doors of
the theatre opened and now no one took any further notice
of him.   He saw a policeman at the side of the road and
thought it well to return quickly to the café.   'I didn't do
very well,' he said.   He folded a pound note and placed it on
the tray.

'You're very kind, but it's no use, you know,' the man
said.   He shivered a little.

'Nothing's any use,' Renn said.

'You're born and brought up—educated—I suppose that
cost the country something.   You even fight for them,
though that wasn't all bad.   In the end you're not wanted.
There's no room for you in the country.   What I want to
know is—why don't they kill you if you're nothing but a
nuisance ?   If they've nothing for me to do, if it's true I'm only
in the way, a disappointment to my wife, and no need for me
to live, why not painlessly get rid of me ? '   He spoke with
excitement.   'I could kill myself, of course, but, do you know,
I have a prejudice against that ?   Besides, I should have to

do it clumsily and as cheaply as possible. No, no, it's their responsibility, but they won't take it. Why ? '

A stout woman, followed by two others, stepped out of a car at the main entrance to the theatre. They were furred, jewelled, and so well made up that each face was as like the other two as the three balls of dung in the road.

' It seems there's plenty of room for those women, but not for a healthy man of twenty-eight,' Renn said. ' Are you healthy, by the way ? '

The other only smiled. ' Do you remember coming back from Gommecourt that night ? '

' You were carrying their rifles for three men,' Renn said.

' They were heavier than this tray. When I take it off I feel that my neck has broken.'

They parted outside the café. Now I shall have to avoid Shaftesbury Avenue at this time, Renn thought. He hated himself for having thought it. He looked back. His old sergeant was being moved on by the policeman. Renn walked quickly away, uncertain now whether he wanted to see Louis and Rachel. They would talk to him about a Labour government and how in time everything would be changed and become decent. But how will that save my sergeant ? he cried. In time he'll be dead—or too done to care.

He crossed the road and stepped on to a bus. With luck, he thought, I can catch the last train to Hitchin. He caught it, and sat looking through the window. In the dusk, houses, then trees and fields, slipped past him like driftwood swirling in brown water. It was dark when he walked down the road from the station and stood outside his mother's house. There was a card in the window. He stepped closer to read it. Plain Sewing Done Here and Mending. He opened the door and whistled, then walked into the sitting-room. His mother was seated with a book in front of her at the table in the window, her tongue pressed between her teeth, as a child reads. She's not understanding a word of it, he thought. He glanced at the book, and saw that it was a schoolbook, one of his own, a dryasdust history of Europe in the Dark Ages.

His mother looked at him without surprise. ' I was just going to write to you,' she exclaimed. ' Luckily for us I made bread this morning.' She closed her book with an air of relief and came round the table to him. She was so moved that she forgot to kiss him.

' You're still too thin,' she said, smiling. ' You ought to live with me. I miss you, too. There's no one to answer my questions. Even before he had his stroke your father was not very talkative, as you know. Do you know, this is a terrible book you studied, Davy. It says they burned whole villages in France and when the wars ended people were starving.'

' We have certainly progressed a good deal,' Renn said. ' I never noticed it before.'

' You haven't changed,' his mother said. ' Last Monday your headmaster stopped me in the street to ask after you. He said you were always his best pupil, but he was afraid that you had no respect for authority.'

' He was wrong, I had too much,' Renn said, smiling.

Mrs Renn was gaily opening cupboards and setting plates and knives on the table. ' What do you think ? ' she laughed, ' I found your bowler hat in the loft yesterday. Do you remember when you left school and went to work in London ? It was a few months before the War. You came home to see me in July and when I opened the door there you were, wearing the bowler hat. You looked frightful in it—like a little boy playing at shops. I was afraid to ask you about it. Afterwards—when you enlisted—I put it in the loft, thinking, now he'll soon forget it.'

' I remember it quite well,' Renn said. ' I bought it as soon as I went to London. I thought I needed one, and I couldn't wear my cap in Regent Street, could I ? '

His mother looked into the cupboard again. ' Would you like me to make an omelette ? There are four eggs. My left-hand neighbour gave them to me for the socks I mended. Her husband wears five pairs a week. He's very anxious about his looks. At night, she says, he places strips of sticking-plaster over his worst wrinkles. I suppose he has to in these times. You don't tell me anything in your letters. Are you happy ? Is your work going on well ? Now that you are an editor you will be sought after by other people. Do you like that ? '

' Very much indeed,' Renn answered.

CHAPTER XXIV

HERVEY LOSES A PART OF THE GROUND GAINED

1. *Three days in August 1921*

THAT year the summer was dry and hot. The commons round London smouldered and the streets smelled of earth. It reminded you that the paving stones covered what had been fields in a livelier England.

Hervey's northern-bred bones melted in this heat. She grew thinner and lazy, and formed the opinion that London is no place for a Christian soul.

Penn told her that his holiday had been allotted to him for the second week of the month. He went to spend it alone in Dorset. The day after he came home again there was forwarded a letter addressed to him in Dorset. It was laid with Hervey's, and happening to glance at him as she gave it up, she saw a most curious look on his face. She saw it—and immediately forgot it. It meant no more to her eyes than a change of light on the wall. Penn took the letter to read it in his own room.

She went to bed and fell asleep, being tired. Towards the morning, but while it was still dark, she awoke suddenly.

A thought had spoken in her ear. She was asleep when it began speaking and awake before the words were all out. That letter is important for you, it said. She lay for a moment still and awake. The stillness was as it were visible, enclosing her bed and the room between its hands. Also her mind was still. She was vividly conscious of her body lying in the bed.

After this moment, she got up, without reflection, and went into Penn's room. She felt her way to his coat, which was on the chair by his bed, felt in the pockets for the letter, took and fetched it to her room, and read it, standing with her hand on the bed-rail. It was a short letter, the words poor and foolish. But it made so clear that at first she did not see it that Penn had been a long time the writer's lover and they had spent the first week of his holiday together. There will be other letters, she thought. She went back to Penn's room, not troubling to be quiet or careful, and peered along the shelves until she found a collar-box stuffed with letters. When she was taking it Penn half awoke, and she spoke to him. He went to sleep again.

Again in her room, she looked at the letters until she found one signed in full, 'Len Hammond,' but did not read them. For the first time an overwhelming excitement seized her. She felt charged with it, and as though she would burst apart. Also for the first time since she awoke, she began to look at what had happened. She cried out, 'I'm free, I'm free.' Then she fell on her knees and prayed to be kept from mean thoughts. Her prayer formed itself: 'I had to steal these letters because Penn would not have told me any of the truth—but don't, my God, let me be mean in using it.' She felt cold. Suddenly she began crying. Tears rushed from her and fell on to her hands. She was torn with them and shook from head to foot. 'But I'm old, I'm old.'

She got into the bed for warmth. She did not know why she had cried but it was at this moment, when she was saying 'I'm old,' that a much younger Hervey began to take possession of her. This girl—she was about nineteen—did not know that Hervey had come to an end of her husband and of her love and respect and passion for him.

Hervey was always methodical. She lay there, stretched out stiff and straight on her back, and planned, not vaguely, but most precisely and patiently, what she must do, as if it were a matter of life and death that she should say this, and do that, from the moment of rising. I must sleep now, she thought. But when she closed her eyes it was as though she had turned on a light in a curtained room. Her mind was clenched on itself. She was forced to repeat her plans over and over, until her brain felt as though it had grown to her skull.

Now the light began to stream into the room, but she was still so cold that she could not help shuddering. It came to her to go into Penn to get warm.

Penn half roused when she came in, then, feeling the cold of her body, he drew her closer to him and tried to warm her. His hands moved over her. 'Do you mind?' he asked suddenly.

She was seized with grief. She would have wept again, but forced herself to be quiet. Penn felt the effort of her body and said gently: 'What's the matter, my love?'

'Nothing, nothing.' She was overcome with shame for her act of treachery.

After their breakfast together she went out as usual but did not go to the office. She believed that the girl was living at Tonbridge in Kent. She went directly to the station and looked up the trains to Tonbridge. One started in half an hour. She sat down to wait, her hands folded. Now and then her lips moved as she rehearsed carefully questions she would ask. Was it because she was tortuous or because she distrusted him, that the idea of questioning Penn himself did not occur to her? Above all, I must be calm and polite, she thought. She was pleased to find that she had so much lucidity. It seemed a proof that she was not much hurt.

How strongly and clearly I am thinking, she thought. It was true, but she did not know that she had gone mad.

At Tonbridge she stood trembling in a station telephone booth looking up the Hammonds. There were only two in the book, one a butcher. She called on the butcher first. His name was not Hammond and he had no daughters. The streets were untidy with the traffic of a small town and so airless that the sunlight stood in her way like a wall. She kept asking people to direct her to Dean Road. It was outside the town, and when she reached the house and found there an old rude woman she did not know what to do. Her tongue felt thick and she had trouble in speaking. ' Do you know any other Hammonds living in Tonbridge ? ' ' No ! ' She went back to the station, and to London.

For a long time she trudged about the streets in the sun, uncertain what to do. She felt very hungry and went into a small café. As soon as she had sat down she began to tremble, so violently that she was afraid people would see it. She ordered tea and bread and butter. When it came she drank eagerly but her throat closed against the food. She got a mouthful of the bread and had to put it out into her handker-chief when she thought no one was looking.

In the early evening she was walking across the Green Park and saw T. S. Heywood at her elbow. ' I had to run after you,' he grumbled. He looked at her. ' What's the matter ? '

' Nothing, I'm hot,' Hervey said. She spoke slowly because each word had to be dragged from a great depth.

He made her sit down. He noticed that she kept putting her hand to her throat. ' Do you know a good lawyer ? ' she said.

' I can send you to mine. Who d'you want punished ? '

' Why, no one,' Hervey smiled. She yielded to a strong impulse. ' I find I can divorce Penn and I don't know where to set about it.'

T.S. did not answer at once. He felt a prick of annoyance that she was taking it badly. But she's unreasonable, he thought, irritated.

Almost for the first time he had the feeling that she was a woman : a female creature. In the same moment he wanted hotly to comfort her. He laid his hand on her knee. ' My dear Hervey,' he said tenderly.

Hervey pushed his hand off and snarled at him. He was horribly startled and thought, She's more like a young wolf. He felt that if his hand had been any closer she would have bitten it. It put him at ease with her again : he asked no questions, wrote down the address of his lawyer for her, and told her to mend the sleeve of her dress.

Q

That was like Philip, she said.

She went home, talked to Penn a little, and went to bed.

During her sleep her mind seemed to be feeling its way quickly through darkness. In this forced march it came to this memory and to that, until her life came about her like a swift heavy rush of earth down a hillside carrying away villages and the roots of trees.

The next day was Sunday. Penn asked her to go out, but it was too hot, she said, too hot. She could not face so burning a light. Indeed the sky was white hot and the sun pressed down on the streets at the level of faces like a sheet of brass. In the evening she could not longer hold in, and she went into Penn's room and stood by the table, her head thrust forward, and said: 'Why didn't you tell me you were in love with this Hammond?' Penn did not say anything. He stood at the other side of the table and looked at her. 'If you'll tell me about it, I can divorce you and you can have her in peace.'

To her astonishment Penn began to cry. 'Don't you love me, then?' he said. He wiped his tears with the sides of his hands.

Hervey frowned, trying hard to understand him. 'Please, what has that to do with it?'

'Don't divorce me—don't leave me,' Penn said.

'I thought you preferred her.'

'Good God no.'

Hervey leaned against the table. 'Do you want to live with her?'

'Not at all,' Penn said.

She was by now quite out of her reckoning. 'I think you had better tell me who Len Hammond is,' she said, staring.

Penn did not speak at once. He removed his pince-nez, wiped them thoroughly with his handkerchief, dried his face with it, adjusted the glasses to his nose, looked at her through them, and said gently: 'The girl I used to dance with in Canterbury. I told you about it at the time. She was a V.A.D. then.'

Hervey felt a cold excitement, the pure satisfaction of the mind in completing a figure. Her body trembled, dissatisfied. 'It's been nearly three years, then.' She grew crimson. 'How did you—when you left the Air Force—did you write to her? How did you see each other?'

After a silence Penn said: 'I got her a job in the office. She's gone now—left a month ago: her mother wanted her at home.' He paused. 'You saw her there once.'

Hervey thought she had been struck on the breast. 'Oh!' She stepped back, feeling for the support of the wall. 'When I asked you, Who is that?' She spoke so softly that it was as if she were sighing, alone in the room. 'Oh, I didn't know being deceived was like this.'

'Don't be childish, Hervey,' Penn said.

'That day it was I went home. I suppose you were with her then. You would be with her that night.'

'I suppose so.'

'You must have laughed at me, the two of you. My coming in like that—and asking—that was a good joke.'

'Don't be foolish, my dear.'

She tried to defend herself against the word. 'You both knew, and I didn't. You looked at me together, both knowing.' She clapped her hand to her mouth.

Penn threw up his hands. 'I can't argue with you in this state.'

'Don't try,' she said swiftly. 'I shall begin to laugh at you. You look very silly yourself, undressing in front of your typist. You're so long and thin.'

'Much obliged,' Penn said stiffly.

Hervey felt miserable again. 'What I don't like is your creeping between bed and bed,' she said. 'Why did you have to fetch her to London, Penn? Tell me, tell me now.'

'I wanted to do something for her,' Penn said. He frowned at her absently. After a moment he added: 'I can't see that it was any worse to have her in London. After all, I'd had her. I couldn't alter that, could I? Mind you, I didn't mean it to start again.'

Hervey looked at him.

'I thought I was strong enough to see her without falling, as they say. In fact, though you won't believe me, I had decided to prove it, by bringing her up here and not touching her. Rash of me, as it turned out—but there you are.'

Such dreadful words, Hervey thought. She pressed her hands on her chest. 'You could have given her up when you were demobilised.'

'Yes, I could have given her up. I suppose I didn't want to.' He looked at her to see how she was taking it.

Hervey sat down. She pressed her hands on her knees to hide their state from him. 'It was worse,' she said. Penn came across the room to her. 'Oh Hervey, I was mad,' he said quickly. She smiled to keep him from touching her. 'Nothing of the sort. You couldn't stay mad for three years. Or make so many neat plans.'

'If I'd known I was going to risk losing you through it——'

'You haven't lost anything,' Hervey said instantly. 'You threw it away.' This phrase comforted her, but not for long: running back and forth, her mind snatched a straw from the vast heap in front of it. 'That man you made me ask here— who was your sergeant. Did he know that you were—that you had her then?'

'In Canterbury? Yes he knew.' Penn hesitated. 'I couldn't help that. When we moved to Lympne she came to my room sometimes.'

The words started up a dozen frightful ideas in her. 'When you were in Canterbury, you asked me to stay with you one week-end,' she said, trembling.

'You enjoyed it,' Penn said.

'I wish I hadn't gone,' Hervey cried. She sprang up. 'It's too much. I think he must have smiled. The next week-end it would be your—your concubine.' As red as fire she rushed out of the room.'

Her own room had a chill empty look, as if she had been away from it for a long time. It has changed, she thought. She began to walk up and down. She arranged the curtains.

She set the chairs at a fresh angle. She looked into books and pulled drawers open.

But this was what her mind had been doing since yesterday. It had dragged out so much that there was nothing now but a litter of old dresses, books, broken shoe-laces, letters, pieces of torn ribbon, between this moment and the one nine years ago in which she had said—it was growing dark and they had been quarrelling, and she had offended him—' I love you, Penn. Didn't you know ? ' Poor Hervey, he had said ; and seized with shame, she thought, It was all a mistake, I shouldn't have said it. She could scarcely see him, but in the darkness they touched ; she did not kiss him, she was too clumsy, she bent her head awkwardly and felt his touch, there, on her right temple.

' But don't come in here, not into this room,' Hervey said aloud. She walked quicker, she was almost running, to shake off the awkward young creature. It was useless. She came in, she listened, she saw what had happened. But she understood nothing. She supposed that it was happening at the same moment as the other scene, and she suffered as if her lover had turned from her to the other woman that evening, under her very nose.

Hervey ran to the shelf where she kept her unfinished novel, tore out a blank page, and began to make notes of her feelings. She wrote down what she had said and felt. As soon as she had finished and laid the paper away, she burst into tears.

Another thought jumped into her mind. She dried her face on her sleeve and ran into Penn's room. He was standing looking through the window with an unhappy air. What can he be looking at ? she thought. She tugged his arm. ' You didn't come straight to me when you were demobilised. You stayed with her first. How long ? '

Penn cleared his throat thoroughly. He blinked at her. ' About a week, I think. Does it matter ? '

' Why didn't you write to me that you were falling in love with her ? I would have come—yes—and argued with you.'

' I'm sure you would,' Penn said.

' Running to a person called Len, behind my back,' Hervey
sneered. She spoke in a loud rough voice. ' How was it
you didn't warn me ? ' He is a stone, she thought ; he has no
kindness for me.

' You said—you must remember, Penn ?—you would tell
me certainly and instantly.'

' I know I did. But it isn't possible. And I believed you
were very pleased with your life. One doesn't reason these
things out, you know.'

' There must,' Hervey said, ' come a moment when you
decide.' The past rose in her again and choked her lungs.
Your enemies are much kinder to you than your friends,
she thought—you expect treachery from them and sometimes
you get something better.

' Oh no,' Penn said. ' Oh no. Dear me, no. By that
time it's a great way too late to reason about it.' He saw her
face and said hurriedly : ' You know, you're capable of it
yourself, poor Hervey.'

' Not of such *careful* meanness,' Hervey cried. She looked
at him, not troubling to hide her agony—it had made her
look old, with blotched wrinkled eyelids.

' I thought it would be all right to have her when you
weren't there.'

He did not know what to say to her. This is getting me
down, he thought. He watched furtively her hands, trembling
and the palms pressed over her knees.

' You must have been much in love,' Hervey whispered.

' That's where you're wrong, my dear. I loved her very
moderately.'

Hervey was struck with despair and surprise. ' You didn't
love her and you let her do this to me ? ' she said, staring.
' What a lot you must think of me ! '

He saw that she had lost the last remnants of her sense of
reality. He wanted to help her—he was in need of help
himself, this was very painful to him—but she was beyond
help. He felt sorry for her. He moved closer and tried to

put an arm round her shoulder. ' I'd give anything to undo this,' he said. There was a great deal he could have said, he had thought about it, but he saw she was not in a state to listen. He tried.

' I'm not ashamed of what happened. There was nothing mean about it—about my feelings for her. If you're imagining anything like that—I didn't pretend that I wanted to marry her. She was happy to have me on any terms, and I suppose I was too. But if I'd thought for one moment that you would find out, and be hurt, I wouldn't have had anything to do with her.'

' How can you go on talking when I'm feeling like this ! '

' I think you're taking up a wrong attitude to it. I haven't very much respect for conventional morality.'

Hervey's mind gave a short blind jerk, like a laugh. ' Were you defying herd morality ? ' she cried. ' You didn't achieve much except herd immorality, did you ? It's not unusual.'

His anger flared up for a moment. ' I'm delighted you feel like that about it.'

She had punished herself. ' Yes, it's usual enough,' she said in a low voice. She tried to become calm. ' Yet I suppose all women think, It won't happen to me. I suppose men feel the need for changes. I myself—I felt it myself. It's a pity. It spoils things.' She smoothed her dress. ' Isn't it queer ? I'm poisoned with jealousy.' After a moment, she said : ' I can't help knowing that it would have been better, easy to bear, if you had told me. Being startled or disappointed is one thing—women should be able to face that, I think. Being lied to and deceived is something different, worse.' Looking at him, she felt in herself a flow of hatred and bitterness. She wanted to hurt him, to humiliate him for ever and ever. At the same time (it was her mother's harsh voice) she thought, There never was a fool but found some woman ready to be a bigger fool.

' I've always respected you, my dear.'

' Nonsense,' Hervey said. She felt a contempt for him. ' You don't respect anyone you're so easily able to deceive.'

They must often have laughed together over me, she said to herself. Her heart seemed to nip her—she thought for an instant that she would faint. Her sense of humour awoke in time to save her : well, you are a pretty figure of fun, it said. At once, as soon as she thought it, she saw her mother standing there, in a ruched dress. She was angry. 'To go out,' she said, 'to swing on the gate, deliberately, on the Sabbath. You should be *ashamed* of yourselves. I should think you're the laughing-stock of the neighbourhood.' And we believed it, she thought, half laughing, half pitying the heartsick child.

'It's in your own mind,' Penn said.

'You don't know what's in my mind.' She looked at him, pulling at her mouth. 'I might, you can't tell, can you, be thinking about the first time you were with her. Did you think of me ?'

'Don't be silly,' Penn said.

Hervey felt deathly tired.

She stumbled away from him to her room, this time locking the door, and went to bed. Lying down was like falling into a cloud of blackness. She fell, down, and down. The darkness was as deep as the sea ; it lay all round, above, below her. She could hear Penn speaking outside the door. His voice was an immense distance away. She was not being stubborn, she would have answered it, but she was not able to move. She lay bound hand and foot on the floor of the sea. Soon she heard and saw nothing.

In the morning she felt her mind clear and empty, except for a core of hardness. She wrote a brutal letter to the girl's mother. Searching the letters, she had come on the right address, and she took pleasure in placing her sentences like a row of stones. She carried this letter as far as the post office, hesitated, and tore it up.

She felt relieved when she had done it, and yet angry, since she had wanted to harm the girl. But it was no use. She threw the pieces of the letter into a gutter. Women should be kind to women, she said to herself. This gave her no comfort. She was vexed that she had thought it. She stamped her foot, and imagined the girl disgraced (by some other hand), and coming to her for help. She would behave with generosity, yet without mitigating her scorn.

2. *For a time Hervey behaves badly*

A week later she climbed a flight of uncarpeted stairs to the lawyer's office and entered an anteroom and then a room of the austerest shabbiness and gentility. He was a dry kind man. The kindness was as impersonal with him as his boots. It was impossible to believe that he had any life outside this room in which he sat to hear confidences.

He made Hervey sit before him in an armchair covered with black leather, not to show the stains. Now and again he smiled. It was neither pleasant nor unpleasant. It was like talking to a stuffed man.

There was a clerk seated at a desk in the other corner. He was making notes of her answers, and from time to time he bent down and scratched his leg. She felt empty, as though her life were running out of the corners of her mouth. 'Where were you living at that time, Mrs Vane?' The kitchen of her house in Liverpool came and with a ludicrous flapping of clothes hung drying in the garden, vanished, and its place was filled by another room, and another, and another. And in each of them she was living still, as, and with the same impulse, she would until she died, and fell from her mind into the earth. 'When did you suspect that something was wrong?' 'Have you always lived happily?' If I could answer that, Hervey thought, I should have an answer to everything in my life.

'How did you gain possession of these letters?'

'I stole them.'

The lawyer smiled very slightly; a propitious and unnatural smile. He turned over the pages of the letters. 'Letters of this kind are all alike,' he remarked. He handed them to his clerk, who tied a length of pink tape round them.

'I must tell you that they're not evidence against your husband, Mrs Vane, although they were written to him. They're evidence only against the writer.'

He explained to her that—such was the law—she must write to her husband and ask him to live with her again. (But he has never left me, Hervey thought. She stared straight before her, her face wooden.) Mr Vane, the lawyer went on, would do what was expected (he coughed dryly) of a husband in these circumstances. What is that? He would refuse to return. 'I shall ask you to write a draft letter to your husband, and to let me see it.' 'What shall I say?' Hervey asked him. She hid her alarm. 'Just use your own best words,' he answered: 'I don't want to put words into your head. That would destroy the spontaneity.' And then? 'Then we shall bring an action against him for restitution of conjugal rights; he will decline to comply with the order—giving you fresh evidence of adultery. Then we shall begin the action for divorce.'

'Conjugal is a dreadful word,' Hervey said. She moved to the edge of her chair, and only then noticed a large splash of ink on one stocking. You will be the laughing-stock of the neighbourhood, she thought. She got up.

'Is that all?' It was like dropping a stone into a shaft— she listened to it to hear the echo in herself. 'You mustn't see or be seen with your husband,' said the lawyer. He walked with her across the room, and steadied her when she knocked her awkward ankle against a chair.

There were two flights of stairs, bare, worn hollow in the tread of the stair. She placed her foot carefully in the centre of each smooth dip, to be like all the others who had come here. With a dreadful clarity she saw that she was to blame for everything. I have been selfish, arrogant, disloyal, she thought. I have failed through unkindness. To have had so much—days, nights, hunger, ecstasy, cold on hands wet from washing clothes, plans, money in a thin purse—and to see it tied round carelessly with a bundle of papers, as if it were nothing. It was indecent. She thought of Penn. My love, you are no more to blame than I am, she cried. She was filled with dismay at the notion of turning him into the street. It was too callous. It was troublesome.

At the foot of the lawyer's stairs she turned. No one had been following her. ,

She went on, and trotted about the streets for a long time, then went home. Penn was there, waiting for her to warm coffee for them on her gas ring.

He listened with a defensive smile, then said gently : ' Do you want me to go ? '

' No,' Hervey said. There was so much to say she could not say it. She held her tongue.

' Don't send me off, Hervey.' He sat down. The very way he sat was an appeal.

She felt—but she had felt it in the lawyer's room—that she had no heart for this scheming and lying. But she would not put Penn at his ease at this time. She was afraid, cold. I must be very sensible and calm, she told herself.

She felt too deeply ashamed to admit her weakness to that dry lawyer. She thought he would despise her. In a short time he sent her a copy of some long document he called her proof. She did not read it, only looked in it to see whether it was recorded that she stole the letters. It was not. In a note the lawyer reminded her that she was to draft a letter for her husband. Now was the time to say, I can't go on. He will laugh at me with the clerk, she thought. She drafted the letter imploring Penn (he was in the next room) to return, and submitted it.

A day later she had it back—two of her phrases had been corrected in pencil in a pinched hand. She felt sharply mortified. It seems there is a style in these letters, she thought.

She put the letter aside. If she could have forgotten it, forgotten the whole, by losing a finger, she would, at this time, have cut it off. The days passed, with no ease for her— since a part of her mind was beside itself with jealousy. She did not call it that.

She forced Penn to tell her what had happened between

them. 'Where did you stay together?' She avoided the
girl's name.

'Which was the first time?'

'What did you say?'

'Did you talk of me?' She thought that if she knew
everything, the intimate details, of his life with the other girl,
she would cease to be humiliated by it.

She turned the past out, as if it were a bottomless untidy
cupboard, in search of facts. They were rods to her back.
She would be in some place with Penn and ask him in a
quiet detached voice whether he had brought the girl there,
and which day. She cleaned his mind out of all he remembered. Then she would go back in her own mind and try
to discover where she had been on that day.

Penn thought she was possessed. She would be in her
room laughing with him, and suddenly, with barely a change
of look, she would start her questions.

'Did you any time feel unhappy?'

'Certainly I did.' After a moment he added self-
consciously: 'Do you really think it would have been any
more decent if I had refrained? He that looketh upon a
woman. Eh?'

There was too much simplicity and grossness in Hervey
to leave her accept this. 'No one can control thoughts,'
she said. 'They come in, they go out. You can control
your body.'

'But why should you, my dear girl? Why should you?'

'There are times when I can't bear it,' Hervey said. She
spoke quickly and roughly, not raising her voice. He could
see how her face would be when she was old, the bones of the
cheeks jutting, and the flesh sunk. 'I think of you going to
her when I was with you. Of your seeing me off and going
away to her. And I can't put it right. I wish I could tear
out my brain that goes on thinking of it.'

Penn was seized with exasperation and weariness. He
stood up. 'I can't bear it either,' he exclaimed. 'I must
get out, out of this house.'

Hervey hung on his arm to keep him. 'Only tell me one more thing. I'll never ask you anything again.'

'What is it?'

'That first leave, when you came here to stay with me. Two years since. You didn't come to me at once. You brought her up with you. No, don't say anything—it's in one of her letters.'

'What can I do?'

'It's true, then.'

'I suppose it's true, if you read it. Why do you go on thinking and thinking, Hervey? You can't put it right. You've just said so.'

'Do you think I'm old? Am I too clumsy, plain?'

'Good God, how old are you? Twenty-six? You're acting like a schoolgirl in this. You're not plain, you look fine—when you're not crying, or punishing me.'

'Then why did you go to her before me? Can't you explain it to me so that I understand it? I can bear what I understand?'

'I don't know why. For pity's sake, let it rest now, Hervey.'

'I will, I will. Only answer me one question.'

Penn propped himself on the door, waiting. He was sorry for her, and a little unhappy; and sorry for himself. She was more to him, and needed, than anyone. He hoped earnestly she would soon forget what had happened, so that they could live in peace. It's always something with her, he thought, half amused. Before this she wanted a better sort of life; when we were in Liverpool it was Richard—Richard must have the best, he must have this, and have this, he must have everything; as soon as this is over it will be something else: she has no sense of proportion, and no patience—believe me, she hasn't got used to being alive, he thought.

'Did she travel to London with you, when you were demobilised?'

'No. Certainly not.'

' When did she come ? '

' She came as soon as I had found work for her.   I'd promised her to do what I could in that line.   She isn't happy at home.   I was sorry for her, I wanted to help her.'

' Did you go to meet her ? '

' No.'

' I suppose you were awfully pleased to see each other again,' Hervey said.

' I suppose so.'

' Did you stay with her at once ? '

' I can't remember.'

'Think.'

' I can't think.   Wait.   No, I didn't stay with her until the week after.   You were in Danesacre.'   Hervey put her hand over her mouth.   ' There, you see,' Penn said, not unkindly : ' you drive me until I wish I was dead, or deaf, and all you do by it is hurt yourself.   Why can't you let it end ? '

' Where did you take her that time ? '

He told her.

The next evening she took the train to Henley, found out the hotel, and walked in front of it for an hour.   Each time the door opened she caught a sight of the hall.   There were chairs and palms : the staircase went out of it to the left. She became conscious of glances.   She turned and went back. As soon as she was at home she fastened the door of her room and went to bed.   She meant to think calmly, to smile, to fall quickly asleep.   She saw them drive up to the hotel. The door opened outwards.   They crossed the hall, passing the chairs and the ridiculous palms.   A servant had their luggage.   Now they were writing their names—Mr and Mrs Vane.   Did they look sidelong at each other, and smile ? She went with them up the stairs ; there was a corridor ; a door opened, and closed.   No, I can't bear it, she thought. She turned, pressing her face into the pillow.   Scalding tears ran over her cheeks.   ' I must stop, I must stop,' she said. Why have I no pride ?   Her tears were endless.   They ceased and began again. The skin of her cheeks was made sore with them. She sat up. In the darkness she leaned against the wall. She struck her head on it, again and again.

3. *Hervey forms a grave decision*

She had not the hardness of mind to leave Penn. Her heart failed when she thought of living for the rest of her life without him, without anyone. She was much afraid of loneliness.

There were, too, the practical difficulties, the dividing out of their books, the scheming. These seemed to her to need at least as desperate an effort and a hardness as the other.

Towards the end of September—that was five weeks after the first time—she saw the lawyer again. This time there was no clerk listening. With a little anxiety she explained that she did not want to go on. ' It takes too long. There are too many expedients.'

' Perhaps it is so,' said the lawyer.

' I am sorry to disappoint you,' Hervey said.

He looked at her with his blank quietness. ' I'll have a parcel made of the letters.'

' Would you destroy them for me ? ' Hervey said. ' It would be very obliging. You understand that if I have them I might not destroy them. I might do something mean with them.' She glared at him.

' I can't destroy them. I'll keep them in my safe if you like.' He was smiling and unemphatic. He may have thought she was as eccentric as she was shabby. (The bill he sent her was a good balance between legality and mercy.)

When that was done she felt that she had wasted time and money. She was sore in mind. Half of her was relieved that she had not to scheme and visit lawyers, the other half was in a mood to punish anyone. She insulted Penn. He had kissed her, stroking her face, and said : ' I'll do anything you want, my darling.' He was deeply moved and happy : ' I promise you.'

'You promise!' Hervey said. The thought that was always on the watch, to nip her—that he had shared his leaves between her and the girl—squeezed her sharply. With it she lost control of her tongue. She stripped from herself the last rags of decency and human sense. At the end of this spectacle—it had not lasted more than a few minutes— Penn left her and went sadly, and with a certain dignity, to bed. After a time she went to him and apologised humbly. He forgave her. She hurried to her own room, wrote out as much of what she had said as she could remember, and slept.

When she was eight years old, her mother went with her husband to Buenos Aires—going out to the Plate, as they say in Danesacre. She left Hervey at a woman's small school. During the days Hervey did not think of her mother. She was a stubborn child, thinking her own thoughts, not easy to manage. The woman left her much alone. At night, as soon as she was in bed, she began to cry, hard and quietly, and cried herself to sleep. This happened every night of the five months Mrs Russell was away from her children. She was not thinking as she took her clothes off and got into bed, but in a few minutes the image of her mother, as clear and sharp as a ghost, entered the room, and the child began her persistent helpless crying. After the first week the woman gave up trying to silence her. 'She's as stubborn as a pig. I doubt if she's right,' she said. She had tried to punish her by shutting her in her room without food : after eight hours she went in, with milk and a plate of bread ; Hervey took them from her and sent them crashing to the floor against the wall.

What violence—of spirit or flesh—worked on the child worked again in the young woman. It was almost a year before Hervey slept without crying. In the day stolid and careless, David Renn's faithful sergeant or servant, whom he overworked. At night as soon as she was in bed the memory of this scene or of that—with what she knew and could invent—leapt at her mind. Its claws worked in. She tried not to think. She thought of sharp phrases, wrote them, without waiting to light the gas, on a page she would in the morning add to the small pile of them on her shelf. None of it helped.

Yet she formed the opinion that mental agony is easier to bear than physical. This was when David Renn sat with the sweat running off him, speechless. He was so thin you could think it was his skeleton aching and sweating.

4. *She begins to come to her wits*

Hervey knew that if she were to go away for a time, and not to see Penn, she would be cured both of him and of sorrow. It was the seeing him every day, with the thoughts and memories this bred, made time and her thoughts turn back in her. She even knew that she had been growing out of him, when this happened and put her back eight years, to the first year of their marriage. (Even in those days she had had more passion and intelligence, and less sense, than younger girls.) If she could go away now she would be cured certainly. But she could find the courage to go away only if she had ceased to care what he did, and then she would not need to go.

She would be walking in a street, and some common thing —perhaps a girl hanging on a man's arm and smiling into his face—would drive a thought through her as if certain thoughts are no easier than a twitch of the nerves. Each time this happened she thought : I shall never become used to it.

This month—it was October—Penn's father died suddenly, and he slept a week in his mother's house. Now alone, Hervey took the unfinished novel from its cupboard. She was a little embarrassed by it, as if it were a friend lost sight of before the War and discovered years afterwards talking about his cabbages. The young woman whose husband was unfaithful to her had not changed a muscle. Hervey scowled at her. Now you shall suffer, she said. But first I must read my notes.

R

This brought on a fever. She clapped her hat on and went out to cool her cheeks in the air. It was turning to mist in the dusk, so that a street of houses only a short distance away changed body and colour and appeared as a range of blue hills on the near sky. Hervey looked at it and (such is the devious and wilful character of the mind) thought, There is a contemptible sight of vanity mixed in my feeling for Penn. If there were not, I should instantly have forgiven him. There is no such thing as forgiveness. I should have put it away and forgotten it. Perhaps there is no cure for jealousy— but time. Nothing lasts. Not even a great sorrow. I could have sent him away, she thought, looking at a scarlet bus rushing away out of sight. The truth is—(she was for ever beginning a thought or a remark with the words ' the truth is,' but her mind, restless and inquisitive as a cat, contradicted itself sometimes at once ; Penn said that she was dishonest)— Penn is my young days, he is my weakness.

The word brought her to a sudden stop. She blushed hotly.

I am a detestable monster, she exclaimed.

She would never hear of the American again : he had not kissed her a dozen times; yet, there, but for the grace of——. It should have made me forgive Penn, she cried. Her shoe-lace had come undone and she had to stoop to fasten it. There was a way of tying them so that they stayed tied— Philip had shown her, but she had forgotten. It was nothing, but she felt horribly guilty. Forgive me, she said to Philip.

She knotted it up somehow and went on. What I do is always right and explicable, she thought. If Jess Gage was a sin, I sinned against myself. Her mind flooded with light suddenly. It was my very sin, she exclaimed : I took it under my protection. I repented and I forgave myself. Ugh ! I don't like the look of Penn's sins ; they have a sly look, tawdry, greasy. I am vindictive, I keep grudges, she thought ; I have an unforgiving mind. I know well that I ought to forgive Penn. Damme, I can't feel it. Philip, my darling, how you would laugh at me.

Say what you like, she cried, it is more humiliating to have been deceived for a year than for an hour, for three years than for one.

She turned and ran home. The thought of the smooth empty pages in her notebook had become irresistible.

The morning after Penn came home he came into her room in his shirt. He had his trousers over his arm. He asked her to mend the pocket. While she sewed, he walked up and down, talking. His long thin legs made her smile. Naked, they had a foolish air. She saw him approach Miss Hammond in just this state. Her lips tingled. Tears started to her eyes as she began to laugh. She laughed, and bent herself forward over her sewing, laughing, and wiping her eyes. At this moment she heard in her laughter an exact echo of her mother's, harsh, jeering, loud.

Something changed in her in this wild fit of laughter. She scarcely marked the change. It began in her too far under the surface, among the gross clownish impulses that survive in us like old roots. If she had respected him she would not have laughed. But her respect for him had died years before, and its place had been taken for a time by pity. Pity, a creeping root, is all but impossible to dig up. But it can wither. It can dry and cease. It can fail.

There were already days when she thought she had come to an end of caring. She was then as pleased as with a clear morning. Her body felt light and quick, and she talked much nonsense. The day after she would be in a restaurant with Penn and he would begin to say: ' Last time I was here——' and pause, it was almost imperceptible, glancing at her to see whether she had heard; she would know then he had come here with the girl. She would wait quietly for him to cover it with his talk—he liked talking dog French to the waiters; he made puns. She was ashamed to let him know that she knew. She would sit and listen. She wanted him to think that he had been too quick for her. Afterwards she would lock her door and lie staring into the darkness, smiling. ' I am better. You see ? I thought it funny, I am better '; and in a moment she was crying and shaking, nearly mad.

All this time, too, she knew that she would one day come to an end of Penn. As yet she did not feel it. But she half knew that it was the young Hervey who cried tears as bitter as the aloes they smear on children's nails, and struck her head on the wall. She caught glimpses of another, waiting to return, to whom all this would be a dry tale, without sense or colour, a little dust at the side of her mind.

CHAPTER XXV

1. *In Danesacre*

THE church they climbed to—the sea at their left hand—was eight hundred years old. They trod one hundred and ninety-nine shallow steps from the street by the harbour to the top of the cliff. For more than half the way the crouched old houses accompanied them, one above the other clinging to the side of the cliff. The topmost step, worn deepest because here many turned, flowed frozen in a flagged path between the graves to the church porch. They turned and looked downwards to the harbour, to the hills standing round it, to the line of the coast running north in iron cliffs, to the pale sea. The time was twenty-four minutes past ten. They walked towards the church, passing to one side to enter by the outside staircase. The narrow door swung open on a passage that ran towards the gallery. They trod softly this narrow passage between the wall and the high walls of pews. A little light came through low windows. The boards creaked. They passed the memorial tablet for Jake—' To the memory of 2nd Lt. Jacob Russell, Medaille Militaire, D.C.M., M.C., Royal Flying Corps '—on the wall of the gallery at the height of the eyes of passers-by. They came out between the high wooden sides of pews to the carved one Mrs Russell had chosen ; near to the old Garton pew, that now stood empty, like a square roofless room, a cushioned bench running along its walls, the latch of the door set high above the reach of a child's hand.

Hervey looked down into the well of the church. In the three-decker pulpit an old man made the gesture she had seen him make when she was a child. He flung his white surplice over his head and bowed his face in it. This stiff and believing old man stood to her for all those priests who accept, no, who excuse war. Their words, with the words used at the unveiling of war memorials, are the pus oozing over a wound. I could never forgive you, she thought.

She turned from him; but the church she sat in was part of her life; she could not deny it. It spoke to her skeleton, as if this remembered the worn places in stairs, the grain of old wood, the moment—each time as sharp as if it were the first—when a man crossing the moors sees the cliff lying against the sky and the church there waiting. But how could it forget, since all those who lived in her, Gartons, Hansykes, Russells, had so looked at it, from the land, and from the sea, from the beginning when it was first built ? She had read the logs of old ships, long since gone, and the writing, withered to brown like a dead leaf, almost gone : ' at eight in the morning Danesacre church bore W.N.W. distant three miles.' Here is nothing but what is mine, she thought.

The winter sunlight lay by the wall. It touched a corner of Jake's tablet. Hervey wondered how much longer it was to the silence. Leaning a little over the gallery she could see the soldiers drawn up facing the altar. She watched their officer : he made a shut, restless movement of his body when he stood up; he had a thin red face, fair hair, quick hot eyes. He does not care who looks at him, she thought. The sergeant-major standing at his elbow was less exposed—thin, his face thin and hollow, eyes sunken, gleaming, and yet as if they were dead. He had an air not so much cynical as experienced, but he was very quiet with it. He knows the officers thoroughly, Hervey thought; their vanities, their ways, what each can do, their lusts. She imagined an imperceptible mockery under his assurance. He would have known when Penn had his young woman, she thought. She was vexed with herself for thinking it here. She pressed her hands together and looked at the old plain windows. It might be sea or sky she looked at, or it might be sky one minute and sea the next, as if this were a ship. The repeated failures of her will—so that at every turn she came face to face with the same useless thought—made her bitterly ashamed. I behave as if I were only a female, she thought in her shame. This female is a burden to me; why can't she leave me alone? I am weary of her. Life is very confusing. She thought of Jess Gage. It confuses me. If someone had told me five years since that I should be involved to my discredit with an American and crying for Penn's unfaithfulness I should have laughed at him. But I shall use this.

It was like her to try to strike a profit. She hated waste and to fail.

The ex-service men sat with the soldiers. What do they see? Hervey wondered. She thought that one man's brain might hold the side of a trench, and another the face of a dead man, and another the room he lived in; it was a poor cold room—he was very shabby and his face gaunt. The sailors filled three rows. They were apart from the others. Their clothes, fitting tight round their bodies, gave them a queerly naked look. One of them, a little head on a solid broad neck, looked with his smooth face like an animal. The rest of the church was filled with men and women to whom the war had made different gifts, giving to this a death, to another new life, to this one money. There were many people in Danesacre whom the war had fed full with money. Perhaps they came here to thank someone for it.

It has come, Hervey thought suddenly.

It seemed now as if the silence filled the church like the welling of the sea between rocks. The great chandelier hung motionless in it. The tall pulpit, the gallery, the painted pillars, the figures of men and women, stood upborne in the full tide. All all were still. The great ball of air round the walls contracted and pressed on them. The silence drew into itself every quiver of light reflected on the walls and so strengthened it upheld the thin shell of the roof which would have been crushed : which would have fallen on them. This sound I hear is my own heart, she thought.   A splinter of light fell from Jake's tablet. She saw him at the other side of a London street; he was in clumsy khaki, his face was red, he believed he was unwanted. She ran across the road, between the wheels of cabs. She called. She touched him.

Out there, in danger, living with men, he had grown from boy to young man. Then one morning flying over the lines he had been shot at and had fallen dying on to the spoiled earth. He was nineteen. She had not known him very well —as if he had been too like her, too much the voice of her clumsy dreams. He had had ambitions like hers. He had lived a short time here, and a still shorter time in France, and he was dead. She turned here and there in the silence, thinking of the young men she had known until they were killed. She thought of Philip with a familiar grief. He had only a narrow room in her mind but it was his own. How I wish you had not died, she said to him. And now the silence changed, as though a cloud passing overhead were reflected in water. It darkened, and a wave far out at sea gathered itself to fall, to send a shock of water against the shore. Through all that place there was the sense of waiting for something that would happen. No heads were lifted, no eyes that had been closed opened, the ex-service men still stared rigidly before them, the face of the old man bowed in the upper deck of the pulpit was not uncovered—yet the change had taken place. All now waited—but for what? Nothing came. Nothing happened, except that a gun was fired outside and at the back of the church a man lifted his arms and sounded the Last Post. That dreadful sound, a sigh issuing from all those murdered young men, lacerated their nerves. What *is* man ? he spoils and kills, and then laments with a simple, an unendurable grief. The last note ended, slowly, it passed on, it would go over the earth; it would be heard here and there. The ears that were stopped with earth would not hear it. Hervey held the rail of the gallery. She was ashamed to cry, because these were not the first tears she had shed. But now another sound checked her, checked everyone. After a death there are sheets to wash, dirt to clear away ; a shell falls in a group of young men and what is gathered up into a sandbag is as undignified as a dish of tripes. In the musicians' gallery the organist began the first bar of God Save the King. Lurching a line or so behind the choir, the congregation sang one verse and would have sung the rest if the trumpet had not flown out again in the Reveillé. It flew out and up. It set the branches of the chandelier quivering. It jerked the breath in some throats and hardened others. A woman cried aloud the name she had called at intervals since July 3rd 1916. No one answered.

Mrs Russell did not cry aloud. Such was not her habit. For a second when the service began she had glanced towards the Garton pew. Whom did she expect to see there ? The figure of an old woman ? (She had never reflected that her only image of her mother as an old woman was drawn from a picture in a newspaper. It had not replaced the other images.) Her own youth ? That least : too much had happened to her—years spent working like a poor woman, like a slave, the births of children, mending clothes, nursing, counting out shillings, going on voyages, heat and discomfort in foreign ports, illness, pain, anger, ambitions transferred to her children, growing old, growing tired—there was nothing left to remind her of the young stubborn girl who had defied her mother, defied everyone, and for what ? For nothing. For this moment in which she stood wearing a black coat, made loosely since she was growing heavy, and thought of her dead boy. Yet there persisted—as if it had been any one of those coloured prints, worthless, falling between the pages of magazines we treasured in childhood, living still in us more sharply than the masterpiece we saw yesterday—the bright flickering image of a child asleep in one corner of the great pew. It was warm, there were flies droning on the panels : she said, I fell forward. Someone—her mother ?—had laid her down on the seat and she slept.

She looked away again. Covering his face, the old rector was silent. He had been praising those who had died. He had told her to be proud, to be comforted. She listened and thought, He is excusing what has happened. But there could be no excuse. War, for any cause, is inexcusable. There is nothing which excuses us for the beastly ingenuity of our wars. Only fools, only the diseased, think that we are served by killing the strong young men with machines. Mrs Russell looked at the memorial to her son. He hath outsoared the darkness of our night. They were the right words for an airman. He hath outsoared. The red frowning face of a little boy looked at hers. His mouth was black with bramble juice. She spoke to him. He frowned. He was sullen. Then he smiled at her; a tooth was missing, one of his first. He ran away and she followed him. Doors opened and shut, a cab drew up at the house and she got into it. Jake's canvas bag on the seat beside her bulged full, the cake that had just finished baking on top of all. His feet in thick army boots crushed hers on the floor of the cab. He mumbled an excuse. He was silent; his eyes had the remote stare of her own and—but she would not think it—of Mary Hervey's. He was a boy; he was going to make a name: he was going to be killed. The old man's strong unpriestly voice recalled her. She listened. *It is raised in power : it is sown a natural body ; it is raised a spiritual body.* She saw a khaki tunic folded in a drawer. The curtain blew out, filled by the wind. Jerking at the drawer she closed it, she stood up, she went from the room. Her feet dragged on the stairs. I am too done, she thought. *We shall not all sleep, but we shall all be changed.* No, no, she cried. She sat stiffly, immoveable. Her hands lay on her knees. She looked at them. Her whole life was in confusion in her, nothing was at peace, nothing was safe. *You know that your labour is not in vain,* she heard. No, she cried. Take it, take your victory. Take it and give me the living body of my son.

2. *Renn talks to an old friend*

A long way from him, and coming in jerks, as if a door swung open and again to, Renn could hear a bugle giving the Last Post. He heard it without hearing. He was alone in the room. The cessation of sound now gave him, when it was over, a tremor of alarm—as walking by a road at night you come on someone hidden there, pass him, and only then start with fear. For a time his senses had been astray.

He had thought that if you were to write about London it would have to be in the form of an auctioneer's catalogue, or a painting in which the intersection in a certain way of three lines, and with the corner of a newspaper, releases the charged mind. The sheet of paper under his hand was all over his compact writing. He wrote on the margins:

> these things cannot be endured.
> rooms without light, with a W.C. for use of eight families,
> the totty hinge has gone loose again, spoiling the lock;
> children toss scratch yes as they sleep, because of the vermin running in the pillows, in walls, and the marks you see the marks.
> now is the time to buy furs. This exquisitely worked mink.
> worth 300 guineas.
> Seen in Hyde Park with his nurse
> the intelligent young marmoset, Mrs Cammell another well-known hostess.
> adores. now showing
> now drops the crimson spittle, now the white
> This position will be held and the section will remain here until relieved.
> If the section cannot remain here alive, it will remain here dead, but in any case it will remain here.
> No Hands Wanted.
> But that's the after-birth, you must have mutilated—mutilated?—misbegotten something one time

The door opened and his friend Louis Earlham came in. 'I grew tired of knocking.'

'I didn't hear you,' Renn said. He smiled and dropped the paper into a drawer, on the top of several other fragments of *London*. 'How is Rachel?'

'She sent her love and wants you to come to see us.' Earlham paused, looking at his friend with a slight smile. 'We're going to have a baby in five months. Rachel said I was to tell you now because you'd never notice it until the child was born. She wants you to be the godfather.'

'But where will you keep it?' Renn said anxiously. 'You have hardly room for Habbakuk in your flat—let alone a child.'

Earlham did not answer at once. There was going on in his mind a strange process whereby, without anything being lost, or any belief sacrificed, an entirely new form emerges. It is like the shifting of the sea floor—a depression fills the place of a range of hills, new peaks are flung up, a whole submerged island is stripped of life, but the watcher on the surface sees nothing, except a wave that rises suddenly in mid-ocean, rushes over a small ship or two, and sinks back. Already Earlham had accustomed himself to what he was going to do, but not to speaking about it. He felt for words.

'You know that Cohen is starting an evening paper. *The Evening Post*. He is moving over part of the staff of the *Daily* as a nucleus, and he has offered me a job as leader writer. I shall take it, Davy. It's not only for the money. I know precisely how far Cohen's Radical ideas go—not far enough to damage his investments—and I know that I can force some Socialism into those limits. Probably I can do it better this way than if I were using an openly Socialist newspaper. The people will be educated without knowing it. Small homœopathic doses for the million.' He laughed, looking at Renn's face.

'Is Cohen financing the paper himself?' Renn asked.

'Not entirely. I believe Harben holds a share of it.'

Renn lifted a file from his shelf and opened it. 'Harben,

Thomas,' he read aloud. 'Yorkshireman. Born 1864. Chartered accountant by profession. Holds nineteen directorates and eight chairmanships of companies. Chairman since 1918 of the Garton Shipbuilding and Engineering Company. Director of two other shipping firms. Lately bought a controlling share in the Ling Steel and Iron Works on the Tees. Director of Stokes Chemical Works, a subsidiary of the largest armaments firm in the world. A director of the Midland Railway. Of the English Steel Corporation. On the board of Lloyds Bank. Director of a petrol combine. Chairman of a Canadian timber company. Married. No children. Has one mistress, partly German, whom he visits twice a week in the evening. Is at present engaged in reorganizing his shipping interests to avoid the worst consequences, to himself, of war inflation.' He closed the file and looked up at Earlham with a smile. 'What percentage of Socialism do you believe you can squeeze through this gentleman's fingers ? '

Earlham shrugged his shoulders. 'I knew most of that,' he said. 'But you're forgetting that *The Evening Post* is avowedly a *Radical* paper. Harben won't be able to change the policy.'

'He won't need to,' Renn said swiftly. 'When you were inoculated against typhoid you absorbed a certain amount of the poison. After that you were immune to it. That will be your job on the *Post*. Under cover of the smoke screen of Liberal promises and ideas you put up, Thomas Harben and his allies will be able to carry on in ease. Should a time come when they no longer need screening, they will invite you to turn about and admire their fine system of forts and salients and entrenchments. At present you are dupe and decoy duck. Do forgive me. Your illusions are not my business—nor your hopes either.' He turned over the papers on his desk. 'When Harben instructs the financial editor of the *Post* to recommend an issue of shipping shares, will you be allowed to point out facts I'm about to print week by week in *The Week*? In 1919 one of Harben's

companies actually doubled its share capital by an issue of
bonus shares, another increased its ordinary share capital by
200 per cent. in 1917.   Of these one is about to issue four
million pounds worth of debentures at 7 per cent. to pay
the part cost of its reckless buying up of other firms.   These
interest-bearing facts, with those I shall set out in *The Week*,
affect every man woman and child who depends on the
shipping business.   There will be men looking for work for
years of their lives; boys' lives will be twisted; a woman
will die of hunger, another woman will give birth to a dead
child, because Harben indulged himself in an orgy of inflation
during the War.   Did he think it was going to last his lifetime ?   Are you going to open this to your readers ?   Homœopathic doses ?   Why, you even won't be allowed to warn the
anxious middle-class investor that the statement Harben
supplies with his new issue is completely misleading.   It is
nothing more than the balance sheet of a holding corporation
and doesn't tell him whether it is safe to invest his money
in the shares of this or that firm involved, and what share
of the declared profits has been drawn from secret reserves.'
The fine delicate lines of Renn's mouth sharpened this
outburst.   He could seem to smile as he said bitter insulting
things in a pleasant voice.   'You mercenary !' he said
gently.

Earlham looked at him.   'Listen to me, David.   *The
Week* is a luxury.   Nothing else.   You couldn't afford it
without Philip Nicholson's money.   When that's spent you're
done.   You're showing a weekly loss, aren't you ?   The pure
milk of the word.   Who reads it ?   The converted.   Only
the converted.   The little I squeeze through the *Post* will be
heard by millions.   Long after you're silenced.   That's all.
You want to work a revolution.   I tell you it can't be done
that way.   Inch by inch, one step an inch in front of the
last——'

Renn laughed.

A detachment of infantry marched down Fleet Street
with fifes and drums.   The music swept round them, isolating

them in another world. Now destroyed. Earlham went over to the window. ' My God, I was happier in the War than I've been since,' he exclaimed.

' It was certainly simpler,' Renn said.

3. *Harben has an important suggestion to make*

The soldiers had left their barracks at nine o'clock. Shortly after ten they were passing the building which housed Garton's Shipbuilding Company and the shipping firms it controlled. The drums—the fifes were silent—thudded in the Board room. George Ling straightened his back in response. He loved martial music. Obscurely he felt that he and England were safe so long as the drums stammered and fifes shrilled of a morning somewhere.

Thomas Harben lifted his long nose and turned it towards the windows. In this posture his face was all strong fleshy beak. In a moment the beak drove down into the papers in front of him. He had observed Ling's rapture with annoyance. It aggravated the rage he felt at having to explain to this nincompoop that Garton's was already feeling the effects of war inflation. The huge prices paid for tonnage during the War, financed by new issues, the increase of capital, now dragged at it. In his fury he said too much. He had the pleasure of seeing Ling's fresh-coloured cheeks fall with terror. Then he went on to say that the ground position was still good. The reserves hidden away during the War had not been dissipated. From one source and another, the sum of these undisclosed monies went into eight millions. Over-depreciation and over-insurance (ships sunk during the War, *spurlos versunkt*). This year, for two companies, debenture holders and other mortagees would swallow up the last farthing of the net profits, unless (he squinted suddenly round his nose at Marcel Cohen) it was felt advisable to pay a small dividend.

' From what ? Pay from what ? ' Ling quavered.

' From special reserves,' Harben said.

'Naturally you would consider not disclosing the source of this dividend ? ' Cohen said.

'I should certainly consider that.' Harben let himself sink forward in his chair. He was feeling the onset of a violent attack of dyspepsia. This always happened to him after one of Lucy's more elaborate dinners. He had taken all the precautions—a dose of salts before going to bed ; in the morning he lay relaxed on the floor of his bedroom for ten minutes and massaged his stomach with both hands. It was no use. Presently he resigned himself to his pains. In the moment of speaking to George Ling he had decided to go directly to Chelsea and get Lise to give him the cascara and a cup of lime tea. She was lazy. At this hour she would just be up and freshly bathed. He would lie down on the sofa and let her talk soothingly to him until relief came. He had a certain respect for Lise. He had never given her a gift worth more than a few pounds. A long time ago he had offered her an allowance. She refused it with her wide smile. But she asked him to advise her in investing her little money, and in this way he had in a few years made her very easy. He did not know that she had begun now to gamble in shares ; and she was too afraid of rousing his contempt to tell him.

The fine pleasurable image of Lise in his mind faded. In the corner of his eye he saw Cohen take an envelope from his pocket and scribble a short sentence. Instantly his mistrust of the man started awake. How far could you trust a Jew who was also a Radical ? He had found the *Daily Post* useful ; he had used it. His policy was thus : so long as there is a free press, people allowed to read what they like, even silly subversive rubbish, so long he must need an ear in every camp. He did not like Cohen better for owning an offensive newspaper which he sometimes used.

Cohen put the envelope back in his pocket and looked up. His glance travelled from Ling's pitiable face to the face of another director, a Jew. Something passed between them, an assurance not translated into words. Cohen sat upright, pressing his thighs together, and looked at Harben. His eyes, so full, so brown, that they seemed fleshier than other people's, were now alert.

'There is a suggestion I have to make here,' Harben said. 'I have discussed it privately in certain quarters, and it has been welcomed.' He leaned with his arms over the table. 'What I have in mind is the formation of a council, a league, call it anything you like, formed I say to counter the revolutionary doctrines of economic communism. After a war, slump, unemployment, demobilised youths, is especially favourable for the spread of notions. You have psychological unrest, you have a sentimental socialism based on ignorance or denial of economic laws; you have communism itself. I needn't add, you have the fate of Russia. Russia has become a fat breeding ground of economic diseases. Well, gentlemen, I am not inclined to leave the failure and defeat of these forces to chance. Once a Socialist rot sets in, nothing is safe enough, no institution. Not even the banks. If you knew that certain men were mining your factory would you be willing merely to go on running your machines in the hope that the mines would fail to go up ? ' He opened and shut his hands. He had noticeable hands, firm, large, brutal. 'I have in mind an organisation charged to collect news of subversive movements and persons ; to put forward— in the press, throughout the whole country at meetings, through all reputable existing bodies—the sound economic doctrines of private enterpise ; to uphold our great mercantile tradition ; to discourage state interference ; to combat the menace of organised Labour ; to oppose dangerous and sentimental notions of pacifism ; to——'

A faintly puzzled voice repeated : ' Pacifism ? '

'The most complete proof you could want ! ' Harben said smoothly. 'Here you have a key industry—steel—armaments—chemicals—directly menaced by a bosh of sentiment, false assertion, and pure bolshevism. Our national security itself is involved. Pacifism, gentlemen, is not a joke, it is a threat. In my personal knowledge there are men in important

s

positions who are infected with it. It seems not to have
occurred to these influential fools that the spread of their
sentiments would bring us to a condition in which we should
look back at the War as a time of happiness and security.'

The director who was interested in humane slaughter of
animals and worked for it devotedly, spoke. He never said
anything more than Perfectly quite quite, but since he was
uninterested in everything except humanely slaughtered
animals—he had photographs and diagrams of them in all
stages—no one noticed him, saving the secretary, whose
business was to hear everything, and Thomas Harben.
Harben could not endure this man's voice.

' Who's going to pay for it all ? ' George Ling said.
' Eh ? ' His chin trembled.

' Members will pay an agreed subscription.'

' Members ?   You said ? '

' The several industrial and financial interests approached
are the first members. You can expect a sharply growing
membership when the aims of the—I should like it called an
Economic Council—are known.'

' How known ? ' Cohen interrupted. ' I don't imagine
you'll seek publicity.'

' Not in the columns of the *Daily Post*,' Harben said.

' But all this ought to be done by the Government,' Ling
exclaimed. ' A strong Government would make this—these
expensive schemes unnecessary. I support it but I don't like
it. The shareholders will want to know why and how their
money is being spent.'

' Shareholders are only interested in their profits,' Cohen
said gently. ' You have sums which have been transferred
to special reserve before striking profits. Why bring out at
all the item of a subscription to the Economic Council ? '

' A memorandum is being prepared for private circulation,'
Harben said. ' As for the Government—I may add now that
it will be right to attach the Council at various points to the
permanent structure. The Home Office. The Foreign
Office. The police. Certain organisations working already

in other countries.' He yawned suddenly and involuntarily.
' Every vital interest is concerned,' he said.

At this moment the secretary to the Board looked up
quickly. An electric bell rang in the corridor. The footsteps in the room over their heads suddenly ceased. Harben
rose to his feet. All rose, and stood in their places at the table.
One fiddled with his hands. A heavy tear ran across the
side of Ling's nose and dropped on to the blotting-paper.
Cohen stared before him at the window. A tender expectant
feeling rose in him. He did not know what he expected
but he leaned forward, pressing his body against the table, to
be ready for it when it came. At the other side of the table
Harben had closed his eyes in a spasm of discomfort.

4. *Frank sometimes thinks about the War*

Leaving Sally to serve the morning customers, Frank
walked over to look at the new road. It was well begun,
men working at both sides of the cutting, trucks, cement
mixers and what not. He stood for a time looking at the
work, then spoke to a man.

' How much longer ? Oh, next spring maybe or summer,
who cares ? '

' I do,' Frank said. ' I been running a sandwich place on
the old road.'

The other looked at him. ' Better move it here, chum.'

' No bon. They wouldn't have it. I been and asked.
Not good enough, see.'

The other saw. It might have been himself he saw.
Frank moved away and walked the length of the cutting to
the northern end. From here he could see three villages
wrapped in their fields and bare trees. A stream joined
two of them. There were no shadows on the distant fields,
the sunlight too pale and the winter hedges low. The scene
reminded him of Northern France, not of any place he
remembered but a feeling of all that country he came into
behind the line, seeing unspoiled villages and fields and hearing

voices not English but country voices, and for a short time
something he had had in the past closed round him. But it
was changed. So now the familiar English fields were
changed by that country known to him as 'rest.' They
folded into each other in his mind, and sometimes when he
fell asleep he was living with other men in a village of which
he had forgotten the name and country, but all its colours were
stronger and clearer, the woods like flames, the streams a deep
colour like the sky, the hills bold as brass, than any in life.
He was glad and pleased to find himself living in such a place.
When he woke he knew that he had been dreaming; there
were no such colours anywhere in the world. He had never
seen such woods, streams, or hills in any part. He did not
know that neither was there any colour in the world like the
one at which he supposed himself to be looking. It was not
green, not grey, not yellow, not English, not French. Part
of his mind had fallen asleep in France, in 'rest,' and was
dreaming as it looked. He turned and walked back to The
Dug-out.

From this side he had to pass through the village. He heard
the church clock strike : it was like a broken rusty key
turning slowly, round and round, in the lock. There was a
long wide street, which was empty. Two cars drawn up at
the side, the drivers still at the wheel, caught his eye. After
he had passed them, a man he knew came grinning to the
door of the *Spread Eagle* and called out : ' Hurrying ? You
walked slap through the silence, my lad. I saw you afar off,
as it says.'

' What silence ? '

The man laughed and went in. Frank was left standing.
He had remembered just as he said it; and the thought of
himself standing stock still in the middle of an empty street
made him jump. Of all damned nonsense, he said angrily.
He hurried on. Now he walked in a straight line, keeping
to the side of the road, his head down. He was the inner
man of the rank, to the side and in front of him he saw other
marching bodies and felt the pressure on his body of those

coming behind. He felt easy and not tired and he marched without thinking. Someone spoke in the rear file and the words slipped through the ranks like leaves rubbing on leaves.

At the turn of the road he saw the corrugated iron hut—The Dug-out A Good Pull-in—and now he was alone.

An overmastering anger seized him. He had no words for it. Certain words that had been obscene had become old friends by going all through the War with him. In the face of this injustice they were useless. When I came here and when I built our two rooms and when I was putting up the notice and when I fitted the shelf, he thought, I was glad. In a confused way he felt that the higher authority that had taken away his gladness was mean at bottom. We weren't doing anyone any harm, he thought. His shelves, the notice board, Sally's things she was so pleased of, might be so much dirt. No one gave a thought to them. No one. No one in the whole of England.

He reached the Dug-out. The door into their living-room was shut and he stood for a moment in front of the big coffee urn. The shelf behind him was piled with cups and plates. He took a cup in his hand and flung it against the urn and followed it with another and another. 'I'll smash them first,' he shouted.

He was breaking the eighth when the door opened behind him and his wife stood there. 'Frank, what is it?' she said, afraid. He looked at her for a moment, then he went awkwardly to her and put his arms round her and his face in her neck. She drew him into their room. She understood that something in him had been finished when he broke their cups. After a time they talked to each other in low voices, as though someone ought not to hear, and then she got up and went outside and swept up the broken bits.

5. *Two minutes only*

T.S. heard the warning for the two minutes' silence. He was alone at his end of the laboratory and he could not even glance round. The liquid in the second retort had reached the stage he was watching for; he had to move instantly.

His movements seemed mechanical and were not. Although he knew the result, what he was doing was for the first time. His mind had something to do besides watch. At the same time it had the energy to finish off a thought that had been with him all morning. This thought was about his wife. From some feeling of pity for her, because he had noticed she was unhappy and anxious, he had gone to her room when he came home that evening, full of words he meant to say. He opened the door, and closed it again quietly at once.

The silence in the factory, in his laboratory, penetrated to his mind. He moved an arm. The very slight noise he made, of glass against zinc, sounded like a knife dropping. He tilted the retort, waited, judged. The image of his wife in William Ridley's embrace stayed on one level of his mind, like a print tacked to a wall. He felt thoroughly vexed by her stupidity. She should have fastened her door, he said. The contempt he had been feeling for her since was due to that and nothing else. She can have as much of anything as she likes, it relieves me of my responsibility, he thought; but she should have been careful. It might have been any one, one of the servants who came in and saw them. His hand made a swift neat movement. The sun in this corner is in the way, he thought. His eyelids rose and fell quickly. See to it. But she must lock her door. Very distinctly he remembered walking along the High Street after school with his mother, there were boys coming behind them, when he saw that her petticoat was coming down under her dress. She never cared how she looked. When he told her she only laughed, and turned round to look at it. In a low voice he said, ' Do hush, mother.' There were inches of it showing at the back over her boots, it was almost on the ground, he felt very miserable with the disgrace of it. He would never be able to go back to school, never face them. A year afterwards when his mother died he had not forgotten that

day, and before he missed her he thought quickly, She won't
be coming to meet me, I shall be safe. After that he had
been alone until the War and his marriage. He married a
woman twelve years older than himself.

He saw himself standing in front of her at their first
meeting. He had to ask her name. He was awkward with
women, tormented, wanting them to like him and despising
them in self-defence. Perhaps he had bragged in talking to
her. ' Are you turned twenty-three ? ' she asked. She looked
at him with a mocking smile, but with something else in her
look, with a warmth, with pleading. He turned round.
His hand moved over towards the bunsen burner. Now
I'm twenty-seven I look forty, he thought. I haven't enough
life left to cope with her.

He saw himself dressing to catch the early leave train.
Their hotel was part of the station and through the night they
had heard the trains. He dressed swiftly with his back to
Evelyn. When he was ready he woke her and found that
she had been crying. ' What's the matter ? ' he asked.
She gripped him with both arms, pressing him to her in a
useless fear. He saw himself running down the long platform.
Leaves aren't worth it, I don't want another yet. He was
glad to be sitting in the train, to sit and be moved, not to
move himself, to act, to think. Had I another leave ? he
wondered. The tiny flame of the bunsen burner vanished
when he touched the tap. If the end had come before I was
this tired she wouldn't have changed.

A faint shadow wavered across his hand and up the wall,
so faint that it was like a strand of hair loosed in an eddy of
deep water. It was the reflection of smoke from a chimney
below the windows. The works covered about eight acres
of ground. There were no sounds from the yard. He
listened, moved the retort over, and picked out a test tube
from the rack of them at his elbow. Everything had gone
as it should. He noted a figure under those he had written,
and as he slipped the cap on his pen he heard the siren go
off at the gas works. A truck started with an abrupt screech

in the yard. The silence is over, he thought. It occurred to him at once that since his experiment had to do with the first stages in the production of a new highly poisonous war gas it would have been indecent and very silly for him to pause. In the same moment he came to the end of his feelings of spite and humiliation and felt sorry for Evelyn. But she didn't change; it was I that changed, it was the last year, he said. No war ought to last four and a half years. It is too long.

6. *His wife washes her hands*

Evelyn Heywood waited in the window of her room. She was not dressed, she had overslept, and she reproached herself for her laziness. A restless anxiety to be at the office struggled in her against the tension that kept her here, doing nothing, not even opening her letters. Her secretary had already telephoned from the *London Review* to know when she was coming. She felt imprisoned. The door was open, she had only to bestir herself, to dress, to walk out. She felt her thoughts turning in her head and her heart jumping, but she stood motionless. She looked at the river.

There had been a light mist. Now the near buildings were dark, like ramparts, and the farther ones as dim and insubstantial as a vapour, a breath. She saw a barge move slowly at the head of a string of lighters. There was a woman on board, moving between the cabin of the barge and the side. She emptied a spout of water overboard, went away, and reappeared, moving smoothly and swiftly like a brightly coloured shuttle. Evelyn thought, If I could go away, if I could leave everything and lead that woman's life I should be saved. She knew that she was incapable of living such a life, incapable in her over-trained mind and in her weak under-experienced body. There is something rotten in me, she thought; but what is it? She looked down at her hands and imagined that one of them had become soiled since her bath. I must have touched something. Looking down at her hand, as she walked turning it from palm to back, she hurried into the bathroom and there washed both her hands with great thoroughness. She let the water run the whole time and held the offending hand under it. The quick hissing noise of the water filled her ears. She dried her hands, pulled open the door sharply, and heard a bugle and on top of it drowning it the whistles of ships. The two minutes had come while she was in the bathroom and gone. She began to dress, opening cupboards and dropping her clothes over the floor in search of others. When she had finished she looked at the disordered room and rang her bell. ' Clear this up,' she said to the servant; ' put everything away and then polish the paint and the glass. Make everything clean and sweet.' She picked up gloves and paper. Her hands were now shaking. She looked : it was inconceivable that they had become dirty again, yet she saw it distinctly. Dropping everything she held she went back to cleanse them. She wiped and rubbed and plunged them into the hot water and at last she was satisfied.

7. *William Ridley will cc the voice of England*

The silence caught Ridley in the street, outside the offices of the *Daily Post*. He was expecting it, yet when the traffic stilled suddenly about him and a man walking in front stopped and jerked off his hat, Ridley was taken by surprise. He stood still, hat in hand, and stared round him at the immobilised street. A horse's bit jingled. A boy scraped his foot on the pavement. These tiny noises accentuated the silence.

As he waited a strange emotion sprang in him. He felt himself surrounded by friends, and though he saw no face or form and heard no voice, he knew that they were the men with whom he had lived in France. At another time, if anyone had said, of him and them, these men loved each other, he would have laughed incredulously, since he had forgotten even their names. And he would have been right to laugh, in so much as the end of the War ended that love, which sprang from it; but yet he was wrong, since what he then felt, though it died too quickly, was the quckening of a new promise, an assurance offered by one man to others, that since everything else has failed, since there is no help in princes, and none in God, nevertheless help is forthcoming. Help shall be given, ' Nation shall not lift a sword against nation, neither shall they learn war any more.' And if this is a lie, if the seed quickens again and again only to die, then we are all lost and the generation to which Ridley, and Hervey Russell, and Philip, and David Renn, and T.S., and Frank of the Dug-out, and Jake, who was nearly too young for it, belong, will be the last nourished in the illusion of freedom.

William Ridley stood quietly in Fleet Street, leaning forward on his stick, and listened to the silence. He was far from being displeased with a world in which he saw innumerable splendid chances for a man like himself to make good. Yet even in him something had changed. He was not always at ease; now and again he had felt an impulse to hide, to sink himself in the nameless ranks from which he had emerged. So now he surrendered himself to a useless emotion. It seemed useless. Later he began to see that it might have more than one use. But now he stared, with the frank serious look of a child, at the motionless buses, at the boy leaning restlessly against his bicycle, at a sparrow which had lost its head and was trying to balance on nothing. When the guns went off, and the wretched shabby man standing outside the public house began to play the Last Post, weakly and badly, and only the first notes of it could be heard at all, the rest was drowned, Ridley felt tears in his eyes.

He hurried into the doorway of the *Daily Post* and up the far from imposing stairs to the editorial office. He had an appointment with Cohen and yet he did not feel safe about it until, after waiting ten minutes in a dark narrow room, no better than an angle of the passage, he was summoned to Cohen's room. To give himself confidence he assumed a

rude bluff manner.   He sat well at his ease in an armchair,
straddling his legs out, and said :
   ' I can't say I'm impressed by your waiting-room, Cohen.'
   ' It wasn't intended to impress you,' Cohen said.
   ' I'm glad to hear that,' Ridley said.   He covered his
embarrassment under a sly wide smile.   ' Well now, you
asked me to come and here I am—and I don't mind telling
you I don't waste much time running about in a morning.
What do you want ? '
   ' Have you looked at the paper this morning ? ' Cohen
asked.   He spread a copy of the *Daily Post* over the table
and showed Ridley his own name on the left centre page,
under the title of an Armistice Day article he had supplied.
' I like that article,' Cohen said, ' it has the right sound,
good-hearted, sensible, friendly without being vulgar.   Was it
an accident or could you write one a week in the same voice ?
I thought you might care to run about—you needn't do it
in the mornings—looking at crowds, a fight, a football
match, a popular café, the fish market, a fair—choose your
own themes and write about them in a broad, jovial, straightforward style.   Catch hold of your readers by the arm.
Make 'em stare and chuckle, but once in a while don't forget
the lump in the throat.   I want literature, my dear fellow,
something you're not ashamed of writing, but it will have
to please a million readers.'
   ' Like Shakespeare,' Ridley said, grinning.   ' He was
another William.'
   ' Exactly.'
   ' No one can do that as well as I can,' Ridley said.   'There's
nothing niggling about me.   I have unlimited fun and
imagination, absolutely unlimited, and I don't want to write
exquisite polished trifles.   Literature without guts bores me.
I'll tell you something, Cohen, if Shakespeare was alive now
he'd have to write prose like mine.'   He looked into Cohen's
face with an impudent stare.   Assurance sat awkwardly on
him.   ' All you have to do, Cohen, is to tell my agent what
you're willing to pay for them and if it's right I'll turn you

in the best articles you ever printed.' He saw a chance to use up an essay he had once sent to *The Week*. It had been returned to him with a curt letter, and an impulse of spite drove him to say :

' Do you ever see a rag calling itself *The Week* ? '

' I always read it carefully,' Cohen answered. ' I like to know what the smaller rats are busy with.' He smiled, his sharp fine infinitely knowing smile, which expressed contempt for what it had first degraded. ' A friend of ours, Miss Russell, is the assistant editor.'

' That girl's sly and unreliable,' Ridley exclaimed.

' Unreliable perhaps yes,' Cohen said. ' I know her grandmother. You can't trust a woman or a man who is as honest as that ; they're like Liberals, they'll give away the pass, any pass, for the sake of an idea. But no she's not sly.' Hervey's round face, with the too big forehead and heavy jaw, came before him ; it wore a childishly morose air. Involuntarily he smiled.

Ridley left the place in great good humour. He had expected nothing so fine to come of his visit. He went home, wrote an article, making first use now of his feelings during the silence ;   and towards four o'clock ran out in search of his novel. He crossed Vauxhall Bridge and walked on slowly. The river was like dulled metal. He heard an aeroplane and stood looking into the sky, but darkness had thickened over the lighted streets and he saw nothing. The lights entering the darkness turned it to a reddish brown fog which stretched its arms over London. He walked under this canopy, through wide streets and past shops stuffed to bursting with clothes, brass bedsteads, tins of food, and through streets as dark and narrow as canals. In the lighted streets girls strolled with linked arms, women filled market bags, old men peddled matches, boys raged up and down, there was some laughter and an unceasing babble of voices, yet he could never catch anyone in the act of speaking. All the faces, smooth, staring, vacant, intent, lewd, innocent, bold, were silent. At last he saw a girl speaking in a telephone booth and he went into the one next to it to listen. She was young and thin, shabby, wearing a wide hat, a short buttoned jacket, and a narrow skirt. Her hat had slipped backwards, and the line of her pregnant body was visible under her skirt. She was so thin that it was very ugly. Despair, anger, and bewilderment wrote themselves on her face, where nothing else had been written during her few years. 'You aren't coming?' Ridley heard. 'What? Oh but you said. It's the fourth time you haven't.' This was followed by a moment in which she laid her hand over her mouth and listened. 'Jim, I want you so,' she said. 'Jim, you said you——' A start ran through her body and he felt certain that the listener at the other end had gone. It was so. She spoke again, listened, spoke once more, in the voice of a child, and gave it up. He watched her pull her jacket down and go away.

Next he followed a stout woman wearing a man's yellow waistcoat. She showed it to her friend, looking at it herself with eyes as bold and hard as brass, but they were merry. 'Armistice Day last year put his light out. He went and no mistake, and I kept it as you might say when this you see remember me. Lord, he was lively. After m'first I said, I'll have no thinkers or thonkers, give me sister a doer of or what d'you call the word. Be that as it may, I've never been better satisfied. Well, what d'you get married for? Please God I'll find another soon.' He followed this pair into a saloon bar where, by some trick of the lights, the flesh even on fat rosy faces appeared dissolving, so that he saw the bones. This was not pleasant. He went out and saw a boy and girl leaning against a wall : the girl was smooth-faced and aware of herself but the boy expressed bewilderment and agony in the way he lifted his hand and touched her face. The girl watched Ridley as he went by slowly. He went as slowly as he could. The boy was blind and trembling and saw no one.

Next he came to the arches of a railway and saw two men asleep there. They lay with knees drawn up. He turned

back and went into a cinema. It was full and he had to stand
at one side, close to the screen. From here he could see the
organist and the faces of the worshippers. Their eyes were
turned slightly upward. They were adoring a half-clothed
young woman reclined in a room of inexplicable splendour,
where like Aholah in the scriptures she doted on her lovers.
This finished better than anyone could have hoped. The
organ then rose several feet into full view, luminous, changing
from rose to green to blue, and afterwards sank again, to the
delight of the people. You don't see miracles every day, not
to notice them. Ridley went out. There were now so many
walking up and down in the thickish light which revealed
forms but not colours that you could think the houses bred
them. Some had faces without eyes and others were all eyes.
They crowded together. They walked this way and that.
The fog was torn in a few places and he saw a sky neither
dark nor light. He remembered the airman.

In the Albert Hall 1,104,896 scarlet poppies fell from the
roof—a poppy for every British and Colonial soldier who fell
in the War. The trumpeters of the Royal Horse Guards
sounded the Reveillé, a cue for the man operating the spot
lights.

The airman had gone north, taking his way by known
markings, the lights of a railway junction, of a city. He
crossed the Humber at no height, picking up a strong light
placed at the end of a jetty, and flew on by the coast. Here
were old lights, for ships. He passed over Danesacre without
seeing it, all that which had been from time gone a landmark
for way and seafarers invisible to him.

CHAPTER XXVI

A MAN OF BUSINESS

THE year after, in July, Renn brought *The Week* to a quick end. It had lasted two years. He had enough money to pay all debts and after paying them he had left twenty pounds, of which he gave Hervey ten. The nine hundred and ninety-four subscribers to this honest paper, all of whom had a slate loose somewhere, missed it; one of them wrote to ask whether a hundred pounds would be any use to keep life in it.

Hervey was now at a loss. She had saved close on fifty pounds and had finished her novel, which was appointed to come out in August. But it never entered her head that she could live by writing novels.

She was in this state when Marcel Cohen told her to call on Mrs Harben. 'She wants,' he said, 'a secretary to write a personal sort of letters. For that you won't need the shorthand you haven't learned. What possessed you to learn Latin and no shorthand? She has two secretaries of the usual kind. She wants to be able to say to you: Explain that I am devoted to her but can't see her. On that you compose the letter and she signs it. I've told her about you that you have, which is true, the head of an old diplomat on your young shoulders.'

Hervey looked at him, not certain that she was pleased. She thanked him and went home. She tried to see herself entering Mrs Harben's room with a fine confident air. Actually she would stalk in looking—but what do I look like? she cried. She ran to the glass and staring, thought: That gaunt simple face is me. As always she was confused by the thought of calling on a stranger. It offended and frightened her.

She did not tell Penn what she was thinking. It might be a failure. Then it would humiliate her to have talked about it.

When the day came she put on a newly bought hat. This was a mistake. Her head, as round as an apple, offered nothing for an inexperienced hat to cling to. As she walked she felt a familiar sensation in the pit of her stomach. She tried to overcome it by walking slowly. I shall stand as if I were looking not smiling watching to see whether I am to shake hands. My friend Mr Cohen. I think I could do what you want. I think I. Five pounds. Two hundred and fifty pounds a year is less than I. I read French perfectly. And Anglo-Saxon and Latin, but of course you (an amused smile), still perhaps you, I type very quickly I taught myself; I think I have enough experience. I have experience. Here she caught sight of herself in a shop window in Mount Street and straightened her hat. It is easy to imagine that you are a success; it is not so easy to imagine that your hat is on straight when it is in fact over one ear.

So dreaming, she walked past Mrs Harben's house, turned back, rang the bell, and the instant the door opened she said in a loud voice: 'I wish to see Mrs Harben.' While she waited she stared round the room to convince herself that she was not anxious. Mrs Harben came in. She spoke to Hervey with so much kindness that the girl felt for her a passionate gratitude. She smiled suddenly, and Mrs Harben said, also smiling: 'It's agreed then, and my secretary shall write you a formal letter at once.'

Outside the house Hervey drew a deep breath; she could not believe that she had made so good an impression: her cheeks burned and she felt confused and vexed. She could not remember what she had said. She went home. Penn was still out and she could not tell him that she was safe. A warm feeling of relief and happiness overwhelmed her.

The letter came by the last post. It said simply that Mrs

Harben had changed her mind and did not wish to avail herself of Miss Russell's services. She was reading it when she heard Penn's hand on the door. Without thinking she thrust the letter out of sight under the tablecloth. Her heart beat violently but her face did not give anything away. She could only think of one time in her childhood when she let a shilling drop in the street; it vanished instantly through a grating, and she stood stock still and in agony that someone had seen and would laugh or be sorry for her.

She had William Ridley to thank. He was in Mrs Harben's house when she was seeing Hervey. She had had to leave him and go into another room to see Hervey, whom she liked at once. She liked a simplicity and a distance which Hervey had by not caring for people. She was explaining this to Ridley and he said, simply: 'Do you remember my asking Evelyn who it was wrote that sneering article in the *London Review* about you and it was this same Hervey Russell? I told you at the time.'

'I had forgotten it,' Mrs Harben cried.

Ridley had the delicacy not to say another word.

On this occasion he had no foolish impulse to be generous. Hervey irritated him and he felt that she might become a rival, and since he had said nothing but what he thought true his conscience did not trouble him. After all, what had he done? He prided himself strongly on being a good man of business and it was in accordance with business ethics that he had pressed an advantage against a weaker rival. So he felt satisfied with his morning's work. A feeling of pleasure and well-being possessed him. He felt almost kindly towards Hervey, as if she had been the obscure means of making him know his strength.

CHAPTER XXVII

As soon as Penn came into the room he said :

'Shaw-Thomas sent for me this evening and gave me a week's notice.' He looked at her the whole time as he said it. He was pale.

Hervey's first thought was, I must keep quiet and seem not to be startled or anxious. She said in a low voice : 'Why, Penn, what had happened ? Tell me about it.'

'There's nothing to tell,' Penn said. He sat down on the sofa. 'I thought something was wrong. When I wanted to see him last week he made excuses for not seeing me. This evening he said he had orders to cut down the staff. I happen to know he's engaged two new men, so he's a liar. If I hadn't felt so knocked down by it I'd have told him to his face.'

Hervey could not bear the sight of him hurt and humbled. She went quickly across the room and stood close to him, not touching him because that would have made it seem too like pity. 'One of the others must have made mischief,' she said, in a firm voice.

'I thought so at the time. But when I was coming home I thought it over, and I realised that I'd made a mess of everything. These last months I've had all the stuffing knocked out of me. I've made a failure of copy-writing, I failed to get a teaching job, I've failed as a husband—though God knows I've tried to make that up to you. It's been no good, though. I realised it to-night. I'm just useless.'

'You're not useless,' Hervey said.

Penn turned his face quickly aside. 'Everything I've done

290

is no use. I've been walking about for hours, trying to make up my mind to tell you. I feel miserable, Hervey. I feel so sorry for you. Please comfort me.'

She felt her heart ache for him. She flung her arms round him and rocked him against her body, as if he were a child. He was very quiet, accepting it all. She felt she could bear anything for him. In the same moment she remembered that he had had the other woman. If I had known nothing about it he would have gone to her this evening to be comforted, she thought. She trembled and felt that she despised him. Then again she was ashamed, and drew him closer to her, stroking his face. She tried cleverly and subtly to make him feel that whatever he was he was not a failure. It was the kind of work, she said. He was much too intelligent to do it well; it needed a mind more like hers, coarser and less scrupulous, to carry out work of that sort. ' And you see even I could not stand it for long,' she cried.

' I've let you down pretty badly,' Penn said, but he was less wretched.

' All that worries me is I have no work myself.'

' I'll ask my mother to help us.' He frowned. He hated to ask his mother for money, not only because she had so little now, but because she would reproach him and Hervey for living what she called a light life.

Hervey remembered her fifty pounds. Should she offer it ? She closed her eyes—but I may need it for Richard, she thought. She said nothing.

' You are sure you still want me, Hervey ? ' Penn asked.

' You know I do,' she said. It is true, she thought. I'm still fastened to him, and now more than ever.

' I'm a poor sort of husband.'

' You're my husband.'

' Do you still feel like that ? '

' Yes.' Hervey said.

' Will you let me come to you now ? '

' You are all I want,' Hervey sighed.

When he went off to his own room she felt that she had

no strength. She remembered that she had pushed Mrs Harben's letter out of sight under the cloth. Feeling for it with one hand she swept it out and without looking at it tore it in pieces and threw them out.

The next day Penn went off early to see his mother. Hervey waited for him with impatience. She was too restless to work or write. She thought of Richard, of her unmanageable desires and her unabateable ambitions, and again of Richard. My life is in pieces, I am nothing, I have achieved nothing; yet I will, she thought.

When Penn returned he went directly to his room. She waited a moment, then ran after him and looking with an eager face, said : 'What did your mother answer ? '

He hated her to question him. For some reason it made him want to defend himself against her, as if he lost dignity by answering. She knew this but did not understand it, and when she was in a hurry she forgot.

' Dear me, you're very anxious to know,' he said coldly.

' Yes,' Hervey said.

To snub her, he made her wait while he polished his pince-nez. ' You won't like it,' he said drawling, ' but my mother has offered me the money to go to Oxford for three years—and whatever you say, I consider it very generous of her. She can't very well spare the money, but she's got it into her head that a second degree will help me to get back into the scholastic world. I shouldn't be surprised if she's right.'

Hervey did not answer for a time. While he was speaking her mind had become still. It was as if her thoughts sank in it to a great depth, leaving a space in which she was quiet. She held herself in this space. A familiar certainty possessed her, from which, without thinking about it, she would act. She lifted her head and looked thoughtfully at Penn. ' Would you like to go ? '

' I haven't actually thought about it,' Penn said, in surprise and doubt. This was not true.

' Think,' Hervey said gently.

Penn had expected opposition and scorn. He was taken

aback and did not know what to think. All his resentment vanished and with it the half decision he had made, to go. He looked at Hervey with an air of appeal. ' Do you want me to go, my dear ? '

She was implacable. ' I want you to do exactly what you like,' she said in a kind voice.

' I don't know,' Penn cried.

Hervey looked at him with a warm smile. A faint sense of excitement gripped her. Do I want him to go ? Doors opened and shut in her mind, she heard footsteps and voices, a hand touched her face. She started. Who came in then ?

' Do you feel it would be a help to you to have another degree ? '

' I suppose so,' Penn said. He jumped up and began to walk up and down. ' I don't want to leave you to live alone again, pup.'

' Don't consider me,' Hervey said swiftly. ' It only confuses things. Think what you want to do, and then do it.'

' How would you live ? '

' What would I live on, you mean,' Hervey said. She felt a momentary panic. But this finishes me, she thought. I shall have to go back ; and people will look at me and see that I have come to nothing. She was filled with despair.

In this moment of defeat, when she could see nothing that would save her, and no way out except the humiliating way of going home, having utterly failed, she felt a deep satisfaction. It was as if she preferred that Penn should leave her to face defeat ; as if, in the obscure place it had come to, her spirit wanted to be humiliated. Perhaps she wanted also that Penn should do it. She felt almost happy. Perhaps without feeling it more clearly than, when she was deeply asleep, she felt the change from darkness to light, she felt that he was setting her free by his readiness to leave her when she had nothing, no work, and no money, except the fifty pounds she had and he did not know she had. In this darkness where the waiting mind feels its way, where nothing is known and where everything is certain, what voices take up the tale ? She was used to listening. Something will come (someone said) of letting Penn go : better let him go. You're not afraid, are you ? (Here a child laughed—Shut your eyes and open your mouth and see what *they* have brought you.)

She grew aware of Penn's impatience. ' I don't know, but I'll find something,' she said vaguely. ' I always do find something.'

' I'm not sure whether I ought to go,' Penn said.

I won't take the responsibility, Hervey thought swiftly. She looked at her hands. ' You've always accused me of wanting to manage your life for you. This time I'm not going to do anything. I won't interfere. Make up your mind what you want and I'll accept it.'

' Do you think I ought to go ? '

' I think you ought to do what you please. Would you like to go ? '

' I've always wished I had been sent to Oxford.'

Hervey did not say anything.

' Perhaps it's too late,' Penn said.

' You're only thirty-one.'

' I wish to God I'd taken it two years ago, when my father offered. Instead of hanging about here and giving you the chance to say you had given me your job.'

' And your girl a job,' Hervey said.

' I expected you to say that.'

' Well, forgive me,' Hervey said. ' Tell me—do you truly think it will benefit you to have an Oxford degree ? '

' I suppose it will.'

After a moment Hervey said : ' I can go to Danesacre.'

' What to do ? '

' I could write another novel.'

' That's a good idea.'

' It's a fine idea,' Hervey said.

' I could let you have fifty pounds for a start. Mother is taking out nine hundred and fifty for me. I rang up Parke before I came in—he was at Oxford and he says I can manage on three hundred a year. If you're in Danesacre I can spend half my vacations there.'

' Where do you spend the rest ? '

Penn cleared his throat. ' With my mother. Naturally, she's expecting to get something for her money—poor dear, she's lonely.'

' Oh quite,' Hervey said.

' If I do well it's worth it.'

' Why shouldn't you do well ? '

' It gives me something to take hold of. I've been feeling so wretched, Hervey.'

If you could make Hervey think of you as a child or as poor or oppressed, she would move mountains for you. My poor Penn, you shall have everything you want, she cried silently. She was full of love for him. ' Darling Penn, you'll be a great success.'

' I'll remember that,' Penn laughed.

' Remember this, too, then. I may get the wind up some time or other about being left. Don't pay any attention to it.'

' We'll have fine holidays. When the three years are up you shall have your house and all that and you'll be happy and I shall have done something, after three years. I'm not going to think of the three years, I'm going to think of our future.'

Hervey listened to him in silence. In her head the words made a noise like voices coming and going away in a street, the street empty, and the voices coming towards the street lamp and passing it and dying away again.

CHAPTER XXVIII

INTERVAL

1. *I am you reading*

SHE gave up the rooms and went back to Danesacre at the beginning of August. She had close on a hundred pounds, her hoard and the fifty Penn had given her, or Penn's mother. She wrote to thank Mrs Vane, falsely grateful.

Her plans, such as they were, the cover for defeat, did not please her mother. She did not want Hervey to take Richard from Miss Holland. Perhaps she felt it to be unjust that Hervey could so easily take back her son, after how long ? after three and a half years—Jake was killed in 1917. Mrs Russell did not think these things. But she thought with a sudden bitterness that the boy was well enough with Miss Holland; why take him away ? 'You may very easily want to go away again,' she said, frowning. 'Then you would have unsettled him for nothing. You might even find that Miss Holland was not willing to take him back.'

Hervey felt herself flinch. That sound in her mother's voice cowed her. She became a child tense with fear before the thrashing no tears would avert. She poked her chin forward in unconscious mimicry of her mother. 'I'd rather have him with me,' she repeated. 'I can take rooms in a house near hers, in the fields. He can go to her for lessons.'

'You must do as you please,' Mrs Russell said coldly.

'I can write in the mornings and when he is asleep.'

'Miss Holland has been getting him into good ways. You'll find he behaves much worse with you. I shouldn't be surprised if he begins his bad tempers again.'

' He behaved well enough with me when he was a baby,' Hervey said.

She went out of the room and upstairs to her bedroom. She was trembling with anger and dismay. She was a grown woman, she was a child, she had offended, she would be thrashed shortly. Shutting the door of her room, she put her hands over her eyes and tried to stiffen herself. She was uneasy and ashamed. When she was out of favour with her mother she remembered that she was living here because she had nowhere else to live. She had no husband, no room that was her own. If I had been a success no one would have said, You are the wrong person to bring up your own child, she thought, with shame and growing anger.

The smell of wood smoke came into the room. She looked out. Pale wisps and spirals rose from a heap of green in the field. The strong sunlight pressed down the flames. In the house someone struck a note on a piano, then a run of notes. Her mother's voice tried over a line of a song. It came out loud and strong for a moment, weakened suddenly, missed a note, then ceased.

She's not vexed, Hervey thought. At once she wished her mother had finished the song. Why did she stop ? I know why, her voice felt weak to her, she couldn't reach the notes. Hervey clenched her hands. She could not bear the thought that her mother no longer felt certain of her voice. How she used to sing then, she thought. Loud and clear, drowning the uncertain voices of her children, Mrs Russell sang *The River of Years* and *White Wings they never grow weary.* They stood round the piano to listen. Her foot pressed on the pedals and her hands, the fingers a thought swollen, struck boldly the notes. Bright with pleasure, her eyes followed the words as she sang. A fury of love and pity overcame Hervey when she remembered it. Why aren't you young now ? she cried. Her throat felt hard with grief.

Her mother was at the centre of her life. She rebelled against her, at times with dislike, but she was bound to her by a love in which bitter and hurting things were drowned.

There was no one whom she admired as she admired her mother.

She watched the wind rushing down the field of long grass. The grass lay over like waves rushing in green and silver under a ship. Again her heart was near breaking with grief. She loves these country things so much ; she ought to live for ever, not to die and lose them. I too—all the pain and discontent and the striving will be as if it had never been. She gripped the edge of the window. Why can't you live for ever ? she said furiously, seeing her mother's hands. You must, I tell you.

She went downstairs. Her mother was still in the front room. A woman in a thin grey coat had come in and was sitting there. She had a lean tired face : she sat with her hands folded, smiling in an unlistening way when Mrs Russell spoke to her. The contrast between the two women startled Hervey. Her mother was older and frailer than her friend, yet she had more life in one hand than the other woman in her whole body.

'You shouldn't do it for them,' Mrs Russell was saying, in an energetic voice. '*I* wouldn't, Mary. I wouldn't work like that for anyone living. Tell them you can't do it.'

The other woman listened with an uneasy smile. 'It's the first week this season I've had all my rooms let. You can't do what you like when you take visitors. They leave you and go elsewhere if they're not satisfied. And it's a short enough season.'

'Nonsense,' Mrs Russell said. 'Visitors or no visitors, season or no short season, I wouldn't *do* it.'

Hervey sat quietly and listened. For a moment she had an extraordinary feeling of love and understanding of all such tired, anxious, unattractive women, coming, with pro-pitiatory glances, into rooms, going away, shutting doors, opening and closing windows, drawing blinds up, drawing them down again at night or against the sun, turning down the tops of beds, preparing trays, climbing with them up flights of stairs, answering bells. 'We see you have rooms to let.'

'What do you charge?' 'Is the water hot?' 'Is this facing the sea?' 'Is it quiet?' Is life nothing but bells and stairs and trays of food? Is the grave quiet? The woman's thoughts and feelings rose in pale wisps and spirals in Hervey's mind. You are living in me, she thought. I could speak for you, I could lie in your bed and wear your clothes; I am you.

2. *Night image*

Hervey lived with Richard in the country, where the valley of Danesbeck begins to narrow entering the hills. They had here two rooms in a house within walking distance of Miss Holland's. In the morning Hervey wrote at her third book and again in the evening until past midnight when her eyes were falling into her head with sleep. She wrote quickly and easily about fancied events, having no respect for words. Certain thoughts and feelings started an excitement in her brain, and she was under the delusion that this had some connection with literature.

In the afternoon Richard was with her. She played with him and took him out. Her pride in him was excessive. He was tall for his seven years, brown as a berry, his eyes wide, a deep bright blue, with black heavy lashes. He was quick, graceful, and lazy. He hated to exert himself. Hervey took such care of him as never was, and yet she had no pleasure in talking to him. She was herself too young to talk to a child. She wanted company of her own age.

She did not know what Richard was thinking when they walked. He was apt for silence as a Trappist or she was. He gave no more than half an eye to the real world. Once he told her a story about a young bird, but it was no bird, it was himself. They went here and there, the careless-walking, shabby young woman and her handsome child, in woods and meadows, each fast in his own mind. When Richard talked she listened, anxious to please. He only listened when something she said amused him.

One hot day they sat down under a tree beside a stream.
'Once I was disappointed,' said Richard suddenly. 'I was
in the Christmas bazaar by myself and I met an old lady
who knows me. She said, "Would you like to go and
refresh yourself at that stall? Have you some money?"
I said No, but she thought I said Yes, and she said, "Then
why don't you go and refresh yourself?"'

'That was a bad day,' Hervey said. She looked at him
with a smile. At the same moment she thought, I wish I had
enough money to travel, I have never seen Spain. The shutter
of a foreign house was flung open and a hand set a pot of
herbs on the sill. I should be happier if I were not greedy.
Can I possess myself in patience? I shall work harder and
harder, I shall learn Spanish. She watched her son trying to
make a raft from the tough dry reeds. He had a little skill
and no patience. Now she was seized by an irrational fear
that something terrible would happen to him. The more
radiant living creatures are the less use life has for them,
she thought. Rousing herself from this old nightmare she
tried to help him to plait reeds, but her fingers were as
awkward as his and the reeds broke. 'We might try the
Lord's prayer,' Richard said, frowning.

'Do you think it would help?' she asked.

Without answering, he repeated it. He looked at her
face when he was saying it, and at the end he said: 'What do
you think of it?'

'Well, I like it,' Hervey said.

'Yes, I think it's a good one myself. My throat hurts.'

Her mind jumped, then steadied into silence. She looked
into his throat, but nothing showed. But they went home
and in the night he woke and woke Hervey and said: 'But
my throat does hurt.' There and then Hervey got up and
dressed herself, to be in good time. There was diphtheria in
the town, many cases. Before the doctor she sent for came
she made her mind up that if Richard had diphtheria he
should stay with her. No isolation hospital for him, she
thought.

And so it was. He had that diphtheria and Hervey was so certain the woman of the house would let him stay that the woman did.

He had it lightly, yet Hervey would watch the first nights. She took a chipped saucer and floated a night-light in it, and put it near her chair. Her chair stood between the light and his bed, in the narrow cave hollowed out of the surrounding darkness. She could think that outside the country lay as wild and harsh as when the Danes landed and burned the first town, leaving charred ash of timber and at the edge of the cliffs the blackened stones. That sound might be branch grinding on branch or it could be—they ran their cruel ships on to the beach and afterwards there was the smoke curling about the walls the dead sons the mess the stones the mess of blood on the stone. Richard slept without moving. She folded her hands and thought of her book. She had begun to suspect that she was a foolish writer, taking excitement for feeling and ideas for thoughts. I ought to write simply, she thought. I exaggerate events in my mind. When I think, She is dying, it is I who am dying, and I pity myself. A thought of Penn jumped into her mind. The truth is I have never forgiven him for bringing that girl to London. It is a year since I knew and I am a fool. Where did they go the first time ? Did they go together ? Did she go first ? Did he open the door and see her waiting for him ? Was she ready ? It has broken me : I'm old. I don't want to think of it. I don't want to think. *Stand close around, ye Stygian set, with Dirce in one boat convey'd*. Oh no, oh no no no no I won't think about it I won't look *Sweet day, so cool, so calm, so bright*. Please not. What are they doing ? What are they saying ? The truth is, there is no one in the whole world no person nothing you can trust. Make a note of it for the future. *Bist du mit mir*. She felt her body contract with hot pain. Scalding tears ran over her cheeks. I loathe them, I am sick with my loathing. Why are we like that ? It is foul like worms like dying like earth. She thought Richard had moved. She was still at once and looked. She had not made a sound, but it came to her, Could what I am thinking disturb him? That quieted her. Richard slept on and she sat without moving, thinking of her book, until he woke.

He asked her in what he believed to be an invalid's voice what time it was. 'About six,' Hervey said. The windows were open but the blinds hung without moving. Hervey pulled them up and at that the sun came in, it was like a stamping horse.

'Now give me my little friend,' Richard said. She felt under the pillow and in his bed and found that old bear; it was very flat and looked to be dying, or else it was only shamming. Richard embraced it indifferently. 'I didn't sleep a wink all night,' he said, looking at Hervey.

'You've been asleep for ten and a half hours,' Hervey said.

He was much offended and said coldly: 'That's not a great deal for a boy.'

Hervey made him comfortable and went downstairs. She brought him milk, honey, and white grapes. To watch him drink sent a thrill of joy through her. She held the cup and it seemed that her own strength was feeding him.

He had not been ill at all. He lay in bed and drank milk, ate eggs, fish, fruit, honey, and grew rosier daily. There was a bottle of Valentine's meat juice on the washstand. Hervey had bought it because it was costly, but he liked it and she fondly thought it the better for what it cost. She had been told that he must lie still and to keep him lying on his back she read to him hour after hour, until her penny whistle of a voice cracked. Richard was without mercy. As she read she thought of herself walking in London with Philip and T.S.; of lighted rooms filled with famous writers and she was famous, her witty talk made her accepted of the accepted; of Vienna which she had not yet seen, of yellow houses near the quay in Antwerp where when she was a child she walked and came into a narrow street into the Place Verte in sunshine with the flower women the shop where they ate the cakes the rue de la Mair the Place de la Mair the trees the tall schoolboys in socks and blouses the open trams the music at night the people walking under the trees in the darkness the few lights what are they playing her mother's clear voice like a sudden fountain Un Rêve Printanier in memory of early days.

The day when her second novel came out was five days after Richard fell ill, and she forgot that was the day. The next morning she remembered it. Perhaps there will be a letter about it, she thought. She waited for the postman. There were no letters for her. The next day and the next there was no letter. A complete silence had fallen on the world, as if Danesacre were the only place that had survived a new flood.

On Sunday morning she was reading to Richard as usual. Suddenly she heard her mother speaking outside. ' Hervey ! Are you there ? I want you.'

Startled, she closed the book and ran over to the window. Mrs Russell was standing under the window showing her a newspaper and smiling.

' It says here your book is fine and exquisite. A masterpiece. Wait, I'll read it to you.'

She was full of excitement and elation. Her eyes shone, as blue and living as a girl's. She was quite joyous, quite gay.

Hervey's heart slid under her ribs. Well, it's certainly not a masterpiece, she thought. But she was pleased the book had been praised. A warm feeling of confidence and satisfaction spread through her. She listened, gripping the window sill. Now I have done something, she thought, now she is pleased with me. It was the same feeling, hardly changed at all by time, that had seized her when the scholarship came to her and again when she got her First. It was half excitement, half relief, as if she had felt that she could now rest a little before she made a further effort to please her mother. Those first triumphs had led to nothing, they must have come to seem like failures to her, like a poor end, she thought. This is different. Something begins. Now, here begin the life and works of Mary Hervey Russell. A strange exciting

sense of power came to her; she laughed, looking at her
mother, who had finished the review and was waiting for her
to speak.

' Thank you for bringing it,' she said.

' I always knew you would do well,' Mrs Russell said.
' I didn't expect anything so good as this, though.'

The words filled Hervey with love and sudden fear.
Don't expect too much of me. She could scarcely endure to
see her mother so pleased with this tiny success. You have
had so little, and you should have had everything, she thought,
hurt and angry.

' It's only one review,' she muttered.

' There'll be others,' Mrs Russell said.

Will there be any money? Hervey wondered. ' If the
book sells I'll buy you something you want and can't afford,'
she boasted.

A short time after she had an affectionate letter from
Penn, enclosing several reviews, all long and praising. She
was pleased by them. The letter ended with the words,
' I hope you are happier, my love. I have been a bad husband
but I do love and admire you, and I will not if I can help it
do anything to wound you again.' Strangely enough she felt,
as she read it, a certainty that she was cured of Penn. I don't
love you but I am used to you and I am bound to you, she
thought. Am I a coward? Am I afraid to be alone?

Later she came by chance on a review which said her book
was the silliest ever written. This impressed her more than
any. She did not wholly believe it but she went to school
with it for her good.

After waiting a month or so she wrote in great fear to
Charles Frome, and asked him whether the book had earned
any money. He sent her by return a cheque for a hundred
and seventy pounds. This kindness she should have been
more obliged for, if she had not been too astonished by her
own merit to notice his.

CHAPTER XXIX

FEBRUARY 8, 1923

1. *Two of Class 1913*

HERVEY was in Danesacre six months before she left it again. She had written a third novel. An uncontrollable impatience with her quiet life possessed her. She must have eaten knives, as they say.

Leaving Richard with Miss Holland for three days, she went up to London. This journey was a score of journeys, one sliding into another in her mind as the train left Danesacre, the water in the harbour grey, the sky the colour of grey water, the iron-bound moors, coming then into the sodden Midlands and the air growing flat and heavy as they came south. She was travelling during the War and the corridors were crammed with men in clumsy khaki, talking, smoking, lying asleep; she had heavy Richard in her arms; she was alone, going eagerly to London to make her fortune; she was alone still, with no fortune but with unmanageable desires and unabateable ambitions, with a new dress and an old coat, with twenty-eight years gone and with nothing done and all to do. To look at her as she sat with a forbidding air in her corner of the carriage you would not think she had so many journeys in her.

She reached London after dusk and spent the evening walking with herself, in an indescribable excitement squeezed from the crowded irregular streets, the lights and darkened doorways, the gaiety, the furtive faces, the misery, the colours running pell-mell over restaurants and theatres, the smells, all that whirl of stone and cataract of bodies caught in the forms they assumed for one moment one evening in February 1923, once and once only, then and only then.

In the morning she was with T.S. He did not look pleased at her, and she felt embarrassed. But when they were going along he looked at her and said : ' Upon my word, Hervey, you're the only person I want to see. Why don't we live together ? I think I could stand you four days out of five.'

Hervey laughed and felt easy again. He asked why she had let Penn run away to Oxford. An impulse to abase Penn made her say : ' He arranged it without asking me.'

' Did he ask you how you were going to live ? '

' I can look after myself,' Hervey said. She felt ashamed of her evil impulse and said quickly : ' I advised him to go.'

' But why ? '

' I don't know.' She frowned, trying to tell the narrow truth. ' I wanted something to happen. I wanted Penn to leave me by myself so that perhaps something would happen.'

' What did you imagine would happen ? '

' I don't know.'

' Are you satisfied ? '

' No. Yes.'

In a moment T.S. said : ' I wish my wife'ud leave me.'

' Can't you leave ? ' Hervey said. She looked at him.

' No, I ha'ant the energy, Hervey. If she kicked me out I'd go happily—but I don't think she wants to be left with her William. Can you imagine a woman bringing herself to embrace William Ridley ? That face and gross body. Inconceivable. Most women are damnably unfastidious, if you don't mind my saying it.'

' Do you mind much ? ' Hervey said swiftly.

' Did you like it when Penn——? '

' No. Leave me out.'

' I agree. There isn't a comparison. I haven't your curiously physical imagination. Also I'm sorry for Evelyn, and I'm tired. Her mind is no help to her ; she should have married a tower of strength.' He burst out laughing. 'When I came back in 1918 I wanted a mother, not a wife.'

'It was a bad war.'

'Bad for you, Jake, Philip, David Renn. Good for Thomas Harben.'

'Can't we save ourselves from the Harbens?'

'Not in this world.'

'I forgot. You're working for them.'

'Forget it again.' He put his head down and smiled. 'You can't quarrel with me, our Hervey. I know you better than if I was in love with you. Funny, ain't it? I suppose I'm the only man who knows how anxious you are to please people. You'd agree with the devil, wouldn't you?'

'Only to his face,' Hervey said. 'Not if I were quietly in my room writing about him.'

'Why to his face?'

'People confuse me. When I'm with people they confuse me. My mind is not suited to go much into company.'

'You can't bear to be laughed at, can you?'

'No,' Hervey said. She knew that she shrank from ridicule with a nearly insane fear.

'I used to think you had a masculine mind. Nowadays I realise that the only male virtues your mind has are thoroughness and slowness. In every other way it's a woman's mind—clear, logical, bitter, ironical, and nasty. But, my poor Hervey, you have a masculine heart. It becomes possessive and domineering with your equals, and as soft as water with the young and weak. It is the cause why you are shocked by cruelty. Not only is your heart a polite heart, but it has imagination. You're lost. By the way, have you enough money or do you want me to lend you some?'

'I have enough for three more months.'

'Cross your heart?'

'Cross my heart.'

'Talking to me doesn't confuse you, does it?'

'You're my only friend,' Hervey said in a serious voice. 'There were three of us with Philip.' There was a glass

behind the next table : two men got up from it and went
out, and she could see herself and T.S. in the glass.   A curious
emotion seized her, as if she were seeing their younger selves
seated there before the War.   In that reflected room Philip
could come.

'Class 1913,' T.S. said.

'We ought to keep together.'

'What is left of the company will advance in loose formation.   Or not advance.'

'I shall advance,' Hervey said.

'You can count on me in any personal way.   You can't
count on me to turn Socialist with you.   That's all moon-
shine, my dear.   It used to be a religion.   It is an establishment.   It used to have martyrs.   Now it has respectable
leaders of Trades Unions.   I saw your friend David Renn
yesterday.   He talked like a Communist.   Don't deceive
yourself, I said.   Communism is no go in this middle-class
country, and even if it were, even if it were, they don't want
you to help them.   Or you.   Or me.   Don't think you can
belong to a new age by going to meetings in shabby rooms,
sitting round deal tables, and addressing the others as
" comrade."   You're not their comrade.   You're mine but
you're not theirs.'   His face twitched.   ' A new age is no
damned good to me.   I shan't understand it and I shan't like
it.   Class 1913.   It was a fine class and it lived in a damned
fine world.   Hear me.   I'm bragging.   I know what England
was like in 1913.   You can keep the change.   Maybe you
don't know yet where you belong, you and David Renn.
Comrades?   I've s—seen comrades!   I'll tell you both something.   The world you're part of, bone of, is finished.   You're
a Socialist.   Very well—you believe in reason.   You believe
you can reason people into tolerance and good will.   I tell
you that's a dead dream which stinketh.   The new age is
being prepared by unreason, to be brought in with violence,
to maintain itself by violence.   In that day reasonable people
will be swept aside.   This is something you don't know yet;
you will know it, and you won't like it.   This isn't the world

I was born into, you'll say. Nor is it. Your world's finished,
I tell you.'

He pushed his cup aside and put both hands on the table.
He had been sending his nails into the flesh. She could see
the marks there.

' I don't believe you.'

' As you like. You will, though.'

' Your world may be finished. Mine isn't. Not yet.'

' Comrade Hervey Russell.'

Hervey laughed. ' If it weren't for Richard, I don't mind
what happens.'

' There's always Richard. Do you think you love anyone
else ? '

' My mother. You.'

' Brass before and brass behind, Never cared a —— for any
other kind ! Hervey loves me. When are you going home,
Hervey ? '

' To-morrow,' Hervey said. She hesitated and said : ' I
have a letter from your wife in my pocket.'

' I don't want to see it.'

' She and I had a quarrel of a kind. Now she asks me to
go and see her.'

' Go. Why don't you ? '

' I shall say the things I don't mean.'

T.S. laughed at her. ' You'll take them all back afterwards.'

2. Reconciliation of opposites

She sat in Evelyn's room and listened, with surprise and
growing unease. She felt embarrassed and vexed. What you
are saying is not true, she thought ; and even if it were you
ought not to say it. She kept her head down, avoiding
Evelyn's eye.

' You know, Hervey, I was very fond of you,' Evelyn
said. ' I can't think how I let you quarrel with me.'

Hervey looked at her without speaking. She could not

believe that Evelyn had an affection for her.   Nor could she believe that Evelyn would give herself the trouble of lying about it.   Hervey's pride and her sense of decency were outraged.   This woman must be going off her head, she thought gloomily.   It is very trying.   She was repelled, uneasy.   Do I look as foolish as I feel ?

'Actually I'm a very lonely creature ;   there is only one other woman I love,' Evelyn said.

'You're very kind,' Hervey mumbled.   I must look at her with a candid gaze.   It isn't true ;   she is pretending to feel this nonsense.   Can she be telling the truth ?   She did not attempt to understand Evelyn.   The more intense the older woman became, the less warmth Hervey felt for her.   A sullen resistance sprang in her.   Beside Evelyn's elegant airs she felt uncouth, shabby, an awkward schoolgirl.   At the same time she felt a contempt.   These emotional words disgusted her.

'I hope we shall always be friends,' Evelyn said.

'I hope so, too,' Hervey answered, with a clear look. Her quick warm childish smile contrasted with the gloom in her voice.   She was ashamed of herself for taking part in this pretence.   She felt that it was a pretence.   Yet in part of her mind she knew that Evelyn was actually moved—she knew this, but she could not feel it and she did not for a moment understand or enjoy it.   Outwardly, she was pleased, underneath she felt cold and stupid, a block of wood.

'Now tell me about yourself,' Evelyn said.   'I'm told your new novel is good.'

'No.   There are one or two true pages '—she was thinking of pages about herself and Penn—'the rest is false.'

'It is selling, isn't it ?   You'll make plenty of money.'

Hervey did not think that two hundred pounds would seem to Evelyn 'plenty of money.'   She was about to say so, when an unpleasant Yorkshire instinct pulled her up sharply : don't let her think you poor, it said.

'It has sold very well,' she said, with an air of reserve.

Evelyn glanced at her.   She may have felt the lack of

warmth in Hervey. A flicker of malice came into her gaze, and yet she wanted Hervey to like her—she had been telling part of the truth. 'When your husband was here the other day he told me that the book was in its tenth thousand.'

Hervey felt a pang of alarm. She had not known, Penn had kept it from her, that he was seeing Evelyn. She wiped all surprise out of her face and voice. 'That was during his vacation.'

'Yes of course,' Evelyn answered. 'We were dining at the same house, and after dinner he talked to me for a few minutes and I asked him to come here. He would tell you about it, of course.'

'Yes,' Hervey said.

'I liked him much better, Hervey. In fact I think he's very charming and intelligent. I'm sending him some books to review for me.'

'How kind of you,' Hervey said. She felt that there was something else to come. Her hands trembled.

'He's in the greatest trouble about you, Hervey. He feels that you'll never wholly forgive him for making love to that dancer. And he loves you so deeply. Everything he said to me about you proved that. He has the deepest admiration for you. For your talents. I said I was sure you were much too wise to allow an incident with an actress, however young and charming, to weigh on your mind.'

An actress? Hervey thought. Dancer? Surprise and bewilderment had almost made her lose hold of her mind. She felt it becoming blank. Evelyn's voice went on gently : 'You know, my dear, so many men had these affairs during the War. Hysterical women. I rather agree with you that he should have dropped her when he was living with you again—yet, after all, is it important ? He didn't care for her in any deep way. I am sure you are the one woman he loves.'

A cynical amusement filled Hervey. So for Evelyn's benefit the buxom young V.A.D. had become a dancer, an actress. How like Penn that was. She began to laugh inside

herself. She laughed, and yet it humiliated her. She felt
tired, as if she could not go on. Why has he confided in
Evelyn whom he scarcely knows ? And he knew that she
was not my friend, she said to herself coldly. She felt that
something in her had been damaged by it.

‘ You’re not going to turn him off, Hervey ? ’

‘ Of course not,’ Hervey said. She smiled, looking at the
other woman with an indifferent stare. She would rather
die than let Evelyn see that she had been taken by surprise.
Or that anything Penn had done hurt her.

‘ I feel sure he never meant to betray you. I suppose it
happened to him. He’s a boy, for all his twenty-eight years.’

‘ He is thirty-one, he will be thirty-two in June,’ Hervey
said. Her contempt for Evelyn grew stronger every moment.
But she felt hopeless, and bitter against both of them, against
the woman, and against the man who had not the common
decency to hold his tongue about himself. He is soft and
loose, he has no dignity, she thought, bitterly. She sat with
a fixed smile.

‘ He showed me the letter he was sending you about your
book. You don’t mind it, do you ? ’

‘ Not in the least. Why should I ? ’ Hervey said. Now
I am too tired, now I am done with him, she said to herself.
She felt that she disliked every living human being. Her mind
shrank from people, from speech and contact with them.
She wanted to hide, to run back to Danesacre. I can stand
my own people : I can’t stand these spineless literary blokes,
she thought. A smile, the reflection outwards of the bitter-
tasting Yorkshire humour, crossed her eyes. Her face held
its stolid expression, stolid and at the same time evasive, as
if she were only half attending to what she heard.

Evelyn looked at her with quiet satisfaction, in which there
was also a little pity. Though there was nothing to be seen,
she had felt Hervey flinch under her words. This gratified
and made her feel tender towards the young woman. She
wanted to do her some kindness. With real delicacy she
began trying to discover whether Hervey needed money, or

work.   She herself needed a literary secretary : she thought that perhaps she could use Hervey and help her with the one coin.

But here she was bested by Hervey.   The girl's shrewdness came up at once : she would not say that she wanted work. She had the quickness to know that if she said that, Evelyn would make her an offer and it would be a poor one.

She sat and listened with a reserved smile, and shortly rose. ' I must go,' she said, in her light voice.   Her voice had scarcely altered since she was a child.   Either you liked it or it annoyed you ; it vexed Evelyn now, to have failed to manage Hervey as she wished and then to hear her speak in this thin pure voice.   She slides out of one's hand like water, she thought, at a loss and vexed.   Her self-importance was roused.   To punish Hervey she said good-bye to her with a snubbing dignity.   It had no visible effect.   Evelyn was left standing with her dignity in her arms.

Not for the first time, and against her will, she recognised a massive quality in the young woman, enforcing respect. It was not true, she thought, that Hervey slid out of your hands.   You came up roughly against a blank wall in her, and found that she had gone.   It disconcerted.   With sudden certainty Evelyn thought, That young woman is indifferent because she mistrusts everyone : she has raised her bridges, she is cut off from the rest of us by her own act.

4. *The Romantic*

Penn was waiting for Hervey in the brasserie of the Café Royal.   He had come up from Oxford only to spend an hour or so with her, and while he waited he watched eagerly the people at the other tables.   He loved to come to these places, to feel about him the threads of lives supporting a web round his own.   It gave him substance.   His mind sucked in sounds and colours like taking a stain, and only to contemplate this stain gave him pleasure, as if he had put it there by his efforts.

He knew why Hervey was late—she wanted to be sure that he would be waiting, not to have to walk shyly to a table and to sit at it for a few moments alone. Queer creature. He hoped uneasily that she was not going to reproach him for not writing to her oftener. She wants this, she expects that, he thought, but all the time what she is wanting is to punish me for that business. He felt a sharp pity for Hervey because he had made her cry. At the same time the thought of the other young woman stirred him. The two impulses did not interfere with one another. They flowed warmly and naturally in him side by side. Now one now the other drew his senses.

He did not like to think of Hervey in tears. When a painful thought entered his mind he got rid of it as swiftly as possible. Poor love, my poor love, he thought: deeply moved, he thought, After all it has brought us closer together. And this soothed and softened him.

He had a copy of Hervey's novel on the seat beside him. It had been entrusted to him by an undergraduate who wanted Hervey to sign it. Penn had talked a great deal in Oxford about his wife. He was unconscious of lying when he described incidents and triumphs that had never happened. They happened in his mind at the moment he was describing them. The more he could praise Hervey to these young men and make her seem fine and marvellous, the easier he felt. It fed his love and his resentment. He loved her; he was never free of her in his mind. And he deeply resented her. He did not know how deeply, nor from what source he drew his impulses of hate and anger. When he praised her writing he belittled it by adding that she could not have done it without his help.

Despite himself he knew that he had disappointed her in some way more profoundly and irremediably than by his unfaithfulness. Her life with him had disappointed. But for this she would have forgotten the other. He did not admit it. He said that she was discontented and restless by nature: no human being could have pleased her: and in this way he refused his responsibility, as he had always refused responsibility for their two lives.   Her unhappiness, her certainty that she had been cheated, were (said he) her fault. This was true. That on another level of being the fault was his he did not admit. He could not admit it. It remained, a heavy and unrecorded item in the sum of their lives, falsifying the balance.

He had a letter from Len Hammond in his pocket. It was the first she had written him since, half to please Hervey and half glad to be saved from what was becoming nearly a responsibility, he had ceased going to her. It was a sad letter. She missed him, she was lonely living at home; she missed his talk as much as the other things : ' dear Penn, you were the only clever intelligent man I have ever known, and you have spoiled me by this for other men.   After knowing you, they seem dull and usual.'   Poor Len, poor loving unhappy Len.   A deep tenderness was freed in him, like a spring. It soothed and refreshed him. She will believe that I have forgotten her if I don't write, he thought.   Or that I am callous. He could not endure the thought that he would be diminished in the girl's sight.   Already the phrases of his reply to her letter were alive in him.   If he had not momently expected Hervey he would have scribbled them down, so eager was he to comfort and be comforted.   And if she wanted it, he would see her.   Not as before, not to have her, but only to comfort her and to prove, to himself and her, that he could withstand the temptation.

On the seat beside Hervey's were two books Evelyn had sent him that morning. They came as he was leaving his rooms and he had not wished to leave them behind.   In the train he looked at them and thought of the moment when he would lay one carelessly on the table before Hervey with the words :

' I'm reviewing this for the *London.*'

Already he saw himself become indispensable to Evelyn. She would rely on him more and more, until the day when she would suggest his joining the staff as her assistant.   Assist-

ant literary editor to the *London Review*. Literary editor,
Mr Penn Vane, the well-known critic, essayist, and *bon
viveur*. He smiled, then checked himself quickly. Thank
God I don't need success, he thought solemnly: I can be
happy without it.

Hervey came into the room. She came a few steps and
hesitated, looking for him. Well he knew that air of stiff
self-possession: it meant that she was ready to sink into the
ground, in an agony of doubt at finding herself alone here.
He stood up in his place and waved. He could see the sudden
relief in her face.

She seemed small coming towards him. For a moment
the fumes of his self-destroying egotism cleared and he saw
her as, when she was most nearly free, she was—eager,
mistrusting herself, shy, clumsy, too sensitive, too proud,
buying liking with affection and services. He saw that
neither her pride nor her kindness saved her. She is as
awkward as a child, he said to himself; and he saw her
learning and forgetting not to expose her greenness to every
wind. But now she had seated herself at the table. She
dragged her hat off and laid it between them, in the careless
way that vexed him. That intractable forehead showed all
too plainly since she had taken to brushing back her hair.
Childlike? He glanced at it and at her long stubborn jaw
with a revulsion of feeling.

Hervey folded her hands and looked at him with her sudden
intimate smile. Had he, she asked anxiously, been long here
waiting for her?

'Of course,' Penn said. He spoke with self-conscious
humour at the waiter. 'Luckily I realise that women have
no sense of time.' The man returned a civil grin, which
pleased him and he was again softened to Hervey. He
squeezed her arm.

Hervey disliked this clowning so much that she could not
look at it. She kept her head down. When the man went
away she asked hurriedly whether he was happy at Oxford.
At once he began to describe the intrigues surrounding his

election to a certain literary society. One man had sworn to keep him out. 'And I know why the swine is doing it,' he said, in an arrogant voice. 'I fairly showed him up at dinner the other night, when he was talking of piloting an aeroplane. You don't know the rudiments of flying, I said to him. And I proved it.'

Hervey listened to him with a feeling of ironical wonder. Would he never realise that he created the hostility he met? People liked him at first sight, for his easy amiable manners, his flow of talk (even though his stories were not true). To buy only a moment's triumph he turned their liking to enmity, but then he did not know what had happened. He is insensible, she thought. Even that was not true.

He now looked at her with a complacent smile. She felt that she no longer admired him. To have lived through so much, the timidities of first love, the delight, the shame, poverty, ecstasy, the birth of a son, to have had so much, and after so much to sit here, to look, to feel, to think that this man's nostrils are gross and impudent, that he is too familiar with strangers (the grinning waiter), or offensive without cause, that he is not known or too cruelly known—I know the hands the face the tongue the voice the words, she thought. From to-day I should like to think, I don't know them. Or I have not known them.

But she was ashamed, and thought, I am denying the person I know best in the world.

Looking for something to say, she saw the books. 'I have just seen Evelyn. She said you were going to review for her.'

'Yes,' Penn said. 'As a matter of fact, these two books are review copies.' He gave her her own book to sign. 'Not a bad start, I think. I'm glad now I didn't write any hack articles for other papers. If you don't mind my saying so, pup, that thing you had in the *Daily Post* last week fairly dripped sentiment. I blushed. You won't do your reputation any good by it.'

'I know,' Hervey said. 'But it was ten guineas.'

'Not to be sneezed at,' Penn smiled. 'Never mind, my

dear. The day I finish with Oxford we'll settle down somewhere and you shall write only masterpieces.'

' I'll look forward to it,' Hervey said.

' By the time I leave I shall have a reputation as one of the
few real critics. Though I say it myself, I know how to
write really subtle criticism. It may not be as impressive as
writing novels but in a modest way it's useful, it's useful.'

' Good critics are infinitely rarer than novelists,' Hervey
said. He had made her, as he could, feel sorry for him.
She hoped with sharpened anxiety that Evelyn would like
what he wrote and would praise him. She had only a little
faith in Evelyn.

To give him pleasure now, and so that he would not lose
it if things turned out badly for him, she began to say, Why
not write an entire book of criticism ? ' You could do that
at the same time as your reviews, and it would be a more
solid achievement.' He was very willing to do this, and she
began to plan it, using for her notes the wrapper of one
of Evelyn's books. In these few moments they were good
friends and she thought, How foolish I was to marry ; we
went on very well before, and we could now, if it were not
for the burden of intimacy.

He had to hurry back to Oxford at six o'clock. And she
went off to see David Renn. She walked quickly along the
lighted streets. At night London is diminished by the weight
of darkness about it, and the people against whom one brushes
are smaller and spectral. To walk then alone is to fancy
oneself a ghost. This ghost of Hervey went on, thinking of
her husband. Suddenly she thought, A woman is living whose
knowledge of him is as intimate as mine ; for three years
she knew better than I, since she knew that they were deceiv-
ing me and made plans to see each other ; was taking her to
himself ; she knows many of my secrets (why should he hold
his tongue ?) and she will know this of me as long as she lives.

She felt herself growing hot, her heart thudding. An
indescribable bitterness and anguish filled her and the nerves
of her chest ached. It was Penn did this to me ; it seems to

be impossible. It is unbearable. I want now to forget.
I can't believe it. I can't forget it. That it should be me.
There were plans, secrets, thoughts in their minds of me.
I am mad with bitterness. Why, tell me why Penn did this
to me. Tell me now. To have an excuse for clapping her
hand to her chest she drew her coat over it. Now she passed
a spectre who made the same gesture. Now she was crossing
Trafalgar Square, where the fountains were still. At once
words springing in her mind falling returning echoing
comforted her. *The fountains are still. Are not my fountains
still ?*

5. Husband and wife

T.S. found his wife's room empty. He waited for her in
the window, where he could see the river, the lights along
the river, and on the south side a line of buildings that for all
he could see were walls leaning on darkness. God be thanked
for ships, he thought. If we had always had aeroplanes we
should have had less need of rivers, and London Paris Vienna
and all their sisters might have hung dry tongues out of their
mouths. At night the Thames is the second loveliest river,
running as dark under its reflected lights as when the Romans
first laid eyes on it. These died in any case. Before the
Romans there were savages living not too comfortably down
there. Civilisation advances some thousand years ; and there
are still shivering half-starved men trying to live through a
February night on the bank of the river. God be thanked
for picric acid. Some February evening the aeroplanes will
come and the whole thing will go up in dust and flame.

He heard his wife come into the room, and turned round.
A curious impatience seized him. He wanted to punish her
for having made him a fool and at the same time he did not
care to see her again, he was indifferent and tired. These
contradictory impulses fought in him while another, which he
did not recognise, stood and watched. He saw that she was
slightly disconcerted to find him in her room.

'Are you expecting a visitor?' he grinned. 'One of your devoted young writers?'

To his surprise she looked taken aback and frightened. 'Surely you are not afraid of me?' he said gently. 'Come, this won't do, Evelyn.' He found a difficulty in speaking, as though he were short of breath. He had never seen her look like this. He was sorry for her, but behind this pity, as it might be a quiet ante-room, his mind was in tumult with bitterness and resentment. His head felt hot. He controlled with effort a strong impulse to hurt her. Shall I tell her that she is being used by Ridley? He knew precisely how to humiliate her, with what words.

Looking at her, he said: 'You're less intelligent than I thought, my dear. No—believe this. I looked up to you, you know. Your self-assurance and all that. Now I realise that was a fake. Actually, you're on the defensive; bored; very very clever without being especially intelligent.'

'You've changed too,' Evelyn said.

'I know. Poor Evelyn.'

'Was it only the War?'

'I daresay.' He felt that he would lose control.

'You lost interest in me. I might not have had a husband.'

'So you had to fill my place,' T.S. said. He bit on a shocking epithet for Ridley. 'Sorry,' he said, smiling and looking into her face. 'Forgive an old soldier. But your own want of taste shocks me. I at least never wanted to make use of you to better myself.'

'You're intolerable.'

'I know, I know. But there you are. You can't tell what effect these human joinings and disjoinings are going to have until they've had it. Indeterminacy of emotions. Mark you, I don't pretend to understand it. Why should I, because I know the precise shape and texture of let's say your thigh, and I know that you breathe with a sort of bubble when you're falling asleep, and I know certain gestures you make in the act, why should I mind Ridley knowing? We're still not civilised. But of course marriage is uncivilised

—only fitted to animals or saints. Could you conceive any worse form of relationship for two intelligent beings than one that forces each of them to know whether the other takes cascara, coughs, spits, scratches ? Upon my word, I can't.'

' Please go away,' Evelyn said.

He felt as though he had talked himself empty. There's a fine dish of tripes for you, he thought, looking at his words. Has she the right to be offended ? Of course. One should preserve appearances.

He went away.

Evelyn sat still, and heard him go out of the house. She had come in the last moment to feel angry; but it was a double anger, with the feeling that she had been spared. He should have said nothing. He should have said more. She was left at a loss. It was as if he had judged her only as a woman and contemned her—as cruelly as if he had pitied her for being deformed or old. For such scorn, and such pity, she had no defence.

The door opened and William Ridley came in. He was wearing a new thick coat, in which he looked fat. He stumped across the room to his chair, sat down, thrust his legs forward apart, and smiled at her.

' You look rare and glum,' he said, smiling. ' Anything wrong ? '

' Nothing,' she said gently. ' Let me see, was I expecting you ? Is there anything I wanted to ask you ? '

' Never you mind about asking me anything,' Ridley grinned. His mood of excitement and exaltation lifted him above snubs. At these moments he obeyed easily the rule he had made for himself on coming to London—to remember that since all but a few people accept you at your valuation the higher you put it the better. He was actually deeply impressed by himself, but at the same time he had to deal with an unseen traitor—the lonely miserable squirmings of a Ridley no one except himself had seen. And just because this squirming creature existed, William Ridley was ready

x

to despise a woman who had surrendered to him, even when he was overflowing with gratitude to her. Already he had begun to feel that Evelyn was scarcely worth devotion—and this feeling was far from being soothed by the suspicion in his mind that as a critic of literature she rated him a great deal lower than she had yet allowed herself to say.

' I came in on my way home,' he said—not giving himself the trouble to remind her of what she had certainly not forgotten, that this was his hour and day for coming—' yes, to tell you I've started writing that novel I told you about. I'm about ready now to do something'll make people sit up. I was telling Lucy Harben about it this afternoon. She thinks I've got a grand scheme for it. I've learned a lot in the last four years. You know the book I mean, don't you ? about a London restaurant, full of action and humour and characters, hundreds of characters, a real human book— absolutely original; none of your old stuff. I can do it, and I don't know any other writer who can.'

Evelyn saw this enormous book rolling towards her, with descriptions of faces and family parties and love scenes, with inventories of pantries and kitchens, with comic events, with speeches in character, corpulent, leg-slapping, something for all tastes and nothing for thought.

' I'm sure that is true,' she said in a smooth voice. She looked at him with an insulting air of amusement and irony. Seized with despair, she was thinking, Long before he finishes this frightful book he will have finished with me. For a moment she felt herself slipping into a darkness. But this darkness had been close to her the whole time, from the beginning of her separate life as Evelyn Lamb, the well-known critic. She felt herself slowly being isolated, and however eagerly she ran towards this and that physical contact, hoping to lose herself, to be reassured, the dread sense of isolation increased. For a short time after her marriage she imagined that at last she had ceased to be alone, but this idea too failed her and with the increasing dryness of her life she saw the whole world fading about her, into a darkness in which no

voice could reach her and her hand would encounter no
seeking hand. She glanced at a picture standing on the floor
against the wall. ' Have you noticed my Van Gogh ? ' she
said languidly. ' I paid too much for it, I daren't tell you
how much.' She went over to look at the picture, laying her
hand lightly on Ridley's arm. I look old this evening. The
oil, the herbal packs over my eyelids, rest, sleep ; why do I
take this trouble ? who will see me ? She curled her finger
in the folds of her dress. Tell me, what shall I do ? what
shall I ever do ?

6. *David Renn talks to his friend*

Climbing the stairs to David Renn's room Hervey thought,
I couldn't live in this place. The smell of dirty walls, of
bodies, pervaded the house. She had walked through a
warren of streets, passed houses in which there were as many
people as maggots in a piece of rotten cheese. In parts of
London it is possible to forget that other parts are as disgusting
as a badly-placed latrine. The street in which Renn lived
had a comparative air of decency and reserve, and yet it stank.
She had passed a Fun Fair on a piece of waste ground, a
shelter of corrugated iron, with wooden horses, slot machines,
and a mechanical organ. Drawn by the music, and the lights,
and by their penniless state, two little pallid girls stood in the
entrance. Otherwise, it was not patronised.

Renn seemed pleased to see her. He had set the table
with a clean tablecloth, a teapot, cheese, a loaf, and a few
biscuits. Hervey was impressed by the neatness of the room.
' Do you keep all this clean yourself ? ' she asked.

' Certainly. What did you expect ? I don't like living in
a disorder.'

' Then why do you live in such a street ? ' Hervey asked.

' For two excellent reasons. It is cheap. It puts me on
the side of the poor. I couldn't call myself the comrade of
these people if I lived in middle-class comfort in Bloomsbury
or Hampstead.'

'You wouldn't feel you had to sleep in a cancer ward because you were trying to cure it.'

'Clever,' Renn said, with a smile. 'But false.' A stain of colour showed itself under his cheek-bones. 'People speak of these streets as a blot on civilisation. False! You don't say of a man with leprosy on his hands that it's a blot on a healthy body. You say he is a leper. The slums of the poor are a leprosy. The social body isn't a healthy body diseased in spots—it is a leper's body. I'm beginning to believe that Europe is, too. Look at this from Germany.'

He showed her three photographs. First—black troops stopping a young German woman in the streets of a Ruhr town. Second—a poorly-clad man running with a load of paper, his week's wages, to change it into food. The value of the money fell even as he ran. Third—the body of a university professor of literature found lying in his room, dead of starvation.

Hervey looked at them without speaking. Renn said: 'What are you writing now, Hervey?'

'Another novel,' she answered awkwardly.

'Don't you know you haven't any right to write novels unless you put into it this slum and those black troops being used to bully Germans? We shall pay for both crimes.'

'Propaganda novels,' Hervey said. She pushed the photographs gently aside.

'Who writes any other kind?' Renn said in a sudden voice. 'Whether you know it or not, you're being used. You're either soothing or rousing people. You're persuading them that all's for the best in the best of possible worlds. Or you're warning them. You're telling them lies or truths. You're——' He stopped, biting his lip. 'Well, I'm a madman,' he said calmly. 'Have some more tea.'

Hervey pressed her knees together. They had begun trembling because she was afraid to say what she was going to say. Until this moment she had supposed that she still cared sharply about what was being done in Europe under the ægis of a dirty Peace. Once she had cared—enough to lie awake at nights, to go hungry so that she could give a little money to murdered Austria. Now incredible. It must be six months since I looked at a foreign newspaper, she thought. Why should I care ? All her passion of anger and pity had gone into nothing. It was finished. The photographs shocked her, but they did not make her burn with anger. But for coming here to-night she would never have seen them. Without thinking, she had closed her ears and turned her eyes from the spectacle of Europe being driven as an ox is driven towards the next war. It was too much. It was unendurable. Why watch it ? Eat, drink, work, for to-morrow you die again. I have my work to do, she thought sullenly. The thought that her next novel was certain to be a success flitted through her mind.

She looked at Renn. ' I can't write the kind of novel you want.'

' Why not ? '

' I don't know enough. What's more, I don't want to know.'

Renn jumped up. ' You've changed too much. Why, I don't know you. Are you going to spend the rest of your life to become a popular novelist, as if nothing mattered but your making a fat income ? You'd better go back to advertising. There's money in it.'

' I must make an income,' Hervey said. ' I have a son.'

' You have a son,' Renn mocked her. ' You have given birth to a charming piece of cannon-meat. Don't you see, you poor young fool, that if you let them, if you don't watch and listen and protest, they'll kill your son as they killed Philip and the others ? It must look funny from above. The war graves with their unpleasant tenants and the nurseries with theirs. I hope there is a God.'

Hervey's face had flushed an unlovely red. ' I have only a certain energy. I can't earn money for Richard and worry about Europe as well.'

If she could she would have explained to him the sudden drying up of her passion. For a time she had cared. For a time she had looked with deep horror at pictures like these now lying under her arm. They came into the office of *The Week*, and drove her to write with angry bitterness. They haunted her dreams. Then one sudden day it was all gone. Her mind was voiceless about Renn's three pictures.

'I can't help it,' she said roughly. She pushed the photographs towards him. 'I don't like these. But—I don't feel anything. It's no use. I have to live my life as best I can. You can't live it for me by telling me what to feel. I must find my own way. I'm lost now. Everything I know is turning and flying apart.' She looked at Renn with a childish smile. 'You don't know what awful confusion my mind is in, now, in these days. Imagine a pond after someone has stirred about in it with a stick.'

'Talk to me again when it settles,' Renn said.

Hervey stood up. 'Good-bye.'

'You're angry.'

'No. I haven't enough dignity to be angry.'

'Hurt, then.'

'No.'

She went away quickly, afraid that he would see how little she liked being snubbed by him. Her cheeks still burned.

After she had gone Renn could not at once get rid of her. He was surprised by the anger she woke in him. After a time he began to think that she would always anger people by her mingling of shyness and mulish obstinacy. He saw her, her listening face, the eyes a clear sky, and behind the clearness a storm of obstinacy gathering, to come down when least expected. Her virtues will offend more than her faults, he thought. Then, his anger cooling, he was sorry he had treated her with so much harshness. She is very kind, he thought, generous, and in the end she is honest. But it is too late to take back what I said; and besides—she will forgive me.

He cleared the table and sat down to write to his mother. But first he looked in his notebook at a column of figures, added the total, and compared it with another figure he had in his mind. The difference between the two figures was what was left of his savings. It was like the skin that shrank each time its owner uttered a wish; by now it was horribly small, scarcely large enough to make a glove.

'It is disappointing I cannot come down,' he wrote, 'but you know what it is with a new job. I enjoy the work, but I have to keep at it very close until I have earned a holiday. I am not sure when that will be, but one of these days you will be sitting reading by the fire, with your tongue between your teeth, and I shall walk in. You really must cure yourself of that habit. One evening when I startle you by coming in without warning you will nip the end of it off, and that will be a serious misfortune. Do you remember when I was living at school I used to rush home during the afternoon break, running all the way through five streets and arriving out of breath and unable to utter a word. One day you jumped round when I came in, and the soup you were stirring boiled over; you did not hear it at once and I could only point and point and you thought I had gone mad, and in your alarm you let it go on pouring over until I got my breath. My word, how I hated that school. Thank you for the cake. The ones I buy at—' (he had to stop a moment to remember where one can buy cakes) '—the place we had tea when you were up here, Buzzard's, are not the same thing. By the way, you can give up wondering—my leg doesn't hurt at all these days. I have just had a friend, a young woman, to supper. You would like her—but don't encourage any romantic notions, she's married, and in any case I shouldn't want to marry her. She's too erratic. I want someone quite soothing and gentle and as round as an apple.'

He ended the letter as he had been ending these letters once a week for fourteen years, exactly half his life, and folding the two £1 notes inside the sheet he closed the envelope, addressed it to Mrs. Renn, 5, The Street, Hitchin, and propped it against the tea cannister for the night.

He had given up his second room, and he slept now on the

couch. Usually when he was undressing he talked to himself,
or to anyone who was prepared to listen. 'You know, my
dear Renn, you ought to have explained to that young woman
that what is wrong with her is that she lacks a sense of values.
She doesn't know whether she is looking for truth or success.
You can't have both, not in this age. The truth is unpleasant. Who wants to be told that the next act is a squalid
tragedy ? If you want success you must join the saxaphonists.
A little nearer the end you can still play *Nearer my God to
Thee* and gather up the pennies thrown you by your deeply
moved and tearful audience. Now if our Hervey would
make up her mind what she wants——'

'Our Hervey is very slow.'

Renn glanced up. 'Oh, is it you ?' he said, pleased.

Philip leaned against the wall and looked at his friend with
a smile in which there was some irony. 'You have so little
patience,' he remarked.

'But there is so little time,' Renn said.

'What do you mean, so little time ?' Philip retorted.
'Time for what ? *I* hadn't much time, it's true, but the
human race didn't die with me, and there will always be
someone to enjoy living as well as I did.'

'That's no use to me,' Renn said sadly. 'I mean it's
awfully pleasant to talk to you, and it's decent of you to come
in like this—by the way, why are you wearing khaki ? it's
out of date, people will think you can't afford anything new—
but I'd rather you were alive, one can't say you showed much
politeness in dying in just the way you did ; and then, these
visits are a little uncertain, and to speak coarsely they have
too little body for my liking. As for all this talk of yours
about time, it doesn't reconcile me in the least to living in a
lunatic asylum.' He went on talking for several minutes,
amusing himself by proving exactly how out of date and
wrong-headed his friend's philosophy was ; stooping to take
off his shoes when he looked up again Philip had gone.

7. *As the night darkened*

As the night darkened Frank came out of The Dug-out and stood looking along the road. There was a faint glow on that part of the horizon to which he was turned, and to-morrow morning they would move that way and by night the glow would have closed round them. London. Two rooms in a street in the north-east of London, and a job which he did not expect to like. Lucky to touch it, he said, without conviction.

The carrier's cart with their furniture on board stood close to the hedge, the shafts resting across two boxes. He seated himself between them on one of the boxes. During the day he had been burning pieces of tarred wood and that salt odour lingered in the air. It flowed into the February smells of wet grass and frost, at night rising thinly from the un-quickened earth. As a child can only believe in what it sees he could not believe that something was over. Well, it's finished, he thought; here we are and here, in a manner of speaking, we aren't. But while he still breathed this air, thin, faintly acrid, cold, and felt under his hand the shaft of smooth worn wood, he could not feel a change.

Looking at The Dug-out he saw one window darken; a moment later a yellow glow came in the other. Sally had carried the lamp into their room and was undressing for bed. She had set the lamp by the window, but in his mind he saw it standing on the chest of drawers now wedged into the cart. A moment, and he remembered that the room was empty of all save their bed and the lamp. A feeling of uncertainty invaded him. Where had she stood it? Now he could not see the room in his mind. Empty, it did not exist. In a shadowy fashion other rooms filled its place and he saw a room in which he had been a child, and through that, like a reflection in water, the room into which a dozen dog-tired men had crowded at the end of a day's march. Which room? He could not have been sure. But there was a lamp, and outlined in that fine glow the face of a boy called—he remembered the name with excitement—Angus. Beyond that evening no memory of him remained, and he did not know whether he had died or lived; but only to have recalled a name from that time filled him with a deep excitement and satisfaction, as if something which had been left unfinished had now, with ease, been completed and could be put by.

He came back to himself and felt the cold, and the shaft under his hand. He stood up. By some road—it should have started from that room full of soldiers—he came to the morning when stepping whistling out of The Dug-out he saw the captain lying out there with his head on his arms. No one seen him that time but me, he thought. He moved stiffly towards the hut. In the first room his father-in-law was asleep or lying still in the darkness. He opened the other door softly and went into their room. Sally had been crying but she was asleep.

The darkness deepened after midnight. It pressed down the sleepers as if they lay in deep water. Their life died in them to a semblance, vague and distorted. Yet, imperceptibly at first, a current began to flow through the darkness, altering its nature. The blind surface of the water changed, but so weakly that you would not know whether what slipped over it was a ripple or the first actual breath of reflected light. The night turned. To the few watchers it was as if a signal, unseen by themselves, had brought the world about at the moment when it was voyaging out of sight.

The new lightness made itself felt in the senses even of the heaviest sleepers. Children and old people, between whose sleeping and waking life there is a briefer passage than for others, felt it quickest. Richard Vane opened his eyes and called out. This happened before he remembered that he was in his bedroom again in Miss Holland's house. He put his hand out and felt the quilt, and remembered. The handle of the door creaked slightly. Now she will speak, he thought. ' Richard ? ' He did not answer her. He could hear her slow breathing but he did not see her. Now she is listening, he thought. After a time he heard her move, and the door closed. He lay without moving, his eyes open.

At the same moment Mrs Russell woke smiling, with the words, 'For always and always,' on her lips. She remembered her dream at once, and her happiness vanished. She had been walking along a road, and her son had come to her and said, 'Mother, I've got the house I wanted.' She walked with him as far as a gate, and along a drive bordered with trees. The house was neither large nor small but it had fine windows and the rooms were all lofty and well made. He took her from room to room and she admired here a cornice and there a fine cupboard and from every window there were views over the country. It was the kind of country she liked, with tall trees, meadows, and in the distance a range of hills. 'I'm sure I love trees,' she said. 'Well, mother,' Jake answered, 'they're your trees, and this is our own house. We're going to live here together. You see I'm quite well and safe and I shan't want to go away again.' Mrs Russell was filled with joy. Her son, whom she had thought dead, was alive. And this house was what she had always wanted. She turned to look again at the rooms. It was growing dark and suddenly she thought that Jake was in another room. She hurried to go to him, but the passage was longer and darker than she had thought it. A little anxiety now laid its finger on her happiness but before she had found him she awoke.

A man standing on the platform of Danesacre lighthouse could now see that the lamp behind him was diminished. The darkness had become opaque and as the beam entered this dull element part of its strength was sucked from it. The first veil had been lifted from the sea. The sky appeared less close to the earth. Now Sally woke and finding it still dark and her hand near her husband's she slept again. Hervey Russell slept with her arm over her face. She was surprised to find herself able to rise on her toes like a ballet dancer. All her life she had wanted very much to be able to do this, and now without effort she was dancing turning on her toes like a leaf on its stalk, in an ecstasy of pleasure and lightness. The music to which she turned came from within her, yet was as strong and clear as a fine orchestra. She could pick out the different instruments, shuddering with pleasure when the great middle notes of the violins sprang through the centre of her body. With precision and lovely ease her body played through the third Brandenburg concerto while she spun on her toes across the waxed boards. Surely I have never been so happy, she thought.

CHAPTER XXX

JUNE 1923

1. *They used to sell good linen*

HERVEY took Richard to the gate of Miss Holland's house.
' Don't come for me at twelve,' he warned her. ' A boy of
my age can fetch himself from school.' The day before was
his eighth birthday.

' Very well,' Hervey said. ' I'll wait for you at home.'

She did not go home then, but took the Guisborough road
to the moors. The morning was clear and warm, with the
softness and light winds of early summer. The leaves of
trees and hedges were an intense pure green, and translucent,
with the sun shining through them as though it shone through
water. In the garden of a cottage tulips and wallflowers
were as thick as paint. Before she reached the moor there
were no more cottages. There was the dry moor, with the
first fern leaves, and the peewits crying ' Whereaway ? ' like
the ghosts of sailors.

She walked quickly, until she came to the top of the moor.
In front of her it ran north-east to the coast with its scanty
villages and hard-set iron works. She turned her back on
that and sat down looking towards Danesacre. The valleys
were like the troughs of waves with the hill ahead rising in
a great sweep as green as a wave to the other moors. ' You're
a beauty, you are,' she said, looking at what she could see of
Danesacre. It was as much as anyone crossing the moor from
this side on any clear day during the last eight hundred years
would see. I ought to be glad to stay here, she thought.
But she was not.

She wanted to go back to London, a city which in other

333

ways she hated, because she had there the sense of things happening round her and within the reach of her mind. She was too young to wish for anything better. Well, even a young tree can have deep roots, but it feels the wind more than an older one. In the moment that her heart lifted to the sight of Danesacre on a clear morning she thought, I am buried alive here, I hear and know nothing. Yet she thought, I shall always come back here.

She put a hand into her pocket and drew out a letter which had come that morning. It was from Penn. His careless fingers had folded up with the letter a scrap of paper on which he had noted the various things he had to do in London. Half-way down the list Hervey read: Len 6.30 Marylebone Hotel. She was very roughly shocked and found it hard to think. She leaned up against the wall holding the letter, and after a moment or two she was able to think quietly, So he has gone to her again.

He had agreed readily with Hervey that their situation would be unbearable unless he gave up this Len Hammond. She knows too much about me already, Hervey said to him: and I can't face the prospect of your telling her that I have cried a great deal and been angry with you about her.

She read through the letter for the third time. He has of course told her now that I cried, she thought. To quiet herself she said out loud: ' He wasn't able to give her up because he wanted her to think well of him. He had to put himself right in her eyes.' She knew that was not the whole story but it was enough. For the rest, she was forced plainly to know that her needs and wishes meant very little to Penn. She had needed time to recover some confidence in herself: nothing so takes the pride out of you as being deceived, easily and for a long time, by an intimate. If I could have had this one promise to me kept, I should feel less humiliated, she thought.

A feeling of extraordinary bitterness seized her. She sat looking at her hands and thinking, I can't put this right.

She put her hand over her mouth. All my breast aches, she thought.

Many sharp thoughts came into her mind as she sat there, and at the end she felt a quick exhilaration, unlooked for, but it comforted her. It was something to know where she stood, and that was alone. Thinking, I shall do something with my life yet, she lay down with her face to the ground.

After a time she turned round and looked up at the sky. It was cloudless except for the small and lovely clouds out to sea. She watched a bird turn and stoop as a ship leans over to the water. 'Whereaway, whereaway?' she mocked it. A strange happiness filled her. She stood up and looked once more at the two lovely valleys before turning home. She had come to no decision about her future, and she was alone as she had never been, yet had in her mind a feeling that something would soon happen.

In the early evening of that day she walked to her mother's house. Mrs Russell was on the moment of going out to buy new linen and she turned and went with her. They were going to an older part of Danesacre, where Mrs Russell had her first house as a young married woman.

'I bought my first sheets at Peirson's,' she said. 'They were plain fine linen. That's twenty-seven years and I have them now. I worked an R in red cotton in the corner.' She looked with remote staring blue eyes at a young woman drawing a needleful of red cotton through white linen. The years of her life, children, foreign harbours, a dead son, grief and happiness, were still folded in the sheets tumbling from her knee.

'I had scarcely any money,' she said suddenly. 'Your father was out of a ship for half a year after I married him. I couldn't bring myself to buy poor linen, so I took what money I had and went to Peirson's and asked for old Mr Peirson. I told him that I would buy two pairs of their fine sheets if he would take half the money now and the rest as soon as I had it. He said " Choose your sheets, honey, and pay me when you like." I chose the finest and he brought them to the house himself.'

'That was kind,' Hervey said.

' I suppose my mother had spent hundreds of pounds on linen in his shop,' Mrs Russell answered, in the dry voice she used in speaking of Mary Hervey. ' The linen cupboards were one woman's work. There were there a hundred and thirty-eight shelves, of cedar wood, each marked with a date when that linen on it was bought.'

She pressed her lips tightly over the words. Glancing at her, Hervey saw that two pairs of Mr Peirson's finest linen sheets were the symbol in her mother's mind of that vast cupboard, just as her six Chippendale chairs stood for the solid and great dignity of Mary Hervey's house. In everything she did, Mrs Russell had had that inachievable grandeur in view. It had burned up her life.

They were walking between the harbour and a row of tall faded houses. The life had ebbed from this part of the town, and the gardens of the houses were like stagnant pools, filled with pampas-grass and laburnums, and their narrow paths edged with shells brought from the seas at the other side of the world.

In the harbour the tide was far out, and gulls stepped delicately on the grey mud, their wings flashing as they rose, to settle again on a post or a grounded cobble. Across the other side of the harbour the oldest houses stood up in that bright air with the clearness and fineness of the shells. At the water's edge Garton's shipyard was sunk into its old decay after a flicker of life during the War. Danesacre people had put money into it then, to lose it. It was a vain enterprise. Life has gone too far past all such fine places, where men lived in what they made.

As they climbed the steep street towards Peirson's, Mrs Russell had to stand still to rest. Her lips were blue. She could scarcely stand. Hervey looked at her in an agony of fear. ' What's the matter with you ? ' she asked.

' Nothing, except that my heart is getting old,' her mother said.

' Well, you should rest,' Hervey said. She was almost angry with her mother for feeling worn.

They went into Peirson's shop, where Mrs Russell could rest. As they waited, a smile, pleased and expectant, softened her face. The man brought out bundle after bundle of sheets, spreading them out over the counter. She fingered one after another in dissatisfied silence. Her mouth worked, as it did when she was losing patience. She had so little patience with imperfection.

'Are these the best you have?' she asked coldly.

'These are the best we stock,' the man said. He looked at the sheets anxiously as if to incite them to do him credit.

'But I used to buy very good linen here,' Mrs Russell exclaimed. The corners of her mouth came down, and her eyes started at the offender. At these moments her voice was overbearing and sarcastic.

'We should have no sale for anything better than these; it's quite good linen,' the assistant answered. His manner showed that he was afraid of her. Hervey was sorry for him.

'We'd better leave it,' she said in a low voice to her mother.

'Yes, I'm afraid I must,' Mrs Russell said. She relented her manner a little towards the assistant as she rose, but left him scared. Outside, she stood looking at the faded familiar houses, made unfamiliar by time, and time's accomplice. 'I never would have thought it,' she cried. 'Never.' She gripped Hervey's arm. 'In those days,' she said, 'every captain's wife knew a piece of good linen when she bought it.'

'You can send to London for your linen,' Hervey said.

'Ay, and pay London prices,' her mother retorted. She tossed her head. There was no one to recognise young Sylvia Hervey in the gesture. 'Nay, I'll make out with what I have. I daresay it will last my time.'

2. *A chipped saucer*

Hervey had no confidence in herself as a writer. She could not believe that money earned by writing novels was as safe as the money her grandmother Mary Hervey had made out of ships. The builders of good ships were, except in a Crisis,

sure of their livelihood. Not so the writers of books.
Between one novel and 'the next you could lose your wit
or your audience. It was a chancy life. It was unsound,
the one quality in a man's work or way of life Hervey Russell
could not do with. A vagabond in spirit, she despised
vagabonds.

She had finished writing her third novel and had begun
laboriously to type it from the nearly illegible manuscript.
Her money was almost done and she was little comforted to
think that she would receive a hundred pounds when she sent
the MS to Charles Frome. What is a hundred pounds to a
young woman with ambitions and a son ?

The more she typed the more cruelly certain she was that
this novel would fail. There was not a tear in a dozen
chapters. This was because her last novel had fountained
tears. She was now so ashamed of it that she had thrown
sand over all her emotions and written a book as dry as a
desert.

She sat typing eleven hours a day. Her back ached.
When she stopped for the day her thoughts typed themselves
in her head. On the eighth day, when she had done typing
and correcting, she carried the script to the post. It was
seven in the evening. There was a veil over the heavens,
with the feeling of thunder coming from the land.

She put Richard to bed, all the time thinking, I'll have a
good cup of tea. Penn said once that if she were dying and
one said, Hervey, here is a good cup of tea for you, she would
sit up and take it.

She carried the cup into the garden. The veil was now lit
over the sea by the downflowing sun. A strange heavy light
lay over all, so that on a distant hill each tree and moving
creature was as clear as a threat. It was now high tide and
the estuary was full of water, but a breath had covered the
surface of the water so that it reflected nothing, no bird
shadow or cloud.

So waiting, Hervey turned her saucer round in her hand
and felt the chipped edge. At once, as if the chipped saucer

and the fear were the same thing in her mind, she thought that Richard might be ill, and though it was absurd, since she had just seen him fall swiftly and softly asleep, she ran back into the house to look at him. He was asleep and well: all she had for her trouble was the moment of certainty that nothing so beautiful could escape.

She sat down. He was ill, she thought, in this room, and I had a chipped saucer for his night-light. There was a tiny circle on the floor and another on the ceiling. It might be a room or a cave, and the darkness beyond it concealed either Danes or country lovers idling past, and always at one moment or the next, by this or that sudden stroke, death. (She looked at the window. It was open, and the first knocking had begun in the distance. The storm is at the other side of the moors, she thought. She bent her head to listen.) He had diphtheria lightly, she thought; but the anxiety she had felt was not light. It sprang from a deep source. A clap of thunder reminded her of the shells she had heard crashing into the town from the German ships. A sharper terror flowed in over the old and she thought, If there were another war I couldn't save him. She felt a mad fear and anger. So must the woman in the cave, she thought, have felt, when, crawling back after the raid, she saw the smoke lipping the lintel and the blood the mess the thing done which cannot be undone, the end.

Rousing herself from this nightmare she went downstairs. On the table was the letter from Evelyn. It had lain there three days, while she typed. She took it up. In this letter Evelyn offered her five pounds a week to work for her as secretary, but a secretary of a particular kind. She must come between Evelyn and the tiresomeness of her friends, write to one, find out books for another, meet and send away satisfied persons whom Evelyn could neither offend nor endure. So, wrote Evelyn, you will save my reputation and my health, and write better books yourself for knowing more of the world.

She pulled a long face over the letter. This five pounds

a week is too good to pass, she said to herself. But she distrusted Evelyn. And to have to do with many people exasperated her. They set her in a quiver. They pulled her mind to pieces with their monkey's fingers and put her to the trouble of assembling it again. Yet despite this she knew that she would take Evelyn's offer. She had not the hardihood to refuse. It gave her the margin of safety she needed for her son.

He has outgrown Miss Holland, she thought: I shall find a better school for him near London. Her thoughts flew so far ahead of her that she saw a tall young student walking with books in his hand across some green quadrangle in Oxford. With such a forehead he will be a scientist or a statesman, she thought.

The light had changed. Now from a clear sky the last rays of the sun blessed the earth. A multitude of clouds, coloured like tropical fishes, swam in the depths of the sky. The storm has passed over, Hervey thought.

She went out and walked in the field by the estuary. I shall write a book every year and make money which I shall save for Richard. I shall have a fine house. But she detested houses, and the thought of owning one crushed her down with despair.

It was for Richard that she would have one. Everything was for Richard. In her bitterness against her husband she would not deny him the right to share their house, but she would not welcome him. He is seeing Miss Hammond now, she thought. Her hand flew to her breast, to the ache there. Every intimate memory she had of him was flavoured by the thought that he had once deceived her. She could not think near him without coming on this hidden bitterness. It poisoned their life. I shall never look at him again with pleasure, she thought. At once she was sorry for him— because he had ruined himself with her. Poor Penn, she said to herself. Whatever else had died in her, the familiar need to comfort and reassure him was still there.

She had the honesty to say aloud: 'You once hoped he would leave you.'

It is true that if you think with sufficient energy about an event it will at last happen, not (as you might suppose) because you have created it, but because it was all the time in your nature. But the logic of the mind has one fatal flaw. It starts in a wish. And so the moment an imagined event emerges into the real world, time seizes on it and gives it a twist that deforms everything. A spring you had supposed dry overflows, the imagined ground gives way, and down you go. How could I have guessed that I should cry every night for a year ? she said. Jealousy is a disease which we should catch as seldom as possible. It is probably incurable— but all the same one gets over it. What is important is to remember that no one is to be trusted. To trust yourself to a human being is only to ask to be betrayed. She lifted her head, smiling. Oh if only I can remember that, she said.

She went in and went to bed, and slept, but dreamed of Philip. They were together in some place and she had to go away, to leave him there. She told him over and over that she would come back. She wanted to make him think that she was not leaving him. It's only for a time, she repeated. She told him that she would rather live with him than with anyone, and he only smiled, kindly, with disbelief and love. She woke, and found that she had cried as she slept.

3. *Death is an incident in life*

In the morning an extraordinary thing happened, and for a few hours she believed that her life had changed.

Her grandmother Mary Hervey wrote asking her to come, and to come at once, since she was old and there was not a great deal of time but there was only a little time. The letter had been sent on, her address found by Mrs Hervey's lawyer. For a moment, as Hervey read it, she was the ashamed clumsy schoolgirl, begging Mary to take her into the firm. Whatever her mind could say to it, her body had not forgotten that frightful humiliation. She felt as though it had happened yesterday.

She saw and heard Philip saying : ' If I could I'd send you your fortune by post. From Philip. With love.'

A sudden rage blotted every other emotion. ' After all these years. I don't want anything from her,' she said.

She looked at Richard, and as the writer had known they would the closing words of the letter paid all. ' I should like it very well if you brought with you a photograph of your boy.' Her heart turned in her side. If she will do something for Richard I will forgive her anything, she thought.

Her grandmother's new house was seven miles from Danesacre by the moor road—six, from her present lodging. She decided to walk the distance, so that she would not come there until the afternoon but could start at once. She could not wait.

She left Richard at Miss Holland's. Walking, on that road, with the moors turning their great shoulders to the sky, and then the lines of the farther hills folding in, one below the other, falling to the valleys, she thought of everything that could happen. Once she ran, because of the excitement. Her happiness was so great that it was hardly she kept quiet. Towards the last of the way she could only think that she was safe. Now every step she took brought her closer to the moment in which she would say to herself, Now Richard can have everything. When she reached the first gates she stopped to dust her shoes : to her vexation one had sprung a crack during the long walk. She went in, past the pines, to the drive proper, and so up to the house. Her heart was beating to choke her, and she felt empty inside her.

The double doors of the house were open. As she hesitated on the step a man came forward, she supposed a head servant. She found that it was hard to speak. ' I am Miss Russell and I wish to see Mrs Hervey,' she said stiffly.

The man was looking into her face. ' Mrs Hervey is ill.'

' Yes ? ' Hervey said. She felt as though she had fallen out of the world. She stood in the midst of nothing. ' I should like to see someone,' she said, in a moment.

The man left her standing in the hall and went by another

door into the garden. She looked through the window and
saw the light falling on the hedge in such a way that it seemed
full of holes through which the light poured. She heard
steps behind her and swung round. A young man came
towards her. She stared at him, at first sight pleased by his
looks, the eyes quick and kind, nose finely and lightly arched,
the mouth short and fine.

'We're cousins, I think.' He smiled at her. 'I'm
Nicholas Roxby. First cousins.'

Suddenly she wanted to make a good impression on him,
but felt dull and awkward. She suffered in feeling herself
exposed to his glances, to be liked or despised. Following
him into the drawing-room, she could think of nothing more
to say than : 'I came to see my grandmother.'

'She's ill,' Nicholas said.

Hervey felt in her bag and took out the letter. She kept
her hand over it. 'Is she very ill ? '

'She's dying, I'm afraid.'

I must go, Hervey thought. She was at the end of her
courage in this house. It was an agony to her to push herself
forward. But she made another effort. 'Is she too ill to
see me ? '

She heard Nicholas answer that Mary Hervey was speechless and dying. She did not say anything. By now she was past
caring what he thought, except that she would die of shame if
he saw that she had expected something from this visit. She
forced herself still, her face showed nothing. All at once
she could have laughed, knowing what she had thought on
the way here.

'Well, *I'm* alive,' she said.

She stood up to go. Her hands were full of the things she
had emptied out of her bag to reach the letter, with them the
photograph of Richard. Nicholas picked up a bunch of keys
she let drop. 'Stay to tea,' he said. She felt an impulse to
talk to him, to say no matter what, if it came from the heart.
But, no, she would not stay in this house. She marched
out, walking quickly yet blindly, her head dropped forward.

Now that she was outside, and had got nothing, she felt a rough gaiety. No one must ever know about this, she thought with passion : no one *shall* ever know. Courage came back to her. She laughed, she was almost happy, except when she considered what a dull poor figure she had cut before her cousin. Then she stood still with vexation in the road, frowning and biting her lip. She wanted very strongly to stand well with him. As she walked, she kept him before her mind, with so much eagerness that she forgot how awkward she had been. With the whole force of her massive clumsy mind she wished to see him again.

She gave a thought or two to her grandmother, that arrogant old woman, near her end. So long and strange a life, and now to become nothing. This thought angered her, denying the life in herself. She could not believe that she would die.

A narrow track crossed the moor at one point, leaving the road out of sight. She took it, and so missed the car in which her mother was hurrying to Mary Hervey's house. But it came into her mind to wonder if they had sent for her mother. Again she thought with hot anger of Mary Hervey. If she had been kinder my mother would not have had to work so hard or do with so little, she thought ; and her heart ached for her mother, that she had had so little. What's it been for, all your work and struggle ? she cried. But wait, wait : that rich old woman did nothing for you, her daughter ; *I*, your child, will give you everything. So she went on, not even caring to keep her shoes from being worse scratched by the heather.

She came to the turn of the road above Danesacre, where she could see it. The sky, so blue, so calm, dissolved into the sea. The town appeared new, though it was a thousand years old, the roofs shining in the light, the grass on the cliff edge greener than that close at hand. Hervey sat down on the ground to look at it and to think over her plans. I shall accept, she thought, Evelyn's offer, I shall write and work ; in a few months I shall have enough to take a small house near London, with a garden for Richard; there I shall live quietly, more like a scholar than a novelist. It was an excellent plan, yet when she had tested it thoroughly on every side, and approved it, and told herself that at last she was on the step of making her fortune, she found her heart still waiting, and impatient, but for what ?

VIRAGO MODERN CLASSICS

The first Virago Modern Classic, *Frost in May* by Antonia White, was published in 1978. It launched a list dedicated to the celebration of women writers and to the rediscovery and reprinting of their works. Its aim was, and is, to demonstrate the existence of a female tradition in fiction which is both enriching and enjoyable. The Leavisite notion of the 'Great Tradition', and the narrow, academic definition of a 'classic', has meant the neglect of a large number of interesting secondary works of fiction. In calling the series 'Modern Classics' we do not necessarily mean 'great' — although this is often the case. Published with new critical and biographical introductions, books are chosen for many reasons: sometimes for their importance in literary history; sometimes because they illuminate particular aspects of womens' lives, both personal and public. They may be classics of comedy or storytelling; their interest can be historical, feminist, political or literary.

Initially the Virago Modern Classics concentrated on English novels and short stories published in the early decades of this century. As the series has grown it has broadened to include works of fiction from different centuries, different countries, cultures and literary traditions. In 1984 the Victorian Classics were launched; there are separate lists of Irish, Scottish, European, American, Australian and other English speaking countries; there are books written by Black women, by Catholic and Jewish women, and a few relevant novels by men. There is, too, a companion series of Non-Fiction Classics constituting biography, autobiography, travel, journalism, essays, poetry, letters and diaries.

By the end of 1986 over 250 titles will have been published in these two series, many of which have been suggested by our readers.